Praise for *Acts of Love and War*

vivid, immersive novel about a remarkable woman helping refugees in a bitter, heartbreaking war. I couldn't put it down.' Gill Paul

'A love story with a twist; a war story with a difference. *Acts of Love and War* is a heartrending tale of love, courage and sacrifice . . . inspired by the real lives of aid workers, International Brigaders and Spanish civilians, Maggie Brookes has crafted a beautiful, compelling story of hope and humanity in war.' Nikki Marmery

'This amazing book has everything in it: love, war, history and relevance to today. Gripping.' Russell Kane

gripping, panoramic tale of the very human cost of war . . . *Acts of and War* is vividly told: at once epic and intimate. Be prepared to lose our heart in the simmering heat of war-torn Spain.' Miranda Malins

Immersive and humane . . . one of historical fiction's most lyrical and intelligent voices.' Rachel McMillan

'A heartrending but inspiring novel . . . insightful and moving.' Katherine Clements

'A moving and unputdownable story of bravery and endurance.' Judith Allnatt

'Accomplished and expansive.' Ann Morgan

'A beautifully woven tale . . . Extraordinary events sensitively told.' Lucy Jago

'Emotionally captivating and authentic . . . an unforgettable story.' Susan Meissner

I insist you read this intelligent empathetic novel. You won't regret it.' Frost Magazine

Also by Maggie Brookes

The Prisoner's Wife

Maggie Brookes is an ex-journalist and BBC TV historical documentary producer, turned novelist and poet. She relishes uncovering stories about the strength of women and the power of friendship and love in the most terrible of circumstances. *Acts of Love and War* is about love and courage in the brutal Spanish Civil War. *The Prisoner's Wife* – based on an extraordinary true story of WW2 – was published around the world in 2020. Maggie taught Creative Writing at Middlesex University for thirty years and has had six poetry collections published under the name Maggie Butt.

MAGGIE BROOKES

Acts of Love and War

PENGUIN BOOKS

PENGUIN BOOKS

UK | USA | Canada | Ireland | Australia
India | New Zealand | South Africa

Penguin Books is part of the Penguin Random House group of companies
whose addresses can be found at global.penguinrandomhouse.com

Penguin
Random House
UK

First published by Century in 2022
Published in Penguin Books 2023
001

Typeset in 12.19/14.5pt Fournier MT by Jouve (UK), Milton Keynes.
Printed and bound in Great Britain by Clays Ltd, Elcograf S.p.A.

The authorised representative in the EEA is Penguin Random House Ireland,
Morrison Chambers, 32 Nassau Street, Dublin D02 YH68

A CIP catalogue record for this book is available from the British Library

ISBN: 978–1–529–16045–1

www.greenpenguin.co.uk

For the brave people who give humanitarian
aid all over our troubled world.

And for Matilda, Katie, Amy and Tim – everlove.

Let us then try what Love can do.

William Penn
(Prominent Quaker, founder of Pennsylvania,
14 October 1644–30 July 1718)

Historical Note

The Spanish Civil War (1936–1939) divided a nation and set family members against each other as they took violently opposing views about religion, class, democracy and Fascism. Those on the left believed that the landowners and Catholic Church had kept the country in medieval poverty and ignorance. Those on the right feared that Spain would become communist and atheist.

In 1936 a left-wing Republican coalition was elected and the right-wing military immediately moved to stage a coup. This sparked fury among mobs who went on the rampage, murdering clergy, burning churches and seizing land and property. The right wing gathered behind the Fascist General Franco and the conflict quickly descended into a war between the democratically elected Republicans and the Fascists who strove to overthrow them.

Despite an international non-intervention pact, Hitler and Mussolini came to Franco's aid with massed troops, bombers and fighter planes. In support of democracy and in fear of the spread of Fascism, about fifty thousand left-wing men and women travelled from all around the world to join the Republican 'International Brigades' and Stalin sent them weapons.

Franco expected his military coup to be quick, but a raggle-taggle Popular Army of peasants, factory workers, trade unionists and the International Brigades held him at bay.

Apart from the Nicholson and Murray families, and Concha, all the major characters in this novel were extraordinary real people. They are listed in full in the Author's Note on page 401.

Prologue

Hertfordshire, England, 1921

Lucy was sitting in her favourite place, halfway up the mahogany staircase, with a doll laid across her lap. From here she could see all the comings and goings of the house. She watched as her father opened the front door and light flooded into the panelled hall, fixing that morning in her memory forever, as if that was the day someone wound the clockwork and her life began.

Her father ushered Mrs Murray inside and took her to the drawing room. Behind her came two boys, silhouetted in the doorway against the bright day beyond: a bigger boy holding tight to the hand of his little brother. Jamie and Tom stood still for a moment, on the threshold of Lucy's life, and then moved cautiously forward into the unknown hall. As they walked towards her their dark outlines blushed into colour and rounded into flesh.

Lucy thought one of them looked a little older than her and one a bit younger, perhaps seven and four. The bigger boy, Jamie, wore a school uniform with blazer, tie and short trousers. The small boy who gripped his hand was dressed in a sailor suit. As light fell on to their faces from the landing

1

window behind her, Lucy saw Jamie's lips were clenched hard between his teeth in the effort not to show his feelings, while Tom gazed all about in a mixture of fear and curiosity. They were as unalike as two brothers ever could be. Jamie had his mother's blue eyes, sandy hair and freckled skin, while Tom's eyes were brown as his hair; Jamie was skinny, as if he'd grown too fast, while Tom was square and solid; Jamie was pale as a china doll, whereas Tom was all aglow.

Lucy knew these were the boys who were coming to live in the little cottage next door. The boys with the dead father. She turned over the thought in her mind like a shiny new penny and imprinted on its reverse side she found the fact of her own dead mother.

She watched as the boys became accustomed to the relative darkness of the wide hallway and caught sight of her on the stairs above them. When their gaze met hers, something seemed to catch in her throat and an unfamiliar shiver ran through her. She set aside her doll and stood up.

Later they told her that rays of sun from the landing window illuminated the blonde curls which encircled her head. But all she would remember was the way they stopped and stared as though she was a vision, as though she could become the fixed point in the turmoil of their lives. As though she would save them.

HERTFORDSHIRE
October 1936

1

Lucy was chopping the top off her boiled egg when Tom burst into the dining room through the French windows. His hair was standing on end as if he'd just sprung out of bed, and he was waving a newspaper in his hand. Lucy laid down her spoon and glanced nervously at her father, Captain Nicholson. He wouldn't like this interruption to his breakfast.

'It's come,' yelled Tom. 'The call has come.'

Lucy's father looked up from deboning his kipper, and wiped his moustache. 'Good morning, Thomas,' he said drily.

Tom stopped momentarily on his dash round to Lucy's side of the table, and seemed to notice Captain Nicholson for the first time.

'Oh yes, good morning, sir.' He knelt by Lucy's chair, stabbing the newspaper with his forefinger. 'Look, look, the call has come at last. I'm going.'

Lucy pulled the *Daily Worker* from his grasp to keep it still enough to read the call for volunteers to fight for the Spanish Republic. The headline made her insides lurch with fear. She turned to him, taking in his conker-brown eyes, bright with excitement, and his whole face alight with joy. How could something which gave him such pleasure feel like a stone in her stomach?

'Going where?' asked Captain Nicholson, giving up on his kipper.

Lucy laid a warning hand on Tom's sleeve, but he shrugged her off and leapt to his feet, pacing around the room, unable to keep still. 'To Spain. I'm going to Spain.'

'Oh no you aren't!' Captain Nicholson snapped. 'Ridiculous boy! Sit down.' His eyes flashed to Lucy, who was moving to Tom's defence. 'And you. Be quiet.'

Lucy subsided, biting back her words for now, biding her time to intervene on her friend's behalf as Tom slowly pulled out a chair and sat on it, laying the paper on the table in front of him. Lucy saw her father disapproving his unshaven chin, unbrushed hair, untucked shirt and sweater awry. Tom had obviously hastily yanked on some clothes and run round from next door to tell her the news as soon as the paper had been delivered. She loved his impulsiveness, but wished he'd checked to see if she was alone.

Captain Nicholson laid down his cutlery. 'Now then, what's all this nonsense?'

Tom leaned forwards. 'It's not nonsense. It's really not. This is my chance to do something to help. It's what I've been waiting for.'

Lucy could see her father's face starting to redden as he struggled to maintain control.

'I'm not certain I get your drift.'

Tom brandished his copy of the *Daily Worker* again. 'It's

a call to go and join the International Brigades, to fight Franco. I've got to go.'

Admiration ran through Lucy, turning almost immediately to a twinge of sickness at the thought of Tom hurling himself into such danger.

Captain Nicholson jabbed the table with his finger to emphasise each word. 'You. Will. Do. No. Such. Thing.'

Tom ran his hand up through his unruly hair and Lucy could see he was making an effort to sound reasonable. 'But with respect, sir. I am going. I have to.'

Lucy's father rose to his feet. 'You are nineteen years old, Thomas Murray. You have no idea what a war is like. You will stay here and finish your degree and that's an end of it.'

Tom stood up too, shoving his chair back so hard that it fell over.

'I know I don't know anything about war, but I have to go. I can't just sit around and do nothing.'

Lucy waved a hand, and tried to cut in. 'Calm down, both of you!' But neither of them was listening. Her chest churned with divided feelings – the urge to support Tom against her father wrestled with horror at the thought of him going to Spain and getting killed, but she knew there was no chance of being heard anyway when Captain Nicholson was in full flow.

'That's precisely what you have to do,' he yelled. 'Go back to that LSE place and finish your degree. You are not going to fight for those damned Reds. It's not your war.'

Tom paced the room, fists at his sides. 'Yes it is. If we don't stop the Fascists in Spain they'll be everywhere.'

Lucy's father reached across the table and grabbed Tom's

Daily Worker. Before Tom or Lucy could stop him, he ripped the paper in two. Tom leapt across the room and snatched it back. They stood glaring at each other, an upper-cut length apart. They were about the same height, but Tom was young and muscular, while Captain Nicholson was overweight and middle-aged. There was little doubt who would come off worse. Lucy jumped up to stand between them, holding tight to Tom's right arm. They'd never come to blows before, despite plenty of arguments, but maybe this would be the first time.

'I'm going!' shouted Tom.

Captain Nicholson drew himself up taller. 'I forbid it!'

Before he could think, Tom spat back. 'You aren't my father!'

The words fell like a pebble into a pond, sending out ripples of shock and Lucy looked anxiously at her father. Emotions chased across his face and his jowls wobbled as he struggled to find the right reply.

'Go on,' she silently urged him, 'tell him what you really feel. Say – I know I'm not, but ever since I brought you and Jamie and your mother to live in the cottage next door, you have been like a son to me – so please don't go and get yourself killed.'

She watched as her father opened his mouth to speak, then closed it again. His Adam's apple lifted and sank, and he swallowed twice, as if gulping down all the things he might have said. Then he tugged at his moustache and blinked hard, and those two gestures turned on his mask of self-control.

He picked up a fork and stabbed at his kipper. 'I don't know what your brother will say about you going to fight for those priest-murdering savages.'

Lucy and Tom's eyes met. They both knew exactly what Jamie would say.

'Maybe he'll talk some sense into you.'

Lucy raised her eyebrows. Surely her father knew that whatever Jamie suggested would immediately make Tom rush out and do the opposite. If anyone was to prevent Tom going and getting himself killed, it would have to be her and Tom's mother.

She thought of the furious arguments which had ripped apart the air in the Murrays' kitchen ever since news of the Spanish Republic began to appear in the papers. Lucy and Mrs Murray had been interested in the rights for women and the push for education which the Republic espoused. Tom had provocatively said England should be a Republic and religion should be banned. Jamie had yelled at all of them. How could they not see that the Republic was against God?

'What does your mum think?' asked Lucy, pulling Tom towards the front door.

'I haven't told her,' he muttered, turning to her, whacking the torn newspaper against his leg in barely controlled fury. 'I wanted to show you first, because I knew you'd understand.'

Lucy checked her watch and calculated there would be enough time before she had to leave for work. 'Well, let's go and tell her now.'

Tom was ahead of her on the path as she banged the door behind her, but once they were out of the gate she turned right rather than left to the Murrays' cottage. She knew he needed to let off some steam before they could talk.

'Race you to the bus stop,' she called over her shoulder, tearing ahead.

They ran through the familiar village street in the misty October morning, past the greengrocer's and the butcher's. Tom was hampered by the fact that he was still wearing his bedroom slippers. They dodged between the early commuters on their way to Welwyn station to go to work in London.

Lucy reached the bench at the bus stop first and threw herself down, puffing slightly, tucking her curly blonde hair behind her ears. How many times had she sat here with Tom, talking him out of some mad plan or calming him down after a row with her father or his older brother?

He slumped next to her, the precious newspaper now scrunched in one hand. 'I didn't have shoes on,' he explained, holding his slippered feet out in front of him.

'I knew that,' she smiled. 'And you haven't shaved or brushed your hair.' She sniffed. 'Or washed.'

He edged an inch or two away from her on the bench. 'Sorry. No. I was too excited.'

'All right, show me what it says.'

They pored over the paper, holding the torn page together, and Lucy couldn't think what she might say to stop him going, but for now she knew she just had to let him chatter on.

'You do understand why it's important, don't you, Luce?' Tom pleaded. 'Schools and women and peasants and education and everything.'

Lucy thought about the number of times she had defied her father and ignored Jamie's disgust to go with Tom to pro-Republican meetings. They'd been going ever since July when they'd heard about General Franco's brutal Fascist army sweeping up through Spain, destroying all the good work the Republicans had done since their election. She'd been most impressed by Dolores Ibárruri, the fiery Spanish politician known as La Pasionaria, whose face lit up with fervour as she spoke.

She patted his arm. 'You know I do.'

'OK, let's go and tell Ma. Will you come with me?'

Lucy and Tom hurtled into the kitchen where Mrs Murray had been cooking Tom's breakfast, and Tom wordlessly passed his mother the newspaper. She quickly scanned the headline, and her pale face seemed suddenly much older than her forty-three years.

'I feared this day would come,' she said, smoothing the ripped page out on the kitchen table. 'Where's my glasses?'

Lucy found them on the sideboard and passed them over, giving her hand a reassuring squeeze. Mrs Murray pressed back and they both knew they would do everything they could to prevent Tom going off to war. They stood side by side, with their shoulders just touching as Mrs Murray carefully read the article. Tom watched anxiously, drumming his fingers on the table. Mrs Murray looked up and removed her spectacles.

'Oh, Thomas!' she pleaded. 'Surely there will be other men to go? You are only halfway through your degree.'

'You've only just started the second year,' added Lucy.

'You could maybe finish the year and then see?' suggested Mrs Murray.

Tom clicked his tongue impatiently. 'Don't you understand? It's now. It has to be now, if we have any chance of stopping Franco. You know what those vile bastards are doing to women in every town and village. We have to stop them taking Madrid, and this is our chance.'

Lucy tried another tack. 'But surely they'll want men with experience? Older men who were in the Great War? What good would you be?' She tried to force a laugh. 'I don't suppose they need economists!'

'Cheers, Luce! Thanks for the vote of confidence. You've forgotten I can shoot a rifle. I learned at school, thanks to your father! And I can handle myself. I learned that on a rugger pitch. I think I really could help.'

'Being able to handle a rifle didn't save your own dad, did it?' Mrs Murray cut in.

Tom twisted his hands in exasperation. 'Oh, I might have known you wouldn't understand.'

'It's just that we love you,' his mother said.

'You can't speak Spanish,' Lucy hazarded, grasping at straws.

'I can a bit, from when Jamie taught us both. I know you were better at it than me, but that was because I was only doing it not to be left out.' He cleared his throat. '*¿Dónde está el burro?*'

Lucy couldn't help laughing, and told Mrs Murray, 'It means "Where is the donkey?"'

'Very useful, I'm sure,' said Tom's mother.

Lucy gave Tom a playful shove. 'We all know where the donkey is! He's here in this room.'

Mrs Murray pulled a rueful smile. 'I dread to think what Jamie is going to say when he gets home tonight.'

Out of her front bay window, Lucy watched Jamie walking up the road from the station that evening at his usual time, and as ever with his nose in a book. It was a marvel that he didn't bump into a lamp post, or step out in front of a car. He always left his job as a subeditor at the *Catholic Herald* on the dot of five, and caught the 5.15 from Moorgate. You could set your watch by him; quite unlike Tom.

Even as small boys they'd been opposites. By the time they had arrived in Welwyn seven-year-old Jamie was filled with a quiet determination to be a continuation, almost a reincarnation, of their dead father. He had grasped hold of the few things he knew about Robert Murray and dressed himself in them: his father had been a Catholic, so Jamie found the local Catholic church and went to Mass every Sunday on his own through hail, snow and burning heat. His father had been a soldier who laid down his life to save his superior officer, Captain Nicholson. Jamie burned with desire to somehow become a hero as well, to become worthy of him. But four-year-old Tom had none of Jamie's admiration for their father's sacrifice. He was simply furious that Daddy had died and left them. All their lives would have been so different if Private Murray had simply saved himself.

Lucy slipped out the back of her own house, through the gate in the fence which her father had made when the boys were young, and was in the kitchen next door with Mrs Murray and Tom before they heard Jamie's key in the lock.

She and Mrs Murray exchanged an anxious glance. They knew this was not going to go well. The brothers never saw eye to eye on anything, but on the question of Spain they were as opposed as it was possible to be.

All three heads turned towards the kitchen door as Jamie opened it.

He surveyed them guardedly and laid his book on the table. 'Uh-oh! What's all this? Some sort of deputation?'

Mrs Murray filled the kettle to give herself something to do. 'How was your day?' she asked in a voice which was supposed to sound normal, but Lucy noticed had a tight squeak in it. 'A brew before your tea? It's nearly ready. Toad in the hole.'

Tom moved about the small kitchen like a caged animal and Jamie sat down cautiously. 'Yes, a cup of tea please. Now who's going to tell me what's going on?'

Tom and Mrs Murray both looked at Lucy, always the peace-maker and go-between, and Lucy knew there was no hope for it, so she sat across the table from Jamie.

'It's Tom,' she began.

'I thought it might be,' Jamie said drily. 'Has he been sent down, or got a girl in trouble, or lost a fortune at cards?'

'Cheers,' muttered Tom.

'None of those,' said Lucy slowly. 'Something you'll think is worse.'

Jamie stared at her with his piercing blue eyes and seemed to read her mind, as he always did. 'Please tell me he's not signed up to go to Spain?'

Lucy reached out to place a restraining hand on Jamie's wrist.

Tom stopped pacing. 'Not actually signed yet, but I'm going to.'

Jamie's voice was dangerously quiet. 'You certainly are not.'

'I certainly am!'

Jamie stood to face Tom across the kitchen table. 'No

brother of mine is going to fight for those murderous com-mies. You know what they've done, don't you? I've shown you all the stories: beheading priests, doing God knows what to nuns, murdering monks . . .'

'I know what stinking propaganda and lies your Tory papers are peddling,' spat Tom.

'It's the truth. You just refuse to see the truth when it's staring you in the face.'

Lucy tried her teacher voice on them. 'Stop it, boys. We all need to sleep on this, and talk about the pros and cons tomorrow.'

'There are no pros,' said Jamie. 'It's perfectly simple. If he goes to fight in Spain, he's no longer my brother.'

'That's perfectly fine by me,' yelled Tom. 'I don't want to be the brother of a Fascist.'

The kitchen suddenly seemed terribly hot.

Lucy turned to Tom, removing her cardigan. 'You know Jamie's not a Fascist.'

'I'm going to Spain, and that's all there is to it,' Tom shouted.

Mrs Murray's voice could hardly be heard. 'Please, laddies. Just talk about this reasonably.'

Lucy lost her temper with the pair of them. 'You are both impossible! I'd like to knock your heads together. Stop it at once.'

Jamie's voice was steel-edged. 'If you go, I'll cut off your allowance. You won't have a penny, and you can starve to death for all I care.'

His words hung in the air, and they all froze. Tom picked up the newspaper and flung open the back door.

'He doesn't mean that,' called Lucy, shooting a dagger-look at Jamie.

But Tom was gone, out of the house, without a backward glance. Mrs Murray stood in the doorway, looking after him, twisting a tea towel in her hands.

Lucy turned to Jamie. 'You could at least have listened to him, talked about it.'

'Listened to what? All that bloody Red-worshipping, when he knows the facts.'

'The facts are complicated,' said Lucy. 'We all know that.'

Jamie left the room and ran up the stairs. The two women could hear him rummaging in his bedroom above their heads. They raised their eyebrows to each other.

'His scrapbook,' said Mrs Murray, and Lucy sighed.

The papers, cinema newsreels and radio news had been full of the conflict for more than six months. The only stories which ever pushed Spain off the front pages were those about the King's affair with Mrs Simpson. The whole of Britain was obsessed with the Spanish war and opinions were sharply divided. Most of the British press and all the newsreel companies were stridently anti-Republican, fearing that communist fervour would spread from Russia to Spain to Britain. They had latched on to the Republicans' hatred of the Catholic Church.

As part of his religious faith, Jamie had always taken an interest in the politics of the Roman Catholic countries, so it had not been surprising when he chose to study Spanish at Oxford. And it was even less surprising how fervently he'd railed against the Republicans back in July when mobs had gone on the rampage, burning churches and committing atrocities against the priests who they believed had kept them in medieval darkness and ignorance.

That's when Jamie had begun to cut out newspaper stories and paste them into a scrapbook.

Lucy gave Mrs Murray a hug and ran her hand over the older woman's faded hair. It would have been the colour of Jamie's once, shot through with coppery highlights, but now seemed washed out by care.

'Maybe Tom won't go,' Lucy said hopelessly. 'Maybe we can persuade him.'

Mrs Murray laid a head on her shoulder in despair, as they heard Jamie thundering back down the stairs.

He threw the familiar scrapbook down on the table in front of them.

'Look, go on, just look!'

Lucy had seen all these articles before, but she knew she must placate Jamie before they had any chance of dissuading Tom, so she opened the scrapbook, which blazed with headlines he'd snipped out of newspapers.

Jamie turned over page after page of cuttings from the *Daily Mail* in July and August 1936, only three months before, prodding the words with his finger for emphasis: RED WOMEN BUTCHER SPANISH PRIESTS; FAMILY BURNED BY REDS; REDS DROWN 447 IN WELLS; REDS' SHOW OF SKULLS IN A ROW; PRIESTS AND MONKS TORTURED BY REDS.

'Enough,' she said. 'Enough. I know that all these awful things happened.'

'One more,' he insisted. 'Just so you don't say they're all from the *Daily Mail*.'

He flipped through the book. 'Here. This one's the *Daily Mirror*.'

Lucy forced herself to look at the page. PRIESTS BEHEADED AND NUNS STRIPPED NAKED BY MOB the headline screamed.

'It's terrible,' she whispered, and she meant it; it was more terrible than she had words for. How could people do that to each other?

Mrs Murray laid cups of tea down in front of them both, and Lucy spooned in sugar.

Jamie's face was scarlet with anger. 'You know all that's true and you still side with Tom?'

'I'm not on anyone's side,' Lucy protested. 'I know the mob did all those things in the early days. But the Republic's done so many good things too.'

'How can evil people do good things?'

'Everything is always so black and white to you. The world is more difficult than that.'

'Not to me it's not. They are evil Antichrists, and Tom wants to be one of them.'

'I could try to explain, but I know you won't listen.'

'I'm not interested in listening to you defending the indefensible.'

Lucy felt exhausted by it all. 'Oh Jamie,' she sighed.

Jamie gathered up his scrapbook. 'I'll be in my room if anyone wants to talk sense.'

'Oh Jamie,' echoed his mother, but Jamie had left the room.

Both women were silent, then Lucy took Mrs Murray's hands. 'You are so cold,' she said. 'Here, have my tea. I'll pour another.'

'You don't think he'll really go, do you?' Mrs Murray's eyes searched Lucy's. 'Tom won't go to war? Into that war.'

Lucy shook her head, but it seemed horribly likely. She'd watched him at the rallies and meetings, seen how his eyes shone with missionary zeal.

She lifted her head and sniffed. 'What's that smell?'

Mrs Murray leapt to the oven door but, as she opened it, black smoke furled out. 'It's the toad in the hole,' she cried, yanking out the pan. 'I don't suppose anyone will want it now.'

And as if that thought was the last straw, she threw her apron up over her face and wept.

2

Back in her own house, Lucy began to rapidly cook a chop for her father's dinner. It almost seemed like a dream now that before Captain Nicholson had lost most of his money three years ago they'd had a cook and a housekeeper who came in every day. Lucy hadn't known then how books and skirting boards and door-tops gathered dust; hadn't known the weight of the iron or how difficult it was to dry the sheets on a rainy day. She was ashamed now of the way she'd taken so much for granted – the way food magically appeared in the house, and meals materialised on the table. Just three years ago she'd been on the brink of achieving her dream. She only had to pass her exams to go to university and become a doctor. All her teachers agreed she would sail through. She would heal the sick, and make the world a little easier for as many people as she could.

And then came the day when her father had told her and the Murrays that all his savings were gone, and there would have to be big changes.

First he said their cook and housekeeper would have to go. Sixteen-year-old Tom would have to come home from the minor public school of Wellington in Somerset which Captain Nicholson had been paying for, and go instead to the local grammar. Jamie was on a Catholic scholarship to St Benet's in Oxford, so the change in their fortunes barely affected him. Mrs Murray had held a job in the local haberdashery shop since they'd arrived in Welwyn and had always insisted on paying some rent for the cottage. She was prepared to accept Lucy's father's generosity to her boys, but never wanted to be any more beholden to him than necessary.

Her father cleared his throat. 'I'm afraid you will have to leave school and go to work, Lucy.' He was staring fixedly at a point just beyond her left shoulder. 'I'm very sorry but there won't be any university for you. There's no point for a woman anyway. You'll only get married. So I thought you could teach perhaps, here in the village, so you can be home early and do whatever needs doing in the house.'

For a moment she'd stood speechless. It was as if a great iron door had clanged shut on the sunny country of her future. She opened her mouth to speak, but her father met her eyes with that commanding-officer expression which told her there was nothing she could say or do.

Jamie quickly indicated to her to go next door with Mrs Murray and Tom, while he stayed to reason with her father. Jamie had always been willing to fight Captain Nicholson for her, and usually managed to talk him round.

In the cottage, they waited in strained silence for Jamie's return, but as soon as she saw the pallor of his face, she knew it had been in vain.

'I begged him,' said Jamie, 'literally begged him. I reminded him you'd wanted to be a doctor all your life, and you would be a marvellous one. I told him you were too clever, too bright and sharp to be relegated to be an untrained teacher in the village school. I really, really tried.'

Her eyes were brimming with tears, and she couldn't speak, but Lucy believed him.

'But it's worse than we thought,' he continued. 'When the stock market crashed in 1929 he began to borrow money, and now he's in the most terrible debt. He owes more than you can imagine. Your house might have to be sold.'

'If he'd just let me stay at school and take my exams, perhaps I could get a scholarship like you,' pleaded Lucy.

Jamie shook his head in misery. 'I said that. I said maybe there was something I could do, that I'd get a job in the evenings and holidays, anything to let you stay on. When he said no to that, I offered to leave university myself and get a job. I wouldn't mind what happens to me. But he's adamant. He says it's not just the cost of your medical training; he needs whatever wages you can bring in right now. I'm so sorry, Lucy.' His face was twisted in anguish at his own failure to save her dream, as though it was his dream too.

Lucy sobbed in Mrs Murray's arms and both the boys patted her shoulders. When she'd cried herself out, Jamie had given her his handkerchief and sat close, with his forehead leaning on hers, as if in that way he could share her suffering.

A few days later, when Captain Nicholson had spoken to the head teacher of her own school, who also pleaded in vain, and then to the headmistress of the village infants' school, who had agreed to take her on, Lucy was back in the Murrays' kitchen.

Jamie took her hands in his across the table. 'I know it's not the same as being a doctor, but you can still do good as a schoolteacher, you know,' he said earnestly. 'And you'll be a marvellous teacher, and the children will love you and look back on what you've given them all their lives. There are so many children here who need your help. Poor children who'll never have any other chance in life.'

She'd smiled wanly, thinking he was the person who understood her best in the world.

Tom crouched down at her feet and assumed a falsetto voice. 'Please, miss, teach me to read, teach me to write, I'll love you forever, so I will.' And Lucy, who could never resist his antics, gave a hoot of laughter, reached out a foot and tipped him over. He rolled on to his back and waved his arms and legs in the air like an overturned beetle. 'Please, miss, a big girl pushed me.'

'Ridiculous!' muttered Jamie.

'Get yourself up,' said Mrs Murray indulgently. 'You'll make your sweater all dirty.'

So Lucy's life had changed overnight from schoolgirl to teacher, from a carefree seventeen-year-old to cook, cleaner, housekeeper. Each day she bought groceries on her way home from school, rolled up her sleeves and began to make a fish pie or cheese tart. Heavy things like potatoes were delivered on a Saturday by the greengrocer in his van. Saturdays were also wash day for Lucy, pulling out the copper to boil the sheets, and the mangle to squeeze the water out of them.

Her dream of becoming a doctor had been the obvious conclusion of her lifelong desire to mend things. Jamie and Mrs Murray had always been her allies in that, helping her to feed a baby bird which had fallen out of its nest, or bind up the broken leg of a kitten. Aged nine, Lucy had rescued the kitten from a group of older boys who were torturing it, down by the canal. She'd heard the pitiful mewling, and peeped between their legs to see them poking at the injured animal with sticks. Without another thought she steamed into the centre of their circle, elbowing them out of the way, swooped up the kitten in her arms and turned to face them, all towering over her.

'You should be 'shamed,' she yelled. 'You are disgustin' bullies.'

And they were so surprised that they let her pass, to take the kitten home and nurse it back to health.

It was the same with people. If she saw another child being picked on at school, she would immediately befriend them, seeking them out in the playground, sitting with them at lunch, her very presence signalling to the other children that they could no longer be nasty to her new protégé.

It was a terrible grief to be told that she would never have the opportunity to be a doctor and learn how to mend broken humans: never be able to save women like her mother from dying in childbirth; never prevent other girls from growing up without a mum. She'd even suggested becoming a nurse, but her father had refused to allow her to live away from home.

So Lucy went to work as an infant teacher, and Tom transferred to the local grammar school where his sporting prowess and general clowning soon made him popular and filled their house with boys who lived nearby, many of whom sighed over his blonde seventeen-year-old neighbour.

That was all three years ago. Since then, Tom had won a scholarship to the LSE and Lucy had become accustomed to her life as Miss Nicholson, the teacher. At first she'd resented being incarcerated in the dingy Victorian schoolrooms and was determined to hate teaching, but despite herself she discovered a pleasure in the company of small children. Their imagination, creativity and honesty energised her. Every day they did something which made her laugh, and she couldn't help responding to their unguarded adoration of her. It didn't take her long to realise that people can be damaged in many different ways, and that teaching might give her the means to support girls and boys who were suffering in ways other than the physical.

She had an intuitive knack of recognising a look she had first seen on Jamie and Tom's faces on the day they arrived in her life which told her that children were bereaved, or uprooted, or oppressed, and they needed her to help them. She knew she had fallen in love with Jamie and Tom from that first moment, instantaneously and unreservedly, in the way that only small children can bestow their affection, and nothing in the intervening years had dimmed her initial devotion. But now she also found room in her heart for inventive Joan with her skinny arms and legs, Alfie who laughed all the time but wore shoes which were too small and had socks which were more darn than knit, Jean who was the youngest of a family of fierce redheads, Harry who always begged for her apple core, Gladys who couldn't get the hang of reading until

Lucy realised she needed glasses which her parents couldn't afford.

Although Captain Nicholson's fortunes were much reduced, Lucy knew very well that they weren't as poor as so many people in those dark years: the parents of many of her pupils, the Jarrow marchers and three million others without work. It smarted when her father seemed to find dribbles of money to supplement Tom's scholarship, but she had realised many years ago that the boys were everything to him and she was next to nothing. After all, she was the baby who had caused the death of his wife. Perhaps she should have hated the brothers for getting the fathering she lacked, but right from the start she had loved them too – Jamie for his pathetic determination to be the man of the family, and Tom for his playful nature. She couldn't resent Tom for getting the support from her father which she hadn't received. It wasn't his fault.

*

Now, Lucy pulled the brush furiously through her hair and stared at herself in the dressing-table mirror. In the ten days since the call had appeared in the *Daily Worker*, she and Mrs Murray had cajoled and pleaded with Tom, but failed to change his mind about going to Spain. She could hear Tom and her father downstairs, and knew she was expected to join them, but how could she possibly say goodbye to one of the boys she'd loved since she was five? She was too angry with herself for her failure to dissuade him, and too terrified at the danger he was heading into.

She heard Tom's voice at the bottom of the stairs. 'Luce, come on, I'll miss my train.'

26

I hope you do, she said savagely to herself in the mirror. Her grey eyes flashed like knives. I hope you miss your train, and they turn you down for being too young and unreliable to get there on time.

Her hand halted in the brushing as she heard him on the stairs, taking two at a time in his usual way. He burst into her bedroom, and she swung round.

'Haven't you ever heard of knocking?' she snapped.

He raised his palms in half-hearted apology. 'It's time to go,' he said. 'I'm just leaving.'

Lucy slammed the brush on to the dressing table. 'Well, I wish you weren't.'

'Don't start all that again. It's decided.' He was standing next to her in two strides, vibrating with excitement. 'I'm going, and that's that.'

He came close behind her, took one of her curls and twisted it round his finger, as he had done since he was a small boy. Usually she found this endearing and he knew it. It reminded them both of when she was five and he was four, and she was his only friend. Now she shrugged him away.

'Get off me.'

She stood up, knocking over a jug of hair pins, but he didn't step away, so they were standing uncomfortably close, and her heart began to thump in her chest. His eyes locked on to hers, and he raised his hand to her head again, but instead of wrapping a curl, he grasped the back of her neck and quickly drew her face to him in a fierce kiss. With his other hand, he pulled her body tight against him, and despite herself she was kissing him back, feverishly, desperately, as though she had always been waiting for this.

Captain Nicholson's voice came from below, 'Where's the damned boy gone now?' and he began to lumber up the stairs.

They were both trembling as they pulled apart. Lucy searched Tom's face to try to fathom what this must mean. He had kissed her once before, when he was twelve and she was thirteen, but although she had never forgotten it, that kiss had not been anything like this.

'Don't go,' she said.

'I have to.'

But she thought she detected a new hesitation, a new anguish in his voice.

Captain Nicholson was in the doorway. 'Ah, there you are Tom. Your mother's waiting. And Jamie.'

Lucy and Tom exchanged a look. So he had persuaded Jamie to come and say goodbye.

Her father shepherded Tom out of the room and Lucy caught sight of herself in the mirror. Her cheeks were flushed, there was a fire in her eyes, and her hair fluffed out around her heart-shaped face. She thought she looked almost pretty.

Very well, she thought, lifting her chin. This would be the memory of her which Tom would carry with him. Perhaps it would bring him back.

They all stood awkwardly on the crazy-paved front path. Tom opened the gate and passed through, and was out on the street with his small leather suitcase, while Mrs Murray, Jamie, Lucy and her father remained in the garden. Tom clicked the gate shut between them. They all looked at him in his cavalry twill trousers and red tie, with his hair brilliantined to a dark shine, and his hat resting on his suitcase until he had kissed them goodbye. Lucy could feel Mrs Murray shivering beside her though the day was not cold. Tom leaned over the gate and shook hands with Captain Nicholson. Then Lucy stepped forward, offering her hand, but he grasped hold of both her shoulders, pulled her into him and kissed her loudly on the lips. She felt Jamie's eyes on them, taking this in, but she didn't look at him as she moved aside to let Mrs Murray through.

Tom hugged his mother tightly over the gate and whispered, 'Don't worry Ma!' into her hair. As he let go of her, she staggered, and Lucy took her arm to steady her. Tom picked up his suitcase and turned to leave.

'Your brother. For God's sake, shake hands with your brother,' barked Lucy's father and Tom swivelled again. Captain Nicholson gave Jamie a shove and the brothers' fingers met in a flaccid shake.

Wiping his palm down the leg of his trousers, Tom settled his hat on his head and walked away, rapidly, without looking back. When he reached the corner, Lucy thought he might turn and wave, but he didn't, and she would have run after him if Mrs Murray hadn't slumped against her.

'That's that then,' said Jamie, as though his infuriating little brother had never existed.

Lucy felt Mrs Murray begin to shake with tears. 'How could you take leave of him that way?' she asked Jamie, but he just shrugged and strode across the low picket fence which separated Lucy's garden from theirs.

Embarrassed by all the emotion, Captain Nicholson cleared his throat. 'Well, I'll leave you women to, umph . . . I've got to . . .' He waved a distracted hand and scuttled back to the house, leaving the two women gazing through their tears in the direction where Tom had disappeared.

That night Lucy lay in bed, picturing her lovely Tom marching off to war, fighting in muddy trenches, his flesh being torn apart by the steel of bullets or bayonets, until she covered her face and wept. And that kiss. Where had that come from, and what did it mean? It wasn't the sort of kiss a brother would give a sister, and her response had been very far from sisterly – a world away from how she'd felt about the unexciting kisses from her few short-lived boyfriends.

When she had cried herself out, she crept to the bathroom to wash her face, and on the landing she was stopped in her tracks by a sound downstairs. She edged stealthily down the stairs and pushed open the dining-room door. At the table with his back to her and an almost empty bottle of whisky in front of him, sat her father. The strange sound was deep, muffled sobs, coming up from the pit of his stomach.

Lucy had never heard a man cry before, and especially not her father. For a moment she wondered whether to go to him, to put her arm around his shoulder, to comfort him as she would comfort anyone in distress. But she knew it wasn't her he wanted. It had never been her. Jamie and Tom's father, Private Murray, had died from the gas he'd inhaled saving Captain Nicholson's life, and in paying his debt of honour by taking care of his saviour's sons, her father had pushed her aside. Jamie and Tom had become the centre of his world and taken every ounce of the love which should by rights have been hers. There was nothing Lucy could do to win him back.

She stepped away from the door and mounted the stairs

again, with fear for Tom pounding in her head. Back in bed, she twisted her head against the pain of loss, and remembered when Tom was about seven and he'd been teetering on the edge of a bank over the stream, trying to recover a fishing net he'd dropped. As he tottered on the brink, she'd reached out, grabbed him by his collar and yanked him back. She was a year older than him and it was her job to save Tom from all the scrapes he got into.

'You almost strangled me,' Tom had complained, easing his shirt from his throat. 'There was no need for it, I'd almost got the net and I knew perfickly well what I was doing and wouldn't have fallen in. And now the net is lost forever and your dad gave it to me and he'll be cross and you are a stupid girl.'

He'd pushed past her and gone back to the house on his own, even though they were meant to stay together.

Lucy had studied the lost net, and then looked around her until she found a long branch. Holding on to a willow trunk for balance, she'd fished for the net and pulled it back up the muddy bank to where she could lean down and grab it. It was her job to make things right and she had, though Tom took the returned net from her without a word of thanks.

She sat up in bed as conviction hardened in her. She had failed to talk him out of signing up, but that was just a boy's bravado. Perhaps when he was in Spain and had seen the reality of war at first hand, then she might be able to persuade him to leave the fight to others and come home. It became clear that there was only one thing to do. She would have to go to Spain and bring Tom back, whether he liked it or not.

3

Dusk fell earlier and earlier as October became November, reflecting the dreariness in Lucy's days without Tom to make her laugh, to dance her round the kitchen, to take her to political meetings. She knew he could be self-centred and unreliable, but his enthusiasm and good cheer were infectious and always lifted the spirits of those around him. Now Lucy felt the light travelling further and further away from her, leaving her in deep darkness.

In all the outward ways, life was unchanged. Lucy went to her teaching job at the local infants' school each morning, Captain Nicholson set off for his office and the two of them came together in the early-evening gloom to eat their meal. They ate mostly in silence to the tick of the big grandfather clock, and he never thanked her for cooking. When he turned on the wireless and settled down with his newspaper Lucy slipped through the back gate to the Murrays' house, as she had done for years. But it wasn't the same without Tom. The space in her life where Tom had been seemed like a tangible thing, and every moment of it confirmed her resolve to go to Spain and bring him home. She had no idea how that might be possible, but began to make preparations.

The day after Tom had left, she'd asked Jamie if he would start to teach her Spanish again, as he'd done in his university holidays. Then she'd been a keen pupil, finding it good to have something to sharpen her brain. It always gave her joy to please Jamie and she basked in his admiration as he praised her quick learning. Tom had tagged along to the lessons too, though he never did any of the homework Jamie set and couldn't conjugate a verb to save his life. Lucy suspected he was only there because he couldn't bear to see her and Jamie doing something from which he was excluded. The lessons had often disintegrated into a shouting match, with Jamie calling Tom a lazy dunce and Tom accusing him of being a hopeless teacher.

Without Tom's disruptive presence at their Spanish lessons, Lucy learned fast, and it was obvious that Jamie was enjoying the hour they spent together every evening just as much as she was. They sat together at the kitchen table, and Jamie loosened his tie. He'd brought out all his old college books and sat close to Lucy as they worked through them. Lucy felt as if his mind was joined with hers, filling it with new knowledge.

But as the days passed, Lucy found it increasingly difficult to force herself out of bed to go to work. A cold fog hung about the streets, and the church steeple was lost in the grey cloud which also seemed to have swirled its way into her head. People turned up their collars and drew their scarves round their throats as they appeared out of the mist and vanished into it again. And though she was a good teacher and enjoyed the company of the children, somehow she could no longer put her whole mind to her work.

Every morning she pulled aside the curtain which hung inside the front door, to look for a letter from Tom. Each day there was a moment of hope and a crash of disappointment, until on the tenth of November a letter lay there in its airmail envelope with Tom's familiar, scrawly handwriting addressed to Miss Lucy Nicholson. She stuffed it quickly into her bag, leaving the house without calling goodbye to her father, and almost running around the corner, where she could open it unseen. Her fingers were trembling as she pulled the thin paper from the envelope and she blessed her stars that she'd thought to stuff the stationery into his case.

Tucking her hair behind her ears, she read as she walked.

6 November 1936
Somewhere in France

Hello Luce,

Well, this is an awfully big adventure already. I can see you frowning at me, so yes, I do know that I'm heading into a war, but at the moment I can't help enjoying it all so much. (Don't tell your father.)

I'm on a train going down through France, so my hand-writing is probably going to be a bit jumpy. There. Like that. Let me try pencil. That'll be less blotty.

The countryside here is not unlike Hertfordshire, with gentle green hills and homely villages and bare trees standing

34

sentinel over it all. In my carriage are three other volunteers, but we aren't supposed to know each other, so we just keep exchanging little looks and lifted eyebrows when some funny French thing happens. Someone got on with a live cockerel! A bit later an old lady boarded – as wide as she was tall, and dressed all in black, with a black headscarf – and unwrapped the biggest baguette you've ever seen, and laid it over her ample lap, and then stuffed it full of ham and cheese and we must all have been staring at it and possibly drooling, because she carefully broke us off a bit each, gabbling away in French. I understood some of it, but I could see the other blokes didn't and that suddenly seemed so funny to me that I had to press my nose against the window and pinch my arm to keep from laughing. How we would have got the giggles together, Luce.

But I'm jumping ahead, and maybe I should tell you all about my adventures from the beginning. You know I wrote in after that piece in the Daily Worker, *and they told me to go to London, taking my passport and £5 8s for my fare to Spain, and find the Communist Party HQ in King Street, Covent Garden. I'm sorry I took off so suddenly. I didn't want to spend too long saying goodbye to you and Mum. I didn't trust myself to turn around and wave. I hope you understand.*

Covent Garden is a bit of a run-down area of London, smelling of rotting fruit and vegetables, and there were about twenty men gathering there, looking pretty shifty. Mostly about my age, but older men too, and mainly I'd say labouring men, in flat caps and mufflers, like they'd heard there might be work and were waiting to be hired.

The door opened and we all crammed into one room where we had a talk from Harry Pollitt of the British Communist Party about taking this seriously, and going for the right reasons and understanding that we might not return. (Don't fret, old girl, I promise I will.)

Well, I've never quite been a communist, but the excitement buzzing around that room made me feel like leaving the Labour Party and joining up. No, no, don't worry, I didn't! Not yet, anyway.

Then we were taken one by one into a little side room for an interview about our political allegiances and motives. I wasn't sure what I was supposed to say about political allegiances, so I just told him I'd been a socialist ever since I started university. The question about motives was easier. My interviewer was a very serious young man with steel-rimmed spectacles, and he leaned across the desk and I'm sure his eyes twinkled a bit when I said, 'To fight those Fascist b——s, and save the Spanish revolution.' I think it must have been the right answer because he just moved on. I suppose they have to identify spies in the midst of us.

He asked me if I had any dependants, and I thought about Mum, and whether I ought to mention her, but Jamie can look after her, so she's not just dependent on me, is she? And I dare say your father wouldn't let her starve, so I just crossed my fingers behind my back and looked him straight in the eye and said, 'None. I'm free as a bird.'

Then he asked me about my physical fitness and I told him about playing scrum half and doing a bit of rowing. He seemed to think that would be good enough. Last of all he asked me if I had any 'special experience', and I suppose

I must have looked a bit puzzled by that, so he prompted me: had I done any first aid or ever handled a weapon, or organised a trade union and did I speak any languages, and I told him I spoke a few words of Spanish, though my brother was the real linguist. I did get a first-aid badge in Scouts, but I didn't mention that. I hope they are going to have better medicos than me. All I can remember is how to tie my scarf into an arm sling. I thought about telling him I was an economics student, but I couldn't really see how that would be any help in a battle. All that calculus gone to waste. He looked like he'd sucked a lemon when I mentioned being in the Cadet Corps and I suppose that marked me down as a boy who'd been to a posh school, even though it wasn't my choice to go there, but he seemed a bit more positive when I said I knew how to strip down and handle a rifle. I haven't done it since I left Wellington, but I expect I can remember how.

After he'd finished scribbling down answers to my questions, he sent me through to another room, where there was a doctor (or a man in a white coat anyway – I assumed it was a doctor, ha ha!) who told me to strip and gave me a rather cursory physical examination, like could I touch my toes and could I read some numbers on a chart on the wall, and then asked me to get dressed again. I saw him give a big tick on a piece of paper, so I knew I'd been passed fit for service.

I went back to my college digs that night and looked around my room, knowing it would be the last time for quite a while, and that felt rather queer. So I started packing, and that brought back the thrill of it. I'd done what the letter said and bought two khaki shirts with pockets, and a pair of shorts. Though surely it won't be weather for shorts? And all the while, it was running through my head, I'm going to Spain, I'm going to Spain. Then I stood in front of my little bookcase and tried to decide which books to take. I put in too many and the case wouldn't close — it's just that little brown one — and had to take them out again. Guess what I chose in the end? Hugo's Spanish in Three Months Without a Master *obviously, but the rest I'm not going to tell you. Let me know your guess when you write. You will write, won't you? Write soon. Send it to the Communist Party HQ in London.*

Then one of the fellows who shares my digs knocked on my door and suggested we went to the pub for one last drink. So we did, and there were some other chaps I know in there who insisted on buying me drinks and slapping me on the back because I was going off to fight for freedom and democracy. I don't mind telling you I felt pretty pleased with myself by closing time.

The next morning I dressed in some corduroy trousers because that was what most of the volunteers had been wearing, and left off my hat. I do so want to fit in with them and they were wearing flat caps, not hats. When I pulled my door closed behind me, my stomach gave a funny little lurch, and I wondered what I might have seen by the time I opened it again.

Back at the CP HQ we were given weekend boat-train tickets to Paris. They have to be weekend tickets because most of the men don't have passports, and if you've got a weekend return you can go to Paris without one. We were given a bit of French money, and told not to spend it on drink or women! So, as it was Friday night, we all caught the Underground to Victoria, and we'd been told just to go in pairs and 'behave like tourists' so we didn't draw attention to ourselves. I was with a rather weedy-looking type, who was a union man from a Lancashire mill. At Victoria we stood about waiting for the train, trying to appear nonchalant, and spotting other little groups of men who we'd seen in Covent Garden. Two blokes were on the wrong platform, and apparently a guard said to them: 'The International Brigaders are over there.' So much for looking like tourists!

I can't tell you how exciting it was to climb on to that train and settle down, then to board the ferry and cross the Channel in the dark and then to take the second train to Paris. I was the only one of our group who could speak any French, so it was down to me to get coffee for everyone at Calais and on the train. We were met at the Gare du Nord, and taken to a hostel. It was a bit of a fleapit, but I suppose I'm going to have to get used to worse than that!

Some of the other blokes went out on the town, and came home drunk, and they were sent packing in the morning — back to Blighty. I sat in a café with the man from Lancashire and bought him a French beer which he didn't like and let him tell me about his life. There's so much I didn't know about the way most people survive, about back-to-backs and knockers-up and never having money to see a doctor. I feel ashamed. This is going to be a real education.

The next day we were taken to the Paris CP HQ and given breakfast and another medical examination and a

Spanish ID card. They've stamped it with the word 'Antifascista'. I'm so proud of that card. I keep taking it out and reading it when I think nobody's looking.

And now we're on a train south again. Heading towards Spain. Imagine that! After all these months reading about it and talking about it and shouting at Jamie, I'm actually on my way!

Fondest love,
Your Antifascista Tom

P.S. – I'll write separately to Mum. Don't let Jamie get hold of this letter, will you?

The church clock struck 8.45 a.m. and Lucy ran the last few steps into school. As she hung up her coat she thought how this was exactly the kind of letter she would have expected him to write before that kiss: a loving, brotherly letter. Fondest love! What did that mean?

4

Every evening Lucy lifted yesterday's copy of *The Times* out of the waste bin beside the fireplace, where her father had left it. As their dinner was cooking, she rolled and twisted some pages of the newspaper into firelighters. Once she'd made a little heap she laid them carefully in the freshly swept grate, with the wooden kindling and a few lumps of coal on top. When she had touched a match to the paper and the flames were catching, she would hold the unused double pages across the chimney opening to draw the fire. As she did so, she would idly read the articles in front of her.

On the nineteenth of November, she knelt in front of the fireplace with her arms outstretched, listening for the crackle of fire behind the paper, and watching that it didn't catch light, when her attention was drawn to a letter from the Society of Friends about Spain.

The sufferings of the children . . . she read as she rocked back on her heels. *Havoc . . . Bombings from the air . . .* She whipped the hot sheets of newsprint back towards her. The one nearest the fire was scorched and she dropped it on to the hearth as she folded the letters page small enough to handle and carried it to the light from the window.

Untold miseries are being inflicted on the child population of this unhappy country, not only by wounds and death, but also in shattered nerves and ruined health. It said that Quaker Relief was working with Save the Children International Union and the International Committee of the Red Cross to evacuate children from the worst war zones. A thousand youngsters had already been moved to holiday camps or 'colonies' in safer Spanish districts or in France, but thousands more needed to be evacuated in what it called *the impartial rescue of children.* It gave an address and requested donations for the cause.

Her throat dry with excitement, Lucy forced herself to read the letter again more slowly. Surely it wasn't an accident that she had stumbled on these words, which seemed aimed at her alone? After she'd read it for the third time, she held the page close to her heart and thought of the boys and girls in her class. It could be Joan who had witnessed her parents killed by a bomb; it could be Alfie whose home had been destroyed and was now forced out on to the road; it could be Gladys packaged off to a children's home where there was nobody who knew her, let alone anyone to love her.

Only a week before, Mrs Murray had shown her pictures in the *Daily Worker* of Spanish children killed by General Franco's bombs, and now those terrible images fused with this letter in *The Times*.

The fire in the hearth might have failed to catch, but another had been lit in her mind and it burned with a bright flame. *The impartial rescue of children.*

During dinner that night Lucy could hardly contain her excitement. It bubbled and boiled up inside her, as if any second she might burst out with the shrill whistle of a kettle on the hob. She could barely swallow the cauliflower cheese she'd cooked.

As soon as Captain Nicholson had opened his copy of *The Times*, Lucy slipped next door to show Jamie and Mrs Murray the newspaper cutting, already soft from handling.

'You always have a gleam about you, Lucy, but tonight you are positively glowing,' Mrs Murray observed.

Jamie studied her hard. 'You can't be thinking you'll go to Spain too? You've never been further than London on your own.' He didn't say, 'You're a girl!' but Lucy could see him thinking it. He always wanted to protect her, but now it was time for her to stand on her own.

'Don't pour cold water on me, Jamie Murray, or I won't come here and tell you my secrets any more. You sound just like my father.'

She turned to Mrs Murray. 'I could be of real help over there. I know I could. And when I'm there I could look for Tom and bring him home.'

'But how would you manage it, dear?'

'I'll be twenty-one in January, and then I get the allowance from my grandmother. It's only £50 a year, but I think that would be enough to live on in Spain, don't you? And when I'm twenty-one my father can't tell me what to do any longer.'

'That's true,' agreed Mrs Murray. 'It probably doesn't cost much to live there. And I've got some savings I could lend you for your fare.'

Jamie looked from one to the other of them, and his horror about the plan was written clearly on his pale features. 'But it would be dangerous, Lucy. You'd be going to a war zone. I wouldn't want you to get hurt.'

Lucy turned the full beam of her joyous smile on him. 'But the children, Jamie. The children need me.'

After a mostly sleepless night, Lucy sought out Ruth, one of the other teachers at her school, just two years older than her, and the only Quaker she'd ever met. Lucy wore her own religion lightly, going to St Mary's every Sunday with her father and Mrs Murray, more because it was the centre of the village community than from any strong faith. She had taken all she needed from Christianity – the notion that she was put on earth to help others. She had no idea what Quakers might believe, but knew that Ruth exuded an enviable kind of calm.

Ruth was on playground duty, bundled up in a brown scarf and gloves, when Lucy showed her the cutting.

'Yes, it's really bad in Spain,' said Ruth.

'I want to go,' Lucy blurted out. 'I know it sounds stupid, but I feel this letter was written to me, telling me I have to help.'

Ruth smiled. 'I think it was written to raise money for the cause.'

'Well I haven't got any money, but I have got myself. And I know about children.'

'You certainly do.'

Ruth picked up a ball which had rolled to her feet and threw it back to a group of boys.

'There's a speaker about Spain at Friends House in Euston next month.' She could see Lucy was looking puzzled. 'It's the Quaker headquarters. Our official name is the Society of Friends, and we call ourselves Friends, but most people know us as Quakers. I'll take you if you like.'

Lucy squeezed her hand. 'Oh yes. Yes please!'

A childish wail rose from the corner of the playground and the two young women hastened to investigate.

It was mid-December before the next letter arrived from Tom, and so cold in the house that Lucy had to get up early to make sure the range was full of coal before she went to school. She heard the post drop through the door and her heart flipped.

1 December
Barcelona. España!!!!

Dear Comrade Luce,

I'm now in Spain, in Barcelona, in a little hostel near the main street, La Rambla. God, Luce, you'd love it here. I wish you were with me.

So, the train chuffed down through France to Perpignan. And by then we'd given up pretending to be tourists, and were all sitting more or less together. We are mostly young but there's some men who served in the Great War and a lot of union organisers. Miners and suchlike. Your father would call them Reds or 'Bolshy types'. I'm going to like them very much.

Perpignan is a pretty place with palm trees like Torquay. By the sea, I think, but we didn't go there. We went to a café for wine and food. The wine was quite vinegary.

Just as we were beginning to think we'd be spending the night in the café, a Spaniard came, possibly the smallest man I've ever seen. And I was very pleased that I could understand what he was saying. Well, some of it anyway. I've been brushing up on the train. He told us we'd be picked up by a bus, so we sat down by the roadside for a few hours, and it was quite cold and I felt an idiot for packing shorts. I hope nobody ever sees them. I was glad of my corduroy trousers.

It was starting to get dark before the bus turned up and it was the oldest thing I've ever seen – almost looked like it ought to be horse-drawn – but we all piled in. I wish I hadn't brought a suitcase too. Most of the men have kitbags, which looks a lot less poncey. I look like I'm going on a holiday. Everything marks me out as a man with a privileged upbringing, but the others don't seem to hold it against me.

The bus took us on twisty-turny roads up and up in the mountains, and I was really suffering from car sickness, so had to open a window and hope I wouldn't show myself up. Most of the other men were smoking and that made it worse. It was all right as long as I didn't think of that wine I'd just drunk. The wine is stronger than British beer.

I don't know how long it was, and I wouldn't say if I did, just in case this letter falls into the wrong hands, but it felt like a lifetime we were on that bus. And then, finally, it stopped, and we all tumbled out. I took deep, deep breaths of mountain air. I could tell we were high up because it was so cold, and there was snow on the ground, but it was too dark to see anything else, except thousands of stars. I put on all my shirts on top of each other, and my sweater and my jacket, but I was still very, very cold. The Spaniard came round to us handing out rope-soled shoes – no more than

46

slippers, really, with canvas uppers. They are called alpargatas. I noticed for the first time how badly shod most of the other British men were, though one chap was wearing brogues which wouldn't have been much good for mountaineering. Luckily I'd brought my walking boots – you know, the ones I had from the Lake District holiday – so although I politely accepted my pair of alpargatas, I shoved them in my suitcase when the Spaniard wasn't looking. I felt a damn fool carrying a suitcase, I can tell you, but didn't want to leave my books. And, did I say? I've got a picture of you. The one taken at your cousin's wedding: you were laughing your head off and wearing that blue dress I like, though of course it's grey in the photo.

Anyway, then it started to get serious. The Spaniard told us there must be no talking and no smoking and we must walk single file behind our French guide. That sobered us up, I must say, and we were looking all about us and listening for border guards who might have stopped us crossing, and our ankles kept nearly twisting over on the rocky path because we couldn't see where we were putting our feet. Almost as soon as we set off, it began to rain, icy rain, which might have been sleet – driving into our faces.

Even with gloves, my hand holding the suitcase was frozen, and I had to keep swapping, and ram the other deep into my pocket. Some of the men didn't have gloves, and I felt a chump for leaving my hat behind, just because I was trying to fit in. My hair was soaked and freezing rain was running down my face and neck.

We must have walked, or rather tripped and stumbled, in the darkness for about two hours and then the guard stopped ahead of us and, because we were in a line, we all bumped into each other. It would have been funny if it wasn't so frightening. He shushed us furiously and whispered that we should all be completely silent, because we were near the border.

We could just about make out white painted rocks and boulders which glowed faintly in the moonlight, and we understood that this side of them was France and the other was Spain. We fanned out, and as we approached the rocks I could feel the men on either side of me speeding up, and I did too, and in the end we were all running for the last few yards, expecting a shot to ring out any second.

And then we were past the rocks, and they told us to stop running because we might fall off a cliff. Well, that stopped us pretty quickly I can tell you, and we were all laughing and slapping each other on the back, because here we were. We'd made it into Spain!

Not that our joy lasted very long, because we had to trudge further, down another treacherous track for about an hour, and the rain was now much more like snow, and our feet were numb, and the sleet was melting into the neck of my jacket and dribbling down my back.

Eventually we came to a track that was wide enough for a vehicle and there was a lorry waiting for us, and we all clambered aboard, and sat in the back of it, huddled together and shivering, and everyone tried to light cigarettes while the lorry was bumping us around like spuds in a sack.

And now, here I am in Barcelona, and my God, Luce, you should see it. It's everything we dreamed the Republic would be. Every building has a flag flying from it – either the red flag, or the red and black of the anarchists, or the *red and yellow stripes of the Catalan flag. (Barcelona is in Catalonia and they speak a separate language and the Republic is giving them independence. Fancy that! The Welsh miners who are with us think that's a great idea.)*

So imagine all the flags flying against the bluest sky you ever saw, and it's like a fiesta everywhere you look. There are revolutionary posters blazing red and blue pasted up on every wall and in the small gaps between them people have painted the hammer and sickle or the initials of the revolutionary parties. The buses are all red and black and even the bootblacks' boxes have been painted red and black! Then there are the people – everyone dressed more or less the same, no well-dressed people at all, everyone wearing working-class clothes, or blue overalls or some kind of militia uniform. There are women fighters too, Luce – you'd love to see them. They look so splendid in their corduroy knee breeches and zipped woollen jackets and their flashing eyes. I've got myself kitted out with a leather jacket and a forage cap and a red and black handkerchief to wear around my throat. I look very dashing, and because I'm so dark, I often get taken for a tall Spaniard. Please send woollen socks when you can. All the socks here are cotton, and no use at all. Tell Mother to send anything warm – flannel shirts, wool underwear.

Almost the best thing is everyone addressing each other as 'comrade'. If I go into a shop, they don't call me 'Señor' and the polite form of 'you', they look me in the face, like an equal, and call me 'comrade' and the familiar 'thou'. Nobody says 'buenos días', it's always 'salud!' All the shops and cafés have notices saying they've been collectivised and you aren't allowed to tip waiters any more. In the centre of town, the road called *La Rambla*, there are loudspeakers bellowing revolutionary songs day and night. Nobody seems downcast and there's a thrilling sense of equality and freedom. It's what I came for, Luce. We can't let General Franco and his Fascists take this away.

I have to admit there are signs of war too — all the buildings are in disrepair and (don't tell Jamie) every church has been gutted and there are gangs of workers taking them down stone by stone. At night they keep the lights in the city low in case of bombing raids. There are long bread queues — bread is really short because all the wheat-growing area is in Franco's hands. And there's not much meat or coal or sugar. The only sort of meat is a bright red sausage which gives you the runs. (Sorry.) And you can't get milk at all. How I long for a cup of tea with milk! I drink tiny cups of thick black coffee now.

And there are refugees coming in by train from the areas where the fighting is. You'd want to take them all home with you, especially the children.

So here I am, Luce, and our train is taking us south tomorrow. Yes, I'm a bit scared about what I'm going into, but now I've seen it with my own eyes, I'm even more sure that it's worth fighting for. I promise I'll be careful and keep my head down.

Don't forget to ask Mother to send socks and warm things. She can send them via the Communist Party in London. And letters too. Please write. And please give Mother a hug, and have one for yourself.

Night night, comrade!

Tom

* * *

Not even *fondest love* this time, thought Lucy, folding the letter into her pocket. Now she was just a comrade. But now she had a plan. She was going to Spain to join the Quakers, and as soon as she was there, she would be the comrade who would bring him safely home.

5

By Christmas Lucy's resolve to go to Spain had hardened diamond-sharp, and she focused on her Spanish lessons with absolute concentration. Jamie was surprised at the speed with which she progressed and, as always, she glowed in the warmth of his approval.

Ruth had taken her to the meeting at Friends House in London, where she'd heard speakers talk movingly about the plight of the refugee children in Spain. What they were told was heart-rending. Thousands of women whose husbands and fathers were away fighting on the front line had taken to the roads with their offspring to escape the bombing which preceded the approach of Franco's brutal army. As those refugees converged on towns which were already poor and desperate, the Republican government struggled to feed and house them. To make matters worse, many children had been orphaned and were now alone and vulnerable in strange places.

At the meeting Lucy listened intently to a couple called Alfred and Norma Jacob who were going out to Barcelona, where thousands of refugees were heading. They were both Oxford graduates, only in their twenties and with a young son and daughter, but had been chosen because they were Quakers who had already lived in Spain and spoke fluent Spanish. An older woman called Edith Pye and her translator Janet Perry were also about to leave on a fact-finding mission. Edith was a dumpy little ex-midwife with a Somerset accent, the kind of woman you'd pass in the street and barely notice. Lucy was thrilled that women were involved in such important positions. She had expected that only men would be allowed.

On the train home, Lucy said, 'I felt a bit conspicuous in my red hat and gloves.'

'I'm sorry, I should have told you that Quakers like to dress soberly,' said Ruth.

Lucy realised she'd never seen Ruth in bright-coloured clothes, always in grey or brown, and had thought it was just personal taste.

'Would you be interested in coming to the local meeting house with me?' asked Ruth. 'It's in Welwyn Garden City.'

Lucy laughed uncomfortably. 'If it's like a church service, I wouldn't know when to stand up or sit down. Jamie dragged me to Catholic Mass with him a few times in my teens, but I couldn't make head nor tail of it.'

Ruth raised her eyebrows in amusement. 'I can promise you it's nothing like a Latin Mass. We don't have any priests or vicars. And there isn't any standing up or kneeling. We just sit in silence.'

'No hymns or sermons or readings or prayers?' Lucy was astonished.

53

Ruth shook her head. 'If anyone feels moved to speak they will do, but otherwise we just sit quietly together. It's very peaceful.'

'I normally go to St Mary's,' Lucy said doubtfully. 'But all right. I'll come.'

A thought struck her. She remembered Mrs Murray telling her that she'd had to convert to Catholicism when she married Mr Murray, even though she reverted to her Protestant roots when he died. 'Would I have to become a Quaker if I wanted to help them in Spain?'

Ruth laughed again. 'No, it's not like that. We don't have any creed or doctrine. Nobody tells us what to think.'

Lucy liked the sound of that. 'What do you believe, then?'

'It's quite simple, really. That there's a light, of love I suppose, or God or whatever you like to call it, in everyone, in every human being. And that makes every person valuable.'

'I see,' Lucy said slowly. 'So that's why you are pacifists.'

Ruth nodded. 'It's why we oppose war and slavery, and so on. Why don't you come and see? You'd be very welcome. And someone there can write you a letter of introduction to the Jacobs in Barcelona – if you're really serious about going.'

Lucy grinned. 'I've never been so serious about anything in my whole life.'

The festive season without Tom felt empty. He'd always been the one to choose Christmas trees and lug them home for both houses. Then he'd helped Lucy and his mother decorate the trees, singing carols loudly and often with the wrong words till they all fell about in giggles.

On 25 December, Lucy got up early to light the fires and

put the pudding to steam in the clothes-washing copper. She knew that Mrs Murray would be next door peeling potatoes and preparing the swede and carrots. The two families always shared Christmas dinner, cooking half of it in each house, and gathering around the larger table at the Nicholsons'.

By 8 a.m. Jamie would already have gone to his Catholic Mass, and Lucy wondered if he would be praying for his brother. Mrs Murray would be alone and Lucy knew they were both thinking of Tom, of where he was and how he would be marking the day, both desperately hoping that he was safe. Lucy wiped a tear from her eye and wished they could just pretend Christmas wasn't happening.

At least it felt normal when Lucy, Captain Nicholson and Mrs Murray walked to church together and took their usual pew. Tom had given up coming with them some years before, saying it would be hypocritical now he was an atheist. But it was some comfort to Lucy to sing the old familiar carols and shake hands with her friends and wish the other villagers a happy Christmas.

Over dinner they dutifully pulled their crackers, donned their paper hats and read each other the riddles. Jamie tried hard to engage everyone in conversation about topics of general interest – the abdication of course, and poor King George, and the Croydon air crash. Mrs Murray chattered on in a falsely bright voice about what the customers in the shop had said about that devil Mrs Simpson, how some of them liked her clothes and one of them had been to Cannes where the couple were now living. The one subject they studiously avoided was the war in Spain.

Lucy had rearranged the seating for the four of them so

there wasn't an empty chair, but her eyes kept straying to the place Tom usually sat. Captain Nicholson carried in the plum pudding, poured brandy over it, and set fire to it. Tom usually loved to do that, and they always exclaimed at the blueness of the flames. This year they all watched the flames die away and said nothing.

After dinner they exchanged their gifts. Lucy's father presented her with a surprisingly attractive silk scarf in misted blues and mauves and greens, which she suspected Mrs Murray had chosen. Jamie had bought her a petite English–Spanish dictionary. Mrs Murray gave her a pocket-size folding photograph frame made of leather, in which she had put a hand-tinted photograph of each of the boys. Jamie's classical features looked as if they had been painted in the soft pastels of watercolour, whereas Tom's red lips and brown hair seemed to have been rendered in oils. It was just as they were in real life and would be perfect to pack in a small suitcase.

The largest and most carefully chosen parcels this year had been posted to Tom. Each family had sent one containing warm clothes of all kinds, with chocolates and other modest treats. The parcels had gone to the Communist Party in London, and from there would be transported to Marseilles and by sea to Valencia. Although they'd been parcelled up in good time, nobody knew if or when they might arrive. Both families had received a card from Tom, drawn by one of his comrades-in-arms. It sat in pride of place on each mantelpiece.

After they'd cleared away dinner and washed up, they all gathered in the living room for half-hearted word games, until Captain Nicholson fell asleep and began to snore loudly.

Mrs Murray stood up. 'I think I'll just pop home for a little nap. I'm feeling quite tired after all that lovely food.'

With evident relief, Jamie suggested a walk to Lucy and she hurried to get her coat, hat and wellington boots.

Once away from the village, they paced side by side through the woods, and their comfortable silence was calming after all the forced conversation of the day. The leafless trees dripped from earlier rain, and the wet earth gave off a rich, mulchy smell as they walked. Where the path came out of the woods and overlooked ploughed fields, Jamie paused for a moment. Lucy was gazing out over the countryside and felt his eyes on her. When she looked up, he was assessing her shrewdly, but she also sensed an excitement.

'I've got something to tell you,' he blurted out. 'You mustn't repeat it to anyone.'

His usually pale face was flushed, and her first thought was that he had a girlfriend nobody knew about and he was going to announce his engagement. It would be so like Jamie to keep the girl a secret, Lucy thought, and a pang of jealousy stung like a slap. The strength of her own reaction took Lucy by surprise, but she tried to arrange her face into a mask of pleasurable anticipation.

Jamie started to walk again, striding off down the muddy path which ran around the field. She hurried to keep pace with him.

'The *Herald*'s correspondent in Spain is coming home, and I've persuaded them that I should go in his place. I didn't want to say anything before, because I wanted Mother to have one last Christmas before I go too. I'd be filing copy for all the Catholic papers, and trying to get stories in the nationals too – though they'll have their own men there. But it's a great opportunity. I won't tell Mother till tomorrow, till Christmas is over, but I couldn't wait any longer to tell you.'

He stopped again and scanned her face anxiously. 'What do you think?'

Lucy was still trying to realign her thoughts. 'It's . . . it's . . . a surprise,' she stammered.

'Why would it be a surprise?'

He set off so fast that she almost had to run to keep up with him.

'You know I've wanted to go,' he continued. 'To shout the truth about the Catholic cause to all the corners of the earth, ever since this all began. It was only that the *Herald* already had a man there. It's like all my life has been coming together to this end – if I hadn't kept my last promise to Dad, and hadn't stayed a Catholic, I'd never have learned Latin, never got the scholarships to Ampleforth and St Benet's, never learned Spanish, never got the job on the *Catholic Herald*. It's all been mapped out for me because I was true to myself and true to my promises. You do see what it means to me and that I have to go, don't you?'

Lucy's head spun and she felt as if she needed to sit down. It seemed such a short time ago that she'd had almost the same conversation with Tom. Although the brothers were so unalike to look at and held such radically opposing views, they were so similar at heart, she thought, both pig-headed, stubborn idealists with an overblown sense of their own destiny. It was bad enough that Tom had gone. It would be a complete disaster if Jamie went to Spain too.

'Surely there are other reporters out there?' she argued weakly.

'But hardly any of them speak Spanish like I do, and they're probably not Catholic, not understanding that this is a crusade – a modern crusade against the powers of darkness.'

Lucy sighed, seeing him clad in armour with a great red cross on a tabard, and unquenchable zeal written all over his face. At least he wasn't planning to go to fight, she thought.

'But won't it be dangerous? Won't you have to go where the fighting is?'

'That's what Mother will say. I thought you at least would be glad for me, would understand that this is everything I've been waiting for. You know me better than anyone in the world.'

They turned back off the path into the top corner of the woods, and he stumbled slightly as they entered the dark of the trees. She grabbed his elbow to steady him.

'Of course I understand. I was just . . . a bit surprised, because I thought for a minute you were going to say something else.'

'What on earth would that be?'

She laughed at herself. 'I thought you were going to tell me you had a secret girlfriend and were going to get married.'

He stopped abruptly and gazed down at her in amazement. 'How could you think that?'

She shrugged. 'You had girlfriends at college. And I don't expect you to tell me everything.'

His blue eyes bored into hers as if he was searching for something. 'But don't you know?'

'Know what?'

'That you've always been the only one for me.'

Lucy had a sudden memory of them when she was about six. She had been playing hospitals on the lawn with Tom and a row of dolls and teddies. They often played this game and, being a year older, Lucy was in charge and enjoyed bossing Tom around. When Tom became bored, he pretended to be a kitten, and made her scratch his belly. His capers always made her laugh. At the age of eight, Jamie obviously thought the hospital game was babyish, but stood watching them, hating not to be included. When he finally asked to play, Tom had said, 'But we are the doctor and the nurse, so who are you? You are nobody.' Even then, Lucy had registered the stricken look of dismay on Jamie's face and tried to be kind, suggesting 'Maybe you could be the man next door?' But Jamie had stalked away and Lucy had realised for the first time that the two boys were rivals for her affection, and she had power over them both.

So yes, he was right. She had always known he loved her. It was always Jamie she turned to with her problems, always Jamie who understood, who seemed to know her own mind before she even knew it herself. But was that the kind of love he meant? She nodded slowly and he reached down and tucked a stray curl back under her red hat.

'The other girls were just me checking, measuring them against you. And nobody could hold a candle. And I hoped it was like that for you, with the boys from the Young Farmers and church.'

Lucy nodded again. He was right, of course. Her few

boyfriends had seemed lumpen and stupid compared with Jamie and Tom.

'I want to marry you, Lucy. You know that, don't you?' He looked down at the muddy path. 'I'd go down on one knee, only . . .'

She caught hold of him, laughing. 'Don't do that, you idiot! You'll get filthy.'

'I'd do anything if you'll agree to marry me.'

Lucy felt hot and confused. 'I'm too young to marry anyone. I haven't had a life yet.'

'Is it Tom?' Jamie didn't try to keep the jealousy out of his voice. 'Is it that you won't marry me because you want to marry Tom?'

She couldn't lie to Jamie. He would see clean through her. 'I don't know,' she said, taking his arm. 'I just don't know.'

'Did Tom ask you to marry him, before he left?'

Lucy stammered, 'No, no. Of course not. He's only nineteen!'

'I couldn't bear to lose you.'

'When we both get back from Spain,' she said. 'Then we'll know for sure.'

'I've always known for sure.'

He pulled off his gloves and stuffed them in his pockets, then softly took her face between his hands. He looked deep into her eyes and she felt as if her soul was known to him. Then he bent and kissed her lips, so very gently that her insides seemed to melt.

Pulling her in close to him, he whispered, 'I love you. I've been waiting to tell you that since I was seven years old.'

She buried her face in his tweed coat, and muttered, 'I love you too,' because it was true, had always been true in its own way, and she wanted so much to please him, and it seemed too terrible not to say the words back to him.

They stood in the woods for a long time, listening to the drip of the trees, and a blackbird singing somewhere far off. Then they drew apart and Jamie's face was ablaze with joy.

'Promise me this at least, will you – that you won't marry anyone else till the war in Spain is over?'

She easily promised that she wouldn't. She had no intention of marrying anyone.

'I'll wait for you for as long as it takes,' he said.

'I know you will.'

He took her gloved hand in his. 'Come on, let's get back. They'll be wondering where we are.'

She was suddenly afraid. 'We won't tell them anything, will we?'

'About us? Not if you don't want to. It's enough that I've told you how I feel and that I can write to you and call you "my love". This is my best Christmas present ever.'

It would be nice to be called 'my love', Lucy thought. A whole lot nicer than 'comrade'.

The next morning Jamie told his mother he was leaving for Spain, and two days later they were gathered round the front gate again to say goodbye. He kissed Lucy's cheek in a brotherly fashion, and she was glad he wasn't making any public claims on her. They watched as he walked to the end of the road, where he turned and lifted his hat and blew a kiss to her and his mother before he too was gone.

6

January 1937 was mild, wet, grey and depressing, and Lucy didn't know how she would have got through it without her pupils, who trod on her toes and hugged her legs and made her laugh. She knew she would miss them dreadfully, but told herself sternly that they were children with roofs over their heads and warm clothes and food. She had to go and help others who had none of those things.

The newspapers were full of the Spanish war, and every night Lucy sat with Mrs Murray as they listened to the news on the wireless, and pored over a map of Spain, trying to understand where the fighting was worst. Franco was trying to take Madrid. It would all be over once he'd captured the capital city. Lucy remembered La Pasionaria and her slogan, '*¡No pasarán!*' – they shall not pass.

Mrs Murray had decided that once she was left alone, she would go to visit her family in Lanarkshire, Scotland, and might even stay there. Neither of them mentioned her plans to Captain Nicholson. At weekends they worked quietly together, packing everything into tea chests to go into storage. Both women felt as if they were in limbo, fearful for their boys, longing for letters from them, and waiting for Lucy's twenty-first birthday on the eleventh of January when everything would change.

Lucy had been to Thomas Cook's and worked out the route by which she would travel to Barcelona, down through France and across the border by train. She had studied the railway timetables so often that she'd almost memorised them. Mrs Murray had insisted on giving her the money for her ticket and Lucy had changed some of her own savings into French francs and Spanish pesetas. Her stomach felt tight all the time with a mixture of anxiety and excited anticipation of the adventure she was about to embark on.

Ruth had written ahead to Alfred Jacob in Barcelona, and one of the elders at the Quaker meeting house had given Lucy a letter to carry in case the other didn't arrive. Lucy had handed in her notice at the school, and sworn the headmistress to secrecy. She'd had her hair cut in a shorter bob than usual so it would be more manageable. The shorter her hair, the closer the curls sat to her head and the easier they were to subdue into something which looked like a permanent wave. She had washed and ironed her four plainest dresses – two woollen and two cotton, all made by Mrs Murray over the years. The winter ones were plum-coloured and dark green, the summer ones mauve and pale blue; this was the frock Tom liked. She would wear the green dress to travel. It might be lucky. Her new silk scarf would look well with any of them.

She decided to take one brown belt and her sensible lace-up

shoes with the half-inch heel. When summer came she would buy sandals in Spain. Her only books would be the Spanish dictionary Jamie had given her for Christmas and a Catalan one he'd bought when she'd told him she was going to Barcelona, plus Palgrave's *Golden Treasury of Poems*, which was portable. She had to be able to carry her own case easily. She would be an independent woman on a great adventure and she was impatient to begin. Before she folded and packed the hinged photo frame, she kissed each of the pictures of the boys and swore she would bring them back alive. Now all she could do was wait.

At breakfast on the first Sunday of January, she steeled herself to tell her father she wouldn't be going with him to St Mary's but to the Friends Meeting House with Ruth instead.

'Just to see what it's like,' she said casually, buttering her toast.

She held her breath, expecting a tirade about Quakers being yellow-bellied conchies who ought to be taken out and shot, but Captain Nicholson gruffly said, 'Brave men. It was the Friends Ambulance Unit that picked up me and Private Murray. We wouldn't have made it if they hadn't dashed out with stretchers to carry us back behind the lines. They had to run with us, ducked low because of snipers. And they got us back to the field hospital in double-quick time.'

Lucy took a breath of surprise. He'd never told this story before.

'They're pacifists, the Quakers,' he continued. 'But not cowards.'

* * *

65

Lucy and Ruth caught a bus to the Friends Meeting House in Welwyn Garden City, and as they looked out of the window at the drab, sodden countryside, they talked about Barcelona, which seemed so alive and vibrant in their minds by comparison. They knew it was the heart of the Republican area and the city where many of the refugees were heading. Ruth said she'd heard that Alfred Jacob had set up a canteen at the main railway station.

'They have women and children arriving there at all times of day and night, and they've been allowed to serve hot milky drinks to them while they wait to be taken to the Refugee Receiving Centre. There are three English chocolate companies supplying cocoa: Rowntree's, Shuttleworth's and Cadbury-Fry. Cadbury's gives the most. They're all Quaker companies, you know.'

Lucy shook her head. There seemed so much she didn't know.

'They started serving the drinks on Christmas Day, in the early hours of the morning, with just eleven children who'd come from Madrid where the fighting is worst. It must be such a long, hard journey. They must be so frightened. Now there are hundreds coming every day.'

Looking out at the neat houses of Welwyn Garden City, Lucy found it was hard to imagine living through such turmoil. But Barcelona was where she had to be. She knew it with every fibre of her being.

Ruth introduced her to a few people before the meeting began and they welcomed Lucy warmly. She was glad Ruth had told her about sober clothing and she hadn't worn her red hat and gloves. Then she sat and listened to the tick of the big clock and a robin singing outside, and the occasional winter coughs of the people around her. She thought about Tom's kiss and Jamie's proposal, and how bewildering it all was, and she thought about the refugee children, and what horrors she might see, and shut her eyes and prayed that she would be strong enough to bear them, and that Tom and Jamie would not be killed or wounded before she'd managed to persuade them to come home. And she thought about hot cocoa and how she'd like one right now, and that her bottom was starting to feel uncomfortable on the hard seat, and was startled when someone stood up and cleared her throat.

Three people spoke in all. One talked about her week, and how kind her neighbour had been. Another recited a poem. Lucy slowly felt the agitation of the last few weeks begin to subside. A grey-haired woman struggled to her feet and read something written by William Penn who founded Pennsylvania. Her eyes met Lucy's as she read, '*Let us then try what love can do.*' Lucy felt a jolt of electricity up her spine, as though William Penn had reached out of the past and spoken to her directly across four hundred years. In her head she replied to him, 'Yes, I'll try. I'll go and see what love can do.'

When it was over, tea and biscuits were served, and Ruth introduced her to more people and, for the first time, she heard herself say aloud, 'I'm going to Barcelona, to help with the children. The refugee children.'

'She can speak Spanish,' said Ruth proudly, 'and she's a wonderful teacher.'

Lucy tensed herself for their reaction, but nobody told her she couldn't, or mustn't or shouldn't. They simply offered kindly advice and support, and said they would 'hold her in the light'.

At last it felt real. She was going.

The day before her birthday a third letter arrived from Tom. This time it wasn't dated and had no location.

Dear Comrade Luce,

I can't tell you where I am for obvious reasons, and I don't know when it will get to you, but letters seem to arrive here quite quickly, so please write back. The CP in London will know where to send it.

We are now in an International Brigade training camp 'somewhere in Spain'. It's a bit warmer than Barcelona.

It was so thrilling the night we left the city. Red flags and torchlight and songs roaring out on loudspeakers and us marching off to the train with knapsacks on our backs (I sold my case) and rolled blankets across our shoulders. Did I tell you I bought a Sam Browne belt and a holster and a hunting knife and a leather jacket? I look quite the outlaw!

The train was packed full of soldiers, International Brigaders like us, from so many countries – Hungary, Yugoslavia, Romania, Poland, Finland, France – and Germans and Italians who hate what Herr Hitler and Mussolini are doing; and Spanish militia men and women looking rather shabby and exhausted.

Coming south on the train took a long time, and we could see how much the countryside has suffered. The fields were full of last year's crops which had never been harvested. And orange trees and olive trees. Going the other way we could see great waves of refugees, heading for Barcelona. So many children, Luce. It would break your heart. The train was so slow-moving that fresh oranges were passed through the windows by boys running alongside.

And now we are in a training camp on a rolling plain of vineyards and unharvested wheat fields. We're in a village with the remains of a large stone church which is used as a latrine. (Don't tell Jamie.)

We are No. 2 company of the Batallón Inglés, which basically means everyone who speaks English. The Irish don't want to be in with us, and I think they are going to join the American battalion when that's set up. No. 1 company is already up at the Front.

There's a village hall where most of us sleep and also sit on the floor for lectures on things like gas drill and cleaning our billets and how to judge distances when throwing a grenade and Spanish lessons. And we have weapon-stripping practice and meetings and discussions there. You should hear the debates! We've got a Political Commissar as well as a military commander, to inspire us with discipline and loyalty. But we don't need that. We know that we are here to defend a noble cause, to fight the good fight. You've never seen such enthusiasm, such solidarity. We are full of splendid spirits, in such great heart.

I've already met some men I think I'll get on with: Frank Graham who was a student in Sunderland, Charles Goodfellow who was a miner from Bellshill, John Cornford who's a poet and Miles Tomalin who's a writer. There are lots of Welsh miners, and you should hear them sing!

New men arrive all the time, sometimes in twos and threes, or as many as fifty. We've all been given temporary ranks till we've been in action. Then you get promoted by how well you did. Imagine that! Not what school you went to or how rich your father is! And the officers and men all get the same pay. We have got some officers who were in the Great War and we have to address them as 'Comrade Captain'. And we are allowed to debate their orders with them. I wonder what your father would think of that?

The food is terrible. Really greasy, with olive oil slopped over everything, even eggs. It gives you real tummy trouble, I can tell you. We get a quart of water a day each, and plenty of wine.

No. 1 company of the Batallón Inglés is still in the front line, helping to hold Madrid, and we are getting fed up with training. Some men 'desert to the Front' because they want to get stuck in. But they say it won't be long now. We aren't going to let Franco win.

Please send woollen socks and chocolate. Parcels are getting through and I got your letter about the Quaker people coming out to help with the refugees. They certainly need all the help they can get. And I got Mother's, thank you. Give her a kiss from me, and have one for yourself. Don't let her worry about me. Have a happy Christmas, won't you? I don't know what it will be like here.

In love and comradeship, Tom

Have a kiss for yourself. What kind of kiss would that be? Lucy wondered. And if it was a passionate kiss, not a brotherly one, would she have to stop him, now that she'd said she loved Jamie? She shook her head. She couldn't think about that just now.

70

It seemed he hadn't yet had the letter in which she told him she had decided to come out to Spain. Lucy hugged herself with the thought of how pleased and surprised he'd be. 'Good old Luce,' he'd say, she was sure.

If it hadn't been a school day, Lucy's twenty-first birthday would have been a dismal affair. She was bitterly disappointed not to have a letter or a card from either of the boys, but her despondency lifted when the headmistress struck up the opening bars of 'Happy Birthday' in assembly and all the boys and girls riotously joined in. Ruth had secretly arranged for each of the children in Lucy's class to make cards for her, and slipped into the classroom to orchestrate the presentation of them. As one after another handed her their scrawled images, Lucy was deeply touched, and hugged them to her, realising with a pang how much she was going to miss them all. At the end of the dinner break, Joan and Jean solemnly handed her a fistful of snowdrops and grass, saying, 'It's a bookay Miss Nicholson,' and tears prickled her eyes.

In the evening, when she arrived home, Mrs Murray had already cooked a meal for the three of them and lit the fire and even baked her a cake. Over dinner Lucy's father thought it was funny to present her with a gift-wrapped package which turned out to contain the 'key of the door'. Of course she already had a front-door key and was tempted to ask him how he thought she came home from work and cooked his dinner and cleaned his house without one. But she stretched her face into a smile. Soon she would be gone from here. She just had to gather the courage to tell him.

* * *

Mrs Murray had offered to be with her when she broke the news, but Lucy thought if she wanted him to treat her as an adult she would have to face him alone. She waited until he had finished his favourite pudding on the night after her birthday to ask him how the allowance from her grandmother's will would be paid to her.

'You don't need to worry about that,' he said indulgently.

'Oh, but I do,' said Lucy.

'Why's that?' asked her father. 'I'll draw it on your behalf and it'll be jolly useful to help with the debt.'

'It's not *the* debt,' said Lucy slowly, 'it's *your* debt, and I need my allowance because I'm going to Spain.'

Captain Nicholson's jaw dropped open like in a cartoon and Lucy almost wanted to laugh.

'I'm going to Spain to bring back Jamie and Tom before they get themselves killed, and while I'm there I'll help with the Quaker relief work with refugee children.'

'That's ridiculous,' he stammered, his face pale with shock. 'Pointless. It's a war. No place for a woman.'

'Tell that to the refugee women,' Lucy retorted.

'What do you think you can do? One foolish girl can't possibly make any difference.'

Lucy had calculated that her father would be more pleased at the prospect of having the boys back than angry with her for going. But she had forgotten the financial question.

He made a hurumphing sound. 'And the household needs your teacher's wage.'

Lucy gave her father all her salary every month and he handed her a little back for what he called 'gewgaws'. Her wages were virtually invisible to her.

She forced herself to remain calm. 'Well, I'm going. Next Monday. It's all arranged.'

'Oh no you are not, my girl.' His voice rose to a bellow. 'You live under my roof and you'll do as I say.'

Lucy pushed out her chair and stepped back from the table, away from his red, furious face.

'I'm twenty-one now,' she said quietly. 'And I don't have to live under your roof a moment longer.'

'You are still my daughter Lucy Nicholson, and you do as I say,' he roared.

Lucy could feel her own anger mounting and she struggled to control it. 'You never cared about me, never took any interest in me. All I am to you is a pay cheque and a skivvy. Well, I've come of age now and my life is my own.'

A vein pulsed in her father's forehead as he stood up and took a step towards her. 'You will do as I say,' he repeated.

The words were out of her mouth before she had time to think of the consequences. 'You are not my commanding officer,' she said with slow emphasis, and gripped the chair-back.

Her father stared at her with astonishment, as if really seeing her for the first time. And though she was terrified, Lucy lifted her chin and met him with a defiant gaze. He was used to being obeyed. For three long seconds Captain Nicholson didn't move, and then was the first to drop his eyes, muttering, 'Stupid woman.'

He turned and almost ran out of the room into the darkness of the hall.

Lucy waited until the front door banged and then subsided into a chair, trembling all over. It was done.

* * *

Only Mrs Murray came to the train station to see Lucy off. Her father had left the house before breakfast that morning, leaving a note by her plate, which told her how the allowance would be paid to her.

She had turned it over, but there was nothing more, no 'Be careful' or 'Love from Father'. Nothing. Lucy folded it carefully and slipped it into her handbag with the letter of introduction from the Friends and her tickets. As she opened the front door, the postman was outside and handed her an airmail letter. Lucy almost grabbed it from him. Jamie's handwriting! She would read it on the train.

Mrs Murray kissed her through the train window and wished her Godspeed, and told her to write frequently. 'You know you are like a daughter to me,' she said.

Lucy spoke through a constriction in her throat. 'And you are the mum I never had.'

All the accumulated sorrow of goodbyes welled up in the older woman's eyes. 'Come back safely. And bring my boys back too,' she said, as the tears spilled down her cheeks. 'If you can.'

She stood on the platform and waved until the train was out of sight, and when Lucy could see her no longer, she pulled up the window to keep out the cold January air, wiped her wet cheeks on her sleeve, and sat down to open her first letter from Jamie. Her heart leapt at the first words.

My darling Lucy,
I can't tell you what joy it gives me to write that, so I'm going to write it again: my darling Lucy. It feels as though I've been hiding something all my life, which I can now – at

last – bring out into the light. The Spanish poet Lorca wrote, 'To burn with desire and keep quiet about it is the greatest punishment we can bring on ourselves.' And now I have lifted that punishment from my heart and I feel free for the first time in years because I can say – you are my darling.

And though I wish you were here and I could hold you tight and whisper those words to you, I'm also glad that I can't see you pulling that mocking face, where your mouth forms a little moue. You are too far away to make fun of me, as you always do. Well, now it's all out in the open between us and I am filled with gladness. And I shan't mind you teasing me as long as you love me too, and don't marry anyone else while I'm away.

You were quite right that you are too young to be married yet; only, I do love you so much. And now I can picture you laughing at me again, throwing your head back a little and your eyes filled with twinkles and your curls bouncing in merriment at my expense. Well, laugh away, it won't stop me loving you.

I will tell you about my journey. I wish you had been sitting next to me on the train in the window seat, pointing out everything to me in your lovely, quick way. But I wouldn't have seen anything, I would have been watching your reflection in the glass, the way your eyes light up with interest and excitement at every new thing.

It was quite an adventure, taking the train to Portsmouth and finding my boat to Lisbon. On board the ship I settled myself on a table with a Portuguese priest who spoke Spanish. When he heard that I was heading to Spain to report for the Catholic Herald he began to tell me stories *that I couldn't repeat to you, but made my blood run cold. Worse than anything in those newspaper headlines I showed you. He said seven thousand monks, nuns and priests have been slaughtered. There are skulls of nuns decorating chapels.*

They seemed to be tales out of the Middle Ages, acts of unimaginable barbarism. How can people treat each other so? I feel my life has been so sheltered, so quiet, and I've never known any really bad men or women, not people who would do the kind of things to each other that I've been hearing about. I don't understand how Tom can support the devils who committed such atrocities.

And then we were in Lisbon. What a city! I think I will take you there on our honeymoon and we'll stay in the swankiest hotel, not the smelly hostel I went to.

In Lisbon I was introduced to a French film crew from Pathé News, heading to the same place as me, where all the journalists are together. They were very excited that I spoke perfect Spanish, and asked if I would be able to help them with interviews and so on. They had room in their van, and we drove across Portugal together and into the part of Spain which has been won back by Franco.

It feels as though this is what all my life has been leading up to and I am certain this was God's plan for me. Now I can hear you mocking me again, and asking why I would think myself so significant that the omnipotent deity should have a plan for little me. But I do believe that, with all my heart. And I think He has a plan for you too, and I pray it is for you to be my wife and bear my children.

I know my father would be so proud of me. I want to be a hero like him, but hopefully not die like him. Because I want to come back and take you in my arms, and make you my wife, my darling Lucy.

I'll write again as soon as I'm settled and can tell you all about what's happening. I'm so glad that I'm here to tell the truth to the world, even if it means leaving you for a while, my beautiful, wonderful Lucy.

I love you more than I can say.

Yours for ever,

Jamie

Lucy read the letter twice and her heart was beating fast. In all her life she had never been loved like this. She felt as if she was sitting in front of a roaring fire on a cold winter night and glowing in its flames. She dismissed the small doubt which nagged at her, asking if she loved him in quite the same way, and smiled to herself as she thought how she would tease him for his extravagant romanticism.

BARCELONA
January 1937

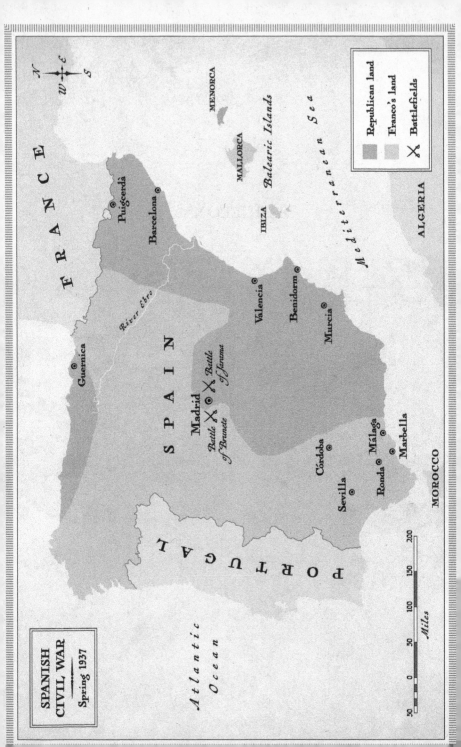

7

Lucy had never been further than London on her own before, and she tried hard to tell herself that the fluttering in her stomach was excitement, not nerves. As long as she kept her head, everything would be fine.

The middle-aged man in Thomas Cook's had been anxious about her travelling on her own – 'You do know there's a war on, miss?' – but she'd told him she was going to visit her brother. It was almost true. The travel agent had wanted her to stop overnight in Paris and Béziers, but Lucy said firmly that she'd sleep on the train. She'd always been a good sleeper; it would save money on hotels and save precious time and she wouldn't have to admit to herself that she was afraid of finding her way, alone in a French town. So he had written her careful instructions in spidery handwriting about how to negotiate every step of her journey.

The ferry crossing to Calais was relatively calm, so she spent most of the time on deck, pulling her coat around her, with her new black beret holding her hair out of her eyes, chatting to other passengers, watching the white cliffs shrinking away from her and the coast of France advancing with its promise of foreignness. She'd been to France before but never further than Honfleur, where her father had taken them all for a holiday in better times. The Thomas Cook man's instructions about crossing Paris from the Gare du Nord to the magnificent chandeliered Gare de Lyon were simple to follow, though the loud French crowds and the men who looked her up and down with frank appraisal were more daunting in reality than in her imagination. Luckily she only had to use her schoolgirl French to buy a baguette and a coffee when the sausage rolls and corned-beef sand-wiches she'd brought from home were long gone. She looked all about her, inhaling the unknown smells, fizzing with adrenaline.

And now she was on a train chugging along the Rhône Valley, passing pretty French villages with picturesque churches. As she looked out of the window, her mind roamed around her own internal mysteries: Tom's kiss and Jamie's declaration of love, and which of the brothers she loved the most. Was it wicked and unnatural to think she loved them both? Perhaps it would all become clear in Spain.

Snow-topped mountains rose in the distance on both sides of the track. How she wished she had someone to point them out to.

The French family in her carriage talked to her and she nodded and smiled even though she didn't understand every-thing. From time to time she stretched herself and went to stand in the corridor. Occasionally two or three young French or British working men would pass her. She heard a Welsh and a Liverpool accent. Why would they be going to Spain if not to join the International Brigades? She longed to ask them to take a message to Tom but thought it best not to speak to them in case all of them were thrown off the train. The non-intervention pact meant that going to fight in Spain was illegal in France as well as Britain, though of course the Germans and Italians were ignoring the agreement in order to help Franco.

The rhythm of the train made her sleepy as twilight fell and she dozed for a length of time which might have been minutes or hours as they travelled ever further south, only rousing herself to read the station signs as they halted in Nîmes and Montpellier and people struggled on and off. The man in Thomas Cook had told her she must see the cathedral in Béziers, but it was dark when they passed through.

At dawn she woke with a stiff neck and her beret lopsided to find the train skirting the Mediterranean coastline with its deserted beaches and marshy lakes, where flocks of pink flamingos stood one-legged in the shallows. Imagine that! She had seen flamingos! If only Tom or Jamie were here to tell. The grandmother of the French family offered her cheese, which she took, and an onion, which she declined. How Tom would have loved to watch the old woman tucking into the onion as though it were an apple!

She was sorry to see the family go when they alighted at Cerbère, and the grandmother looked long and hard at her and promised to pray to the Holy Mother for her safekeeping. A prickle of unease crossed Lucy's scalp as the enormity of heading into a war zone began to impress itself on her.

* * *

Lucy knew the train would dive under the Pyrenees at Cerbère in France and emerge at Portbou in Spain, and as they entered the tunnel, her stomach clenched in a mix of excitement and dread. She was almost there.

They emerged from the tunnel and she blinked at the bright sunlight as the train drew into a small coastal town dominated by an enormous railway station. Standing and stretching, she grabbed her luggage and stepped down onto the platform. For a moment she looked up at the huge iron and glass roof which arched above her, straddling the tracks. Its resemblance to King's Cross gave her a sudden jolt of homesickness. But she couldn't stand still, as the disembarking passengers pushed her forward towards the building which housed the passport office. The border guards who shepherded them into line were speaking Catalan with a smattering of instructions in Spanish and French. Nobody spoke English and she felt very insignificant and far from home.

She presented her passport at a window and it was checked by a disinterested border guard. She had been worried that the non-intervention pact might mean she would have trouble entering Spain. After all, that was why Tom had climbed over a mountain pass and Jamie had travelled via Lisbon, but the guard looked from her photograph to the young woman in front of him, gave her a flirtatious wink and waved her through. He obviously didn't seem to think a smart señorita like Lucy was on her way to join the International Brigades. Stepping away, she glanced around quickly for the young men from Wales and Liverpool, but they were nowhere in sight. Perhaps they'd left the train at Cerbère and were crossing the border on foot? She whispered a silent prayer for their safety as she followed the crush of people through the building and out to a wider track – Iberian gauge, the man in Thomas Cook had said. She climbed into the broad train which would take her to Barcelona and settled herself in a window seat. The other passengers eyed her with frank curiosity, so as the train pulled away she gazed studiously out of the window to avoid their stares. Steam from the engine clouded past, and as it cleared a snowy mountain dominated the skyline. She felt how far she now was from Hertfordshire, from her father and Mrs Murray. It was electrifying.

More and more people climbed on to the train as it chugged slowly – oh so slowly – towards Barcelona. Everything was different – the clothes, the smells of the people and their garlicky food, the loudness of the Spanish and Catalan voices crashing over each other in waves. She tried to follow conversations, but everything was too fast and heavily accented. Men stared at her with unguarded admiration, and one sitting opposite kicked the edge of her shoe until she tucked her legs back out of his reach.

Eventually the train pulled into Barcelona station, almost twenty hours after she'd left Welwyn. She didn't know how long she'd slept, but she wasn't tired; her brain was buzzing and the butterflies in her tummy were spiralling. Massive vaults of steel rainbowed over her head as she walked towards the cream stone building with eyebrow-arched windows at the end of the platform. She thought it looked like the façade of a medieval palace.

It was easy to find the Left Luggage to deposit her case and a Ladies to wash her face and comb her hair, though, to her horror, the toilet was simply a hole in the ground which she had to crouch over. If it was like that in a main-line station, she dreaded to think what she would find in the countryside. She stood on the crowded concourse feeling very alone for a moment, with women examining her clothes and hair, and men jostling too close as she looked around for Alfred Jacob's canteen. She knew it was situated on the platform of the main line from Madrid. Then she spotted it: a large waiting room with the red and black Quaker star and a hand-lettered notice in Spanish and Catalan, welcoming refugees. Smoothing down her creased coat, she pushed open the door. The waiting room was empty except for a young man and woman sitting at a table near the door. Warmth and the smell of chocolate engulfed Lucy as she recognised the young man with mousy hair and blue eyes, even though he looked smaller than he had done on the stage at Friends House.

'Alfred Jacob,' she said, with a flood of relief, holding out her hand.

The man looked surprised for a second before he stood and smiled. In English with an American accent he said, 'You must be Miss Nicholson? Lucy? We weren't expecting you for another couple of days.'

The striking young woman who sat beside him nodded in agreement. She had jet-black hair, crimped in waves and secured at the back of her neck. Her high forehead and thinly plucked eyebrows gave her an aristocratic look which belied the friendly roundness of her face and body.

'This is Margarita Ricart,' Alfred said.

Margarita looked shrewdly at Lucy and fetched a chair. The conversation switched into Spanish as they asked her about her journey. Margarita was small with quick movements and

86

laughter in her eyes. Alfred was slightly formal and seemed a little wary of this non-Quaker who'd come all the way from England to help him. Lucy knew he was an Oxford-educated American, but she couldn't detect that in the way he spoke Spanish. His accent was as perfect as Jamie's. She could tell they were both speaking deliberately slowly to enable her to understand, but she also thought Alfred was testing her language skills. He indicated the empty waiting room.

'We never know what time the trains will come, so one of us has to be here all the time. It's mostly staffed by a rota of local women who'll arrive soon. But they all speak Catalan and most of the refugees only speak Spanish.'

'Well, now I'm here to help you,' said Lucy. 'I can start at once.'

Margarita put her head on one side and looked closely at her. 'You must be tired.' And as she said it, or because it was said with sympathy, Lucy felt the tension of the last twenty-four hours ebb into exhaustion.

She nodded. 'If you don't need me right now, I could take my case to the hostel, and return later?'

At that moment a bespectacled Spanish man entered, nodded to Lucy and crossed quickly to kiss Margarita on the mouth. Margarita introduced Domingo Ricart, her husband. All three of them were not much older than Lucy – in their early thirties at the most, she guessed. Margarita addressed both men.

'Now you are here, why don't I take Lucy to the YWCA and explain everything to her?'

Lucy liked her already.

* * *

87

Margarita took Lucy to collect her case and led the way through the cathedral-like arching domes of the station out into the street.

'Are you too tired to walk?' asked Margarita, in a deep, gravelly voice which seemed out of keeping with her small body. 'It's about half an hour.'

Lucy assured her she would be keen to walk after so many hours on the train, and she was eager to see the city which Tom had loved so much.

He was certainly right about the colour – the flags and posters were everywhere. She passed one showing European, African and Asian soldiers, with the slogan ALL THE PEOPLE OF THE WORLD ARE IN THE INTERNATIONAL BRIGADES.

The streets were crowded with people walking quickly, as if they were late for an appointment. They were mostly dressed in overalls of blue or brown. Many of them stared openly at her as they passed.

'It's your hat,' laughed Margarita. 'Republican women don't wear hats. And a Basque beret. They are trying to work out if you belong to some unknown militia group.'

Lucy hastily shoved it in her handbag.

'And now they will be admiring your beautiful hair,' smiled Margarita. 'You can't win!'

As they walked, Margarita explained that she and her husband had met Alfred at the YMCA where Domingo worked. Domingo had been so impressed by Alfred's ideas about pacifism and the refugees and it was such a complete meeting of minds that he'd soon invited Alfred to live with them. Lucy was unable to tell how Margarita felt about that arrangement.

Her Spanish was too imperfect to understand nuances of inflection; it was hard enough just to translate the words, and even though Margarita spoke slowly, there were many phrases Lucy didn't grasp, although she found she could pick up the general drift if she concentrated hard.

Margarita said that she and her husband were fluent in Catalan as well as Spanish and it had been their pleasure to introduce Alfred to the right people to help him. The authorities were doing everything they could but they were grateful for any assistance with the flood of refugees who poured into the city each day. Alfred had quickly identified that the lack of any milk in Barcelona affected the children badly, and had raised money through Quaker Relief to set up the canteen giving hot drinks to children as they arrived. Margarita was proud of the way Domingo had persuaded the authorities to release five spacious 'requisitioned' warehouses free of charge to store the powdered milk and cocoa which had quickly begun to come from England.

Lucy was looking about her as she listened, impressed by the orderliness but shocked by the poverty of the city. The streets were clean, but many of the children who played in them were wearing the kind of ill-fitting hand-me-downs she'd only seen before among the poorest English children.

Margarita led her across the Avinguda Diagonal, which reminded Lucy of Oxford Street or Regent Street, with shops beneath imposing public buildings. The tree-lined pavements on either side were each the breadth of a road.

'It's the widest street in Barcelona,' said Margarita with native pride. Lucy thought it was probably the biggest in the world. She hadn't pictured such grandeur in this communist–anarchist city.

The shops were open but there seemed to be no food or

clothing for sale; most windows had displays of military ware, knives, water bottles and gun belts. The majority displayed a revolutionary poster, often of Dolores Ibárruri, La Pasionaria, or her slogan for the untrained army of peasants, factory workers, trade unionists and International Brigaders defending Madrid: '¡No pasarán!'

'I heard her speak in London,' said Lucy, and Margarita cocked her head on one side questioningly.

'My friend Tom took me. He's here now, with the Batallón Inglés.' Pride and fear mingled in her voice as she added, 'There, I suppose, defending Madrid against Franco, though he's not allowed to say.'

Margarita studied her for a second, and Lucy thought it was best to be honest.

'And his brother is a journalist – but on the other side.'

Margarita sighed heavily. 'It is not unusual for families to be split in this way, for brother to be fighting against brother. War is an evil thing.'

They crossed the street to avoid a long, snaking queue of women.

'A bread queue,' said Margarita. 'People spend many hours each day standing in line for bread or for fuel. It's rationed and fair, and the government does what it can, but there simply isn't enough.'

For the first time Lucy wondered if she would go hungry herself. This was something she'd never considered. She indicated the intricate paper designs on all the windows they passed and Margarita explained they were to stop the glass shattering in a bombing raid. Hunger and bombing. Lucy swallowed hard. Was she really prepared for this?

She switched her case to the other hand. 'Is the bombing bad?'

'Not as bad as Madrid. But the blackout is too patchy, so when the siren goes, they turn all the electricity off at the power station. I'll bring you candles and matches, and you must buy a torch. And tonight I'll give you a Friends armband with the Quaker star. It helps people know who we are.'

'But I'm not a Friend,' said Lucy.

'Nor am I.' Margarita smiled. 'Or maybe we both are.'

Margarita left her at the YWCA reception desk. As Margarita was on the YWCA board she had managed to secure a small single room for Lucy, knowing she might be working all night and it would be impossible to get enough sleep in a dormitory. She promised to return at 9 p.m. – the earliest the next train might arrive.

'I can't wait to change out of these clothes and wash,' said Lucy.

'Get some sleep,' Margarita advised. 'We might be busy till dawn.'

The tiny room was sparse but clean. There was a hook on the back of the door to hang her dresses and coat. Lucy unlaced her shoes and then, despite her excitement at being here in the city she had dreamed of and so much closer to the boys, and her intention of washing her dress, she lay down fully clothed on the narrow iron bed and fell into a deep sleep.

Lucy was grateful when Margarita collected her that evening. She'd barely had time to change her dress and didn't think she would have found her way back to the station in the dark, even though the roads ran on a grid system and Margarita had shown her the most straightforward route.

Welwyn would have been deserted by nine o'clock, except for a few men coming and going to the pub, but here the streets were as busy as daytime and the station was thronged with people. Tom had been right; nobody was well-dressed. She wondered if all the rich people had been killed, but didn't like to enquire. Instead she asked about the refugees, and where they went when they left the railway station.

'Tomorrow I'll take you to the Refugee Receiving Centre at the stadium,' said Margarita. 'That's where they go to be registered and processed. And later perhaps we'll visit some of the children's colonies.'

Lucy already knew that many of the youngest refugees were being housed in children's homes or colonies, like Dr Barnardo's in England, which made it easier to feed, clothe and educate them.

'I was a teacher in England. Perhaps I could help with classes, or in the Quaker office, when there are no trains?'

'I'm sure Alfred would be glad to have your assistance. There is so much administration, you wouldn't believe. He prefers to have local women working in the canteen, and has a good rota of Boy Scouts and women's groups, but the refugees only speak Spanish so he needs a Spanish speaker with them at all times.'

As they re-entered the railway station, Margarita halted for a second to adjust one of the combs which held up her hair. 'I'd cut it off like yours,' she sighed, 'but Domingo likes it long, and you know what men are like.' She rolled her eyes expressively, and Lucy laughed. It seemed she would have a friend in this strange city.

'Are you married?' asked Margarita, and Lucy found herself explaining that she'd never found anyone as special as Tom and Jamie.

Margarita looked at her quizzically.

'So these boys from next door, they are like brothers to you?'

Lucy wriggled uneasily. 'Well yes, and no. I can't remember a time when I didn't love them. Tom is fun and Jamie is caring,' she said, as if two adjectives could sum up the complicated twisting fibres of both men, rooted down in the very core of her. Her Spanish was not good enough for this conversation. She tried again. 'Tom makes me feel alive but Jamie understands me.' She thought 'mercurial versus steadfast', but couldn't translate those words.

'And do they both love you?'

Lucy hesitated only for a second. 'Yes, I believe they do. In their own ways. Jamie asked me to marry him, and Tom kissed me like he wanted me.'

Margarita whistled softly. 'But which one do you really adore?'

Lucy shook her head. How could she explain it to someone else when she couldn't explain it to herself? Jamie would be a perfect husband and father, but Tom had an energy which radiated excitement. 'I don't know. Sometimes one and sometimes the other. One for one reason and the other for another. They are so different from each other, and I love them in different ways. I just hope they don't kill each other before I can take them home.'

Margarita's carefully plucked eyebrows lifted almost into her hairline, and Lucy flushed as she understood how strange and shocking it must seem to love two men.

At 3 a.m. a packed train arrived from besieged Madrid and officials steered an exhausted straggle of women and children towards Alfred Jacob's canteen. There were perhaps sixty of them, some carrying suitcases and wearing fashionable outfits which wouldn't look out of place in London, and others in the long skirts, headscarves and shawls which Lucy thought of as peasant clothes and carrying bundles tied with string. They queued for the hot chocolate which two Catalan women were handing out. Lucy and Margarita were wearing Quaker star armbands over their dresses and some of the refugees glanced suspiciously at the unknown symbol.

Lucy watched Margarita for a moment as she moved down the line, exchanging a word or two with the haggard women, welcoming them to Barcelona, patting their shoulders and assuring them they would be fed and housed tomorrow. Then Lucy began to do the same, bending to the children and asking their names and where they had come from, admiring a doll here and a toy car there, briefly touching their dirty hands or tangled hair. Some looked half-starved and she was sure they must have lice.

One woman indicated a child who pressed close to her and said, 'She's not mine. I found her in the ruins. What can you do?' The girl's eyes were dark with trepidation, and Lucy wondered what horrors she had seen. Other children half-hid behind their mothers' skirts, trying to work out if this white-faced, fair-haired woman in the plum-coloured dress meant them any harm. None of them strayed from their mothers, or seemed inclined to play with each other as normal girls and boys would. Lucy thought they were unnaturally quiet.

When all the women and children had been served, Margarita brought Lucy a cup of hot chocolate, which she took gratefully. She had lost count of the hours since she'd last eaten. As she drank her own cupful Lucy watched the way the youngsters wrapped their fingers round the mugs of cocoa and inhaled before sipping the milky sweetness. She realised how clever Alfred had been – he was not just giving them much-needed nourishment, but the smell of chocolate also seemed to carry an assurance that here they were safe, here things would be better. She hoped this would be true.

On Lucy's first full day in Barcelona, Margarita took charge of her. 'I'm going to show you how it all works,' she said, and Lucy couldn't miss the pride in her voice.

Lucy already knew that the newly arrived refugees were taken to the Receiving Centre at the stadium, and that's where Margarita began their tour. She was obviously well known at the offices and greeted with respect by the director, who talked Lucy through the system they'd set up. Incoming refugees were registered on a card index, and when they were ready to move on from the stadium, the card was updated with their destination and what assistance they had been given to get there. Lucy understood how important this would be for men trying to find their families in the future. Some women and children were sent to villages, further from the main danger of bombing in Barcelona city. She was told that more than fifteen thousand young people had already been placed in farms, villages and children's colonies. Orphans, or those who had become separated from their parents, automatically went to the colonies, but many mothers chose to send their children to a colony, bearing the pain of parting in the knowledge they wouldn't be hungry or cold. Lucy wondered if the women went to look for their husbands, or to help as nurses near the front line or to join the fighting, and with what unbearable sorrow in their hearts.

'I should like to see the colonies,' said Lucy, and Margarita nodded. They would visit some soon.

The director accompanied them to the dormitories — mostly beds for women and children, but also some married quarters for a few old couples who had lost their homes but not been separated. Lucy looked at these people, sitting or lying on their beds, and although this place was clean and they were out of the weather and being cared for, she tried to imagine how it would feel to be forced to flee the home you'd lived in for forty or fifty years, with only the few items you could carry, and to find yourself on the road not knowing where you would end up or where your next meal was coming from.

Margarita showed her the huge dining hall, the infirmary, the rest ward. Lucy thought it was intelligent of the Refugee Committee and the doctors to recognise that sometimes people were not ill as such, but unable to do anything for themselves without time to adjust their damaged minds. One young woman, nursing an infant, looked up at her with blank despair in her eyes. Margarita saw the look between them, and gently propelled Lucy onwards.

She was shown the spotless swimming pool and showers and then they went out into the low winter sunshine on the stadium steps where small groups of children sat, each with an adult.

'This is where they have their school,' said Margarita, shading her eyes. 'We know that education is the key to everything, and their minds need to be occupied with things other than the horror they've seen. Having lessons gives them structure and normality.'

Lucy heartily approved.

They walked slowly up and down past the groups. Lucy noticed some children were dressed well, perhaps having come less far, or from wealthier homes, while others were in stained sweaters with runs and pulls in the knitting.

Her eye was caught by a little girl with a blue bow holding back her dark hair. She had laid down her paper and looked close to tears. Lucy crouched down beside her and looked to the teacher for permission, who motioned her to sit. She picked up the girl's page and saw she was having difficulty making her letters. Her pencil was clutched awkwardly in the right hand, as if it was a knife she would use to stab the paper.

'Which hand do you use to catch a ball?' she asked and the girl waved her left. Lucy fitted the pencil into her left hand and the child looked apprehensively at the teacher, who nodded approval.

'The nuns didn't let me,' whispered the girl before confidently drawing a line of 'A's across the page with her left hand, and beaming up at Lucy.

Margarita watched carefully. 'You will enjoy visiting the colonies,' she told Lucy as they left the stadium. 'Most of them are run by a teacher with Montessori training. I think you will get on well.'

On the way back to the YWCA Margarita asked when Lucy had last heard from Jamie and Tom. She was obviously fascinated by the idea of Lucy's two beaux.

'Tom's not in the front line yet,' Lucy told her. 'At least I don't think he is.'

Margarita frowned. 'The International Brigades are taking heavy losses in the battle for Madrid,' she said gently.

Lucy's stomach twisted in anxiety. 'I know. I don't think I could bear it if he dies.'

Margarita patted her hand. 'We all have loved ones at the front.'

When they arrived at Alfred Jacob's office in Calle Caspe, Lucy was put to work with a complex ledger of orders which showed Alfred was in charge of the supplies of dried milk funded by the British Friends and also tins of condensed milk sent by Save the Children in Geneva. He was angry about the condensed milk.

'I had a report done by Cadbury's about the nutritional contents of dried milk versus condensed milk, but she didn't even read it.'

Lucy soon gathered that 'she' was Mrs Small, the Save the Children representative, who had now returned to Geneva. Alfred obviously couldn't stand her.

'The condensed milk is £60 a ton, but the tins are so heavy that each costs 275 pesetas in freight!' he fumed. 'We could feed so many more children for the money if we used powdered milk. But she wants everything done her own way.'

Lucy nodded. She could see from the books that the condensed milk was working out twice as expensive. Even refugee support was more complicated and political than she'd realised in England.

Alfred's blue eyes flashed with irritation. 'The refugees aren't the only hungry children in Barcelona. I want to expand the canteens into the poor districts. There hasn't been any milk in the city since October and the local children are starving too.'

'But aren't the authorities doing anything?' asked Lucy.

Alfred nodded but explained, 'They are doing all they can. There just isn't enough without the supplies from abroad. Mothers with children under eighteen months old are entitled to receive milk from the Casa Maternologia, but only four hundred mothers can be supplied and rations have been cut from five tins a week to two.'

Lucy felt a surge of energy; she was here and would do whatever she could to help. For the first time in her life she had purpose.

Lucy assisted in the office for most of the day, apart from a short siesta after lunch, and then returned to the station canteen to greet the next trainload of refugees. As she gazed into the weary faces of these women, she wondered what their lives had been before and how she would cope with being uprooted and moved around the country like cattle.

By the time she was back in her room at the YWCA, she was exhausted. But shortly after she'd climbed into bed, she was jerked awake by the shrill warning of an air-raid siren. She leapt to her feet, terrified, and tried to turn on a light, but it didn't work. She remembered Margarita telling her the electricity was switched off at the mains during a raid. She shoved her feet into her shoes, and pulled her coat over her nighty, then groped her way out of the bedroom and down the cellar-dark stairs, clenching her teeth with fear. A crowd of other women burst from a dormitory, pushing and bumping into each other, and the stairwell echoed with a high-pitched chatter of anxiety and the play of torch-light. She concentrated on keeping her footing.

In the dining area, candles had been lit and the girls crowded round the tables. Someone switched on the battery-powered radio and an announcer called out, 'Catalans! Catalans! Keep calm! Serenity! Keep calm! There are two enemy aircraft circling overhead, go to your shelters!'

Lucy's heart was pounding. Where were the shelters? Had she come all this way to be killed by an air raid on her second night in Spain? Nobody else seemed to be scrambling for these shelters. Did they even exist?

The wireless was turned down and everyone sat and listened for the enemy approach. Lucy strained her ears but couldn't catch any sound of aircraft and certainly no bombing. Eventually the cook put her head outside and announced there was no sign of the planes. They had gone away.

They all made their way back to the bedrooms in the dark and Lucy resolved to buy a torch first thing in the morning.

She lay in bed, too agitated to sleep, wondering if her boys were lying beneath bombers dropping death out of the sky. Or even if they were already dead. She couldn't help picturing Tom's lovely, energetic body, spreadeagled over the edge of a trench, with bloody gore leaking from his guts. She imagined Jamie holding his gentle fingers to a wound in his head, as the life drained from his eyes.

No! She must not allow herself to think like this, or she would go mad. She must not dwell on imagined horrors when there were so many real ones right in front of her. Instead, from now on, she must concentrate on things she could help to change. If she was to survive her new life in Spain, she must direct all her energy to the children, like that poor little left-handed girl at the stadium who might have been dragged from a bomb shelter or the ruins of her home and then been on the road for days and nights, with nothing to eat or drink. What nightmares must she suffer? Until Lucy could get to Jamie and Tom and persuade them to return to England, she must focus only on the children.

8

Lucy was rapidly accepted by Alfred Jacob as an invaluable member of his team as the scale of the Friends' ambitious operation to run children's colonies and canteens threatened to overwhelm him. Lucy worked in the office in the mornings and in the first few afternoons Margarita took her to meet the important people who she would need to know to arrange the movement and storage of donated food.

'They will pay attention to you because you are my friend,' said Margarita, laughing. 'And they will remember you because you are a pretty English girl.'

On their way to meet the key officials, Margarita showed off a little of her birthplace. Lucy was interested to discover that there was a medieval labyrinth of streets in the heart of this grid-patterned city. The fortress-like black stone buildings had windows and balconies which faced one another across winding alleys where the sun never reached, and a sickening smell of drains hung over the whole dismal maze. It made Lucy shiver to think of lives eked out in the grim darkness of these slums.

Margarita led her up the wide steps of the cathedral and inside was almost impenetrable gloom, hiding those who were still sneaking in to pray. Lucy was glad to leave it and be taken out on to the broad promenade known as La Rambla with its plane trees, seats, newspaper kiosks, shoeshine men, flower stalls and perpetually moving crowds. In the bright winter sunshine it seemed a world away from Welwyn.

On other afternoons Margarita took her to visit the children's homes, or colonies as they were called, and at night Lucy became part of a rota for the station canteen. It was tiring work and she slept soundly, and soon began to feel at home in Barcelona. As she walked to work Lucy often saw angry crowds of women protesting about the bread shortages and once she drew back into a doorway and watched as the protests were roughly broken up by the police. The food-rationing system simply couldn't cope with the number of people flooding into the region. Alfred estimated there already were more than 350,000 refugees in the city.

The air-raid sirens went off every few nights, and there was panic in the canteen at the station among the refugees who had come from places like Madrid which had suffered frequent bombing. Lucy's job was to keep them calm and usher them to the nearest shelter. Having a practical task kept her from worrying too much about herself, especially as most were false alarms.

Ten days after her arrival the sirens went off at 3 a.m., just as the cocoa had been issued to the newcomers. All the lights went out and women and children's voices were raised in terrified cries as they asked each other where the shelters were.

The Friends had bought a megaphone, and Lucy stood on a chair and bellowed into it, 'Be quiet. Keep calm,' until the hubbub subsided. She turned on the red torch which they kept with the megaphone and waved it over her head. 'Follow this light and I will take you to the shelter.' She climbed off the chair and felt the crowd surge towards her, threatening to crush her and each other.

'Make way,' she yelled into the megaphone, half-tripping over a bundle of clothing. 'No pushing.'

They parted to allow her to reach the door.

'Keep calm, and everyone will be safe.'

As she quickly led the way towards the shelter, the deep rumble of aircraft shook the air and she glanced up at the arching iron roof above the tracks, shuddering as she pictured the spears of metal which might fall on them if bombs landed close by. Searchlights played across the sky and she could hear the *ack-ack* of anti-aircraft guns from the direction of the docks. The refugees behind her pushed forward like a wave, with moans and cries of fear.

At the entrance of the shelter she stood aside and let the crowd sweep through, calling, 'Go slow. Mind the children.'

The crash of bombs landing down by the coast shook the city, and for a moment terror overtook Lucy. This was war and she was in it. She had a desperate urge to shove people aside and push her way down into the safety of the shelter, but she controlled it. When the last of the night's refugees had been swallowed down the steps, she turned and shone her torch around the station concourse. At first she thought it was empty and then the beam picked out the crouching form of a boy of about four or five, huddled beside a platform entrance. In a dozen strides she had reached him and swept him up, carrying him in one arm as the metal structure vibrated to the explosion of another bomb.

Down in the shelter the noise was deafening, a cacophony of shouting adults and crying children. She eased her way through the crowds and the small boy clung to her, burying his face in her shoulder. Finding a place between two families, she settled down with her back to the wall, and sat the child on her lap. Her fear slowly subsided as she focused on the boy.

'What's your name?' she asked, and after a moment he lifted his head and looked at her. His eyes were brown with flecks of gold, like a tiger's eye.

'Jorge.'

'That's a manly name for a little boy.'

'I am six and a quarter.'

As he spoke, she saw his front tooth was missing. Of course he was six, though so small for his age.

'Ah yes,' she said thoughtfully. 'Now I can see you are. And where do you live, Jorge?'

He recited the address in Madrid which he'd been taught in case he was ever lost, and then his face crumpled. 'But we don't live there any more.'

'No,' she said. 'Now you are in Barcelona.'

He looked around him. 'It's the same, with the bombs.'

'Who did you come with?'

'My big sister Maria and my auntie, but I lost them and another lady found me and she forgot me when the bombs came.' His eyes were great pools of despair, but he didn't cry. Perhaps all his tears had been spent, Lucy thought.

'Well, my name is Lucy and tomorrow I'll take you to the Refugee Centre. They might know where Maria is. Will that be OK?'

He considered her seriously. 'Yes, OK.'

His eyes moved over her, as if learning her, and he pointed to her Quaker star armband. 'What's that?'

'It means I'm your friend.'

He reached up to her hair and patted it. 'Why is your hair yellow?'

She shrugged and smiled. 'It's just how I am.'

He nodded sagely. 'OK.' Then he snuggled closer into her, and his thumb found its way into his mouth, and soon he was asleep.

Although she quickly became uncomfortable, Lucy moved as little as possible till the all-clear sounded and she had to wake him. At first he looked startled to see her, and then remembered. 'Lucy with the yellow hair.'

Lucy took him straight to the stadium and watched as they took down all his details and wrote them on a card. They told her he would be taken to a colony in the north of the city and hopefully one day be reunited with his family.

'And now you are going to leave me too,' he said to Lucy, and her heart turned over.

'You are going to go to a nice place with other children, and I will come to visit you.'

He looked very hard at her with his old man's eyes in his child's face.

'I don't think you will,' he said, as he let himself be led away.

* * *

106

Letters from home began to arrive within days of Lucy reaching Barcelona. First, of course, was a chatty missive from Mrs Murray, telling her about packing up the house for her return to Lanarkshire. She had arranged to stay with her sister until she found work, and couldn't wait to go now all three of 'her' children had departed.

Lucy's first letter from her father was a complete contrast and as unemotional as she would have expected. He went so far as to say the house was 'different without you', but ruined the possible inference of that by telling her that, although he was managing the cooking and cleaning, he was thinking of moving next door to the cottage and asking Mrs Murray to stay on as his housekeeper, an arrangement he thought might suit both of them. When Lucy wrote back, she didn't comment on that, but spent her two sides of airmail paper telling him about her work in Barcelona.

Letters came too from friends in Welwyn, curious about her exotic new life, but Lucy had so little free time that her answers were very short. No letters came from either Tom or Jamie.

With the station canteen running smoothly, Alfred Jacob was busy on the next step of his plan, to open canteens for the poorest Barcelonian children, who were suffering from the diminishing food supplies because most of Spain's agricultural land was now in Franco's hands.

Margarita said to Lucy, 'Have you seen the cats?'

Lucy looked puzzled. 'No, I don't think I've seen a cat since I arrived.'

Margarita nodded. 'Exactly. They've all been eaten.'

She said the boys and girls of Barcelona weren't just

hungry, but developing rickets and tuberculosis. 'Their mothers are terrified of them catching measles. It has a hundred per cent death rate and spreads so fast through the refugee centres.'

Lucy hammered away at the typewriter, sending letters to everyone she could think of to raise more money. She organised the storage and distribution of clothing and blankets from the USA and England, and donated by better-off Catalans. The British biscuit makers Macfarlane's and McVitie's agreed to donate supplies. Quaker Oats offered to send porridge oats.

The station canteen gave the children half a litre of cocoa each, and even though the taste of English hot chocolate was unfamiliar they seemed to relish it, and their eyes became round O's when they were also handed two English biscuits.

Seven hundred boxes of milk, cocoa, sugar, biscuits and oats arrived and were distributed not just to the canteens but to the refugee centres which had been set up in the church of Sant Felip Neri, the gloomy Durán Asylum and ex-convents across the city. Alfred and Margarita's husband Domingo worked closely with the Ministry of Health and the Regional Committee for the Aid of Refugees to ensure that nobody starved to death.

On the eighth of February the southern Spanish town of Málaga fell to General Franco and the stream of refugees travelling north became a river. Many of these refugees were the poorest people, looking to Lucy like medieval serfs in their long skirts and shawls, sometimes wearing clogs rather than shoes and with sacks slung across their shoulders to keep out the rain. Most had been forced out on to the road with no money, bringing only the rags they stood up in. Those who made it to Barcelona told Lucy and Margarita the escaping lines of refugees had been strafed by German and Italian planes. Lucy could not believe such wickedness existed in the world. Surely Jamie couldn't know this was happening and still support Franco? The Red Cross, city council and militia groups helped with a boatload of 3,500 refugees which arrived from Málaga. Then Basques and Asturians began to arrive from the beleaguered northern provinces. Lucy worked longer and longer hours, only stopping when she couldn't keep her eyes open.

The authorities took Alfred Jacob to look at an empty fire station in the Sans district which they agreed to redecorate as a canteen for the poorest inhabitants of Barcelona. On the night before opening, Alfred and Domingo helped to set up tables, while Margarita and Lucy went down on their knees and scrubbed the floors. Alfred had enlisted the help of local women to run the canteen. That way he knew they would keep coming and the mothers would understand it was a safe place to bring their little ones. There would be a doctor on duty to look at the sickliest children, and warm clothing would be distributed to those who needed it.

By the morning everything was ready. Pounds of powdered milk had been mixed with water, cocoa and sugar and heated in huge cooking pots to feed an estimated eight hundred children under the age of six. Margarita took Lucy by the arm, and they watched as the doors were opened. A long line of women stood outside, holding babies in their arms, with toddlers clutching their skirts. The women carried bottles and jars to fill with the precious milk and cocoa. Lucy noted again how quiet the queuing children were, how listless, how pale, how unlike her pupils in Welwyn. When she asked their ages, she realised the skinny Catalan six-year-olds were the size of English four-year-olds.

A local woman had the unenviable task of turning away those who had come too late or weren't named on the list. On the second morning the queue began to form before dawn.

Alfred and Domingo badgered the authorities to let them open a second canteen in Calle Carmen in the notorious fifth district. Mrs Petter of the Save the Children International Union was put in charge, and she refused to use local helpers, preferring instead to pay staff she had chosen. She also insisted on using condensed milk rather than skimmed, and set up a special depot to water down and heat the canned milk. A thousand children could be given milk and porridge each day here. But it still wasn't enough.

On the first day of opening at Calle Carmen, Lucy watched a group of five or six weeping women hold up the wasted limbs of their babies as they were turned away. She turned to Margarita in anguish. 'What can we do? What can we do?'

Margarita clenched her teeth. 'Just work harder, write more letters, set up more canteens, I suppose.'

Margarita went back inside, but Lucy stayed at the entrance, watching one woman who held back slightly from the group. When the others had left she still hovered close to the canteen. She was dressed in skirts to her ankles, a black headscarf covered her hair and she cuddled an infant wrapped in a grubby shawl. Lucy thought she could have come from a Bible story; she could have been Mary escaping into Egypt with her baby son. As Lucy approached, the girl lifted her head. Close up she was younger than Lucy, perhaps no more than seventeen, and her gaunt face was filled with despair. One of the baby's arms hung from the shawl, thin as a twig. Lucy's heart contracted. Perhaps it was already dead.

'Come with me,' she instructed, and the young mother followed her round the building to a side entrance.

Lucy touched her arm, fleetingly. 'Wait here please.'

Inside, Lucy hurried to find the doctor, her fingers drumming impatiently on her own wrist as he gave cod liver oil capsules to a worn-looking woman with five children.

Before the next family could approach, Lucy stepped forward and softly asked him to come with her. He could read the urgency in her voice and followed at once.

The doctor took the unmoving bundle from the girl's arms and gently unwrapped the shawl. Lucy held her breath. At the feel of the air, the baby let out a thin, plaintive cry and Lucy exhaled in relief. As the doctor hurried into the canteen with the infant, its mother looked back at Lucy over her shoulder, mouthing, 'God bless you.'

Lucy leaned against the wall of the building, looking about her at the milling crowds. That girl was only one, and there were so many. So many.

Margarita also took Lucy to visit some of the children's colonies which were being supplied with food and managed by Alfred Jacob's team. They were mostly in the big houses of the rich which had been abandoned as they fled to their country estates. The houses were clean, airy and painted in bright colours – a blue dormitory in one, a yellow dining room in another. There were flowers and plants everywhere, and pottery ornaments and bookcases filled with books. The children seemed well dressed and occupied, though there was something unsettling to Lucy about their regulation haircuts. The girls all had their dark hair cut with a fringe and bobbed just below their ears, while the boys' was shorn very short. Lucy noted with approval that there were plenty of art materials and sports equipment, and no toy guns. The youngsters slept on metal beds with cheerful covers. Each bed had a drawer underneath in which they kept their clothes, books and any personal items. One boy showed her his collection of cardboard soldiers, and another his book of stamps.

She was told that the children all played a part in the running of the colony, making their own beds and taking turns to wait at table, do gardening and care for the chickens and rabbits. There was a cleaning rota. The older boys and girls helped the younger ones.

At one colony the residents were gathered together for what they called a 'Children's Parliament'. There was orderly debate and discussion about the running of the lessons, meals and dormitories. Lucy filed this away for future use; she couldn't imagine schools in England asking the pupils what they thought!

When they arrived at the Los Cipreses colony in Pedralbes, to the north of Barcelona, her heart jumped as she recognised a little boy. 'Jorge!' she called.

He turned and his face lit up with joy. 'You came!'

He ran up to her and then held out a hand and formally shook hers. Lucy was both amused and touched. Jorge turned to his companion and rather pompously announced, 'This is Lucy Yellowhair, and she is my friend.'

He took her by the hand and insisted on showing her around the colony. He was particularly interested in the room where they were producing leaflets on a printing press. Lucy exclaimed in astonishment at the presence of such a machine and the head teacher raised her eyebrows. 'Don't you have these in England?' she asked. 'Almost every school in Republican Spain has a printing press.'

Spain seemed a country of contradictions, thought Lucy, where innovative ideas existed side by side with medieval feudalism, and squalor with lush fashion. The furnishings in the colonies looked like something from Heal's, so different from her own drab Victorian classroom.

'It's all so modern,' she whispered in wonder to Margarita. 'The teaching methods, the equipment.'

'What did you expect?' Margarita smiled with satisfaction. 'We live in the twentieth century too.'

'But in England it's only the children of the rich who would get education like this.'

Margarita raised her shoulders and spread her expressive fingers.

And that's what Tom is fighting for, Lucy thought, feeling a rush of warm pride.

When she left the colony, Lucy shook Jorge by the hand and promised to return.

On the way back from the colony, Margarita told Lucy more about her life. She and Domingo had been married for three years, and shared many interests. Domingo was on the board of the YMCA and Margarita was on the board of the YWCA.

'We are like two halves of one person,' said Margarita, and

Lucy felt a twinge of envy. Would she ever be able to say the same?

Margarita laughed her deep, guttural laugh, tinged with bitterness. 'But now we have Alfred Jacob, so we have three halves. Domingo thought he was the only pacifist in the world till he met Alfred. Now it is like they are brothers. But more than brothers. Soul brothers.'

Lucy looked sideways at Margarita. Is she jealous? she wondered. 'How do you find having Alfred living with you?'

Margarita sighed softly. 'Alfred's wife Norma will come soon with their children. And they will move to their own place. But I will always have Domingo.' She hesitated shyly, and her hand fluttered over her stomach. 'And soon we will have another!'

Not having known Margarita before, Lucy had assumed she was always a comfortably rounded person. She grasped Margarita's hand. 'That's so exciting. When is it due?'

'I am five months gone. I know it's bad to bring a baby into a war, but we are so happy. And this child might grow up to be a peace-maker, a diplomat who will bring harmony to the world.'

Lucy wondered if she would ever be able to joyfully announce a pregnancy, and if so, who the father would be.

Margarita turned. 'What about your young men? Is one of them like the other half of you? Like your soulmate?'

Lucy hesitated. Sometimes one of them felt like that, and sometimes the other. How could she explain it?

'Who do you love most?' pressed Margarita, sounding both intrigued and slightly outraged.

Lucy chewed her lip. 'I love Tom because he is so vital, so

full of life and laughter. And I love Jamie because he is so loyal and trustworthy and understanding. It's as if together they make the perfect person. And some days I feel like I want to be with one of them, and some days the other. It's like if you were a mother with two children. You would love both of them just as much, even if they were so different.'

Margarita raised her thinly plucked eyebrows. 'But the way you love a man is not the way you love your children. And the way you love brothers is not the way you love your husband.'

Lucy thought of the very different kisses the boys had given her. 'No, I suppose not.'

In her father's weekly letter from home, Captain Nicholson reported that he had told Mrs Murray he could no longer afford to keep both the house and cottage running. He'd said he needed to let the house and move into the cottage, offering her the opportunity to stay on as his housekeeper. His indignant astonishment vibrated through the paper as he described her refusal, and Lucy couldn't help giggling as she pictured the scene. Mrs Murray's own letter about 'declining your father's generous suggestion that I should become his unpaid skivvy' made her howl with laughter. Now Mrs Murray couldn't wait to go to Lanarkshire, but she was very worried, particularly about Tom. She hadn't heard from him since a scribbled note written at Christmas, though two letters had arrived from Jamie. She wondered if post from the Front might have reached Barcelona, but Lucy hadn't had word from either of the brothers.

Lucy scanned the newspapers every day for news of them,

and listened to the wireless in the YWCA canteen where she took lunch. There she heard news of the Battle of Jarama to keep Franco out of Madrid. It was well known that the International Brigades and militias were suffering appalling losses. After all, they were barely trained foreigners, peasants, teenagers and trade unionists fighting against General Franco's well-drilled and equipped brigades of Moroccan mercenaries and German and Italian soldiers. Any day, at any time, Tom could be killed. Lucy wondered if she would somehow know the moment of Tom's death. Anxiety about him was like a tight band around her chest.

She hoped Jamie was somewhere safer, behind the front lines. She was less worried about him being physically injured, because as a journalist he wouldn't be as directly in harm's way as his brother. She was more concerned that the pure light of him would become tainted and diminished.

And she worried a little about herself. There were the food shortages and occasional bombing raids, of course, and one night, hurrying home from the canteen through the dark streets of the city, she rounded a corner into a group of young militiamen, lounging on guard duty. She stopped dead for a moment, playing her torch over the faces which turned towards her. They exchanged a few ribald jokes and then began to close in on her, moving silently on their rope-soled sandals and surrounding her. She heard a clatter as one by one they laid their rifles on the cobbles. They would not be needing them for what they had in mind. She shone her torch behind her, and it picked out the dark shape of a man who moved to cut off her retreat. Her mouth went dry and her pulse thundered in her ears. She switched her torch to her left hand and raised her right in the closed fist of the Republican salute and remembered La Pasionaria's call to arms.

'¡No pasarán!' she called, in a small, squeaky voice. And then louder and firmer, '¡No pasarán!' There was a pause, and she could hear all the far-off sounds of the city, but the men around her seemed not to move or breathe.

'¡No pasarán!' she shouted angrily.

Then one of them replied, '¡No pasarán!' and raised his hand in salute, and one by one the others echoed him and fell back to let her on her way, trembling from head to foot.

When she told Margarita what had happened, they agreed that in future she would stay in the canteen until it became light.

After seven weeks with no news, two letters arrived from Tom on the same day in early March. One had been written just after Christmas and had travelled to England and back again.

30 December 1936
Somewhere in Spain!

Dear old Luce,
Well, it wasn't quite like Christmas at home. We had cold corned beef for Christmas dinner. But I can tell you that seemed like a treat compared with our usual oily beans! It was foggy and there was deep snow. I didn't imagine snow

in Spain, but we are high up here. We went out and made a snowman. The locals thought we were mad.

The 2nd battalion, which I'm in, hasn't been allowed up to the front line yet. We are still stuck behind the lines doing weapons training. I'm trying to be patient.

Your parcels arrived in time, and I'm now the warmest chap in the company. The battalion postman is a wizard – he's called Ernest Mahoney, and he used to own a bookshop. He has a little van and he drives up to the front line, no matter what the weather, to make sure that everyone gets letters and parcels from home. I'm wearing three pairs of woolly socks.

You've probably heard it's bad at the front line, Luce, so there's no point in my lying to you. The No. 1 company set out on Christmas Eve. 145 of them went into battle and only 67 returned. You know I told you about the poet John Cornford? He was killed, the day after his twenty-first birthday. I volunteered to send his personal effects to his family – it wasn't much for a life – a few photos, a pencil, a knife and the last letters he got from home. I hope his poems will survive.

Those who made it back got a heroes' welcome from us, I can tell you. We formed up in a guard of honour and cheered them so loud you could probably hear it in Barcelona.

But you mustn't think we are downhearted. We are like young doctors setting out to cure the world. It's a crusade, a brotherhood. I can't explain, but on some days I feel exultant, maybe like hearing the 'Hallelujah' Chorus for the first time, or standing in a cathedral when the sun is pouring through the stained glass, or seeing the ceiling of the Sistine Chapel or something. We have a cause we believe in so

absolutely that our own lives seem unimportant. I can't wait
to get stuck in.
  Not long now.
  With love,
  Tom

Lucy quickly turned to the second letter, which proved
Tom had been alive only a few days ago.

28 February 1937
Base camp

Dear Luce,
  I suppose you've been following the Battle of Jarama on
the news, and you'll know now that we held it and Madrid
is still safe from Franco. Frankly I don't know how we did
it, but we did. And as you can see, I'm still alive.
  The 2nd battalion – my battalion – went up to the Front
in a convoy of trucks with the Dimitrovs from the Balkans,
and the Franco-Belge battalion. The villagers lined the street
and cheered us and some of the women cried. And we felt
pretty good about ourselves. Then we went by train and then
lorry again, up towards Madrid.
  When we arrived in a village, the locals gave us such a
warm welcome – they seemed to have found every egg in the
district to give us! If only they wouldn't coat them in olive
oil! We stopped at a farm which had become the cookhouse
and had bread and coffee. We filled our water bottles and
then we were ordered up the hill. We could already hear the
drum of machine-gun fire, not far away.

We had no idea of the position of the enemy, but we scrambled up the escarpment across a plateau and a dry valley and then we were on a hill looking down on the Jarama River. The blokes who got up there first had christened it Suicide Hill because we were surrounded on three sides. The heavy rifle and machine-gun fire made clods of earth jump up all around us. We set up our machine gun and then found we'd been issued the wrong ammo. There were a lot of jokes about 'non-intervention'.

I can't tell you what the next seven hours were like, except that there's a fear which dries up your mouth and throat when you are lying with your face on the ground surrounded by the flash and roar of shellfire. And then suddenly there's a surge of adrenaline and you forget about fear, and I felt I was fighting for all the poor and downtrodden in the world. I had that sort of wild joy you get in standing up to the bully even though you know you might be beaten yourself.

In those seven hours more than half our battalion was killed or wounded. I don't know what it does to a man to see his friend who was laughing and talking one minute, smashed into a carcass like a butcher's shop, to see a face become a bloody hole. I can't get those images out of my head. I don't know if I'll ever again be the Tom you knew.

The stretcher-bearers were running up and down the hill with the wounded, taking them to our HQ on a sort of sunken road behind the line. That's where we were given hot food and something to drink – the first for seven hours – and had a short sleep. Then we were back again. Day after day. By the thirteenth of Feb there were only 160 men left of 500, and I think I'd accepted that I wasn't going to make it.

One day there was a gap in the line, and we marched out again to fill it, led by an Irishman called Ryan who started singing the Internationale and we all joined in and others from broken units came to join us, and we held the position. And Franco's troops didn't get into Madrid.

Now they tell us we won the Battle of Jarama. But it doesn't feel much like winning when most of your friends are dead.

There's a song they're singing, written by a bloke called Alex McDade. You sing it to the tune of 'Red River Valley':

There's a valley in Spain called Jarama
It's a place that we all know so well
For 'tis there that we wasted our manhood
And most of our old age as well.

From this valley they tell us we're leaving,
But don't hasten to bid us adieu,
For e'en though we make our departure
We'll be back in an hour or two.

Oh we're proud of the British battalion
And the stand for Madrid that we made
For we fought like true sons of the people
As part of the fifteenth brigade.

There are other versions, but not fitting for mixed company. And now we're back at base again. Showers. Delousing. Drinking wine. Sleeping. We held a complaints meeting about all the things that went wrong. And I'm looking at your picture, and thinking of the way you kissed me on that last morning, and I don't think I'm going to make it now, Luce, but I would love to see you one last time. I know your work in Barcelona is really important, but aren't there any refugees further south who need your help? Then if I got a few days' leave, maybe I could come and meet you somewhere?

Would you think about it?

With love,

Tom

Lucy's heart squeezed with pain at the change which had come over him between the two letters. If he had given up hope of surviving, she knew it was urgent that she reach him quickly and persuade him to return home.

9

The opportunity to travel south came sooner than Lucy expected, with the arrival at the end of March 1937 of three English Quaker women: Francesca Wilson, Barbara Wood and Alfred's wife Norma Jacob. Francesca was a teacher from Birmingham who'd been given two months' leave by her headmistress to come to Spain and see how she could help. At first she seemed nothing special, a tall, slim, middle-aged woman with a beaky nose and amused eyes, whose plain frocks had seen better days. But Lucy was soon to discover that an unremarkable-looking woman could also be an unstoppable force of nature.

Francesca's arrival in Barcelona coincided with the peak of the battle between Alfred Jacob and Save the Children about condensed versus powdered milk. An officious woman called Dr Marie Pictet had arrived from the headquarters of Save the Children International in Geneva with her sidekick Mrs Small. Dr Pictet was a nutritional expert and she considered condensed milk to be superior to powdered milk because of its healthful content of sugar and cream. Mrs Petter came from the Calle Carmen canteen to join them and the three women moved as one organism. They had all taken an equal dislike to Alfred, who waved the report from the Cadbury experts to no avail.

Margarita and Lucy tried to act as a buffer between the warring factions, saying they could see both sides of the question, though privately they agreed that Alfred was right, because a greater number of children could be fed if the money was spent on powdered milk.

'He doesn't have any diplomatic skills,' Lucy said to Margarita. 'He knows that what he's doing is the best way, and he won't even discuss anything different.'

The three women from Save the Children didn't seem to appreciate that without Alfred's vision and Domingo's common sense, there wouldn't be any canteens to debate.

The argument then extended to the running of the canteens, and Alfred's conviction that they should be staffed by local women and refugees against Mrs Petter's view that they must be led by people from overseas.

The atmosphere in the office grew more and more oppressive, so Lucy was delighted on three counts when Francesca announced her intention to journey south to Murcia and said she'd be glad to have Lucy's company. Firstly Lucy would be relieved to escape the warring factions among the aid workers; second it seemed right to be heading to where children were most desperately in need and third, she was happy that she'd be closer to both Tom and Jamie, with the possibility of persuading them to leave Spain before they were killed.

In the few days before they departed, Lucy took Francesca

to visit the three children's colonies at Rubí near Barcelona, which were supported by Friends groups in Birmingham, St Helen's and Paris. Francesca brought her camera and took photographs of the clean, neatly dressed children. Lucy wasn't surprised to see the camera because the Quaker medical advisor Dr Audrey Russell had told her that Francesca was a journalist and photographer as well as a teacher.

'The children were evacuated from Madrid,' explained Lucy. 'Slum children who'd never been to school. They were terrified at first, but look at them now.'

'It's impressive,' remarked Francesca, and her eyes glittered behind the camera. 'Photographs of happy children persuade people to donate more money. They can see what good they are doing.'

Francesca snapped away at beaming youngsters in the colony's art rooms and on wide verandas where lessons would take place as the weather grew warmer. Lucy thought the children in the colony now looked much more like her class at home, with rounded limbs and pink cheeks. Only their dark eyes and hair cropped in regulation cuts marked them out as different. For a moment she felt a great homesickness for the pupils she'd left behind.

'Before I left home, someone talked to me about the Spanish Republic fighting for its social experiments and reforms,' continued Francesca. 'They said the Republicans would fight to the death because there was a whole Spanish renaissance at stake. I had no idea what they meant, but I think I'm beginning to understand.'

They stood together watching two five-year-olds trying to carry water from a sink to a bucket for their own serious purpose. They had figured out that they needed to work together to transport the pots of water and hold the bucket still.

'Well, that says it all,' said Lucy, and Francesca beamed at her.

The day before they left for Murcia, Lucy went to see Jorge. He rushed out to meet Lucy Yellowhair, and dragged her straight to see his latest print productions. His teacher said he was making reasonably good progress in class, but slipped away at every conceivable moment to work with his beloved printing press.

That evening she was packing her small suitcase when Margarita knocked on her door. They had agreed that Lucy would leave her woollen winter dresses, coat and underwear with Margarita in Barcelona. She knew it would be much hotter 360 miles further south in Murcia, and summer was coming.

Margarita sat down on the bed, and opened the bag she'd brought with her.

'I've brought you three presents,' she said.

Lucy was nonplussed. She hadn't bought anything to give her only friend in Barcelona.

Margarita took a pair of rope-soled alpargatas sandals from her bag and handed them over.

'I'll keep your lace-up leather shoes for you. That way I know you'll return,' she laughed.

Lucy sat down next to her to try on the new sandals.

'And I brought you this,' continued Margarita, pulling out a soft cotton dress in the palest shade of dove grey. It had pin-tucks all down the front and covered buttons. Lucy could see it had been expensive. Margarita rubbed the round of her stomach, which was pressing against the fabric of her frock.

'It won't fit me this summer,' she grinned. 'Go on, try it.'

Lucy removed her green woollen dress over her head, making her hair stand up with electricity, then unbuttoned Margarita's gift and dropped it down over her petticoat. Although Lucy was taller, the dress fell just below her knees in pleasing folds. The little room at the YWCA didn't have a mirror, but Margarita purred in approval.

'I knew it would suit you even more than me,' she said. 'It's the colour of your eyes.'

She patted the bed beside her and Lucy sat again as Margarita produced a jam jar from her bag with a flourish. The jar appeared to be filled with a squashed creature preserved in formaldehyde.

'It looks like a medical specimen,' grimaced Lucy, hoping Margarita wasn't going to make her eat it.

'This is the most important gift,' said Margarita dramatically. 'I think when you go south you might meet with your Tom or your Jamie.' She pronounced the J in the Spanish way like a guttural H.

'And then you might decide who it is you love as a woman loves a man. You might marry them – or perhaps not marry with a priest, but just in your heart, because in wartime everything is different. And then you will need this.'

Lucy was turning the jar around in her hands, still mystified.

Margarita suddenly clapped a hand over her mouth, and searched Lucy's face.

127

'You do know what happens between a man and a woman when they are married? How babies are made?'

Lucy blushed and nodded. Mrs Murray had carefully explained all the details when Lucy's periods first began.

Margarita laughed her deep laugh and threw up her hands. 'Thanks be to Maria I don't have to explain that!' She unscrewed the jar and carefully lifted up the contents.

'It's a sponge,' she said, and now Lucy could see the holes. 'A sponge kept in vinegar. Do you know about this in England?'

Lucy shook her head and Margarita continued, 'When you think you are going to make love, you take the sponge and push it as far inside you as you can reach. And leave it there for four hours afterwards or eight hours. Just don't forget to take it out. Do you understand?'

'Yes, yes, I understand. What does it do?'

'Sperm don't like the acid of the vinegar. It will help to stop you making a baby if you don't want one.'

Lucy indicated Margarita's stomach questioningly, and Margarita burst out in peals of infectious laughter.

'Sometimes a man can take you by surprise, and you might get carried away and not want to stop to go to the bathroom. The sponge does not work well if it is in its jar under the bed.'

Lucy laughed too. 'I'm going to miss you!' she said, hugging Margarita.

'And I will miss you. I have never met anyone so brave as you, to come so far alone and go now so blasé into the terrible south.'

Lucy patted her friend's shoulder and wondered what she would find in the south and if she would see Tom and Jamie again. Would she ever have to take the sponge from its jar? And if so, who would she be with?

On the day she was leaving, letters arrived from home and from Jamie. She quickly scanned the ones from England first, savouring the pleasure of waiting to read Jamie's. Mrs Murray told her she was now in Lanarkshire and fully reconciled with her family. She had already found a job in a draper's shop, and was paying rent to her sister, though hoped to find a little flat of her own for when the boys came home.

Her father's letter didn't even refer to Mrs Murray's departure, but gave a long and detailed explanation of his dire financial position before telling her he had decided to rent out their house and move into the Murrays' cottage for the time being. 'It's much smaller and I can look after it on my own much more easily,' he said. If that was supposed to make her feel guilty for leaving him, she was afraid it didn't. It would do him good to find out what all the women around him had done for years.

Then Lucy could wait no longer, and set aside the letters from home to open Jamie's.

29 March 1937
Sevilla

My darling Lucy,
  I wish you could have been here in Holy Week, to see the joy people have when Franco has liberated them from the Republic. I was with the French film crew from Pathé-Journal, and also filed copy for all the Catholic papers and the dailies.

It's certainly nothing like Holy Week in England! It went on for eleven days and nights with enormous crowds thronging the streets to see processions like nothing you could imagine. There are about seventy brotherhoods who each take two or three giant 'pasos' from their church to the cathedral and back. The pasos are huge wooden floats with carved scenes from the Passion covered in gold, or giant silver statues of Mary weeping and holding Jesus in her arms. Some of the pasos date from the fifteenth century and it's a miracle they survived when the Reds attacked the churches. Men carry them on their shoulders and they are incredibly heavy and some of the brotherhoods take twelve hours to complete the circular route.

Each procession was led by a giant cross, and behind them came the members of the brotherhood, all barefoot and dressed in white robes with tall pointed white masks with eye holes in them, like the Klu Klux Klan in America, but here they represent penitence. In some processions there were hundreds of these men. Then there were altar boys, and some groups had brass bands with them, but some were in complete eerie silence. One was so long and moving so slowly that it took an hour and a half to pass me.

All the women in the crowds were dressed in black with traditional lace mantillas in their hair, and they were crying or saying their rosaries. It was like really being at Christ's funeral. I'm sure they were also weeping for their own loved ones who've died in this terrible war. It was so moving, Lucy, to see all these thousands of people who are now free to worship as they choose again. It makes me so sure that Franco is on God's side.

I wish you could see it for yourself. Is there any way you could get here? Safely, I mean.

I so much want to see you and hold you in my arms. Perhaps we could even get married here in Spain, though I promise I wouldn't press you on that.

I hope you aren't fooled into believing the false news put out by the Republicans. When you came back from one of those meetings with Tom you said Dolores Ibárruri — La Pasionaria — had claimed that peasant girls were being violated by Franco's legionnaires, mercenaries and Moors, but this is Republican lies — it was Reds and anarchists who mutilated corpses and raped women. And they tell me that the outskirts of Madrid are alive with Republican women militia fighters, stripped to the waist like Amazonian warriors, carrying modern Soviet rifles, with blood-rage in their eyes. You can't possibly think it's right for women to behave like that? I pray every day that Tom will understand the error of the cause he has chosen. I know he means well. And I pray for you, to keep safe and keep doing the marvellous work you are doing.

With all my love,
Jamie

Lucy folded the letter irritably. Why on earth would female fighters be going round bare-breasted? It wasn't practical or rational. She thought she had better get to Jamie soon and talk some sense into him.

MURCIA
April 1937

10

Francesca persuaded Alfred Jacob to lend her a car to drive down to Murcia to see what needed to be done in the south, and Lucy agreed she would share the driving. Truth be told, Lucy was rather terrified at the thought of driving on these lawless Spanish roads, but Francesca's energetic fearlessness was infectious. At the age of forty-nine Francesca seemed almost elderly to Lucy, and she thought, well if an old person like her can do it, I'm sure I can too.

It was now April and although the days started with a freshness in the air, the temperature soon climbed. Lucy was glad she'd only brought her two summer dresses and Margarita's which she would keep for 'best'. Francesca had decided they shouldn't drive for more than three hours a day, because she wanted to see something of the way people lived outside the cities, so they travelled in the cooler part of the mornings and stopped overnight halfway.

Lucy could not have been happier, drinking in every detail of the countryside they passed. She saw orange groves and lemon groves, rice fields where green shoots were just sprouting through the water, and then the road opened out on to the coast. Lucy craned her neck towards the sandy beaches, tumbledown white fishing villages and sea which faded from stripes of deep royal blue at the horizon to palest aqua near the shore. Then the road meandered inland again. Lucy couldn't identify the plants in the fields, but Francesca pointed out date palm, hemp, peanuts, cork trees and pimento. It was thrilling to Lucy to see these exotic species, and it seemed so utterly impossible that this peaceful countryside was in the middle of a war. At the edge of the plain mountains rose, terraced for olives and vines. Everywhere there were fruit trees in blossom and the sweet smell of spring wafted through their open windows.

Lucy soon discovered that Francesca was a great storyteller and she certainly had stories to share. She came from Tyneside, though Lucy couldn't hear any trace of it in her accent, and was the child of Quaker parents but not a practising Friend herself. She'd studied history at Newnham College, and then taught history at Gravesend in Kent.

In Gravesend at the start of the Great War, she told Lucy how she'd come across the Belgian refugees who were fleeing the German army and arriving in great numbers in Britain.

'In the late afternoons I used to take the ferry across to Tilbury where they were landing and in the dim light I saw hordes of bewildered women and children with their treasures tied up in sheets, or sometimes nothing but a canary or a parrot in a cage.' She was told off for 'hanging about' and she asked if she might teach English to some of the Belgian women to prepare them for life in Britain. Her request was granted, but soon this wasn't enough for her; she heard that Quaker Relief was helping civilians in France and she applied to go out there.

She grinned. 'I was interviewed by Ruth Fry at Friends House. I stressed my fluent French and willingness to do any kind of work. But she said, "You are engaged in useful work here. What is your motive for wanting to leave it? Is it a genuine concern for the relief of the unfortunate or only love of excitement?" And I was found out! I'm an adventurer at heart!'

Lucy laughed aloud and wondered what Ruth Fry would think of her motives in heading to Spain to save Tom and Jamie from their suicidal idealism.

Francesca went on to describe the devious way she'd found to get to a POW camp on the Dutch island of Urk and from there to a refugee camp in Gouda, and later to work with refugees in France, Corsica, North Africa, Serbia, Austria, Russia and now Spain. Lucy was awestruck at the places Francesca had travelled to. To think she'd written her off as a drab old woman!

'Aren't you ever afraid?' she asked.

Francesca overtook a slow-moving lorry. 'I have a species of arrogance that this is not my time to die,' she said. 'My insolent confidence protects me from fear.' She glanced sideways at Lucy. 'And what about you – are you afraid?'

'No, not much. Mainly excited and eager to help, but I have two ulterior motives.'

Francesca pressed her and Lucy found it was a relief to tell her new friend about Tom and Jamie as well as her desire to help the children.

'I've met a few of the International Brigaders,' said Francesca. 'I didn't know there were such idealists left in the world. I can't see you talking Tom out of it.'

'No, but I have to try. And in the meantime I am determined to be an enormous help to you.'

They stopped halfway and after their evening meal Francesca ordered coffee with a tot of rum in it, and lit a cigarette.

She had talked while they were eating about her activist women friends, her journalism for the *Manchester Guardian*, the lectures she'd given, the books she'd written about Vienna and Macedonia, and her passionate belief in progressive education.

'I met Sigmund Freud,' she said casually, taking a long draw on her cigarette. 'I didn't like him.'

Lucy felt rather provincial until Francesca echoed Rousseau's ideas about making schools 'into gardens where children could grow', and Lucy thought yes, that was exactly what she wanted to achieve. That's what she knew how to do.

On their second day's journey Lucy drove the car, with some trepidation at first, but soon gaining confidence, while Francesca leaned a lazy hand out of the window, talking non-stop. She sympathised with Lucy's frustrated ambitions to become a doctor, and said she was the only one of her siblings to go to university. Lucy suspected she had worn down her parents until they agreed. It seemed that, like Lucy, she hadn't had a particular desire to teach, but 'what else can a woman do?'

Lucy wondered why she'd never married. Perhaps she'd had a sweetheart who was killed in the Great War? Francesca's explanation was more surprising than that.

'My affairs were all with foreigners who it would have been disastrous to marry.'

She described a failed love affair in Serbia and a deep friendship with a man called Nikolai Bachtin who was disastrously married to a friend of hers. 'If he died I would miss him more than anyone in the world.'

Just as Lucy was wondering how she could bear to leave this Bachtin, Francesca continued, 'This may seem odd to you, but all my adult life I've had this great conscious desire not to cling to any human being.'

Lucy thought how opposite she felt, how she longed to wind herself like ivy around those who she loved and hold them close to her. She had never met anyone like Francesca, with her infectious zest for life but determination to remain at arm's length.

It seemed Francesca's house in Birmingham was a kind of hub for refugees, with boarders and lodgers including a writer called Nikolaus Pevsner. Lucy thought she recognised that strange name. Most astonishing of all, Francesca casually reported that over the years she had 'adopted' or fostered eight teenage girls and two boys, who had been Russian refugees living in Paris.

Lucy risked a glance at her. 'What happens to them when you go away?'

'I have made up my mind to demand nothing from them, to remain detached from them. I have too much wanderlust.'

Lucy didn't know how to reply, and was glad that she now had to concentrate hard on driving into her first big town, Murcia, where the carts and other traffic seemed to follow no known rules of the road.

Murcia looked as it must have done for centuries – an Arab town whose main streets had once been souks and were now thronged with all the poor of the south.

Francesca and Lucy followed instructions they'd been given to the offices of the Refugee Committee. They pushed their way through crowds of ragged, desperate-looking refugees who milled around the building, and inside found four distracted officials, struggling with card indexes and lists. It was almost impossible to hear them above the cacophony of angry men and women yelling their frustration, wild with hunger and anxiety about their families.

Lucy spoke to the man in charge, who shouted in her ear that Murcia was a poor town of sixty thousand people, and it was full even before twenty thousand refugees and soldiers arrived. They had sent the Málagan refugees to five 'night shelters', including one called Pablo Iglesias which was the worst. At the other shelters the refugees were provided with two meals a day, but at Pablo Iglesias they were only given an evening meal and a little milk for the babies. Francesca nodded decisively as though that was what she'd needed to hear, and Lucy said, 'We'll see what we can do.'

Soon Francesca and Lucy were outside the Pablo Iglesias shelter, looking up at the unfinished block of flats and attracting immediate attention. Both of the English women were taller than the refugees who surrounded them and strikingly different-looking with their pale faces, clean clothes and Lucy's blonde hair. Francesca swept in without hesitation, and Lucy followed, jittery with nervous excitement as hands clutched at her and women begged for help for their children. She sailed in the wake of Francesca's confidence. Nothing seemed to daunt her.

As they stepped inside Lucy was appalled at the stench, the din, the filth. It was a huge, incomplete apartment building, nine storeys high. There weren't any windows or doors and the floors had not yet been divided into rooms, so formed vast spaces swarming with women, children and occasional men. There was no furniture, just a few straw mattresses. The noise in the echoing space was deafening: babies crying, boys running from floor to floor, sick people groaning, women shouting. There were flies and mosquitoes everywhere, but particularly in the corridors and unplumbed toilets where human waste swilled about the floor.

They had been told the building held four thousand Málagan people, though Lucy doubted anyone had counted them. As they entered each floor the refugees surged around them, clamouring above each other to be heard. The smell of the unwashed bodies and the reek from the latrine areas made Lucy's stomach churn, but she furiously quelled the urge to retch. One woman was weeping bitterly, saying she had lost her children in the mayhem of the flight from Málaga and didn't know if they were dead or alive; another held out a limp child in her arms and shrieked that her other three children had died and now her baby was dying of fever; another yelled, 'They carry the dead out of here every day.' Lucy looked into the faces of the children who had seen such horror, and for a moment in the pandemonium she felt the utter impossibility of helping them.

But within another hour Francesca had telephoned Barbara Wood, who had moved down to be the Quaker organiser in Valencia. Barbara told her she would send lorryloads of milk, cocoa, sugar and biscuits. Lucy watched Francesca and thought, if she can do this, perhaps I could too. One person can't change everything, but maybe they can change something.

The two women spent the night in a cheap but clean hotel, where sugar bags had been stitched together to make sheets. They were surprisingly soft. Francesca helped Lucy push her bed to the middle of the room under the light fitting, and hung a mosquito net over it. They agreed this hotel would be their base in Murcia, and Lucy dashed off quick letters to Tom, Jamie, Mrs Murray, her father and Margarita, giving her new address. She knew Margarita would forward any letters which came to Barcelona for her.

That night Lucy slept soundly and woke filled with energy and anticipation at what they might achieve. In the morning she and Francesca queued for a shower, but there was no hot water left. Tomorrow, she decided, they would have to get up earlier.

Back at the Pablo Iglesias shelter they found a man in a shabby suit who told them he'd been a government official before the war. He spread his hands to indicate the squalor around him. 'That it should come to this,' he said, with tears in his eyes.

Lucy could hardly imagine how she would feel if she was reduced to living in conditions worse than any animal.

Francesca sent him to gather the details of all the children, and give them tickets for breakfast, but he came back with a list which only had sixty names on it.

Lucy looked around. She could see at least two hundred youngsters from where she was standing.

The man explained, 'They saw you yesterday and could see that you were foreign, so the rumour went round that all the children on the list would be sent to North America or

Mexico or Russia. These people might have nothing, but they won't be parted from their *niños*.'

'That's all right,' said Lucy. 'Sixty children would be a good number to start with, until we have helpers.'

Francesca had asked for volunteer helpers from the Refugee Committee, but she'd been told Murcia was not like Barcelona. Most Murcian women before the war still lived in uneducated seclusion, scarcely emerging from their homes except to go to market. They were not prepared to mix with the 'filthy Málagans', as they called the southern refugees, and catch their diseases.

So Lucy and Francesca set themselves up in the rudimentary kitchen and served the first drinks to relays of girls and boys who brought their own bowls, tin cups or empty bottles to fill with cocoa. The children had to hand in tickets for their hot chocolate and Lucy laughed when she saw one enterprising boy picking up used tickets from the floor and then nipping to the back of the queue for a second and third helping. She could imagine Tom doing this when he was younger.

When they arrived the next morning, Lucy and Francesca could feel a change in the building. They could barely pass up the stairs for the press of people, and had to lock and bar the kitchen door, which left them coughing in the clouds of smoke which billowed out of the stove. There was pushing and shoving, and any orderly queuing system was impossible to maintain. Every child in the building was now clamouring for cocoa.

Francesca visited the Refugee Committee again and that night they sent workmen to hose down the latrine areas with disinfectant, and connect rudimentary plumbing. They cleared a landing, and carpenters hung doors on to it to make a dining room. Tinsmiths fashioned cups out of empty condensed-milk tins. Francesca and Lucy decided that they had enough supplies to feed the expectant and nursing mothers as well as the children. Lucy was amused to hear that in Spanish they were called 'embarrassed and creating women'.

Word spread fast around the shelter and at breakfast the next day, the little ones were reasonably well behaved, but the 'embarrassed and creating women' broke down the new doors and surged forward, shoving each other aside to dip their tin mugs into the scalding vats of cocoa. Lucy's voice, calling for calm, was drowned out by the shrieking of the women as they yanked each other out of the way by the hair.

Francesca said, 'They're like a pack of ravenous dogs.'

Lucy thought anyone might act the same if they were so desperate.

For two days the breakfast was like a feeding frenzy, but by the third day Lucy had bought a megaphone and two English girls had arrived from the University Ambulance Unit. Between them the four women managed to restore order, as the starving refugees slowly realised there would always be enough to go round.

Soon, however, Lucy and Francesca became aware that some children were too sick to turn up for breakfast. They lay on straw, covered by filthy rags, plagued by flies and mosquitoes, their voices so feeble that their cries for water couldn't be heard above the hubbub.

Francesca shook her head. 'This is the greatest misery I've ever seen in my life. And I've seen some terrible sights.'

Lucy was shown a baby who had been born on the roadside as his mother fled from Málaga and whose body was covered with sores. Lucy drove the mother to the civilian hospital but it was overwhelmed and they were turned away.

'There's a man called Sir George Young,' Francesca told her. 'He saw similar conditions in Almería and set up a children's hospital there with nurses from England. Let me see whether I can speak to him.'

Within a couple of days Sir George had come on a flying visit and agreed to fund another children's hospital if they could find a suitable building, so Lucy and Francesca returned to the Refugee Committee and explained Sir George's offer. The harassed officials said they would see what they could do.

The following day Francesca was leaving to assess the situation in Madrid and find out how Quaker Relief might help there. Lucy marvelled at her courage at heading into the heavily bombarded city, and worried about being left alone in Murcia.

Francesca just shrugged. 'I'll be fine. I always am. And I can leave you in charge here. I know you can do it.'

Part of Lucy wanted to say, 'I'm only twenty-one. I can't be responsible for feeding starving people,' but Francesca was appraising her with such confidence that despite her terror she looked her straight in the eye and said, 'Of course.'

11

For the next few days, Lucy struggled to maintain order at the Pablo Iglesias shelter, but she and the two English girls from the ambulance unit stood firm. She overheard some of the Spanish women saying, 'Don't mess with the one with the iron-grey eyes,' and realised it was her. Very well then, she would use all her steely teacherly skills to keep control.

Having learned from Alfred's success in using refugees as helpers, Lucy was keen to find volunteers among the Málagan women to mix the milk and serve the breakfasts. The two English girls couldn't keep assisting with cocoa in the morning and then returning to the ambulance unit to work the rest of the day.

Lucy spent several hours moving around the building, asking about the refugees' experiences. It became clear to her that most of the Málagans came from a kind of horrifying poverty which she'd thought only existed in India or Africa. She hadn't known that Europeans in the twentieth century could be living in hovels, or even in caves in the countryside.

Many owned nothing apart from a cooking pot and the rags they wore, and scraped a living doing the most menial tasks. They had trekked along the coast road to Almería, picked out by searchlights and shelled by warships at night and machine-gunned from the air by day. A woman with a dirty bandage round her neck described the Italian plane which had swooped down on them and strafed them as they fled. Another told her about a Canadian ambulance driver called Norman who raced back and forth along the road picking up the wounded. But whole families had been wiped out. It was said that fifteen thousand people had died trying to escape.

The refugees clustered around Lucy to tell her about the horrors which had devastated their dirt-poor but peaceful lives.

By the end of the day she had identified six women who seemed to have some natural authority and were respected by the others, and she asked if they would help her. Lucy knew that clothing and fabric had been sent to Spain by the American Friends, so she called Barbara Wood in Valencia and asked for some women's dresses and soap and bales of cloth to be sent in the next consignment to Murcia.

When she presented the women who had agreed to help with a new dress each and a bar of soap, they fell on her with embarrassingly effusive gratitude. It was clear they'd never been given anything in their lives. The next day these Málagan women in their enviable new dresses took charge of the breakfasts.

With Francesca in Madrid, and the English girls back with the ambulance unit, letters became an even more important lifeline for Lucy. While Jamie had been away at Ampleforth

College, he had developed the habit of Sunday letter writing. It appealed to his sense of order. Every week he sent a letter to his mother, often with a note to Lucy or her father slipped into it. Now he wrote to Lucy every Sunday, even though the letters sometimes arrived out of order or in batches. Captain Nicholson and Mrs Murray also wrote weekly, even when Lucy was too busy to send anything back but a scribbled note. Her father was proud of his new abilities to 'do for himself', though often asked her when she was coming home. He told her she would like living in the cottage. He never said so, but she knew he was lonely.

Mrs Murray, on the other hand, was fitting in well to her old Scottish community, meeting up with long-forgotten schoolfriends and helping to run the Sunday School. She said the local postmaster was retiring and she was going to apply for his job, as living accommodation was provided over the shop. Where Captain Nicholson's letters were factual, Mrs Murray's were overflowing with emotion – particularly how much she missed her boys and Lucy.

Lucy heard intermittently from friends in England, who were fascinated by her decision to go to Spain, but more occupied with their own lives – their parents, their boyfriends and their jobs. Among her friends, her most regular correspondent was Margarita, who told her all the news from Barcelona, and often made her laugh. When no letters arrived from Margarita for two weeks, Lucy assumed it was a problem with the postal system. When none came in the third week she began to be worried. Surely she would have heard if they'd been bombed? Or had she said something wrong and upset her friend? Her written Spanish was far from perfect.

She shook these thoughts out of her head and concentrated on her work.

All the same, it was a relief when a letter arrived with Margarita's looping handwriting.

My dear friend,

I haven't written because I knew you might try to come back to Barcelona to be with me, and your work in Murcia is too important to leave. I am now up in Puigcerdà with Norma Jacob.

I am sorry to tell you that I have had a miscarriage. I can hardly bear to write the word, but I must accept that it has happened. The pain was terrible, as though I was giving birth. Domingo could not bear to stay in the house and hear me. I fear I made a lot of noise.

They wouldn't let us see our child, but the doctor said his head was the wrong shape and he could not have survived. I feel sick at the thought of something abnormal and monstrous growing inside me for all these months, and then terribly, terribly sorry for my poor broken son. And, I don't mind saying, I feel terribly sorry for myself and for Domingo.

I have cried until I think I can't cry any more. And then I begin to weep again. It is impossible to know where all these tears come from. And my breasts leak milk and that seems the cruellest thing of all when I have no baby to feed.

I didn't want to get out of bed for the first two weeks. I just wanted to sleep and forget. Though every time I woke up and remembered, it was a new agony. Domingo and the others were kind, and brought me food to my room, though I didn't want to eat. Even when they brought me honey cake!

Then the Danish Quaker Elise Thomsen came and sat with me. She told me Domingo was suffering too and I was making it even harder because he was so worried about me. I looked carefully at him the next time he came and I could see he had deep, dark circles under his eyes. So I forced myself to get up and dress and told him he must concentrate on his work. Elise gave me the idea that I should come to Puigcerdà to be with Norma and the two children. The mountains and the clean air are some comfort, and I take long, long walks. Norma is kind but she is not you. She obviously thinks I should 'pull myself together'. You would have understood.

It pains me to see her healthy children, running about and laughing when my boy will never do that, but at the same time it soothes me to hold Norma's little girl Terry in my arms.

I will stay here for another week or two until I feel stronger. And then I will go back to Barcelona and immerse myself in work. I know Domingo is missing me. He writes every day.

The doctor said there is no reason why our boy was not whole, and it shouldn't stop us having children in the future. I don't know if I would dare. When the war is over, perhaps.

You mustn't come to me. I know you would if I asked, but you have so much important work to do. Write to me, and perhaps pray for me and our boy.

With love,

Your friend Margarita

Lucy had tears pouring down her cheeks as she read. Her poor friend. Despite the instruction to stay in Murcia, she wondered if she could get to Margarita by train once Francesca returned from Madrid. She sat down and wrote a long letter, struggling to express the depth of her sorrow and telling her about the work in Murcia. As she wrote about the refugees at Pablo Iglesias she knew Margarita was right and they needed her most at the moment.

As Lucy walked about Pablo Iglesias talking to the families, she couldn't help worrying about the children who were too ill to eat the breakfasts. She brought them water and milk and biscuits, but could see many of them were so weak they were unable to swallow. Every day another child died. And every day Lucy returned to the Refugee Committee to ask about a location for the proposed hospital.

She also noticed a different problem. The adolescent girls who weren't engaged in taking care of their small brothers and sisters hung about in groups, followed around by gangs of boys. Their swearing and snarling kept the boys at bay. But for how long?

Frustrated with the slowness in finding a hospital building, Lucy decided to tackle the issue of the girls. She had read a newspaper article about the Mayor of Murcia, who was a headteacher, so one morning she picked her way through the narrow, twisting passages and sun-drenched squares of the town to his school. She had to wait for two hours while he dealt with a strike of student teachers and when she entered his sweltering, airless office the Mayor was slumped down in his chair as if exhausted. Lucy had prepared carefully for the interview, wearing Margarita's lovely grey dress, and taming her hair with a little olive oil on her brush. She'd even applied a coat of lipstick. As she'd pulled on her Quaker armband it seemed to give her a courage she didn't normally possess. 'You aren't doing this for yourself,' she'd reminded herself sternly. 'It's for those girls.'

The Mayor looked up at her enquiringly, then smiled and drew himself a little taller.

'I have come for your help,' she said, as imperiously as she could manage.

He straightened his tie and indicated the chair opposite his desk. As she sat, Lucy said, 'There are girls, young women at the Pablo Iglesias shelter with nothing to do. I want to give them work and the ability to earn a living.'

He nodded approvingly.

'I am a teacher like you,' she continued, 'and most of the refugees seem to be illiterate. I thought if we could get a few girls together and begin to teach them to read and write, they would be able to teach each other their letters.'

He pulled paper and a pen towards him. 'You are a woman after my own heart. What do you need?'

Lucy took a deep breath. This was her opportunity. 'I need sewing machines, as many as you can get. And needles and thread. I can get fabric. I need a blackboard and chalk and paper and pencils. And perhaps a rota of your teachers who might be able to help after school hours. I won't be in Murcia forever.'

'A pity,' he murmured. 'Can you teach sewing?'

Mrs Murray had taught Lucy to make her own clothes, but she was far from an expert. 'Not really. I saw there was a seamstress with a workshop a few streets from Pablo Iglesias. I thought I would ask for her help.'

The Mayor put his head on one side. 'Be diplomatic,' he said. 'The women of Murcia can be very conservative, secretly religious. They have not embraced the Republic and they are afraid of catching illness from the refugees, and they will be shocked by the language the Málagan women use.'

Lucy could tell she had been given good advice. She wondered if she could push her luck any further. She told him about Sir George and the offer of a children's hospital.

'That would be a miraculous thing,' he said. 'I've heard about the English Hospital in Almería. I'll see what I can do.'

Lucy had heard this too many times before, but he seemed to be serious, and her hope rose a little.

The Mayor stood up and walked around the desk. He shook Lucy's hand hard and then, rather to her surprise, kissed her on both cheeks.

Lucy retraced her steps through the heat of the afternoon. She wondered how unbearable it would be here in August if April was so hot? She hoped she would become acclimatised. Or perhaps by August she would have persuaded Jamie and Tom to return to England. A startling thought struck her. If the boys went back to England would she return too, or would she stay with the refugees who needed her so badly? Would she perhaps become like Francesca, an unmarried woman who spent her life travelling the world forging order out of chaos?

She went back to her hotel to check her dress and her hair before setting out to the seamstress. This time she left the armband on her bed, thinking perhaps it looked too much like a militia or trade union badge.

A thin, bespectacled woman came to the door, looking

angry at the interruption, then took in the blonde foreigner in the expensive dress and ushered her inside.

Lucy blinked to adjust her eyes to the gloom of the shop. She wondered how anyone managed to do any sewing in this light, but then the noise of sewing machines and women chattering drew her attention to a room beyond. The seamstress saw the direction of her gaze and closed the workshop door.

'How can I help you, Señorita?'

Lucy gripped her nails into her palms and tried to adopt Francesca's tone which brooked no argument. 'I haven't come to have a dress made. At least not today.'

The woman pursed her lips. Evidently this was not what she wanted to hear.

'I've come to ask your help,' said Lucy. 'I am an Englishwoman, working with the refugees.'

The seamstress made a noise like pshh, wrinkling her nose in disgust.

'There are girls, young women. I am afraid they may fall into the ways of bad women unless they learn a useful trade.'

The seamstress pulled a face which clearly conveyed 'that's all they are good for'. 'It isn't any of my business,' she said.

Lucy noticed a gold chain disappearing into the neck of the woman's dress. She wouldn't mind betting that a crucifix hung on the end.

'The Mayor has promised me sewing machines. Kind Americans have provided fabric. I just need some good Christian Spanish women to teach these girls how to sew.'

'We don't have the time,' said the seamstress, starting to usher Lucy towards the door. As she opened it and light fell into the shop again, Lucy noticed a shape on the wall where the paintwork was less faded, as if a picture had been removed. Surely a holy picture.

Lucy turned her back to the street and crossed herself. 'Doesn't Our Lord instruct us to care for the poor and needy?'

The woman stared hard at her, as if trying to work out whether this was a trick to expose her secret Catholicism. Then, perhaps seeing only sincerity in Lucy's light eyes, she slowly closed the door again.

' "Love thy neighbour as thyself, and um . . . let the children to come closer," ' quoted Lucy, wishing that all those years at St Mary's had given her something more solid.

The seamstress looked even more suspicious, and Lucy realised her mistake. This woman would only have heard the Bible in Latin, not in Spanish. She wished Jamie was with her.

'Are you a Protestant?' the seamstress asked abruptly.

Lucy laid one hand on the doorknob, and then turned back slowly. 'Surely you wouldn't have it said that a Protestant foreigner was more charitable than a Spanish woman of the true faith? But never mind. I'm sure there are genuinely Christian women somewhere in Murcia.'

Their eyes locked and Lucy thought she had lost, but then, unexpectedly, the woman laughed aloud.

'You may be a Protestant foreigner, but you are wily as a fox.'

Lucy grinned, and her whole body relaxed as the seamstress led her through into the workshop, clapped her hands and announced, 'Señoras!'

The treadling and chatter fell silent immediately. 'What is your name and where are you from?' the seamstress asked Lucy, who told her.

'Señoras!' the seamstress announced. 'This is Lucy Nicholson, from Inglaterra, and we are going to help her to teach the refugee girls to sew. It is our Christian duty, to save them falling into sin.'

They didn't look convinced, but Lucy had no doubt that their formidable employer would persuade them otherwise.

'Lovely dress,' the seamstress commented as she showed Lucy out. 'Don't forget where to come if you need another.'

A few days later, after breakfast, carpenters reappeared at the Pablo Iglesias shelter to cordon off a workshop and a schoolroom on the top floor. One of the Refugee Committee brought Lucy a copy of the local newspaper, turning back the page to an article by the mayor. It said that benevolent women had come from England to help the dying children of Spain. These selfless people were prepared to make a hospital, and it was a scandal that no suitable building could be found for them.

In the afternoon the first two sewing machines were delivered, amid much excitement and interest, and Lucy also received a summons to meet the Civil Governor. She was relieved that Francesca arrived back from Madrid just in time to accompany her to the appointment. As they left Pablo Iglesias the seamstress appeared with two of her staff to give the first sewing lesson.

'You see,' said Francesca. 'I knew you could do it. I should have stayed away longer. You'd have had the whole refugee problem sorted out.'

The Civil Governor took them to see a large white art deco villa in its own grounds, with ten bedrooms, two kitchens, two bathrooms, cool tiled floors and marble stairs, balconies all around and a flat roof. It was ideal for a hospital, but there was a snag. The elderly married couple who owned it were living there. The Governor had a hurried conversation with them in a corner, then turned, beaming.

'It's all settled. They have another house to go to, and we have agreed a suitable rent.'

Lucy was concerned that the old couple had been evicted from their home, but Francesca showed no worry.

'Let's go and have something to eat, to celebrate. I'm famished. And I'm dying for a cigarette.'

Lucy set aside any thoughts of going to visit Margarita as she and Francesca swung into action. In just one week of frenetic activity, the hospital was ready for its first patients. Lucy was exhausted, but felt it had been the most thrilling week of her life. Francesca gave her a budget and she went shopping. She bought pots and pans for the kitchen. She placed an order for thirty beds, and the shop owner promised her they would arrive in days. She set the refugees in the sewing workshops to make sheets and mattress covers, and the Murcian seamstresses produced nightshirts and nightdresses. Other Catholic ladies of Murcia obviously heard about these good works for a children's hospital, and more nightshirts and sheets and sets of clothes for sick children arrived as donations.

Lucy tried to think of everything. She bought combs. She bought card indexes. She bought paper and paints for the children to use as they recovered, as she was sure they would.

The Refugee Committee brought along tea chests carefully packed with fine-quality glassware and china. When Lucy expressed surprise at the expensive delicacy of these items, she was told they had been 'collected' from the houses of the rich who had fled at the beginning of the war. She had nothing more than a slight twinge of conscience at the good use they would be put to.

While Lucy equipped the building, Francesca was concentrating on the staffing. A cook, a ward-maid and a washerwoman were all hired from among the refugee women at Pablo Iglesias. The hospital was assigned a doctor, who helped Lucy and Francesca ransack local pharmacies for the medical equipment and medicines they might need. A nurse arrived from England.

The nurse seemed unimpressed by the fact that this hospital had been constructed from nothing in little more than a week.

'Where are the thermometers and temperature charts?' she asked, and her next request brought Lucy back down from her state of euphoria with a great crash. 'And we'll need screens to put around the beds of those who are dying.'

Once everything was in place, Francesca commandeered a small bus and she and Lucy began to tour all the refugee shelters, collecting the most seriously ill children.

There were so many infants needing treatment that at first the hospital looked more like a maternity ward, full of mothers and babies. But the next week the boys and girls with typhoid began to arrive, many of them delirious and with high fever. Lucy and Francesca took turns on night duty, giving the nurse and doctor time to sleep between their shifts. The English nurse quickly trained her in the special routines for the typhoid patients, the rinsing of the mouth, the constant changing of the sweat-and-diarrhoea-soaked nightclothes and sheets, the washing of the small, shivering bodies. Lucy realised they were shuddering with terror as well as fever and she sang quietly as she sponged them down and dressed them in clean nightwear. This seemed to calm them and many fell asleep in her arms as she sang 'Golden Slumbers' or 'Speed, Bonnie Boat'.

The English nurse explained that typhoid was carried in the diarrhoea and urine, and the children's hands must be washed thoroughly before they ate anything. Fear for her own safety surged through Lucy. She didn't have Francesca's sense of immortality.

'And me?' she asked. 'Will I catch it?'

'Not if you wash your hands between touching their faeces and urine and touching your food,' said the nurse firmly.

Lucy scrubbed her hands raw with the scarlet carbolic soap after nursing each child. She made a pact with God, that if she didn't catch typhoid she would try not to mind the constant itch of the mosquito bites she received in the hospital at night. Sometimes her legs were covered with the ugly red weals. Various people advised different treatments – lemon slices, raw onion, baking soda. None of them had the slightest effect.

During the day Lucy and Francesca were busy overseeing the work of the washerwoman, ward-maid and cook, collecting young patients from the refuges or taking home those who were considered to be out of danger, ordering medicine and the special food which was needed for sickly and convalescent babies and children. Here the International Brigades helped. There were hundreds of wounded Brigaders in the military hospitals in Murcia and the Brigade lorry drivers were very active in finding good food for them. They drove to the coast for fish, and inland to farms for fresh fruit and vegetables, eggs and meat. They were delighted to bring the tastiest, freshest supplies for the hospital.

And in between her shifts at the hospital, Lucy walked back and forth on the floors of Pablo Iglesias, urging mothers to bring their children to see the doctor.

'It's free,' she told them. Or, 'He's a handsome Spanish doctor.' Or, 'There are gardens you can sit in. It's very quiet and clean.' And most of all, 'The food is delicious.' Then she would help an anxious mother lift a thin, mewling bundle of skin and bones from the straw, and on to the bus outside.

Lucy's focus was entirely on the refugees and her work. Only at night in bed did she have a moment to think of Margarita and Tom and Jamie, and pray they were well.

12

Some events are so momentous that whole nations remember where they were and what they were doing when they heard the news.

Lucy was at her hotel, at about 9.30 p.m. on 26 April, resting after a day on her feet at the hospital, when she heard a great commotion in the street. Pulling her alpargatas back on to her sore feet, she stepped outside. People were rushing from building to building, shouting about a place Lucy had never heard of – a small Basque town in the north. A town called Guernica.

She stumbled into the hotel dining room where guests and staff were clustered around the wireless, shushing each other and pressing close to hear the news. It seemed that Guernica, which had no anti-aircraft defences, had been bombed out of existence that afternoon. Monday was market day, and people from the surrounding farms and villages would still have been in the market hall at four o'clock when the residents heard the loud rumbling of heavy bombers approaching. People assumed they were on their way to a military target, but as the first planes appeared over the town they began to drop bombs, sending the terrified civilians screaming to their homes to gather their families and huddle in basements and cellars. Twenty-four German and Italian bombers returned for five major bombing raids until the whole place shook with explosions and the crash of falling buildings. The bombing runs continued for three hours, and fighter planes machine-gunned any civilians who dared to be seen above ground or tried to escape. Very soon the whole town was ablaze. Flames and smoke could be seen for miles around.

The people in the dining room clutched each other, their faces white with disbelief, asking: How many people died? Did you know anyone there? Did General Franco give his approval or were the German and Italian devils working on their own initiative? Such barbarians!

Lucy pulled aside the hotel manager. 'Where is it? Why Guernica?'

He shrugged. 'It's the capital of Basque nationalism, I suppose. It's about thirty kilometres from Bilbao on the northern coast.'

Lucy grabbed her bag and ran to the hospital, knowing Francesca was on night duty and might not have heard the news.

'Oh Lucy!' Francesca sank her head in her hands.

When she lifted her face it was written over in abject despair. 'I thought I'd seen the worst, but bombing unprotected civilians is a new hell. Basque refugees will be pouring into France and Barcelona.'

'Isn't this a war crime?' asked Lucy.

'What do they care? If the Fascists win, who's going to bring them to trial?'

'It could happen anywhere,' said Lucy slowly. 'Even Welwyn.'

Francesca looked grim. 'If Fascism wins here then you are right – one day it might well be London.'

It was the only political thing Lucy ever heard her say.

Within a few days Franco's ground troops were moving rapidly through the Basque region. George Steer of *The Times* and Noel Monks of the *Daily Express* had been on hand in northern Spain, and gave full accounts of the attack on Guernica, including the fact that bomb cases stamped with the German imperial eagle had been found in the wreckage of the town. The *New York Post* ran a cartoon showing Adolf Hitler brandishing a bloody sword labelled 'air raids' as he towered over heaps of civilian dead littering 'the Holy City of Guernica'.

Lucy was incensed at this new horror perpetrated against undefended civilians. She cut out the articles and posted them to Jamie, begging him 'for the love of God' to return home to England, or at least to come and help her with the refugees. She felt quite certain he wouldn't want to remain on Franco's side once he had been told about Guernica.

But before Jamie could reply, a hastily scribbled note arrived from Tom. It simply read, *Guernica. Non-intervention? Bastards.*

When it came, Jamie's letter was also short and seemed to have crossed in the post with hers.

28 April 1937

My darling Lucy,
I expect you've heard about Guernica, but please don't believe everything you read. There are so many lies flying about it's hard to know what is the truth any more. Everything is

distorted in this terrible business of war. I think I am more in sympathy with your Quaker pacifists than I realised.

I can promise you that General Franco says he had no planes up on 26 April because it was foggy. I know they are saying it was the Luftwaffe and the Italians, but Berlin completely denies the bombing. We had a briefing from Brigadier General Queipo de Llano and he said they had evidence that the Reds deliberately dynamited Guernica during their retreat from the city. The front line was only kilometres away and people must have already been fleeing the town. Why would they have been having a market with the front line so close? You must admit it sounds much more likely that the Reds would blow up an empty town to stop Franco's men getting hold of their homes and belongings. I've heard that Republicans are saying three small German bomb cases were found by reporters. General Queipo de Llano says they were planted there by the Reds to try to shift the blame. Did you ever hear of a German bomb that didn't explode?

I believe that there has been a massive lie told to discredit Franco abroad.

I wish you would come to see what it's like in the areas which have been liberated from the Republicans, to hear the stories I hear, to see the women crying over the desecration of their churches and the murder of their priests. I still believe this is a holy war and God is on our side.

Please come. Won't you come?

I long to see you so much.

Your ever loving,

Jamie

Lucy wanted to give him a good shaking. She had always looked up to Jamie, to his bright intelligence and clear-headedness, but now it seemed he was letting himself be duped into believing what he wanted to be true. Her admiration for him stuttered like a candle flame when a door has been slammed.

In early May, Lucy heard from Margarita that the food shops in Barcelona were empty and the ration down to a thousand grams of food per person for ten days. Margarita had returned to the city to help Domingo, but was firm in her instruction to Lucy to continue the marvellous work she was doing in Murcia.

I will never forget our son, or stop thinking about him, she wrote. *But I am all right. And you are needed there.*

She told Lucy that Norma Jacob had joined Alfred's battle against Dr Pictet, Mrs Small and Mrs Petter of Save the Children. Alfred and Norma had decided to resign and return to London unless they were allowed to carry on the aid operation without interference.

But in-fighting among the relief agencies wasn't the only civil war within a civil war to hit Barcelona. On 4 May the newspapers were full of the story of the rival factions within the Republicans whose differences had exploded into open warfare across the city. Five parties known by different acronyms had seized key buildings and opened fire on each other. Barricades were built across roads. The Republican Assault Guards were fighting hand to hand with the anarchists. The crack, rattle and roar of rifle fire, machine-gun fire and hand grenades shook the streets throughout the day and night.

Margarita sent a message to say that the aid workers and canteens were safe.

'Franco must be laughing,' she said. 'The Antifascistas are slaughtering each other without any effort from him.'

Throughout May, Lucy and Francesca continued to work all of their waking hours at the Pablo Iglesias shelter and the hospital. More and more of the refugee women were assisting now, and another nurse had arrived from England. News came that four thousand Basque children had been evacuated to Britain, accompanied by their teachers and priests. Apparently Alfred Jacob was furious. He believed the children should be kept in Spain and fed there.

'They will be better off in England,' said Francesca, taking a deep draw on her cigarette.

'But what about their mothers?' argued Lucy. 'Surely it isn't right to take the children away from their families?'

Francesca looked at her sharply. 'You are too sentimental. You've seen how happy the children are in the colonies. I'm sure I would have been more contented in a colony than with my family.'

Lucy thought perhaps she might have been happier in a colony herself than being brought up by her father, but then she would never have met Mrs Murray and Jamie and Tom.

Francesca had begun to worry that she'd told the headmistress of her school that she would only be gone for two months. If she was to keep her job, she needed to return to work in England.

'When I come back in the summer holidays, I'd like to

set up a colony for boys of about fourteen to sixteen, to teach them to read and write and keep them out of the army.'

Lucy agreed. Far too many of the boys were leaving the refuges, lying about their ages and volunteering for the Republican army. Their mothers, who had already lost husbands, other children and parents in the fall of Málaga, were inconsolable.

'I was thinking we could maybe set up some short-stay colonies down at the fishing villages on the coast,' said Lucy. 'To give the girls and boys some fresh air and a chance to run about. Like a summer camp, with games and crafts and a bit of reading and writing!'

Francesca was enthusiastic and Lucy promised to get it all arranged for her return.

In the meantime an American Quaker, Esther Farquar, arrived with suitcases of clothes and toys donated by Friends in the USA. It had been arranged that she would take over the running of everything from Francesca.

Esther raised the question of refugees on the other side of the front line, in Franco's territory. 'We ought to be helping them too, to show we are non-political.'

Lucy explained that before Alfred Jacob had set up the first canteen in Barcelona, he'd gone to Franco's headquarters in Burgos to offer assistance, but been met with a frosty reception. The Fascists had said they could feed and clothe their own people.

'But that was six months ago. What's it like now?' pressed Esther.

Lucy looked from one of them to the other, thinking hard.

For the week when Francesca was handing over to Esther, she wouldn't be needed so much at Pablo Iglesias.

'Why don't I go and find out?' she offered. 'My friend . . .' she blushed slightly, aware that she wasn't calling Jamie a boyfriend, let alone a fiancé '. . . is a journalist, a Catholic, reporting from Franco's side. He could take me around and I could see if they need help with the refugees and children. If I went as an official representative of the Friends there would be a way, wouldn't there?'

So it was arranged. She would go by boat to Fascist-held Ibiza, and from there into Franco's south. She carried letters of introduction from the Friends Relief Service and Save the Children, and Jamie managed to wheedle an invitation letter from Franco's education minister, which he sent her, along with his own promise to meet and escort her as a reporter from the *Catholic Herald*.

She was going to see Jamie!

13

As Lucy's boat approached Marbella, the white houses of the old town backed by smoky-blue mountains looked like a wonderland after the filth and despair of Murcia. She felt something in her chest lift, as if a dark bird had taken off and flown away. It seemed to promise her that despite her deep misgivings about Franco's Fascists, in this place she would find joy.

Jamie was standing on the quay as her boat pulled in, shading his eyes against the glittering reflection of sunlight off the water. When she spotted him, looking like a caricature Englishman in his linen suit and straw boater, gladness swooped in her. It was so long since she'd seen him. She waved furiously, and he caught sight of her, took off his hat and waved it back.

Then her heart began to beat hard as she realised Franco's feared Falangist soldiers were checking the papers of everyone who disembarked. Most people were signalled to pass through, but one man was taken away under arrest. Lucy knew, with a twist of nausea, that it could be her being frog-marched away to God-knows-what torture or simple disappearance if they suspected her of being a spy. She repeated to herself the Friends mantra: she was here to help children in need, without fear or favour.

It was one thing, though, to say 'without fear' but another thing not to feel it as the unsmiling, imperious soldier scrutinised her passport and then each of the letters. He looked around him.

'Is this Jamie Murray here to meet you?' He seemed to spit out the hard H of the Spanish J. Lucy reached past him to point to Jamie.

The soldier leaned in, so close she could smell his breath. 'We will be watching you. If we find you are not who you say . . .' He made a gesture of a knife across the throat, and Lucy forced herself not to shrink from him, not to run back up the gangplank on to the boat.

The soldier returned her papers and indicated that she should go to Jamie, but she could feel his eyes on her back as Jamie rushed forward and lifted her off her feet, covering her face with kisses. Two sailors nearby whistled and applauded, and one called, 'Lucky devil. Give her one for me.' Lucy and Jamie both pretended not to understand. Lucy looked over her shoulder and saw the Falangist soldier still observing them, saying something to his partner, fingering the holster of his pistol.

'We should move away from here,' she said nervously. Jamie followed the direction of her gaze and grinned at the soldiers with his open, trusting smile.

'Don't worry,' he said in Spanish. 'I'm well known for what

I write in support of Franco's regime. You are quite safe with me.'

Then he laid his arm over her shoulder, picked up her suitcase, and led her away.

As they entered the shadow of a narrow road between buildings, he drew her to him again and kissed her. Lucy was trembling, but whether from agitation or delight, she couldn't have said.

Finally, he held her at arm's length and looked her up and down as if he was memorising every part of her. 'You are such a sight for sore eyes. You look more beautiful than I remember. A bit thinner. But it suits you.' He touched her head. 'Your hair's gone as light and curly as when you were young.'

She relaxed a little in the glow of his attention. Perhaps he was right and she shouldn't be afraid. He had always protected her, and it was a familiar homecoming to allow herself to lean against him. After all she had seen and done in the past four months, it would be a comfort to be the one who was taken care of for a few days.

She gazed at him too and touched his nose. 'Your freckles have all joined up!'

'It's called a suntan!'

The unguarded adoration in the way he looked at her was like stepping from a dark cellar into the sunshine, and Lucy thought, oh I do love him. I do!

'I've found a little hotel,' Jamie said, picking up her case again. Over his shoulder he caught the expression on her face. 'Separate rooms, of course. What do you take me for?'

Lucy hung on his arm as he threaded his way through the crowds at the quayside. And Jamie smiled down at her. 'I want to hear about everything you've been doing. I am so proud of you. I think you might have become some sort of saint.'

She stopped and reached up on tiptoe to kiss his cheek. 'Not quite.'

'Thank God for that.' He turned his head and kissed her quickly, full on the lips.

Lucy washed herself and pulled on Margarita's grey frock, smoothing down her wayward hair. She could hear Jamie moving about in the next room as he dressed for dinner, and there was a thrill of naughtiness at the idea of him so close. She ran a finger over her lips where he had kissed her, and smoothed her dress over the breasts and hips which he had never touched. In her case, wrapped in a pair of stockings, was the jam jar Margarita had given her, with the sponge soaked in vinegar. The thought of it, and what it would mean if she had to unwrap it, caused a flutter of anticipation low down in her stomach.

There was a small mirror in the hotel room, and she stared at herself, trying to see the beauty which Jamie claimed he saw. Her chin still looked too pointed, her mouth too wide, her hair too frizzy. And yet, there was something which hadn't been present in the mirror in Murcia, an excitement which flushed her face and dilated her pupils. The dress really did match her eyes, she thought.

* * *

The food in the hotel was plentiful. There was meat as well as many kinds of fish on the menu, and the bread was soft and white. When their meals arrived, Jamie said grace and then began to tuck in to his paella.

Lucy looked down at the beautiful white fish and heaps of beans and rice on her plate and a wave of sorrow rippled through her. She couldn't eat a thing.

'What's wrong?' asked Jamie.

'This would feed a whole family. Fish! Vegetables! Bread!'

He set down his cutlery and laid a warm hand over hers.

'I know, Lucy. I know you've seen terrible things, and I want to hear all about it. But the refugee families aren't here and you are, and this food will be thrown to the dogs if you don't eat it. I'm sure your families wouldn't hesitate.'

Lucy breathed deeply and began to eat, and though her body was craving the vitamins and minerals, her stomach was not used to such rich fare, and soon told her she'd eaten sufficient.

'You've really been through it, haven't you?' Jamie asked, and the sympathy in his face was enough to bring her close to tears.

She shook her head. 'Not me. I'm fine. It's just what I've seen. And it's not as bad as what Tom's going through.'

A shadow of annoyance passed over Jamie's clear features. Perhaps he'd hoped that Tom wouldn't be mentioned.

He took another mouthful of food. 'How is he?'

So the brothers weren't in contact with each other. Lucy pulled out Tom's latest letter and handed it over. 'I haven't had anything since this. Almost a month ago.'

Jamie smoothed the pages and read as he ate.

15 April
A trench. Somewhere in hell

Dear Luce,

I'm sorry I haven't written. There didn't seem much I could say. You wouldn't believe how wintry and wet it is up here on the plain. Some bloke told me that Madrid is the highest inland capital in Europe. I don't know if that's true, but while it's probably spring down in Murcia, it's an endless winter up here.

What can I tell you? Heavy cold rain. Flooded trenches. Soaked clothes. Sodden blankets. Guard duties. Sniper fire. Mortars. Bullet-chipped trees. Uniforms caked with mud. Boredom. Confusion. Rats that will eat a cartridge belt or a boot if they have half a chance. Excrement everywhere. And bullets singing overhead instead of birds. We don't see any real birds. The only relief is that it's too chilly for mosquitoes and lice. And at least we've got steel helmets, bayonets, maps, field glasses and torches now. But no gun oil. We have to use olive oil. We dirty our bayonets so they don't flash in the light and give away our position.

Then there's the noise. The rumble of distant guns. The deafening clatter of a mass of rifles. The whizz and explosion of shells. Bullets like monsoon rain on a tin roof. The roar and flash of grenades. The constant din does your nerves in. I can tell how close a shell will fall by the whistling sound of it. I take bets on it with myself. And I think about where I will be hit, whether a leg or an arm would be worse to lose. I wouldn't like to go blind. They say you survive if you take a hit in your extremities.

174

In war, only five things matter: firewood, food, tobacco, candles and the enemy. Send food, tobacco and candles. Yes I smoke now. Don't be cross.

I'll tell you what I'm wearing: woollen long johns and a long-sleeved vest, two flannel shirts, two sweaters knitted by Mum, my leather jacket (which now doesn't look so dashing), a trench coat, corduroy breeches with puttees and thick socks, a muffler, lined leather gloves and a wool cap pulled down over my ears. And I'm still shivering. It's too cold to sleep. When we come off guard duty at night we rake together what's left of the cookhouse fire and stand in the embers to thaw our feet.

We get hot food, though, and cigarettes and plenty of wine, thank God, which we drink from goatskins. I didn't realise that the goat fur is still on the inside. That's a bit revolting, isn't it?

It comforts us a bit to know the Fascists must be just as uncomfortable as us. The Italians and the Moors must be frozen to the core. Bastards.

I had three days' leave and thought about coming to see you. But in the end I just slept and ate. It was enough not to be cold and not to be shot at.

We know when the Fascists are coming into battle because they ring the church bells first. That gives us some warning. Idiots.

Our best weapon is a megaphone someone got hold of. At the point where the Fascist trenches are closest we shout, 'Buttered toast! We've got hot buttered toast over here!' and 'You are working men. Why are you fighting against your own class for the rich bastards?' and 'You should see the militia women dancing!' And every night we get a trickle of deserters.

Yesterday I saw some green shoots – iris, maybe, or crocus. So perhaps spring will come. And as long as the people of Madrid hold firm, we will be here to protect them from the Fascists. Do you remember Dolores Ibárruri, La Pasionaria, and her slogan '¡No pasarán! They shall not pass'? I promise you the Fascists will not pass us to take Madrid while I've got breath in my body. Though so many have died, Luce. So many good English boys. At night I say their names over and over to myself, so they won't be forgotten.

Perhaps we could meet in Madrid on my next leave? They say it's 'Mucha alegría in Madrid' – much gayer in Madrid. One of my comrades saw women in a bread queue holding on to each other's shoulders, having a knees-up and singing. 'We Spanish die dancing,' they say. I should like to see that bravery and defiance. It would do me good. Could you get there? I don't know when that will be.

Well, sorry if this is depressing, comrade. Maybe the censor won't let it through.

Everything before Spain feels like another life, and I can't allow myself to think of it too much. But it helps to know you aren't so far away.

Tom

A flicker of relief passed over Jamie's features before he folded the letter and passed it back across the table. He must have noticed that Tom called her 'comrade' and wrote no messages of love.

'I wish you could persuade him to go home,' he said.

'I wish I could persuade both of you to go home.'

He met her gaze and his eyes were blue as a Murcian sky. Lucy thought, he always was the most handsome of the brothers. As if he read her mind, he smiled and took her hand.

'Come on, let's go and join the evening stroll along the promenade. The boys will be looking at the girls and the girls will be looking at the boys, but I will only have eyes for you.'

It could have been the most romantic evening of her life if it weren't for the memory of the horrors she had so recently been living with, and the shock of seeing so many smartly dressed German soldiers, who mingled with the locals, talking and laughing. How could Jamie think Fascism was acceptable? How could he let himself be so blinded to what was really happening? But she bit back the critical words, determined not to spoil their first evening together. She reminded herself sharply that she was here to see how the refugee children were treated, without fear or favour, not as a judge of a political regime.

So they watched the sun set over the sea and she allowed herself to lean back against him, with his arms wrapped around her waist. She was slightly tipsy from the glass of wine he'd given her. It felt as if this was where they had always been meant to be, ever since she was five and he was seven, fitted against each other. Comfortable and right.

Back in the hotel, outside her door, they kissed, deep and delicious. Jamie told her she was the love of his life and the most beautiful girl he had ever seen, but finally he kissed her on the nose and said, 'Go to bed, my darling, we've got a lot to see tomorrow.'

The next morning Lucy wore her Quaker armband over her dress, and as she pulled it on, it seemed to refresh the confidence she'd gained in Barcelona and Murcia and strengthened her resolve to look for the truth. She held her head very high and reminded herself she was here on official business for Save the Children International as well as the Friends Service Council. She carried a notebook and pencil for her fact-finding work, and tried to ignore the itch of the new mosquito bites she'd gained in the night. The hotelier had given her a lemon to rub on them.

A driver in Franco's army uniform had been assigned to take Lucy and Jamie around. He looked uneasily at her armband and she told him firmly, '*Servicio Internacional de los Amigos – Cuáqueros*. Friends Service International – Quakers. I am here to make a report about refugees and education.'

Jamie beamed with pride at the new side of Lucy he was seeing, though Lucy caught the driver pulling a sour face which might have meant 'Protestants!' or 'women!' He held the door open for her to climb into the back seat of the car and then showed Jamie the map of the places they would visit in the next five days – Ronda, Córdoba and Sevilla. It sounded so exotic to Lucy and she knew she would have to remind herself constantly that this wasn't a holiday.

In the car they held hands out of sight of the driver, and opened the windows wide to let the rushing air cool them. They talked and talked as they made up for the months they'd been apart.

Jamie began in his perfect, formal Spanish, telling her about the numerous stories he'd written for the newspapers in England and all the film trips he'd been on with Pathé. He

178

described Father Vicente jumping out of trenches to give the last rites, oblivious to bullets churning the ground, the purple tassel of his beret flying in the wind. With satisfaction he listed the medical supplies which had been donated by British Catholics, and the number of nurses who'd volunteered from the UK. He tried to convey the disgust he'd felt at the sight of stately houses and beautiful churches which the Republicans had left inches deep in human dung. The image of these churches obviously epitomised everything he hated about the Republic – what he saw as the disorder, chaos and filth which sprang from a rejection of Catholicism.

Lucy could see that the driver was listening – how could he help it? She replied in Spanish, and Jamie complimented her on her progress with the language, though said she'd picked up some interesting colloquial habits. She said a few words in Catalan and she saw the driver scowl, though Jamie looked impressed.

Lucy switched to English to tell Jamie all about the refugees in Barcelona and Murcia and the massive task faced by the Friends. Jamie had always been a sympathetic listener and it was a relief to her to pour out the details of the plight of the refugees and the work she and her colleagues were doing to keep the children alive. The road twisted and turned away from the coast and up into the mountains as she told him about Alfred Jacob and Domingo, but as she said Domingo's name she saw the expression of the driver in the mirror, and realised he could understand English as well as Spanish. She would have to be careful, so she changed the subject abruptly. 'But let's not think of that now. How's your mother?'

Of course Lucy had frequent letters from Mrs Murray, but

she let Jamie give her the news about his mother visiting Lanarkshire and being reconciled with her family.

'Just think, I have a whole family I've never seen,' he said, 'who cut her off just because she married a Catholic.'

'If you went home now you could meet your grandparents and cousins. I'm sure your mother would love to have you with her.'

He shook his head. 'I have my work here, and it's important, Lucy.'

She bit her tongue. Now was not the time or place to try to persuade him he was mistaken.

Instead, she turned the conversation back to their childhood and watched the landscape of Andalucía out of the window as it became gradually more mountainous and olive groves gave way to pine forests against a vividly blue sky. She saw craggy peaks with little white villages leaning against rocky outcrops and watched a whole flock of sheep picking their way single file down a track.

In Ronda they were taken to two schools run by nuns, and Lucy could see that all the children were decently fed, neatly dressed and obedient. She took a few notes. The pupils sat in formal rows and learned their lessons by rote. It was very different from the progressive education she'd seen in Barcelona, but she could hardly fault it – it was how most young people in England were taught. She walked around the classrooms and spoke to a few children and teachers, but they had been well drilled and there was little to learn about what might lie beneath their combed hair and shiny shoes. The youngsters' accents were quite different from the Málagan and Barcelonian she was used to hearing, but her Spanish wasn't good enough to tell if these were simply local dialects or whether they came from the rich and middle classes.

'How was it?' asked Jamie, who had been strolling around outside while he waited.

'Orderly and calm.'

He nodded with satisfaction, and she could see again the little boy who liked to have the pencils lined up exactly on his desk and for whom any disruption to the expected time-table of their lives had been deeply disturbing.

'Just like Ampleforth, I expect,' she said, and he began to warmly reminisce about the world of his public school, with its bells and rules which had gone back unchanged for generations.

Their hotel in Ronda had a terrace overlooking the coun-tryside of rolling hills rising to meet sheer, jagged cliffs. Some fields were almost vertical but still cultivated. Close by they could hear a Spanish guitar player. It would have been perfect apart from the insects. The terrace smelled of jasmine and thyme, and canaries in cages sang as if there was no tomor-row. As if there was no war.

They ate cold gazpacho soup and shared a bottle of wine and Jamie began to tell her memories of his father which he'd never shared with her before. Small things: his dad letting him put in the last piece of the jigsaw puzzle; sweeping up the shards of a glass sugar bowl Jamie had broken, and taking the blame on himself. As they strolled around the town and stared down into the famous gorge of golden stone, spanned by its three impossible bridges, Jamie's voice dropped almost to a whisper as he began to tell her about losing his father.

'It was like that – like falling into a deep gorge and not

knowing how I would ever climb out. Tom wasn't so close to him, and Mother was in such a haze of grief that she let your father bring us to Welwyn, away from the house we'd lived in with Dad, and she didn't even seem to notice that your father was trying to take Dad's place with us.'

Lucy remembered clearly how enthusiastically Captain Nicholson had welcomed the boys as the sons he'd longed for but never had. He would invite them in from next door to kick a ball about, introduced them to fishing and, as they grew older, took them to rugger matches. And everything he did for the boys had been a smack in the face to her. When she was still little, she tried to join in the ball games, but was sent away to go and help the housekeeper or cook, until she no longer asked but just sat on the lawn and watched them, whispering words of vengeance to her teddy. She remembered the day her father came into the house humming with two junior-sized fishing rods, and she realised he'd bought two, not three. He loved them, and not her.

But Jamie was thinking of his father. 'It was as if it was up to me alone to keep my dad alive. They tried to stop me – my mother and your father – but I was only seven and I found out where the Catholic church was and went by myself because when I went to Mass, it felt as though Dad would be right behind me if I turned round, smiling with pride and approval. It sounds silly, but it seemed he might lay his hand on my shoulder at any minute. I was close to him there, and had him all to myself.'

'I know. I understand.'

'I think my childhood ended on the day Dad died. Did I ever mention that just before he died, he told me to take care of my mother and Tom? That was the last thing he said to me.'

Lucy's eyes welled up. 'You were such a brave little boy, always trying to do the right thing.'

Jamie wiped away the tear that slipped down her cheek, and then kissed the path of it.

'You were the only light in all that darkness, Lucy. It was you that brought me out of the gorge and back into the sunshine.'

She turned and kissed him, full and deep, realising how little love she had known in her life. None at all from her father who should have loved her most. Jamie's adoration of her was like a downpour of love in a parched desert, and she wanted more of it. Wanted it never to stop.

The next day they drove to Córdoba, and on the three-hour journey they sat in comfortable silence watching the scenery or reminisced more about home. The countryside was flush with new crops, as if the war did not exist. No wonder there weren't any food shortages in the Fascist regions, thought Lucy. They passed peasants working in the fields who lifted their heads and stared at the smart car with the soldier driving the foreigners. The adults wore ragged blue shirts, black trousers and broad-brimmed straw hats and their carts were pulled by mules. A boy was drinking water in the Spanish way, holding a red clay *jarra* above his head and letting a fountain of liquid arc into his mouth from the spout. There were young people working alongside the adults, and Lucy made a mental note that education was not universal. She leaned forwards and asked the driver if they might stop so she could talk to the children, but he didn't take his eyes off the road, and very politely told her that they were expected at the next school in Córdoba.

'Will we visit any refugee colonies?' she asked, and he replied proudly, 'We don't have refugee colonies in Franco's Spain.'

No, she thought, I bet you don't. The Republicans are either dead or in hiding, and all the refugees who weren't killed have struggled north to us.

She twisted her head to look back at the peasant children, so the driver couldn't see the expression on her face. When she had composed herself, she looked forwards again. She was determined she wasn't going to be fooled into believing everything was all right when it wasn't.

The further inland they went, the hotter it became, until the olive trees marching to the sky in their orderly ranks vibrated in a heat haze.

They entered Córdoba, and Lucy caught glimpses of plazas with fountains, narrow white streets, minarets and towers, as if they had driven into *The Arabian Nights*. The main street was lined with orange trees and the bullring dominated the town. There was a flash of river, and an ancient bridge and archway near the school they were visiting.

She stepped out of the car into air which was soupy with heat. The driver told them it was over thirty degrees and Jamie translated into Fahrenheit: 'Well in the eighties.'

Lucy thought she would not be able to stand the heat in midsummer, and finally understood the necessity for the siesta, resting through the hottest part of the day.

After the visit to yet another scrubbed-clean, well-drilled school, she lay on her hotel bed in her slip in the drowsy afternoon, and let the slight breeze from the open window play over her limbs. It was as if Jamie's kisses had brought her body alive, so that every nerve ending was sensitive in a way it never had been before. She drifted to sleep and dreamed they were two columns of smoke, lifting into the air, mingling and merging.

In the relative cool of the early evening they visited the cathedral. Lucy covered her hair with her silk scarf and gasped as they entered the Mezquita, once the great mosque of Córdoba. It was the most perfect building she had ever seen. Hundreds of stone pillars topped with red and white brick arches stretched into the distance like a hall of mirrors. The cool symmetry was infinitely calming. Jamie was busy trying to tell her about the history; the pillars were meant to represent the trees of an oasis – the tenth-century this and the thirteenth-century that – but Lucy held a finger to her lips and moved away from him to wander alone among the columns. It seemed as if the stones had absorbed centuries of quiet contemplation. Here was peace.

Where the Catholic cathedral had been built within the old mosque, it appeared to grow from the original structure, as one culture grafted on to another, opening the oasis up into the towering domes of Western architecture. She sat a long time, absorbing the faith and hope of all those who had gone before. Finally she looked around, and Jamie was there, watching over her, as he always would be if she allowed him.

He put his arm around her waist as they walked out into the rapidly falling twilight, and neither of them wanted to speak, to break the spell, and they each knew the other had felt the mysterious power of the place. It truly seemed they were one soul, thought Lucy.

Over dinner, by candlelight, in a leafy courtyard under a persimmon tree, they looked into each other's eyes, and Lucy felt herself soaking up his adoration, as if she had been a dry sponge and was now plump with it, revelling in it. Then the thought of a sponge made her blush as she remembered the jar in her suitcase, and he pressed her to tell him what she was thinking, but she refused. If he asked her to go to his room tonight, perhaps she would.

As if he read her mind, in that uncanny way he had, he said, 'I'm not going to ask any more of you till you promise to marry me. I know you too well, Lucy. You might be doing it just to please me. And I want you to be sure of your own mind.'

She nodded. 'Actually, I was wondering, if we got married, whether our children would have your Scottish freckles,' she said, and he raised her fingers to his lips.

'I hope they are all girls and they all look just like you.'

'All? How many do you want? I'll be like one of those fat old Spanish women.'

'Hundreds,' he laughed. 'And I'll always love you, no matter how fat you get.'

But he was true to his word and didn't press her again for a wedding date, and neither did he invite her to his hotel room or ask to come to hers. He kissed her long and slow, with a deliciousness she could feel right down to her toes, and they parted, leaving her longing for more. Perhaps that was his intention, she thought.

As she packed her case the next morning, she couldn't find Tom's letter anywhere in her room, but when she asked Jamie he promised he didn't have it. She tried to remember if it had said anything which would give away Tom's position or put the Batallón Inglés in danger, and was furious with herself for bringing it south with her.

'Don't you think it's worrying that it's missing?' Lucy asked him. 'Doesn't it make you worry about Tom?'

But Jamie shrugged it off. 'I expect you dropped it down the back of the bed or something.'

Lucy withdrew her hand from his and looked searchingly at him. 'Why can't you believe anything but good of these people here?'

'They are so genuinely thankful and glad to have their religion back. Franco has given them order and stability again. Surely you can see that?'

On the road to Sevilla, through gently rolling fields of wheat and hay, Lucy thought of her seamstress and knew she would prostrate herself on the floor of the church in Murcia when she was once again allowed to worship there.

If the Republic believed in freedom, surely it ought to include the freedom to worship, she thought. Perhaps neither side in this conflict had got everything right.

Despite the disturbing loss of Tom's letter and Jamie's nonchalance about it, and a growing unease that she was only being shown what the authorities wanted her to see, Lucy enjoyed being shepherded around Sevilla by Jamie. He pointed out the hundreds of orange trees which lined the streets and took her into churches aflame with candles, to show her the *pasos* floats and the faithful at prayer.

'You see?' he urged. 'Do you see now?'

The shops and cafés and restaurants were all open and people were hurrying about their day in a completely normal way. Shop windows were crammed with mouth-watering pastries and cakes. Business appeared to be booming. Lucy noted that there seemed to be no children living on the street, no scruffy urchins. That was good, surely, but it also increased her suspicions that what she was being shown was too sanitised. The driver took them to a back street where Jamie knocked on an anonymous brown door set into a wall. They were admitted to a nunnery and escorted round a museum of sculpted holy scenes before being sold a jar of marmalade, made by the nuns.

They visited two more schools where there was nothing of interest to see, and on the last day they were taken to an orphanage, again run by nuns, where they observed the children taking their midday meal, which seemed substantial enough. Jamie made notes for an article while they were told that these were the abandoned offspring of wicked Republicans but thank God the souls of these innocents were now safe. Lucy bent down and asked some of them their names, and where they came from, but once again the replies were guarded and well rehearsed.

As they strolled through the city that night, Jamie told her how he had always loved her, and her heart expanded and she thought she would never tire of hearing it. He admitted how jealous he had been of her boyfriends.

'Do you remember that dance?' she asked, without any doubt he would know which one she was talking about.

He tutted at the memory. 'You must have been what – sixteen? And you went with that oaf of a farmer.'

188

'Hugh Hamilton.'

'He thought he was the bee's knees.'

Lucy teased him. 'He was very handsome. Every girl at school wanted to go to the dance with him.' Mentally she added *if they couldn't have you*, but didn't want to make Jamie big-headed by saying it aloud. She knew how the other girls sighed over him; his shyness with women gave him a slightly aloof air of unattainability.

Jamie objected. 'But he was stupid.'

'He wasn't gifted with brains. And it's true he couldn't dance like you.'

'He didn't have you to teach him.'

In fact Mrs Murray had taught all three of them to dance, pushing back Lucy's dining-room table to make space. Tom had always been coltish and exasperating, his energy and enthusiasm never quite fitting the rhythms of the music. But Jamie let go of his conscious mind and the music seemed to inhabit his limbs, so he swirled his partner around the floor in effortless synchronicity. Every girl wanted to dance with Jamie, to feel him lift them off their feet so that even the most ungainly and clumsy of them felt fluid and beautiful. Lucy remembered the slight pressure of his hand in the small of her back, guiding her into the next turn. They had moved together as if they were one, and she wondered if that's how it would be to make love to him.

But Jamie was remembering something else. 'You let Hugh take you outside.'

'It was hot in the barn, and every time we went round the dance floor either you or Tom were glowering at us.'

'It was a good job we followed you out, though.'

189

Lucy remembered how thrilling it had been to be taken to the dance by Hugh and how she had basked in the envy of the other girls and the visceral jealousy of Jamie and Tom. It gave her power over them, and she liked that.

She hadn't hesitated when Hugh had suggested they went outside, and led her around the back of the barn into the dark. But then he'd rammed her up against the splintery wall, kissing her too hard, and squeezing her breast so that it hurt. She'd started to push him away, and he'd called her a 'cocktease', and had rubbed his crotch against her. She'd shoved him harder, and he laid one brawny forearm across her chest, pinning her against the barn while he thrust the other hand up her skirt. She struggled to grab his hand and yank it away from her body, and called out for help. He pressed his mouth against hers to silence her, but at that moment, two shapes had fallen on him.

Jamie and Tom dragged him away and rugby-tackled him to the ground, kicking him hard.

Lucy recovered herself, pulling her skirt back down. She could see Tom and Jamie were going too far.

'Stop!' she shouted, grasping the brothers by their jacket sleeves. 'You'll kill him.'

'I'd like to,' growled Tom, aiming a kick at Hugh's thigh.

'Not half as much as me,' panted Jamie, with his fists raised.

Hugh lifted his head. 'Please, I'm sorry. I got carried away.'

'Don't you ever touch her again,' warned Jamie.

'Or else,' added Tom, with one last kick.

Lucy leaned over him. 'And don't you dare try that with any other girl either, or I'll set these two on to you.'

Hugh nodded. 'I won't. I promise.' And though Lucy

didn't believe him, there was little else she could do, so she linked arms with Jamie and Tom.

They didn't go back into the barn, but walked home together. Lucy assured them both that Hugh hadn't hurt her, but she was trembling all over from the shock of his attack and the knowledge that she wouldn't have been strong enough to fight him off. It would be a long time before she would trust a boy again.

Looking back, she realised it was the only time she'd ever seen Jamie and Tom so united in purpose.

'We did get there in time, didn't we?' Jamie asked, tension evident in his voice.

'You did,' she reassured him. Then she stopped. 'Would you still want to marry me if he'd . . . ?'

'Of course I would,' said Jamie, but Lucy thought she could detect a note of hesitation.

During the night there was a disturbance outside in the street and she woke to the sound of running men and a scuffle. A couple of shots rang out and she jolted up in bed, grasping the pillow to her chest, wanting to look out of the window, but not daring. It seemed as if the whole town was silent and listening, as a woman wailed, pleading, 'No, no, he's a good boy!'

The noises moved away towards the outskirts of the city and her heartbeat quieted as she tried to settle. All she could hear was water from the fountain in the hotel courtyard. Just as that was easing her back into sleep, there was a rattle of multiple simultaneous gunshots. She leapt awake and clutched the sheet, certain she had just heard a firing squad. What else could it be? She waited in the dark, but the hotel was silent, as though nobody dared to move or breathe. Eventually the thudding of her heart slowed and she lay down again, but sleep did not return until the sky lightened.

Over breakfast she tried to discuss it with Jamie, but he said he'd slept like a baby all night, and the hotelier just shrugged and averted his eyes. She even questioned the driver, who flatly denied there had been any disturbance and smirked as he suggested it had been a nightmare. Jamie nodded patronisingly, and Lucy fumed, certain of what she'd heard. Determination steeled in her. She was not going to be fooled like him.

On their last night they returned to Marbella, and were once again walking along the seafront, but this time Lucy couldn't enjoy the evening promenade. She had been tense and jittery all day following the flat denials of the events of the previous night. It was going to be hard to leave Jamie and return to the squalor and desperate need of Murcia, but at least there she wasn't being lied to or treated like an idiot. She was frustrated that every attempt to speak to people outside of the schools and orphanage had been blocked by their driver, and she knew that her report would be a whitewash. She felt perhaps she should have worked harder to find out what was really happening under the squeaky-clean surface. When she shared her misgivings with Jamie over dinner, he shushed her.

Later, on the promenade, there was nobody listening so she tried again. 'I didn't feel like I was being shown the real picture when we went to see the schools.'

'Of course it was real, and please speak in Spanish, people are looking.'

She lowered her voice and switched languages. 'It was all too sanitised.'

Jamie shrugged. 'It's just a return to order. You've forgotten what that's like. Why can't you believe what you see?'

Lucy pulled away from him. 'For an intelligent man, you can be incredibly stupid,' she whispered furiously. 'Can't you tell when you're being duped? You only see what you want to see. You only hear what you want to hear. You only believe what you want to believe.'

'Aren't most people like that?'

'But you're a journalist and I expect something better from you. The world is more complicated, and I'd have thought you might be more questioning. Tom's letter was stolen, and someone was killed by a firing squad, and you pretend neither happened.'

They fell silent as two German officers passed them, both with Spanish girls on their arms. 'That's what I mean,' Lucy hissed. 'What about the German forces? They call Salamanca "the German town" and that's all right with you?'

Jamie sighed. 'Maybe the means justify the ends.'

'You haven't seen the ends – the starving children and the bereaved mothers. You should come and see what's happening on the other side of this war.'

Jamie's voice was tight with indignation. 'They shouldn't have turned their backs on the Church.'

'Do you think Herr Hitler has poured troops and the Luftwaffe into Spain and bombed Guernica out of existence to save your precious priests and nuns?'

They reached the end of the promenade and turned towards their hotel. Lucy was walking fast now. 'And the

Moorish mercenaries. Do you think they're here to save the Catholic Church? You are so blind that you can't see the truth under your nose.'

He trailed her back to the hotel, and outside her door he touched her arm tentatively.

'Lucy, please don't let's end like this. I thought this was going to be such a romantic evening. Our last night together for I don't know how long. Can't we make it up? Please?'

But Lucy would not be mollified. Everything she had said about Jamie was also true of herself. She hadn't stood up to the driver or the teachers in any of the schools they'd visited and demanded to see the reality. She was furious with herself as well as Jamie.

'I need to go to bed,' she said stiffly. 'I'll see you in the morning.'

At breakfast they were awkward and silent, and it was almost a relief when they parted at the quayside. Jamie looked distraught as the boat pulled away but Lucy refused to feel pity for him. When she had arrived in Marbella she'd felt like a flower opening under his love. But if the price of his love was the truth, that price was too high for her.

14

June came and the temperature in Murcia soared. Lucy filed her official report about her visit to Franco's territory, which seemed to say next to nothing, then she wrote to Jamie that she was sorry they had not parted on good terms, and she hoped he would open his eyes to what was really going on in Spain. The thought of marrying him receded into the distance. Those first romantic days in Marbella and Córdoba felt like a dream, and she was glad the jam jar had stayed in her case and she'd done nothing to commit herself further to him.

When Francesca left Murcia to go back to her school in Birmingham, Lucy was sad to say goodbye, but Francesca promised to return in August during the school holidays, and Lucy had a great deal of preparation to do in the meantime. She liked the energetic Esther Farquar who took over management of their projects and brought with her generous donations of money and goods from the American Friends. On their first day together at the Pablo Iglesias shelter, Esther saw one of the boxes which the condensed-milk tins came in being borne carefully out of the building, surrounded by weeping women. Lucy explained that half of the refugee babies died. More than ten tiny makeshift coffins were carried out of the shelters every day.

'No wonder all the women wear black,' said Esther.

Lucy continued her efforts to persuade mothers to take sickly children to what was now being called the English Hospital; she helped with the literacy workshops for the young women at Pablo Iglesias and was particularly pleased with the progress of sixteen-year-old and thirteen-year-old sisters Juanita and Carmelita. She also began to travel around the military hospitals. There were hundreds of wounded international volunteers in Murcia at any one time, and they seemed to include men of every nation. The English, Scottish and Welsh soldiers she met had left jobs and families at home to come and fight for the Republican cause, and now they lay in sweltering heat in wards of forty or fifty other men, unable to understand anything their doctors and nurses said to them. Most of them spoke no Spanish, so were in isolation as well as suffering great pain, and they hated the 'greasy' food they were given in hospital.

Lucy spoke to the medical staff on their behalf and the men looked forward eagerly to her visits. Some told her stories about the horror of the trenches which she wished she hadn't heard, always imagining Tom in the scenes they described, while other men had been shocked into wordlessness by their literally unspeakable experiences. She asked all of them about Tom and occasionally found a man who knew him and was able to say he was alive and in good spirits when he last saw him. But everyone reported that the fighting was bitter and relentless and every day she expected to get news that he was dead, or lying in a hospital bed somewhere.

After a day's work sometimes she and Esther would join the evening promenade along the Malecón – the embankment built to stop the River Segura from flooding into the town. On one side rose groves of date palms and oranges. On the other was the rushing brown water and the green Moorish garden or *heurta*, ringed by tawny hills, which would have been beautiful were it not being used as one huge public latrine.

Esther linked arms with Lucy and they both ignored the saucy remarks hurled at them by the gangs of passing youths. They talked about anything and everything. Esther marvelled at Lucy's bravery in coming to a strange war-torn country on her own, not as a representative of any organisation.

'Your mother must be a remarkable person to have a daughter like you,' said Esther.

'I never knew her,' said Lucy sadly. 'She died when I was born.'

While Lucy waited for Francesca's return she also began working on the plan to set up a children's summer camp on the coast. By July Murcia was burning hot, with thousands of people crushed into its streets and hovels, and it stank of excrement. The sun scorched down as she stepped out of a shady alleyway to cross each scaldingly hot square, and the flies were terrible. The lack of toilets in most of the houses meant people simply squatted in the streets. As the human faeces dried in the sun, dust from it blew on to the fruit and vegetables in the market and the number of typhoid cases grew each day. Lucy knew she had to get as many children as she could out of the city to somewhere healthier.

She went to see the Mayor again and he spoke to the Governor of Alicante who had been impressed with the Friends' work in setting up the hospital, and suggested that the quiet fishing village of Benidorm might be a healthful spot for boys and girls. Lucy persuaded one of the International Brigade food delivery drivers to take her there one morning, and they found a white sandy beach flanked by rocky outcrops and backed by palm and pine trees. It had a well of fresh water and a welcoming fisherman called Juan who had lost his own wife and children in the early days of the war. He had a black droopy moustache which made him look like the saddest person she had ever seen. A huge white villa stood amongst the pine trees behind the beach. It was shuttered and closed. Juan told her that the owners lived in Barcelona.

The setting was perfect. Lucy cabled Francesca in Birmingham with a list of what they would need, and Francesca promised to ship it to Spain immediately.

Towards the end of July, two letters arrived within days of each other.

Lucy could feel Jamie's displeasure vibrating through the paper. It made her heartsick to read it and she wished she could rush to him and cover his face with kisses.

23 July 1937

My darling Lucy,
I have written so many letters to you since you left, and then screwed up all of them and thrown them away.
I had hoped by bringing you to Franco's territory that you

would see the world through my eyes, but perhaps it's never possible to force another person to do that.

I have never felt so close to you in my life as I did that night in Córdoba when we walked out of the cathedral and it seemed to me we were of one mind, sharing one soul. But now I think I was mistaken. What I saw there was the complete harmony of the architecture expressing the harmony of religious feeling, which is of course simply love. I thought you felt it too, and we were truly one.

I have thought very much about what you said on that terrible last night. I have asked myself if I'm a fool who only sees what he wants to see. And I concede that Franco's staff are keen to show journalists like me and the film crews the best side of his regime. You ask what has happened to the dissenters, and I fear you may be right to ask that. But I have seen no evidence. I must redouble my efforts to find out if there is another side to the story I am so fervently telling in all my articles. I swear I will do that, for your sake and for the sake of truth itself.

I've thought about the German and Italian troops, and I would vastly prefer that General Franco was not breaking the non-intervention treaty by allowing them to fight on our side. But I do believe many of the Italian troops are fighting for Catholicism, not Fascism. I wish it was possible to be in favour of the Church without looking like a Fascist, but in my head they are quite separate, and I'm not a Fascist, and have never been, and never will be. I just want order to be restored. As for the Moorish soldiers – well, as you saw in Córdoba, the link between the Moors and Spain goes back many generations, and though they can't be fighting for the

Church per se, they are fighting for the soil in which that plant can grow and flourish.

I don't know if you know — this month the Spanish bishops have endorsed General Franco. They are holy men. Can they be so wrong?

On that last night, I had planned to ask you to marry me, here, now, in Spain, and not to wait for our return to England. It was a crushing disappointment to hear what you were really thinking. I didn't sleep a wink that night.

I hope all is not lost. I still love you more than I love life itself.

If your promise still holds true that you won't marry anyone else until we return to England, I will content myself with that.

I am yours, forever.

Jamie

Lucy read the letter over and over, until the paper was creased from the sweat of her hands. She began to doubt herself, wondering if she had thrown away her best chance to be loved, and then relived the sound of shots in the night, the too-perfectly-behaved children, the missing letter from Tom, the German soldiers, and knew she was right. She turned to Tom's letter.

Brunete
26 July 1937

Dear Luce,
I am writing this partly because I want to thank you for all your lovely letters, which mean so much to me, but also as

a record of what has happened here, and all the brave, brave men who have died for what they believe in.

In June we had more time behind the line. We were able to wash and had fresh clothes. I can't tell you the joy of clean clothes! A consignment arrived of English tea and chocolates and books and cigarettes and lighters. I think I told you I have taken up smoking? It helps when you are feeling hungry, and it calms the nerves. We had two weeks' rest between our spells in the trenches, and we went to a small dusty village on a plateau, with cafés round the square. We slept in barns and schools and sat in the sun and read. Miles Tomalin pinned up newspapers on noticeboards, and wrote newsletters for us all to read. I played football every day.

We were allowed to go to Madrid for two days, but no leave beyond that, otherwise I'd have come to see you. We had American visitors, and the poet Stephen Spender came out to speak to us. Imagine that. When shells were dropping so close.

And then into another kind of hell. First the hell of ice at Jarama and now Brunete, the hell of fire. To begin with we weren't down-hearted because Charles Goodfellow, a miner from Bellshill, had proved himself so cool in warfare that he was promoted to second-in-command, and we all trusted him.

When the Battle of Brunete began we were in reserve, watching from the hills — and we could see the advancing columns of men, tanks and cavalry moving over the plain below, as if it was some kind of pageant or toy soldiers. The plain was flat and brown, intersected by rivers marked out in vibrant green by the willow trees along their banks.

Here and there white-painted villages reflected back the glare of the sun.

And then we moved down on to the plain ourselves and discovered that what looked like a flat, brown surface was actually stubbly grass and sandy soil cracked into ravines by lack of rain. It was impossible to dig proper trenches and there was no cover except the willow trees. Every time someone was careless with a cigarette end the stubble caught alight and the smoke drew enemy fire towards us. I can tell you we shouted at the man who'd failed to extinguish his fag end properly!

It was over a hundred degrees for more than twelve hours each day. Everyone burned and blistered, and you drained your water bottle within an hour. The quartermaster dropped food and water to us, and somehow Ernie Mahoney got mail to us in his little van every day. We thought we were going to die of heat and thirst if the constant snipers and shells didn't get us first.

On the second day we took Villaneuva and captured the Fascist quartermaster's stores. That night we had cheese and coffee. And the next day Frank Graham, who was a student from Sunderland, caught and mounted a white horse and rode it bareback to the top of a ridge we called Mosquito Ridge. He looked magnificent!

After that, the Fascists took Mosquito Ridge and they rained down their vengeance. It was like a constant hailstorm of steel from their artillery, plus bombing from the air. We counted three hundred Italian bombers.

Supplies and the wounded were moved by night, mostly on stretchers and mules – can you imagine the bumping of that to a man with gaping wounds? – the Fascists destroyed four of our ambulances.

The heat was intense, not just beating down from the sun, but all around in the air and shimmering up from the ground. I've never felt anything like it, but one comrade used to be employed in a steelworks and he said it was like the furnaces there. We scraped dry river-beds to try to find water to drink. One man found a small pool of water which nobody had touched because it contained a boot with a severed foot still in it. He threw the boot out and drank his fill. Men were staggering with heat, hunger and thirst. The Americans took heavy losses. There are ninety Black American soldiers and they tell me this is the first ever non-segregated US unit. Even they found the heat unbearable.

Our losses are terrible, Luce. Maybe I shouldn't tell you, but on 25 July three hundred of us Brits went into battle and only forty-two stumbled back. So many lovely boys. You would weep. I wish I could weep. I'm dried up like a river-bed. I took a flesh wound, but nothing more, and you mustn't worry about it. They dressed it and it's healing nicely.

Now we are back in a village for a few days – cool and tree-lined. We divide into two types. Some of us sleep like the dead. Others look like ghosts and say they may never sleep again. I'm a sleeper, thank God, though I'm often disturbed by nightmares. On leave we can have our clothes washed and repaired. The women of the villages are glad to do that for us. We all take less than our full army rations and send the remainder to children's colonies. Paul Robeson came and gave a concert. And Harry Pollitt visited. He said

£70,000 has been sent by British miners to help the children of Asturian miners.

Each time I write to you I wonder if it will be the last time. Perhaps I shouldn't say that, but it's true. I look around me for all the fine young men who are missing from our ranks, and wonder why I should be spared.

So, if this is the last time, old girl, I just wanted to say that I still believe in what we are fighting for with every bone of my body, and it will all be worthwhile if only we can win.

Keep your chin up, comrade. Keep writing. And please send cigarettes.

Tom

His letter plunged Lucy into anguish. She had failed to persuade either Jamie or Tom to return home. She had failed Mrs Murray. All she could do now was focus on the children and make sure she didn't fail them too.

In the last days of July, a ship docked in Valencia with all Lucy needed for her holiday camp, and English lorries used by the Friends were despatched to collect it. Great sacks of beans, peas, lentils, rice and sugar were deposited from the Friends' stores and half a dozen convalescing International Brigaders came down to the beach near Benidorm to unload the tents and poles, pots and pans, buckets, mattresses, cutlery and the cases of cocoa, dried milk, jam and bacon which Francesca had sent from England. There were also bats and balls, supplies for basketry and weaving, books, pens, crayons and paper. Juan, the sorrowful fisherman, came to help them. The empty beach was quickly transformed into what Lucy thought looked like a Scout camp as the soldiers and Juan erected tents, dug latrines and trenches for the stores, and built a central marquee, topped with palm leaves.

The International Brigaders pitched four tents for the girls under the pine trees, and three for the boys nearer to the shore. Lucy had her own small tent. When their work was done, the soldiers played in the sea, diving and splashing, carefree as children themselves for a few hours.

Lucy returned to Murcia to gather up the helpers she had identified. A young Spanish girl called Ana was the daughter of Protestant missionaries and she was already helping to teach the other children to read. Sixteen-year-old Juanita and her sister Carmelita had taken readily to the sewing and read-ing classes, but that wasn't the principal reason Lucy wanted them with her. Juanita said she had been plump before the war, but deprivation had removed fat from her waist while leaving generous padding on her breasts and hips. Her long, dark, wavy hair fell over her shoulders and seemed to invite the eyes of young men to her opulent curves and tiny waist. Crowds of boys followed her around the Pablo Iglesias shelter nudging one another and calling out to her. The cheeki-est pushed the bravest into her so they put out their hands to save themselves, colliding with her chest. Juanita snarled and spat at them which kept them in line, but it seemed only a matter of time before they would overcome her by sheer weight of numbers and surging testosterone. Her skinny younger sister Carmelita stuck close to her, guarding her and shoving away the troublesome packs of boys, but Lucy was keen to remove Juanita from danger.

She also chose two seventeen-year-old boys she liked – Julio and Alfonso. Julio was smart and respected by the other children while Alfonso was a slender, timid boy whose eyes glanced off Lucy's in the manner of someone who has been teased or tormented and who longs to be invisible. He too might be better off in another environment, she thought.

The five of them helped her to find the forty girls and boys between the ages of six and fourteen who were to come to live on the beach near Benidorm for the first three weeks. Some of these were children who had simply attached themselves to families in the terrified dash from Málaga, not knowing what had happened to their own parents. One was a girl of about six whose name was not known because she had not spoken since she'd been discovered. It was assumed that her family had all been killed as they fled Málaga. A passing woman had scooped her up and brought her to Pablo Iglesias with her own children.

'She stood on the road crying and crying,' said the woman, raising her eyebrows. 'It turned out this was because she'd wet her knickers. Imagine that! Her family all gone and she's crying because she's wet herself.'

The woman had called her Concha. Lucy stood looking at the child, who had straight coal-black hair cut in a rough bob and a sickly, yellowish face. The girl stared back impassively, as though she felt nothing. Lucy determined to take her, and the woman who had found her sighed with relief.

'I don't think she's stupid,' she whispered to Lucy. 'But she's sullen, with no spark of life.'

Lucy crouched down, level with Concha. 'I am taking some children to the seaside. Would you like to come?'

Concha looked into her and through her with dark brown

eyes which were blank with hopelesssness. After a long moment she nodded briefly and stepped towards Lucy. Her hair fell in a curtain across her face, and she didn't push it back.

'That's all the thanks you get,' shrugged the woman.

Other young refugees were nervous at leaving their remaining families, and the mothers were pitifully anxious as they kissed them goodbye, having lost so much already. They had come to trust the blonde English girl, and the older girls Ana and Juanita promised that the younger children would be well taken care of. It seemed as if all the occupants of Pablo Iglesias came out to watch or hung from the unglazed window frames as the youngsters were loaded into an International Brigade lorry to be taken to the coast.

BENIDORM
August 1937

15

The two-hour drive from Murcia to Benidorm seemed endless and some children were sick in the back of the lorry. But as the doors were opened all that was forgotten as they spilled on to the beach with screams and whoops of joy, running, throwing up armfuls of sand, pushing, leaping, and splashing each other in the shallows. For a moment Lucy wondered if she would ever be able to bring them under control and prevent them injuring themselves. Only the child they called Concha hung back, watching it all, but staying close to Lucy as a shadow.

'Do you want me to call them to order?' asked one of the International Brigade drivers.

Lucy fingered the whistle she'd brought, then held up a hand to shield her eyes and smiled. 'No, let them run themselves ragged. Eventually they'll get hungry, and then they'll come to heel.'

She built a fire and began cooking. Drawn by the smell of the smoke, Juan the melancholy fisherman came over and wordlessly began to help her. Concha stood nearby and watched them.

For the first few days the children ran wild. None of them had any experience of community life and they had only been selected on need. They were greedy, self-centred and quick to anger. Furious battles would suddenly erupt over next to nothing. Maruja accused Luisa of throwing her sandal into the sea, Eduarodo said Daniel had stolen grapes, Carmen insisted that Manola had missed her turn at washing-up. Many of the quarrels were over mattresses or blankets. The girls were the worst, yelling abuse at each other or even locking together, screaming, biting or tearing each other's hair out in clumps. Sometimes it took Lucy and three of her helpers to pull them apart and calm them down.

Most of the children's games were 'playing war', running around with sticks as guns and shooting each other. Lucy thought about banning this but decided that would make it more attractive.

Five-year-old Pepe was a complete anarchist and thief. When everyone else was bathing or eating he would disappear and Lucy would find him with his hands in the cocoa jar. He shrieked like a stuck pig when Lucy washed his hands and face.

The majority of the children seemed happy, but ten-year-old Antonio and eight-year-old Dolores began to weep with homesickness on their first night, and would not stop until Lucy promised to send them back to their families on the next supply lorry. They had seen such terror in their short lives that it now seemed impossible for them to be parted from their mothers.

Concha had attached herself to Lucy and would not leave her side. She reminded Lucy of some kind of cat, small and dark and graceful. She never spoke, but clearly understood everything which was said to her, so Lucy knew she couldn't be deaf. Sometimes she looked as if she wanted to go and play with the other children, but something held her back. And they ignored her, as a being who was alien and different.

On the first night she crept into Lucy's tent and snuggled up beside her. Lucy was determined to be firm and waited until she was asleep to carry her back to her own bed, but over the next few nights she woke to find the child next to her on the groundsheet, or curled at the entrance of her tent in the morning. And often Lucy would be woken by Concha moaning and trembling in terror, with tears pouring down her cheeks in her sleep. Then she folded the little girl into her arms and told her to wake up. 'It's just a dream,' she said. 'Wake up. I'm here. Everything's all right.' Though she knew that everything was not all right for Concha or for millions like her, and the nightmares were not imaginary terrors but the death and destruction she had witnessed, things no child should ever have to experience. As Lucy cuddled and soothed Concha, her crying subsided into hiccups and snuffling, and Lucy drifted back to sleep with the warm child in her arms.

Most of the boys and girls quickly settled, and Lucy saw she had chosen her helpers well. She had assigned each of them to sleep in a tent with their own group of younger children, where they would keep order, comfort them and tell them stories, and the youngsters became fiercely loyal to 'their' helper. Ana was calm and pretty and became a particular favourite among the littlest, who would crowd round her

213

and demand to be played with or taught their letters. The only time Concha allowed herself to be parted from Lucy was when she listened to Ana read. Julio taught ten-year-olds how to chop wood, make fires, draw water from the well and keep from drowning. Alfonso lifted his head and smiled fully into her eyes when he discovered she had ordered art materials for the camp.

'Can I use these too?' he asked, and when she said, 'Of course,' he gripped her hands and kissed them, like a medieval courtier.

Though Alfonso had never had any training, the whole camp soon discovered that he had been born with a real artistic gift, as he sat sketching them and giving away his oddly lifelike drawings. Naughty Pepe was fascinated, demanding, 'Make me a cat. Make me a train,' and Alfonso traded sketches for good behaviour.

Alfonso also took the older children out on to the dark beach at night and they lay flat on the sand while he taught them all the constellations. Lucy noticed that Juanita began to hang around near this boy who was keen to sketch her but never pursued her or pressed uncomfortably close, or even dared to meet her eyes for more than a few seconds.

In order to keep a close watch on the couple, Lucy set Alfonso to work on a project she'd been thinking about for some time. She had ordered plenty of paper and crayons from England, and Alfonso encouraged the children to make pictures of their lives before Pablo Iglesias. Most of them never talked about the horrors they had witnessed, but their images were full of it. Almost every drawing had aeroplanes raining death from the skies, with running people beneath them, or bodies spreadeagled on the ground. One boy drew a square blanket stretched beside the church. When Lucy asked him about it he said, as if everybody knew this, 'That's where they put the parts of the bodies, the bits of people who are blown apart. Arms and legs and all that.'

Concha sat for hours with crayons clutched in her fist, covering page after page with furious scribblings, pressing so hard that the paper was quickly worn thin and the red and black crayons used up. Lucy gathered up the pictures and stored them carefully in her tent.

Juan the fisherman soon took over the cooking from Lucy and she learned how to make many delicious Spanish dishes as his assistant. When she thanked him, he told her that Benita, a curly-haired girl from Madrid, reminded him of his youngest daughter. He turned away as he said it, so she wouldn't see the tears in his eyes. When he wasn't cooking he watched over the children clambering about the rocks, often going in search of a lost child, or dropping everything and running into the sea to bring back a girl or boy who he considered had gone too far out.

The local coastguard called each night to make sure everything was all right, and to tell Lucy and Juan the news of the day. He was shorter than Lucy and completely bald, so his head resembled a shiny hazelnut. He was called Salvador, and he joked, 'What could a boy called "Saviour" do with his life but become a coastguard?'

As she sat with Juan and Salvador, watching the sunset throwing red and gold reflections over the sea, Lucy asked if she ought to set a sentry over the trenches of food, but they both assured her emphatically that nobody would come from the nearby villages to steal from refugee children, however poor they were. It was a matter of honour. The villagers would rather die of starvation than take food from these children who had suffered so much. Salvador and Juan also promised there would be no intruders at the girls' camp in the pine forest.

Lucy found it difficult to reconcile this law-abiding community with everything the newspapers had reported about the rioting and murderous mobs of the first days of the Republic. 'I don't understand it. People are so good now. There is complete order everywhere.'

Salvador the coastguard shook his head. 'You can't think what it was like back in '36. It was *horroroso* – *horroroso*. It was like hundreds of years of fear and resentment came bubbling up together in one terrible explosion of violence. A volcano of fire.'

Juan agreed. 'Some people seemed to have a thirst for killing. They were like animals, like wolves or sharks who have scented blood, and all they wanted was to kill and maim and slaughter. The government had no control over them. Everyone was terrified.'

'*Horroroso*,' shuddered Salvador. '*Horroroso*.'

It seemed hard for Lucy now to believe in the *horroroso*, although there were daily reminders that the war was still raging on. During the early hours of the morning, she would sometimes be woken by the distant rumble of Fascist aircraft returning to their base on Ibiza from bombing raids, and once she even heard them dropping the last of their bombs on to Alicante. Concha clutched her in her sleep and moaned softly.

As Lucy got to know the children, they began to seem the most wonderful beings in the world, who would flash in moments from temper tantrums to hugs and kisses. By comparison Lucy's even-tempered class in Welwyn seemed pale and insubstantial. Within a few days the children had begun to fill out and become tanned and more healthy-looking. Concha's skin had lost its yellowness, and the deep shadows under her eyes were starting to disappear as she slept more soundly. Lucy dreaded the prospect of their inevitable return to the stink and filth of the Pablo Iglesias shelter.

At the end of the first week, as the youngsters sat on the sand eating their evening meal, Lucy told them they would take part in a children's parliament. She remembered the reasoned debate she'd seen at the colony in Barcelona, and wondered if it would look more like a rugger scrum on this beach with these unruly girls and boys. Still, it was worth a try, she thought. The younger children were to take their concerns and suggestions to the helpers, who would be their parliamentary representatives.

A few days later she asked all of them to sit in a semicircle and the helpers began in turn to bring forward their suggestions and ideas. Concha sat with her head buried in Lucy's lap. As a teacher, Lucy had been strict about never showing any favouritism, but every time she moved Concha away from her, she simply crept back.

To her astonishment, the parliament went off with barely an argument – except when Carmen and Manola came to blows over the washing-up. Juanita firmly separated them to either side of her. Lucy was most satisfied with her experiment.

They received several visitors to their camp, who told her that Franco had set up a naval blockade of the Republic's Mediterranean ports, which was making the import of aid more difficult. The guests watched as the children engaged in physical activity in the cooler part of the morning, followed by lessons till lunch, a siesta, then arts or crafts in the afternoon and a swim as the heat of the day diminished. Lucy wanted everything to be perfect for the visitors but on the day when two English nurses came from Alicante, there was a high wind and sand blew into the soup. Another day, Alfonso had been distracted by a painting he was doing and he burned the rice. Despite this, the visitors sat under the palm-roofed marquee and asked Lucy what she needed, making pledges of money or food or firewood. Lucy distributed the money among her helpers, although Juan the fisherman refused to take anything.

One day an Englishwoman came from a delegation in Central Spain. Lucy knew that her approval could mean more financial help for the project, which might allow it to expand. The beans were tender, Juan's sauce was delicious, and there were muscatel grapes for dessert. Lucy beamed round with pride at the children, looking brown and healthy in their little sun-suits and shorts, tucking in to their food without argument for once. They looked so different from the pasty, wild children who'd tumbled out of the lorry from Murcia. Then the visitor looked down her nose and asked, 'Is there a shortage of soap?'

'I brought a case from England, thank you,' Lucy said.

'Then why don't you wash the children?'

To Lucy they all looked perfectly clean from a recent game in the sea. 'But we do,' she said, mystified.

The English lady sniffed and pointed. 'That boy's back looks as if soap hasn't touched it for a year.'

To Lucy's disgust, the woman's delegation did not offer any support. What did a little dirt matter when there were children to be fed and clothed?

After ten days, Francesca came to visit. She had been busy on a project of her own, to set up a farm colony for older boys to keep them from joining the army. She had found the ideal spot in Crevillente and it was already under way.

She observed all the workings of the camp approvingly, and was happy when Lucy suggested the two of them should sleep under the stars at the edge of the water.

'I've found the mosquitoes are less bothersome there,' said Lucy. 'And the sound of the waves lulls me to sleep.'

But Francesca was anxious about the way Concha slipped down the beach in the night to curl up next to Lucy.

'That child has already lost everything. If you let her get attached to you and then leave her, it might break her forever.'

'I know,' said Lucy, wracked with guilt that she'd already shown her such favouritism.

On Francesca's second-last day, Lucy held a sitting of the children's parliament for her benefit. The motions put forward were the usual matters of rotas and food preferences and requests for the little ones to be excluded from particular games because they got in the way. Lucy was trying to teach them beach cricket, which was proving especially popular. But she was startled when Alfonso stood up and said, 'Some of my group have told me they don't want to go back to Murcia. They want to stay here forever. Or at least to the end of the war.' There was noisy assent from about half of the children, while others shouted them down.

The original plan had been to take all these girls and boys back to Pablo Iglesias and bring another set for three weeks, continuing in rotation until the weather broke. Francesca looked thoughtfully around the gabbling, lively circle, seeing the young refugees so changed in such a short time, and Lucy caught her eye and nodded to the shuttered white villa at the back of the beach. Francesca smiled, and Lucy knew that smile meant business.

The next day Lucy and Francesca went to see the Mayor of Benidorm, who knew where the villa owners lived in Barcelona. Margarita was despatched to talk to them, and by the end of the next day she had cabled permission for the Friends to set up a colony in the house.

When Lucy gave the news to the children, there was uproar. She held up a hand for silence. 'The older boys will go with Francesca to a wonderful colony, where they will learn the latest farming methods and other skills to earn a living, but the younger boys and the girls who want to will move into the villa.'

There was animated chatter again, and Lucy waited for it to die away. 'First you must all return to the Pablo Iglesias shelter and ask permission from your families. If your mothers don't want you to come and live in the colony, then you will stay with them. Do you all understand?' The children broke out again into high-pitched, noisy excitement.

Concha's warm, sandy hand crept into Lucy's and she looked down at the little girl, pushing her hair out of the huge brown eyes which looked up at her with a mixture of terror and appeal. Lucy bent close. 'We'll see about you,' she said.

16

Most of the mothers were so delighted to see their children looking well fed and healthy that they gave permission for them to return to Benidorm, in spite of the sorrow it brought to be parted. When news spread round the Pablo Iglesias shelter about these tanned, happy girls and boys, many more parents came forward to beg that Lucy should take theirs to the beach. It was hard to choose just forty from so many in such terrible need.

Lucy was also busy buying the equipment she'd need to establish the children's colony at the white villa behind the beach. The shops and suppliers she'd used in setting up the English Hospital were happy to help again, and many donated pots, pans and even beds. Everywhere she went, Concha was at her side, peeping out from behind her curtain of sleek hair. Lucy bought her a tortoiseshell hair slide and the little girl marvelled at it as though she had never been given anything in her life before. Her hair would have stayed out of her eyes better if Lucy had cut a fringe, but she didn't want Concha to look like an unwanted colony child.

Lucy had asked the woman who'd found Concha on the road if she had permission to take her to the new White Villa colony and the woman had replied with a dismissive flick of the wrist. 'Take her. I've got enough to do trying to feed my own.'

But Lucy still wasn't convinced that she wanted the responsibility for Concha. She had come here to bring home Tom and Jamie, not to adopt a Spanish refugee. What if either of the boys called for her and she had to leave in a hurry? She couldn't promise to take Concha with her. She went to see the Refugee Committee but couldn't tell them the girl's real name or age or where she had lived in Málaga. Alfonso had drawn a lifelike sketch of her, so Lucy left that with details of her height and weight and a small pink birthmark on her left shoulder. Perhaps her family hadn't all been killed, and someone would come looking for her? They entered her into the 'orphans' card index. Lucy hoped that when Concha was living in the White Villa, she would slowly become more independent and would want to remain there when the time came for Lucy to leave.

Lucy had written home to her Quaker colleague Ruth about her project, and the Welwyn Friends had agreed to donate a regular sum, in addition to the donations from her visitors. Now her project had funding, she was able to go to the Mayor of Murcia and ask for his recommendation in hiring two student teachers. Children from the camp and the villa would be taught together until the weather broke and then the teachers would stay on to turn the White Villa into a proper school-colony.

'I want teachers with modern methods,' she said firmly.

'They must be able to help the children learn through games and art, and be prepared to play in the sea and on the sand with them.'

He smiled. 'All my students have modern methods. I will ask Mateo and Valentina. If they say yes, you can come and meet them.'

The funding also allowed her to take on more teenaged helpers from among the older refugee children at Pablo Iglesias, and a second cook to work alongside Juan. For the cook she chose Emilia, a gaunt woman in her late forties, whose clothes hung on her body as though she had once been much fatter. She kept herself apart from the other women, but they treated her with respect, knowing her children had died on the road from Málaga. It didn't matter if she couldn't cook – Juan would teach her – and it would be a pleasure to take her out of the refugee hostel. Lucy would find cleaners from the local village.

She went back to the Mayor's school and met Mateo and Valentina, the stars of his latest teacher-training class. Mateo was a lean young man who shyly said he hoped to be able to introduce drama and dance to the children in her colony. 'As well as the other subjects,' he added hastily. Valentina was a square-built young woman with heavy eyebrows, a faint, downy moustache, abundant hair and a readiness to laugh which seemed to overtake her for no reason. It would be good to have someone with such a merry disposition, thought Lucy as all the arrangements were made. She marvelled that a simple idea was providing employment for so many people as well as a healthy new life for the young refugees.

Once again the International Brigaders helped with

transporting the children and staff and setting up thirty beds in the White Villa, but though she quizzed all of them, nobody had recent news of Tom, and no letters had come through for weeks. They were able to tell her that the remains of the Batallón Inglés had joined with a Spanish battalion and been moved up to the Aragon Front near Teruel, where a new military offensive was beginning. Everyone knew that Franco had now taken Santander and neutral ships in the Mediterranean were being attacked by submarines – probably Italian and German. But they shook their heads when she asked about Tom.

'I'm sure you'd hear if it was bad news,' they offered, and that became her mantra. No news must mean no bad news.

Although Lucy was anxious about Tom and sad about the rift with Jamie, she had little time to dwell on either when she returned to Benidorm in the last week of August with almost seventy children and her new staff. She was busy from waking till sleeping with overseeing the slow taming of the fresh influx of children from Pablo Iglesias, making sure Mateo and Valentina understood the ethos of the colony, mediating the rivalry between Juan and Emilia to come up with the tastiest and cheapest recipes and watching out for romances between her teenaged helpers.

Juanita and Alfonso were now openly a hand-holding couple and clearly infatuated with one another. Lucy felt obliged to have an embarrassing conversation with each of them about the facts of life. All the young helpers had been told that anyone who indulged in sexual activity would be sent back to Murcia. She couldn't afford any irate parents or unwanted pregnancies. She didn't want to lose either Juanita or Alfonso, but wondered if she was taking too big a risk allowing them to remain? Five-year-old Pepe still trailed round after Alfonso but had become much more biddable. She hoped that his constant presence would limit Alfonso and Juanita's opportunities to be alone.

As she bustled about the camp and the villa, she insisted that Concha stay with the other six-year-olds for school and games. Lucy couldn't help a smile of pride to see how quickly the little girl was learning to read and write. Although Concha still didn't speak, the other children were beginning to accept her and chatter to her without expecting any reply. But she still slipped out to sleep by Lucy at night, and Lucy admitted to herself that she liked to half-wake, listen to the swish of the waves and feel the hot body pressed into her back, or the weight of an arm thrown out across her stomach. Perhaps everyone needed the warmth of another human touch, she thought. Then she would turn and secretly kiss the sleeping child.

In mid-September, as both the camp and the colony were settling into mostly harmonious routines, the coastguard's van pulled up in the middle of the day, and Lucy's heart gave a jump as she hurried to meet him.

Salvador looked worried. 'I've brought a message for you. A telephone call to say that your friend Tom has been wounded.'

Lucy staggered slightly, and he held out a hand to steady her. She felt all the blood drain from her face.

'He's alive,' Salvador hastily assured her, 'but it's bad and he's asking for you. They've moved him from the field hospital to Valencia.'

Lucy's thoughts tumbled over each other: how bad, where was he, how soon could she get to him, would he still be alive, could she leave the children?

'Go and get your things, and tell the staff,' said Salvador. 'I will drive you to Valencia. It's my day off and I have some business to do there.'

He was a bad liar, but Lucy wasn't going to argue – she just pressed his hand in gratitude.

She rushed around the camp, and threw a few things into a suitcase. Mateo, Valentina and Juan assured her that they would be able to manage without her for a few days.

'Go to him. You must go,' urged Juan, and she knew he was thinking he would not hesitate for a second if he had a chance of seeing his wife alive again. 'There is nothing more important than the people we love.'

She left Concha in the care of her helper Ana who promised to watch over the little girl.

'She has nightmares,' said Lucy.

'Then she can sleep with me,' replied Ana.

Lucy knelt down next to Concha whose eyes seemed black in her face. 'I promise I will come back,' she said. But Concha already knew that promises couldn't always be kept, and she was crying soundlessly as Lucy was driven away.

Salvador glanced anxiously at Lucy from time to time on the three-hour journey, but understood that she was lost in her own thoughts, unable even to see the beauty of the coast road with its higgledy-piggledy fishing villages, long sandy beaches and impossibly turquoise waters.

Lucy's mind was fogged with worry about Tom and what she would find when she reached Valencia, and also about how the colony at the White Villa and Concha would manage without her if she had to accompany Tom home to England. This would all have seemed so unimaginable to her a few years ago. She might even have laughed if she'd been told they would all be in Spain in the middle of a terrible war. It seemed as if their real lives, the ones they'd planned for themselves, had been whisked away in some macabre magic trick. Or perhaps they were still going on somewhere – the lives in which Lucy became a doctor; where Tom was an economics student, not lying in a hospital bed in pain; where Jamie's kindness and sharp intelligence had not been hijacked by lies.

No wonder the ancients pictured the gods playing games with humans, picking them up by their heads and laughing as their legs flailed uselessly in the air. Now Lucy, Tom and Jamie had been lifted like pawns from one chessboard to another, and all they could do was wait for history to move them to the next square.

Yes, it was true that they had come to Spain out of their own choice, but there had been so many junctions where that choice would not have been necessary: if Germany and Italy hadn't broken the non-intervention pact; if England and France had stood up to Franco, Hitler and Mussolini when they began flexing their muscles. And further back, if Private Murray hadn't died, then Jamie wouldn't have felt driven to turn himself into a small version of a man he hardly knew, and Tom wouldn't have been forced to always take a position of opposition. She was ashamed to think of it but if her father had died instead, then she wouldn't be here at all, and her mother might be alive, married to someone else. So many consequences from Private Murray's single unthinking action.

Lucy shivered to think of the unknown after-effects of the actions she had taken, and saw them spreading out down the years like the bow wave of a ship.

She thought of the refugees at Pablo Iglesias, of their quiet existence before the war, where they worried about the mouldering bread, the milk turning overnight, the pain in their tooth, minor matters of love and death. And then the cataclysm of war had swept over them, flicking some of them off the chessboard altogether, and allowing others to struggle on into the horrific world of the refugees' night shelters. It was said that five thousand people had died on the road from Málaga to Motril; ordinary people with ordinary dreams of ordinary lives, simply wiped out. Why had they died and Concha had lived? How could Jamie think there was a loving God in charge of all this?

She shifted in her seat, and thought how different it might have been to come to this beautiful place in peacetime. It was almost hard to remember that in normal life it was possible to plan ahead, to think: I'll go to see so-and-so this weekend, or visit my aunt, or take a holiday in the Lake District, or get married, or have a baby. It seemed unimaginable that for most people in the world, life was still like that, but war wiped all such possibilities from the map. An air raid, a call to arms, the needs of one refugee child, could derail your hopes and dreams in an instant and send you spinning off in another direction, spiralling out of control.

All you could do was be alive in this moment and follow what your instincts told you, thought Lucy. And be thankful for the million small kindnesses of others who sent money to feed and clothe children they'd never met, for the people who owned the White Villa, for Juan who cooked the beans, for Salvador who was driving her, glancing in her direction from time to time, patting her arm in reassurance.

She lifted her head and smiled wanly at him. 'How far now?'

'Nearly there.'

Salvador pulled up outside the military hospital, which was an old warehouse. 'Come out in two hours to tell me if you are staying or going home with me.'

Lucy leaned over and kissed his leathery cheek. 'Two hours.'

And then the dream-like state of the journey became the clear-brained single-minded need to find Tom and do anything she could to help him hang on to life. She ran into the hospital and the blood in her ears was thrumming, 'Tom, Tom, Tom,' as the young woman on the reception desk dragged her finger interminably slowly down the list of patients to find his name and tell Lucy which ward he was in. Lucy half-walked, half-dashed through the maze of a building, following signs and asking passing patients and medics for directions.

'Let him be alive,' she prayed, 'just let him be alive,' as she pushed open the door to a vast ward crammed with beds of injured soldiers and asked the nurse for Thomas Murray. The smell of disinfectant was almost overpowering, and the air was so hot and still it seemed difficult to breathe. Eyes fixed on her from beds all along the ward. Sweat began to trickle down Lucy's back. The nurse frowned for a moment and then said, 'Ah, Thomas, yes. Are you a relative? We only allow relatives.'

Lucy looked her straight in the eye. 'I'm his sister.'

'This way, then, but I must warn you he is very ill. The wound itself is not so bad, but it was not cleaned properly in the field, and now it is infected.'

Lucy touched her arm, and the nurse turned.

'Will he die?' Lucy forced herself to ask.

Sympathy flickered over the nurse's face before she regained her composure. 'His fever is very high. Tonight perhaps the fever will break, or we will lose him.'

Halfway down the ward, she stopped at the bedside of a man Lucy would hardly have recognised. Tom seemed shrunken under the starched white sheets, apart from one thickly bandaged leg. His hair was lank, his face thin and glistening with sweat, his lips cracked and dry. Her heart seemed to turn over in her chest. Oh dear God, don't let her have come all this way to Spain to watch Tom die!

She quelled the panic which rose up in her. 'What can I do?' she asked the nurse.

'You can help try to bring down his temperature with cold compresses. And give him sips of water. And talk to him.' She lowered her voice to a whisper. 'And you can pray for him, if . . .' She shrugged.

Lucy nodded and pulled out a chair, close to the head of the bed. All around them, men turned in their beds to watch this blonde woman bend over the English soldier.

'Tom, Tom, can you hear me? It's me, Lucy. I'm here now, and I'm going to stay with you until you are better.'

There seemed to be a flickering of his eyelids.

She touched his face and it was burning. She pushed his greasy hair back off his forehead.

The nurse brought a cloth and bowl and showed her where to refill it with cold water. Tom groaned and his body writhed.

'Is he in pain?' she asked the nurse.

The nurse looked at the clock. 'Perhaps. He can have morphia in one hour.'

Lucy wetted the rag, wrung it out and laid it over Tom's forehead, and he moaned again. She opened the window behind his bed, hoping for a cool breeze, but the air which came in was as hot and dry as that in the ward, and two flies buzzed in. The nurse bustled over and closed the window again, tutting.

Lucy laid the damp cloth on one cheek and then the other, and then his neck. She pulled back the sheet. His face and forearms were sunburned to a deep Spanish-fisherman tan, which contrasted with the skin that had been hidden beneath his clothes, which ought to be white, but was pink with fever. His chest and stomach were covered in small cuts that were beginning to heal and bruises turning from purple to yellow and so many bite marks from lice and mosquitoes it was as though his skin had been written with the story of his time in Spain.

She dabbed the re-wetted rag on his bare chest and he shuddered slightly. His body heated the cloth in seconds and warmed the water in the bowl which she had to constantly replace. He was wearing pyjama bottoms which had one leg cut away to allow for the thick wads of bandages around his thigh. She blew gently on to his burning skin to cool it and laid her lips briefly on his hot arm. She spooned drops of water into his parched mouth.

In her head she was saying, 'Don't die, Tom, don't die,'

but out loud she was telling him everything which had happened to her since she'd come to Spain. Just in case he could hear and would know she was there.

He groaned and writhed and she was almost overwhelmed with helplessness.

After a slow-ticking hour the nurse came with the morphia, and he slipped into a quieter sleep, though his eyelids flickered with feverish dreams or nightmares and sometimes he tossed his head. The nurse seemed satisfied that his temperature was not rising any higher.

Lucy watched the afternoon shadows lengthening until it was time to go down and tell Salvador that she would be staying in Valencia. 'Until he is better or . . .' She couldn't say it aloud. Not Tom, not her dearest Tom!

He handed over her little suitcase, and some food and a water bottle he'd brought with him. She hadn't realised but it was hours since she'd eaten.

'God bless you,' he said. 'And try not to worry about the colony.'

The colony! She had completely forgotten about the colony and Concha! Tom was the only thing in the world that mattered. He was the only thing which would ever matter, and she would never ask for anything else if only he would live.

She returned to Tom's side, and slid her suitcase under his bed.

Night fell quickly, and the other patients began to snore. Further down the ward a nurse was sponging the body of another feverish man. She yawned and looked about her as though her mind was on something else.

Lucy continued with the cold compresses, and when she

was sure nobody was watching, she kissed his poor bruised body – as his mother might, she told herself.

At 10 p.m. the doctor came round and stood looking closely at Tom.

'His fever is still too high.'

'He always runs high fevers,' said Lucy. 'His mother would make him sit in a cold bath.'

'I wish we had a cold bath,' said the doctor.

The nurse cut in, suspiciously. '*His* mother? Don't you mean *our* mother?'

Lucy turned her face away to wring out the cloth. 'Oh, please excuse my bad Spanish. It's the anxiety.'

'She can't stay here all night,' sniffed the nurse.

Lucy appealed to the doctor. 'But you don't have the staff to keep applying the cold compresses all night. I can do that for my brother.'

He watched her lay the cool rag over Tom's neck and saw him shiver. 'Just do what you can to bring the fever down. I think there will be a crisis in a few hours. And then . . .' He shrugged helplessly. Lucy knew he meant it could go either way.

'Then I'll find a hotel,' said Lucy submissively, and thought, or, if he dies, I might lie here and howl and never get up.

Laying the cloth on his forehead, Lucy remembered the first time she'd really been aware that he ran high temperatures. When he was twelve Tom had caught scarlet fever from her. She'd had it mildly and soon recovered, but he became so seriously ill that Jamie had been allowed home from school for the weekend, though he was only permitted to look at the bright red face of his brother from the door of the room. On

Sunday morning Jamie had persuaded Lucy to go to Mass with him to pray for Tom, and because she was anxious, and Jamie seemed convinced it would help, she knelt beside him, watching when he got up or knelt down, but not understanding anything of the Latin.

'It's too difficult, like being in a foreign country,' she'd grumbled on the way home.

Jamie was clearly disappointed. 'It's important to understand Latin. It's the basis of so many languages. You can go anywhere in the world and be at home.'

She kicked through the dry leaves and thought quickly. 'Not Germany . . . or Japan . . . or India.'

'All right, anywhere they speak a Romance language. And I could go anywhere in the world to a Catholic church and it would be familiar.'

It started to rain and Jamie pulled his collar up. 'And don't you think it's rather beautiful that people all over the world are saying the same words, in Mexico and Ceylon and even Bulgaria and Sweden?'

Lucy had to concede there was something about that which felt powerful. 'I just hope it makes Tom better.'

Jamie's faith was unshakeable. 'It will. I know it will. I'll go to chapel twice a day at school until he's well.'

As Tom worsened, Jamie redoubled his prayers and Lucy was sent to help Mrs Murray, as she'd already had the disease and at thirteen Captain Nicholson considered she should be learning womanly skills like nursing. Lucy and Mrs Murray took it in turns to sit with Tom, trying to cool his body as best they could. It was agreed that Lucy would stay overnight in Jamie's empty room. When Tom's temperature hit

104 Fahrenheit Mrs Murray ran a bath of cold water and instructed him to get into it.

He was already shivering, and though his throat was almost too sore to speak, he croaked out, 'Are you trying to kill me? I'm freezing. I need blankets.'

But his mother had been firm. 'We need to get your fever down. Just do as I say.'

He had emerged from the bathroom with his teeth chattering violently, but his temperature had fallen two degrees.

It was a constant battle. He tried to pull blankets over him, and Mrs Murray took them away and opened the window to let in cold night air. At 3 a.m. Lucy woke up to hear Tom yelling nonsense. She yanked on her dressing gown and slippers and crept into his bedroom.

'He's delirious,' said Mrs Murray. 'Don't mind whatever he says.'

As Tom sweated and shivered and shouted Lucy was gripped with fear that he was not going to get better. Her heart felt like it was being squeezed between two fists. As she laid cold cloths on his scarlet head and neck, she repeated a snatch of something which might have been a prayer or an instruction. 'Get better. Make him get better.'

Mrs Murray sponged his chest and stomach, and rolled up his pyjama bottoms to cool his legs.

At 4 a.m., Tom's delirious calling slowed to an occasional mutter, then stopped altogether as he slumped into sleep, with his breathing light and shallow. Lucy looked at Mrs Murray and saw she was holding her lips very tightly between her teeth. Did this mean he was giving up and letting go of life? She dipped her facecloth and wrung it out again, fighting to hold back tears. If Mrs Murray wasn't crying, then neither should she. She ran the cloth over Tom's arm, and it didn't come away warm. She felt his skin with her fingers.

'I think it's cooler,' she said.

Mrs Murray laid her palm on his forehead and nodded. Tom inhaled, a great shuddering breath, and both women stood stock-still, watching his face. He held his breath for the longest two or three seconds of Lucy's life, and she held hers too. Then he slowly exhaled, and she exhaled with him.

She and Mrs Murray were frozen as they waited for him to inhale again. How could she carry on breathing if Tom didn't?

And then he did, gently and normally, as a person who is fast asleep.

'Dear God!' said Mrs Murray. 'Never do that to me again!'

Tears began to roll down Lucy's face as she touched her palm to his shoulder, and then brought it to her own forehead, to check his temperature against her own. Although his skin was so red from the rash, his body was no hotter than hers, and his breath was measured and deep.

She watched as Mrs Murray rolled his pyjama trousers back down, and pulled a sheet and blanket over her sleeping boy, smoothing back his hair before kissing his forehead. Lucy longed to kiss him too, to weep against his shoulder, to have him pat her back and say, 'There, there, Luce. Give over now.'

Mrs Murray straightened, and her eyes were wet.

'I think we need a cup of tea,' she said, ushering Lucy out of the room and turning off the light, but not fully closing the door.

'You've been a brick. I couldn't have done it without you. You will make a marvellous doctor. So calm and collected.'

Lucy wiped away her own tears. She didn't feel very calm and collected. She wanted to go and lie down with Tom, to sleep beside him until he woke, but she followed Mrs Murray downstairs.

As she blew across the top of her teacup, Lucy asked, 'Have you seen him like this before?'

Mrs Murray crunched a biscuit. 'All the time until he had his tonsils taken out. Not often since then. And please God never again. It makes an old woman of me.'

Lucy looked and indeed Mrs Murray did look ten years older than usual, with deep circles under her eyes and her hair dishevelled.

'I don't know how you bear it.'

'You bear it because you have to, and because you have a job to do.'

Lucy sipped her tea. 'Can I ask you something?'

'Anything.'

'At a time like that, do you love him more than you love Jamie? Do you feel like you don't love anyone else in the whole world?'

Mrs Murray dunked her biscuit thoughtfully. 'When you have two sons, you love them the same amount, but in different ways. Jamie is my firstborn, and Tom is my baby. Jamie tears the heart out of me with his efforts to be a man like his daddy, even though the irony is that his dad was the spit of Tom, to look at and in character – always joking about, never serious like Jamie. While Tom . . .' she hunted for the words '. . . Tom annoys me and makes me laugh, and it fills me up with love just to look at him. Though I'd never tell him so.'

Yes, thought Lucy, that's just it. It fills me up with love to look at him.

'And then, when one of them is ill, or needs me desperately, I don't love him more than the other, but he takes over my mind, and occupies it completely for a time, as if all my energy must be directed to the one who needs me most.'

'Yes,' said Lucy. 'I understand.'

Mrs Murray smiled at her. 'I know you do,' and Lucy blushed.

Mrs Murray gathered the empty teacups.

'Never be ashamed for loving my boys.'

It was too dark and too early in the morning for Lucy to go home, so she climbed back into Jamie's empty bed. She heard Mrs Murray check on Tom and then poke her head around the door. 'He's sleeping like a baby. You could go to give him a goodnight kiss if you wanted.'

Lucy padded into Tom's room in her bare feet and her nighty. A streak of moonlight fell across his sleeping form, and she tiptoed forwards and kissed his cool cheek. He didn't stir.

A week later, Tom was up and about as if he'd never been ill. Jamie had come home for the weekend again, and his eyes shone with eagerness as he told Lucy he was sure that his prayers had saved Tom's life.

'Will you come to Mass with me again, to give thanks?'

And though Lucy did feel thankful, to the very core of her bones, she shook her head. She had felt too much of an outsider last time.

Jamie's disappointment was palpable. He drew himself up

stiffly and forced his face into a mask of indifference. Lucy always hated not to please him, not to have his radiant smile of approval, and she relented immediately.

'Well, OK then. Just this once.'

When Jamie returned to school, and Tom was well again, he mocked her for going to Mass. They were out walking in the woods. Tom claimed to be birdwatching, but he didn't show much interest in any of the small brown feathered things she pointed out.

'All that gobbledegook,' said Tom, imitating a monkish plainsong. Lucy shoved him playfully, and he pushed her back.

'What do you think made you better, then?' she asked, kicking up the crunchy leaves.

He stood still and was serious. The novelty of that stopped her in her tracks too.

'You did,' he said. 'You and Mum.'

She looked into his brown eyes, on a level with hers, and he suddenly leaned forwards and kissed her on the lips. She jerked back, surprised, but could feel the softness of his mouth on hers, as if it left an impression which would never go away.

Her heart was beating fast. 'What was that for?'

He laughed. 'Because you saved me.'

17

Now, in the sweltering heat of the Spanish hospital, Tom's breathing was fast and shallow again, and no matter how Lucy sponged his battered body, she couldn't seem to cool him. Sometimes a patrolling nurse walked by on squeaky shoes and nodded approval and encouragement. Most of the other men in the ward were sleeping, some snoring and some shouting out in their dreams. Further down the ward a nurse was doing the same as Lucy, trying to cool a feverish soldier, though she often got called away to other patients. Lucy and that nurse each had two candles to see what they were doing, and there was a light at the reception desk, but the ward was otherwise in darkness.

Lucy's eyelids were drooping with exhaustion, but hour after hour she patted the wet cloth onto him, wishing Mrs Murray was beside her. 'I won't let him die,' she promised her silently. She realised love was not a fixed element, but fluid as water or mercury, flowing into every nook and cranny, filling you up, just as Mrs Murray had said. The person you loved the most at any one time was the one who needed you the most. And in this moment her love for Tom was all-consuming.

At 4 a.m., further down the ward, she saw the nurse pull the sheet up over the head of the man she'd been trying to save.

Lucy rose to throw away the warm water and refill the bowl with cold. When she returned, Tom was lying very still in the flickering candlelight with his mouth slightly open.

Oh, no, please no. Please no. Lucy's stomach contracted with a physical pain.

She set down the bowl and bent close to him. He wasn't breathing. She couldn't hear him breathing. She laid her fingers on his forehead, registering that it was now cool not hot.

He had died while she'd been away getting water. He had died in a foreign land without a friend beside him. She had failed him utterly.

Lucy tried to feel for a pulse in his neck, but there was nothing, so she leaned down, laying her ear on his breastbone, and there was his heart, his wonderful heart, beating strongly. *Be-dum, be-dum, be-dum.* Thank God. He was alive. She lifted her head and now could hear his peaceful breathing.

She sank into the chair and bowed her head in her hands, shaking violently.

The nurse must have seen her listening for Tom's heart and hurried over. She took his pulse and smiled broadly. 'One saved at least,' she said.

Tom had survived and he was going to live.

The nurse tucked the sheet back around Tom's body and blew out the candles. 'You'd better stay here till morning,' she said to Lucy, returning to her desk.

In the dark, Lucy covered Tom's salty face with kisses, and wrapped her arms around his body, as she'd longed to when she was thirteen. Then she sat back in her chair, folded her arms on the edge of the bed, rested her head on them, and fell into the most exhausted sleep of her life.

At 6 a.m. the morning change of nursing shift woke her and Tom at the same time. She raised her head and they looked at each other without speaking.

'You,' whispered Tom.

'You,' she replied, entwining her fingers with his.

She was reminding herself of the exact conker-colour of his eyes, the lift of his eyebrows, curl of his hair, his slightly sticking-out ears. His lips were so pink, and the line of his top teeth so straight.

The nurse pushed a thermometer under his tongue and took his pulse, while Lucy tried to flatten her wayward hair. She must look a sight! The nurse turned the thermometer to the light.

'Good,' said the nurse to Lucy, shaking the mercury back down. And to Tom, 'It was very lucky that your sister was close enough to come in. She saved your life.'

A flicker of amusement passed over Tom's features, and he squeezed her hand.

'Very lucky,' he agreed and, in English, 'Thanks, sis!'

Lucy stood up, stretched and retrieved her case from under the bed as a nurse brought Tom a tray with greasy omelette, thin soup and bread.

'I need to find a hotel, and sleep and wash.'

He cocked his head. 'Yes, you look a fright!'

'Charming!'

She gave him a sisterly peck on the cheek.

'Oh, and Luce . . .'

'Yes?'

'I'm starving. Could you bring some better grub when you come back?'

She laughed out loud. The same old Tom.

Lucy emerged into the bright sunshine of a September day in Valencia. It was hard to make headway against the throngs of people. She knew that a town of thirty thousand was now swollen to a million with refugees, and it would be hard to find a hotel room at a price she could afford. She hadn't got the energy to tramp around one hotel after another, so instead took a taxi to the office of Barbara Wood, who was now running the Friends' operations in the town. Francesca had called Barbara on their first day in Murcia and Barbara had been supplying truckloads of food to the Pablo Iglesias shelter and the White Villa ever since. She would be able to recommend a hostel.

But of course Barbara refused to do any such thing. She glanced at Lucy and led her inside.

'You look done in, if you don't mind me saying so.'

Lucy almost fell into the offered chair. 'I've been up all night, nursing my dearest friend.' She paused, then seeing the anxiety on Barbara's face, she continued, 'At four a.m. the fever broke, and he's going to be all right.' And then the tears came, pouring down her face in a torrent she didn't have the strength to hold back.

Barbara put an arm about her shoulder and gave her a handkerchief. When Lucy recovered herself, Barbara announced, 'You'll stay with me for a couple of days. And you can tell me all about Pablo Iglesias and the English Hospital and your White Villa.'

At mention of the colony, Lucy realised with a start that she hadn't thought of it for hours. 'I have to get back to the children.' She looked into the older woman's eyes. 'But it would be so kind of you if I could stay just a little while.'

'Cocoa and bed,' said Barbara.

When Lucy had slept for a few hours and eaten, she found her way back to the hospital to see Tom. As she entered the ward, the other patients began to call out to her in Spanish, 'Hey Señorita, come and visit me.' 'Can you help me with this?' 'I think I love you.' Had they done that yesterday? If so, she hadn't noticed.

At the sight of Tom, turning his head and grinning at her, she was so flooded with love for him it almost stopped the breath in her throat.

He began to wolf down the meal she'd brought, as though he hadn't eaten for weeks, but soon seemed to be full, and pushed the remaining food away, so she finished it herself. He had lost his square shape and become muscular and sinewy, and his dark hair was unkempt. She laid the palm of one hand against his arm, and felt the muscles rippling as he moved. The very fact of him living and breathing was a miracle to her.

When she asked how he'd been injured, he simply shook his head.

'You don't need to know about all that, Luce.'

'You won't go back there, will you? Isn't it time to go home? Surely you've done your bit now.'

He gave her a long look, but didn't answer and she knew

better than to press him, so she began to tell him about the White Villa and the antics of the children, and about Concha, finding she was missing the little girl.

'Typical of you to find a waif and stray,' said Tom.

She felt indignant on Concha's behalf. She was a person, a person who had nobody, not a stray animal. So they fell silent, and Lucy held his hand while Tom dozed, turning over the familiar fingers in her palm, examining his blackened nails and frayed cuticles and an ugly red weal of a gash which ran from his knuckles to his wrist. It was as if his hands now belonged to her and she needed to learn every line in the palm, the bend of every knuckle, the fine black hairs on the back of each one to fix them in her memory. She bent and kissed the palm, and when she raised her head, he had woken and was looking at her.

He folded his fingers around hers and she thought for a second that he would say something mocking, but he just exhaled and whispered, 'I'm glad you are here.'

'Where else would I be?'

They looked into each other's eyes for a long moment, and nothing more needed to be said.

Later, Lucy talked to the doctor about Tom's leg and how long it might take him to recover.

'We'll keep him here until we are sure he is healing properly. In the field hospital wounds are left open and just covered with muslin to keep off the flies. There's a lack of antiseptic, dressings, anaesthesia. This was deep and has a lot of stitches. Some tendons and ligaments may have been bruised or torn, but no bones broken. And all the other cuts and bruises are healing nicely. He's been lucky – this time.'

Lucy shuddered at the implication of another occasion when Tom could be killed outright. She wished the bomb had broken his leg. A broken leg would surely have taken him back to England, and then at least one of her boys would be safe.

'He's been in different hospitals for two weeks,' the doctor continued. 'If he carries on improving, he can leave here in a few days perhaps, but he won't be well enough to return to the Front. Is there somewhere he can go to?'

'He can come to me to convalesce. Near Benidorm on the coast.' She felt a need to tell this doctor that she was not simply a privileged British émigré.

'I run a children's colony – refugees from Málaga.'

The doctor bowed his head. 'Then we are in the same business, Señorita, mending the broken jetsam of this barbarous war.'

She smiled grimly, and he continued, 'Though I hope your refugees do not insist on hurling themselves back into danger as soon as you have made them well.'

'I plan to persuade my brother to go home.'

He looked uncertain. 'I doubt you'll succeed. These International Brigaders are stubborn men.'

Lucy sat by Tom's side for two more days, returning to Barbara's at night. She had arranged with Barbara that Tom would be brought down to the White Villa on a Friends' food lorry as soon as he was discharged. Lucy was going back by train, but Tom wouldn't be well enough to manage that.

'The doc says you saved my life,' he said on the second morning.

'I think that means I now have a say in how you spend that life.'

He hooted in derision, and then gripped his side, where laughing hurt his bruised ribs.

'Not likely.'

'Oh, I thought I had power over you now.'

He looked down at the hand which lay in his and, as he slowly raised his eyes to her face, she felt him taking in the curve of her waist and her bosom in a way other men had often done, but he'd never have dared to do openly before.

'You always had power over me. You just never knew it.'

Tom was still sleeping for much of the time, and when he slept Lucy went around the ward, talking to some of the other patients. It was like the League of Nations on this ward, she thought, with wounded soldiers from all over Europe and America. Some of them she could speak to, and translate what the doctor and nurses were saying for them, but some lay in painful isolation.

After lunch on the second day she stood up to leave, and it felt like a physical stab in her chest to have to say goodbye to him. Dear God, was this how hard it was to love someone?

He took her hand, and peered up at her. 'Do you have to go?'

'I have to get back to the children.'

'Can't someone else look after them?'

'They are my responsibility. As soon as you are well enough to travel, you can come to us. It's all arranged.'

'I don't think I should.'

'It will do your heart good to see them, and the salt water will help your leg to heal.'

He looked deep into her eyes, and his usual jokey mask slipped to reveal a Tom she'd never seen before. 'I'm just afraid I'll never want to leave.'

A ripple of hope passed through her, but she kept her voice casual. 'Then you could stay. The colony is still work for the Republic.'

Tom gripped her hand until it hurt. The words seemed to be ground out of him, through clenched teeth. 'I have to get back to the Front, to my comrades. You might make it too hard for me.'

She knew better than to argue with him. 'Well, you won't be much use to them till you can walk, and you need to con-valesce somewhere.'

She shook her right hand free of his grip, and rubbed it with the left. 'I have to go now or I'll miss my train.'

But still she couldn't bear to step away from him.

'Go on then,' he said gruffly.

She bent to kiss his cheek, but he moved so their lips met and held and she wanted to go on kissing him forever. She straightened up, trembling slightly and turned away. The patient in the next bed called softly, 'Me next, lovely Lucy.'

'See you in a few days,' she said to Tom lightly, though every fibre of her being was screaming at her not to leave. What if he refused to come to the White Villa, and went back to the Front and she never saw him again?

The new, serious Tom looked up at her. 'Not soon enough.'

As she walked down the ward, with her suitcase in her hand, wolf whistles passed from patient to patient. At the desk the nurse said, 'I knew he wasn't your brother,' and Lucy shrugged apologetically.

She looked back over her shoulder for one last glimpse of Tom, who was struggling up to a sitting position to wave to her.

Every step to the station was hard, as if she wore lead boots. Why was she leaving him, when love for him had entered every bone and sinew in her body? She had to remind herself that her best chance of persuading him not to go back to the Front was to get him to the White Villa. And if she knew anything about Tom, her best chance of getting him there was allowing him to think it was his decision.

The ride from Valencia to Benidorm took six hours rather than four. The train was crowded with peasants with sacks of vegetables, clucking chickens carried head downwards, a sack of live rabbits. At one stop a man got on with a sheep. The other people in her carriage passed around wine in goatskins and Lucy took hesitant sips, not wanting to seem rude. Out of the window she saw a group of militiamen, singing as they marched; olive groves; girls wearing black mantillas.

In the late afternoon the train passed through scrubby, drought-ridden hills so unlike the green of England, and white villages reflecting back the harsh sunlight. The coast was rocky in some places and fringed by blonde beaches in others but always backed by the sea with its ever-changing patches of navy and turquoise. The seat beside her was empty, and she wished that Tom was in it and she could lean her cheek against his shoulder, and they could look out together at all this beauty, untouched by the horrors of the war.

As dusk fell, she allowed herself to think about Jamie and how much he loved her, and that she had honestly believed in Córdoba that she loved him in the same way. Perhaps she had been intoxicated by his adoration of her and wanted so much to please him that she had fallen in love with the idea of loving him? She couldn't bear to think of the pain it would bring him when he found out how she felt about Tom.

It was dark long before the train reached Benidorm station, and she pulled her torch out of her suitcase to walk the mile and a half to the White Villa. She'd never done it at night before and was nervous of wild animals or drunken men. But there at the exit was Salvador's coastguard van, and she opened the door most gratefully.

'You shouldn't have come,' she said as he started the engine.

'I had dinner with my auntie in the village, and I knew the train would be late.'

'I'm very glad to see you. I feel quite worn out.' And as she said it, the emotional strain of the last three days made her feel limp with tiredness.

Salvador was trying to see her face and she realised she hadn't told him about Tom.

'He's alive!' she said. 'It was bad the first night, but he's going to make it. And it's all thanks to you taking me there to nurse him. I'll never be able to thank you enough.'

Lucy told him that Tom would be coming to the White Villa to convalesce. 'And if I can I'll stop him going back to fight.'

Salvador grinned approval. 'If anyone on this earth can do it, you can.'

When the car pulled up in front of the villa, first Juan and then the teachers and then a flood of excited children who should have been in bed tumbled out to welcome her, and as they crowded around, she realised that the White Villa felt like home. They were all talking at once, Valentina and Mateo assuring her that everything had been fine apart from all the lights fusing and three boys having sickness and diarrhoea and the flash in the sky of bombs falling over Alicante which had frightened many of the children; Juan wanting to know if her dear friend Tom was alive; Juanita and Alfonso had had a lovers' tiff and weren't speaking; the girls 'telling' on each other – who had pulled whose hair, stolen whose pencil, trodden on whose toes. Lucy smiled and nodded at them all, looking anxiously around for Concha.

'Is Concha sick?' she asked.

'Heartsick,' said Juan, standing aside so Lucy could see her, hanging back in the doorway with her arms folded, obviously not willing to forgive her for going away. Lucy waded through the excitable crowd and held her arms open to Concha who hesitated for just a second before she rushed into them to be swept up in a bear hug. The heat of her small body, her wiry arms tight about Lucy's neck, and legs wrapped around her waist were a welcome home in themselves. Concha buried her face in Lucy's shoulder and sobbed. And though Lucy couldn't promise never to leave her again, she realised she must try. It was a terrible responsibility to be loved with such ferocity.

She shifted Concha to her left hip, and walked into the villa.

18

A week had passed before the rumble of an approaching lorry made Lucy leap up and scatter the mending on her lap. Her heart was fluttering with excitement at the thought of seeing Tom, of having him here with her and persuading him never to go back to the fighting.

She stood on the villa steps, shading her eyes from the low afternoon sun as the driver jumped down and went round to the rear to let down the tailgate.

Slowly, gingerly, Tom eased himself out, feet-first. She'd never seen him in his brown Popular Army overalls before, never seen him as a soldier. The driver helped him down on to his good leg, handing him a crutch which Tom settled under the opposite shoulder. Then the driver moved away and Tom looked up at her, and it was as if the four-year-old Tom met her gaze with the same mix of lively curiosity and fearfulness which she'd seen on the day he arrived in her life. Lucy's heart somersaulted in her chest.

She called her thanks to the driver and hurried to meet

Tom, sliding her arm around his waist, and letting him lean on her shoulder. The solidity of his body and his weight resting on her was as thrilling as if she'd never touched another person before, and she was aware of him in every inch where they pressed against each other. She wondered if it was like this for him. She could smell the sweat from his armpit and she revelled in the sour aliveness of it.

She tried to keep her voice level. 'How was the journey?'

'Rattled around like a bag of spuds. Even my bruises have got bruises.'

She glanced into the back of the lorry, and saw they had tried to make him a nest of blankets to lie on, but it couldn't have been comfortable.

'I sat in the front halfway, but then needed to stretch out.'

Concha ran down the steps and stood in front of him with her arms folded and her feet planted wide, like a small avenging angel. Lucy knew this stance could mean trouble.

'Concha,' she said warningly, 'this is my friend Tom, who has come to stay for a bit. I told you he was coming. I've known him since I was younger than you. And if you are nice he will be your friend too.'

Concha eyed him suspiciously, then Tom stuck out his tongue and made his eyes go crossed, and she couldn't help a peal of low, throaty giggles. It was the first time Lucy had heard her laugh, and she wondered if her voice would have the same peaty timbre when she eventually decided to speak.

'So this is Concha,' he said, and held out a hand. 'Good evening, Señorita.' She didn't take the proffered hand, but ran around and attached herself to Lucy's leg, claiming ownership of her other side.

He raised his eyebrows at Lucy, and she smiled.

'She'll get used to you. Now let's get you inside. Food? Or bed?'

'Both. Simultaneously.'

Tom didn't let out any sound as she helped him manoeuvre up the entrance steps, but she could see how he avoided putting any weight on his damaged leg. Good, she thought. He wouldn't be leaving here any time soon.

They had moved everyone around, so he could have the room next to hers, on the ground floor, not too far from the toilet. The driver followed with Tom's rucksack of belongings and helped Lucy lower him on to the bed.

Concha and some other children and Valentina appeared in the doorway behind Lucy.

'Do you need any more help, miss?' asked the driver. 'Getting him undressed?'

'No thank you. I can manage now.'

An impish grin crossed Tom's face, but Lucy ignored it.

She arranged for Valentina to take the children away and closed the door behind them as he lit a cigarette. Holding it between his lips, he carefully parted the mosquito netting and sat on the bed to unlace his boots. She wrinkled her nose at the smoke but it wasn't enough to stop her stepping up to him and running her fingers through his thick thatch of hair. He grasped her hand and pulled her down to sit on the bed beside him, grinding out the cigarette on the sole of his boot before he drew her into an urgent kiss that left her panting for air and thrumming with new sensations. He tasted of tobacco.

'You and food and bed simultaneously,' he said.

As a way of trying to collect her thoughts and adjusting

to this new way of being with her old pal Tom, she opted for practicality, jumping up to pull off one boot and then the other. His socks smelled terrible. She peeled them off.

'When were these last washed?' she demanded, holding her nose.

'About the same time as everything else,' he said regretfully. 'Maybe a month ago?'

'Then give me everything except your pyjamas and I'll have them cleaned for you.'

'There might be bugs.'

'Then I'll have them fumigated. Have you got bugs yourself?'

'I was deloused in the first hospital. They shaved off my nice beard.'

She couldn't imagine him with a beard.

He grinned. 'I thought you were going to undress me, Nurse Lucy?'

'You can blooming well undress yourself,' she retorted. 'Bug-boy.' This felt more like the normal banter between her and Tom. 'Throw your lousy clothes in this corner, if they don't walk there themselves, while I fetch you something to eat.'

By the time she returned with a plate of Juan's delicious beans and today's fresh bread, Tom was asleep. He'd left all his dirty things with his rucksack in the corner, and wriggled himself under the sheet. Beside the bed was his photograph of her, laughing.

Lucy laid the food and water on a chair by the bed, lifted the netting, leaned in and brushed his bristly cheek with her lips, lingeringly, half-hoping he would wake. She stared down at him, running a finger over the stubble on his chin, accustoming herself to this confusing new intimacy.

On her own way to bed, she looked in again, bringing him a chamber pot, an ashtray and a fresh glass of water. But he hadn't woken. She removed the food in case it attracted cockroaches.

In the night she woke to terrible shouting. She sat bolt upright and her heart banged in her chest. At first she thought they were under attack, that the war had come to the sleepy fishing village of Benidorm, then recognised Tom's voice and ran into the next room. He was still lying down, but had kicked off the sheet and was yelling and waving his arms as if fighting with someone.

She ducked under the netting to stand over him and grabbed a wrist in each hand. 'Tom. Tom! Wake up. It's a nightmare.'

For a moment he fought her and she thought he would overpower her, but then his arms fell limp and he curled into a ball and began to moan softly. She climbed on to the bed behind him and wrapped her arms around him. 'Tom, Tom, wake up. It's Lucy. You're quite safe.'

The moaning stopped and he turned his head. 'Luce? Is that you?'

She held tight to him, pressed into his curled back. 'Yes, it's me. Everything is all right. You are at the White Villa. Nothing can hurt you here.'

He turned over, and dashed tears from his face with his forearm. She slid to the edge of the narrow bed, careful not to touch his wounded leg.

'I get nightmares,' he said. 'Lots of the chaps do.'

She kissed his forehead. 'I'm not surprised. But I'm here now.'

'It was horrible, Luce.' Whether he was talking about the

war or the nightmare, or if one was an extension of the other and it was impossible to know where one ended and the other began, she couldn't tell.

She smoothed his hair, remembering how her father kept his bedroom door closed because he would often cry out in his sleep, and wondering for the first time what scars he carried with him from the Great War. She would write to him tomorrow, she thought, and tell him about Tom's nightmares. Perhaps he would be able to offer some advice.

'Go back to sleep now,' she whispered. But she lay awake a long time, her mind whirling with thoughts of how she could stop him going back to the Front, enjoying the thrill of her body stretched out next to his but awash with guilt for her betrayal of Jamie.

In the morning Juan found Tom clean clothes and stood by while he washed himself. Tom wasn't supposed to get his leg wet. The deep wound in his leg had been sewn up in the field hospital, but at Valencia they said he should leave it another week before finding a doctor to remove the sutures.

At breakfast Lucy saw him rubbing the side of his thigh.

'Does it hurt?' she asked.

He made a face. 'Not as much as it did. My whole leg itches like it's got lice, and the stitches are pulling.'

Concha peeped round Lucy at him.

He held out his hand and showed her the long weal running from knuckle to wrist. 'That had stitches too, but they took them out in the hospital.'

She examined the raised pink line with such serious interest that Tom grinned at Lucy.

'Another doctor in the making.'

He slipped his hand from the table and rested it on Lucy's leg, as though he knew it had every right to be there. She could feel the heat of it penetrating her skin.

Juanita leaned across the table. 'You shouted in the night,' she said. 'Were you in pain?'

Tom shook his head with embarrassment. 'No, I get nightmares. Lots of soldiers do.'

Juanita indicated Concha. 'She gets nightmares too. But not so much now.'

'How did she get rid of them?'

Juanita looked nervously at Lucy as if she had said too much. 'She sleeps in Lucy's bed.'

Tom laughed aloud. 'Well that's a good idea.'

Juanita coloured to the roots of her hair and Lucy gave him a playful shove. 'Idiot.'

Under the table he squeezed her leg gently.

Although it was almost October, the weather was still balmy. The terrible heat of midsummer had departed and now the sun was delightfully warm. Lucy set up two places for Tom to sit or lie and watch the activity of the villa – one in the sun and the other on the shady side of the veranda. He leaned on the balcony rail, looking out at the palm trees and the white sandy beach, and down at Lucy's hand on his shoulder.

'This is like paradise.'

He lowered himself into the chair she'd set in the sun and squinted up at her. 'I believe I've washed up on Aeaea and you are Circe, about to bewitch me to stay for a year and give you two sons.'

'Abracadabra,' she said, waving a finger like a magic wand.

He turned his face to the sun and sighed, but whether from pain or pleasure or the anguish of decisions still to be made, she couldn't tell.

Every time the duties of the house allowed, she would slip back out to the veranda to check on him. Wherever she was in the villa or on the sands, she felt her whole body straining towards him, like a tide pulled by the moon. She wondered if he felt it too.

Several mornings later she found him sitting in the sun. He had taken off his shirt and rolled up the legs of Juan's trousers, and she saw how the bruises on his torso were beginning to fade yellow.

'Does that hurt?' she asked, touching the largest with a gentle finger. It was as if she couldn't resist making contact with him.

'Only when you poke it!'

He caught hold of her hand, glanced around, and seeing they were alone he led her finger to stroke another bruise. 'Try this one. And this one. Tonight you could try kissing them better.'

A clatter of footsteps announced that the younger children were leaving the villa for their swimming lesson.

'Ridiculous,' said Lucy primly, while the thought of kissing his body ignited in her brain. 'I'm going to help.'

'Can I come and watch? The doctor prescribed looking at you in your bathing suit.'

'Ridiculous,' she repeated, but helped him down the steps and on to the beach.

She felt him watching her as she lifted her dress over her

head and folded it carefully with the other clothes on the sand. She stood up tall, holding in her stomach, and let him slowly study her, up and down. When his eyes met hers he pretended to be fanning himself, as if the sight of her had overheated him, and she laughed, running into the waves.

As she supported and instructed the children, she kept glancing up at Tom who was using his crutch to hop along the harder sand at the water's edge. Experimentally, he lowered his damaged leg to the ground and put a little weight on it. Then he rested, and gazed out to sea. He'd always been a strong swimmer, and she was sure he was longing to dive into the waves. She imagined them swimming together in the moonlight, limbs interlacing . . . and then an insistent hand was tugging hers. 'Señorita Lucy! Look what I can do.'

After the swim, she stood near him, towelling her hair dry. He reached out and touched her arm, and his hand was warm against her cool skin.

'You're so brown.'

'I've been doing swimming lessons all summer.'

'I can't wait to get into the water with you.'

Lucy looked into his eyes and wondered if he was sharing her own daydream or if his went much further than she'd dared.

'I'm going back to dress for lunch. Do you need help to the house?'

He draped an arm across her bare shoulders. 'I probably could make it on my own, but this is much nicer.'

It was good to be needed by him, she thought.

In the afternoons, the villa quietened into the lull of the siesta. Lucy and Tom sat on the veranda in comfortable silence and she traced the lines on the palm of his hand, marvelling at their new familiarity. He smoked a cigarette down to its tip and ground it out under his heel. And then the quietness began to feel strange, as if there were too many things they couldn't share. She remembered how she and Jamie had chattered to each other every minute they were together, and then wished she hadn't thought of Jamie because it made her feel so wretched.

'You were at Brunete in your last letter,' she ventured, and he snatched his hand back from her and rubbed the palm vigorously.

'I can't talk about it and I don't want to think about it.'

'I'm sorry.' And she was. Regretful to have spoiled the moment, and also sad he couldn't share his battle experiences, which stood like a wall between them. That and Jamie.

He heaved himself to standing, grabbing his cigarettes. 'I'm going to lie down. I just need to be alone for a bit.'

'Can you manage?'

'I'm not a bloody invalid.' He stumped to the door, and then turned and mouthed, 'Sorry,' and he looked so much like his naughty-then-repentant little-boy self that she couldn't help but smile.

What terrible things her poor Tom must have seen, Lucy thought. She knew she wouldn't sleep, so went to prepare a lesson in which she invited the older girls to compare Homer's *Odyssey* with their own journeys. All that time which had passed since the ancient Greeks, she thought, and still there was war.

Concha stayed close by Lucy wherever she went, particularly if she was with Tom. Her jealousy hung in the air. After lunch one day she sat between them, wiggling her loose front tooth.

'Let me take a look at that,' offered Tom, and she opened her mouth to him.

He gently pressed the tooth with a forefinger, and it folded back almost horizontal in her mouth, hanging by a thread.

'That's ready to come out,' he pronounced. 'What you need to do is pull it down and turn it round and round.'

Cautiously, in case it would hurt, Concha gripped the little tooth and twisted it. Within seconds it had broken free and was in her hand. She held it up for him to see, exploring the strangeness of the new gap with her tongue.

'A perfect specimen!' he declared. 'The tooth fairy will be wanting that to build her fairy castle.'

Lucy spoke English to him. 'I don't know if they have the tooth fairy in Spain! And we can't start giving money to every child whose tooth falls out.'

Tom looked so crestfallen that Lucy wanted to hug him.

'But I suppose we could give them shells,' she said. 'We can find some fairy shells while they are having this afternoon's siesta.'

So that afternoon they meandered along the tideline, choosing the most perfect and tiny shells, and that night Concha placed her tooth under her pillow, and in the morning was amazed to find a miniature pink shell in its place.

When she showed it to Tom at breakfast, and he admired it so seriously, Concha suddenly bent and kissed his hand.

Lucy smiled at Tom over her head, and it felt for a moment as if they were a proper family.

It was getting dark earlier now, and that evening Tom suggested he might try a short walk to watch the sun set. Lucy guessed he needed to escape the constant noise and bustle of the villa; the clamour of thirty children must seem oppressive to someone not used to it. She settled Concha with Ana who was reading a story, and they started out along the beach together. She rubbed her skin with lemon oil. It was supposed to deter the mosquitoes, but didn't really.

Tom was using his crutch, but beginning to put his bad leg tentatively to the ground. She thought he might say something romantic about the vivid tangerine and fuchsia ribbons of cloud in the sky, but his mind was on himself.

'I need to walk more. To get fitter,' he grumbled.

It was on the tip of her tongue to say, 'Why? Just so you can go back and get shot-up again?' but she lightened her tone. 'Good idea. I've been trying to teach them cricket, but you'd be much better at it.'

'I'm going to start some PT tomorrow. See what I can do. My ribs aren't so painful today.'

Lucy sighed. Perhaps it would be safe to talk about the past. 'Do you remember my father trying to teach you to catch a rugger ball? You kept on making him throw it to you for hour after hour, until it got dark, and your mother came looking for you.'

'I was a determined little sod.'

'You always knew what you wanted.'

He stopped suddenly and turned to her. 'I still know what I want.'

With his free arm, he drew her in tight to him and kissed her. It was rough and desperate, as though there was no time to waste, and she was kissing him back in the same way, tangling her fingers in his hair.

He pulled away. 'Sorry, I can't stand on one leg any longer.'

Sitting on the beach they fell on each other again, as if they had been waiting for this all their lives. And now Tom's hands were free, he began to move them over her back and arms, and finally to her breasts, bending to cover them with kisses and biting through the cloth of her dress until she was adrift with longing. He lifted his head for a moment. 'I want you so much, Luce.'

Part of her brain registered that it was want and not love, and suddenly it all seemed too fast, too confusing.

'Hold on,' she laughed. 'I've got to get used to this.'

'I've thought of nothing else since I left England.'

'Just give me a bit of time.'

It had gone too dark to see his face, but she knew the sullen look which came over him when he didn't get his own way.

'I don't know how much time I've got,' he said, scratching angrily at new mosquito bites on his leg.

She stood up, and brushed the sand from her dress. 'Come on. They'll be sending a search party if we don't get back.'

She offered a hand, but he pulled himself up on his crutch, and they walked back to the house in silence.

In the middle of the night, the screaming came from his room again and Lucy ran in to wake him from his nightmare, standing beside the bed and gripping his wrists. For a few seconds he continued to fight whatever was bearing down on him, then clutched hold of her around the waist and shook, holding on to her as if he was drowning, his tears wetting her nightdress. She patted and soothed him, trying to wrap him with her love, and eventually lay down beside him as he fell back into a deep sleep. She began to doze herself until her arm under his neck began to develop pins and needles and she softly untangled herself and wriggled out of his grip. She stood by the bed and kissed him, thinking perhaps she loved him best of all when he was sleeping, then lifted the netting over her head and turned to leave the room. Concha was standing in the doorway and Lucy wondered how long she had been there.

Lucy picked her up. 'Back to bed, you goose. Your feet are freezing.'

Concha whispered the first words Lucy had ever heard her speak. 'I think his mummy and daddy got killed too.' Her voice was deep and musical, like a jazz singer's. Lucy carried her back to their shared bed and sat inside the netting with the little girl on her lap, wrapping the blanket around them both, as the dammed-up words spilled out of her.

'The planes came over and over and we ran to the side of the road but there was nowhere to hide and the noise of the planes and the bullets and people screaming and crying to God and my mother tried to hide me and my sister under her, and my father spread himself over us all and my mother was saying, "Hail Mary, Hail Mary," and my sister was sobbing and the bullets tore up the dirt next to us, and my father yelled out and my mother stopped praying and my sister stopped crying, and then the planes circled back again and shot up the ground a lot more, and I could hardly breathe because every-one had got so heavy on me, and when the planes were gone I wriggled out from under them and when I was standing by them I could see bits of their insides on top of their clothes and everything red, and a hole in my father's head and grey stuff coming out, and I tried to pull at my sister in case she was trapped but she had a hole in her too, and black blood pouring into the dirt, and I started to scream and a man came and took me away from them. And then I wet myself, and I was crying and crying and that woman found me.'

Concha slumped against her and Lucy kissed her head and rocked her, hoping that love would be powerful enough to mend what Tom and Concha had experienced, but fearing they would carry the scars of war all their lives.

Lucy's days at the villa were as busy as ever, as she divided her hours between discussing the menu with Juan, making lists of the remaining food supplies and ordering more to come from Barbara Wood in Valencia, checking the laundry, accompanying one child or another to see the doctor or dentist, teaching her classes and overseeing swimming, while all the time watching for snatched moments alone with Tom.

Juanita and Alfonso came to see her to tell her they wanted to get married and Lucy was dismayed. They were much too young; still only sixteen and seventeen. She should have parted them sooner. Now she would have to send one of them back to Murcia, and separate them until they were old enough for Alfonso to be able to support Juanita. Only then would their families approve the match. But which of them would have to return to the horrors of Pablo Iglesias? When she said this they both wept and Juanita insisted her mother wouldn't care, as long as she was off her hands. In the end Lucy decided they had to go to Murcia to ask their families' permission to marry. She wondered who she would have chosen to marry when she was sixteen: Tom or Jamie? It felt a long time ago.

Tom made himself useful as much as he could by chopping firewood and playing games with the children, who saw him as a hero. Lucy could tell he rather liked their adulation, and at last he had an appreciative audience for his clowning. Concha was warming to him, though she still saw him as a rival for Lucy's affection. More and more, the peal of his familiar laughter would sound on the beach or through the villa and Lucy would stop whatever she was doing and hug to herself the thought that the old Tom was returning to her. If only she could persuade him to stay once his leg was healed.

Sometimes during the day they would pass in an empty corridor and Tom would take her shoulders and push her up against a wall, kissing her till she trembled all over, or till he could no longer balance on one leg, or a small child or one of the adults ran around the corner, and they sprang apart. The adults would smirk indulgently or apologise, but the children didn't notice. At siesta time Lucy and Tom would wait till Concha was asleep and the whole villa had drifted into a hush of suspended animation, and then creep out, far enough into the pine trees not to be seen by the first wakers.

Lying on a blanket on the soft pine needles, with the strong scent of pine and the sound of the waves, their kisses and their desire grew increasingly urgent. Each day Tom ran his hands more freely over her body, through her summer dress, over her hard nipples and round buttocks, and eventually into the cleft between her legs. And she clung to him, panting for more.

Every night he woke with nightmares and she tiptoed in to comfort him, feeling the heat of his body against the length of hers through her thin nightdress, his tears soaking her throat and chest. And each night it became harder to tear herself away from his bed.

19

Just over a week after Tom arrived, the whole camp was woken by the drone of enemy planes overhead. The children who were in tents began to scream, and those in the villa joined their panic. It was the first time the planes had come so close. Lucy grabbed her megaphone, shouted for calm, and ushered all the boys and girls into the cellar. She realised that Tom hadn't appeared from his room, but had to ensure the youngsters were safe before she went to look for him. Why wasn't he here helping? she thought angrily.

When all her charges were counted in the cellar she ran to Tom's room and found him curled on his bed, trembling so hard that the bed rocked beneath him. The planes now seemed to be getting further away, towards Alicante, but she couldn't take any chances.

'Come down to the cellar,' she urged him, but he shook his head.

'I can't let the kids see me like this,' he said, through chattering teeth. 'They think I'm a hero.'

She looked out of the window and listened, as far off the first bombs dropped on Alicante and the tracer fire of anti-aircraft guns ripped through the sky. It was unlikely the planes would return.

She climbed on to the bed behind him, stroking his hair until his shivering subsided and the night-sounds were only the cicadas again.

Tom hid his face in the pillow and refused to speak, so she kissed the nape of his neck before she went to organise the children back from the cellar to their beds.

Each evening, as usual, Salvador came with news of the war. They sat on the veranda hearing the litany of advances and retreats, of battle fronts and generals, of numbers of men presumed dead, of bombs dropped on Alicante's civilians by Franco's planes returning to their base on Mallorca. Salvador and Tom smoked and their faces lit red each time they inhaled.

One night Tom listened with his head hung low, until suddenly in mid-sentence, he grabbed his crutch and set off down the beach at a lolloping speed.

Salvador looked stricken. 'Have I said something wrong? I'm so sorry.'

Lucy reassured him quickly before hurrying after Tom.

She found him sitting on a rock with his head in his hands. Settling beside him she laid one hand on his thigh, just to let him know she was there.

She watched the waves, making small white runs in the moonlight, sighing as they tumbled on to the shore, as they always had done, and always would do, years after she and

Tom were no longer there to see them. As the moon slowly rose higher it cast a silver path across the sea towards the horizon. The regular shushing sound of the waves was calming and when Tom raised his head, his voice was controlled and even.

'I shouldn't be here. With all this beauty. With you. I have no right to be alive when so many of my friends have died.'

Lucy wrapped an arm around his waist, and stroked his side. 'You are convalescing,' she said reasonably.

Tom stretched out his wounded leg.

'I'm starting to feel things again, and you can't let yourself do that. Being here is making me soft. I'll be a danger to everyone if I'm soft.'

She leaned her head against him, thinking, don't go back, then. Please, don't go back.

That night, after his nightmare, he didn't immediately return to sleep, but began to kiss her and she let him run his hands up under her nightdress to touch her naked body, pressing himself against her, hot with desire, until she thought she heard Concha at the doorway and tore herself away.

'Stop now.'

She slipped out of his bed and he rolled over and groaned. She looked at the curve of his back in the moonlight. Perhaps, she thought, there might be one way to keep him from the Front.

A few days later a letter came from Jamie, the first for many weeks.

1 October 1937

My darling Lucy,

I think so much about the days in Ronda and Córdoba, and wonder what I could have done differently. I felt then that we were like two streams merging to become one river, that we understood each other completely and nothing was hidden from us. And now. What? You said in your last letter that you have Tom with you at the villa. I know your aim is to reconcile him and me, but it only makes me wildly jealous to think of him seeing you every day when I can't.

I picture you at the beach, surrounded by children, your hair blowing in the sea breeze, and I'm empty with longing to be with you. I picture Tom eating with you, making you laugh, and other things I can't name, because he always loved you too, and perhaps he will win you with soft words in the sunset. Or not soft words, but something altogether more Tom-ish, more physical. I beg you, don't do anything just because you want to please him. You know he only thinks of himself. If I treated you too much as the Madonna, he wouldn't hesitate to make you his Magdalene. There. I've said it. And if I post this you will see my whole heart opened up to you like glass. And perhaps you will hate me for thinking so little of you that you might allow yourself to be seduced by him.

Confession seems easy on paper, so I'll tell you it's eating me up that I didn't press my advantage when I had it, and now it might be too late. I think you would have been mine that night in Córdoba, when we were so close that we were like an extension of each other. Am I imagining that,

271

deluding myself? And couldn't it happen again? Should I release you from your promise that you won't marry anyone else until we are back in England? I think it would break my heart.

Perhaps it would help if I told you that you have sowed a seed of doubt and as I travel around I notice that nobody at all says they aren't happy with the new regime. Even in paradise some people would complain that the flowers were too bright or the milk and honey too sickly, so that seems strange. And nobody is willing to admit that the Republic might have had some positive ideas. What happened to all the supporters of the Republic? After all, they were elected to power with a democratic majority. I know you have huge numbers of refugees, but surely the Republicans can't all have left?

I remember that day we went to Speakers' Corner in London and saw all those cranks on soapboxes shouting their ideas, and I think about the opposing views of the Daily Worker *and the* Daily Mail, *and I am worried by the lack of dissent here. Though I also wonder which would happen first: freedom of worship under a communist regime or education of the peasants under a Fascist one? For me, the freedom to worship is everything.*

But I am going to travel more around the country, try to get closer to the Aragon Front, try to understand more, try to win back your love.

Your ever-devoted Jamie

Lucy sat with the letter in her lap, and wanted to cry because Jamie was right, and that night in Córdoba she might have gone to his room with him, and now she was on the verge of the same with Tom. Did that make her some kind of bad girl? The lunch bell sounded and she folded the letter and slipped it in her suitcase at the bottom of her wardrobe.

Tom had seen the letter arrive with Jamie's familiar handwriting and he was sulky as they sat together under the pines in the siesta time.

'So. Are you going to tell me what he said?'

'Letters are private,' Lucy said primly, playing with the fringe of the blanket they were sitting on.

'Love letters are. I bet it was a love letter, wasn't it?'

'He said he's noticing that the Fascist regime doesn't allow any sort of dissent.'

Tom snorted in derision. 'It doesn't take a bloody genius to notice that!'

'But you know what he's like about the Church.'

'Opiate of the masses,' said Tom automatically. He began to pick up pine cones and hurl them out across the beach, using a boulder as target practice.

'His religion makes him feel closer to your father.'

'Well, I don't remember "our" father. Jamie claimed ownership of him long ago.'

Lucy ran her fingers lightly up his back. 'Your mother says you look just like him and act like him. She says your voice even sounds like his.'

Tom gave a giant throw and hit the rock. 'Yes! Well, that's ironic, isn't it? I almost feel sorry for Jamie. All that effort to be like Dad, and it's me who takes after him. That must eat him up. And now I've got you too. Does he know that?'

'He's guessed.'

Tom hit the rock again.

'He loves you, doesn't he? He's always loved you.'

And you? thought Lucy. Have you always loved me? Why can't you say it?

She told Tom a little about her trip to the south.

'What was it, then?' he mocked. 'A meeting of true minds?'

She twisted and untwisted two fibres of the blanket fringe and thought – something like that.

He pulled her roughly towards him, kissing her so hard that his teeth were bruising on her lips, and thrusting his hand up under her skirt to prise her legs apart. She pushed him away with such ferocity that he toppled over. She jumped up, rubbing her mouth with the back of her hand, eyes flashing with fury.

'Don't you ever do anything like that again!'

Immediately he was contrite, shading his eyes to peek up at her, just like little-boy Tom when he'd been told off.

'I'm so sorry. I would never hurt you.' He took a deep breath. 'I'm just jealous. I've always been jealous of you and him.' Perhaps that was as much an admission of love as she'd ever get from Tom, she thought. She paced up and down and the anger ebbed out of her.

He tore the flanges off a pine cone, one at a time, not looking at her. 'Has he asked you to marry him?'

'Yes, but I said I won't marry anyone till we are all back in England.'

She waited, but Tom didn't say, 'I want you to marry me.'

The day he had his stitches out, the sun shone and the sea glittered like a handful of flung diamonds and Lucy had to pretend to be glad for him, though it represented being one day closer to possibly losing him forever. The doctor said that ligaments had been damaged and he would walk with a limp for some time, perhaps for the rest of his life. He advised lots of swimming and exercises. Tom asked when he would be fit enough to return to the Front. The doctor raised his head and took in the misery on Lucy's face.

'When you can run faster than a bullet,' he said.

Tom laughed, a sour laugh, without humour. 'I'm no good for anything else,' he said. 'No good for normal life.'

Despair washed over Lucy and the brightness of the sun seemed to be mocking her.

Tom began to put his mind to mending his body, swimming several times a day, out further every time, with Lucy observing from the beach. What if he had cramp? Was he daring death to take him? As she watched his dark head receding and getting smaller and smaller in the bobbing waves, it was as if he was rehearsing for when he would go away, and she could barely breathe until she saw that he had turned and was slowly coming back to her. The anticipation of him going was a sickness in her stomach which prevented her eating more than a few mouthfuls at each meal, and as she pushed her plate away, he would draw it to him, greedily finishing her portion as well as his own.

'Off your tucker, Luce?' he asked.

She sighed. 'Just not hungry.'

'Juan is a genius. I'm going to get him to show me how to make this sauce, and I can show our company cook.'

A great weariness came over Lucy at his determination to

return to the battalion. He was just as bad as Jamie in his dogged inflexibility. She forced herself to concentrate on what he was saying. 'And I was thinking, maybe Juan could get a boat and we could teach the older kids to sail.'

A tiny lick of hope flickered in her. If he could play a greater part in the life of the villa, perhaps he'd stay for the children if not for her.

'You'd be great at that.'

'Another thing I should have been more grateful to your father for,' he said ruefully. 'Teaching us to sail.'

'Teaching you to sail, not me,' Lucy pointed out sharply.

'No, you weren't there,' he said, shaking his head in disbelief.

The nauseating disappointment of that first sailing weekend lapped over Lucy. She had been eight when her father had announced at the breakfast table his intention to take the boys away. She'd paused with her toast halfway to her mouth. Surely he meant children, not boys?

'What about me?' she'd asked.

'No, no,' said Captain Nicholson, blithely swishing his tea around the cup. 'I thought we'd have a boys' weekend, all men together. Camping. Much too rough for you.'

She had thrown down her cutlery and rushed out of the room, hearing her father's 'What's got into her?' as she stomped upstairs and hurled herself on the bed in a storm of noisy tears.

That was the day she had finally accepted that no matter how hard she tried to please her father, he would never love her in the way she needed to be loved. So it became her life's work to please everyone else instead, to make her teachers admire her, her friends choose to be with her above all others, Tom and Jamie to adore her. And now there was one ultimate way left that she could please Tom.

Tom's mind was obviously still running on his own relationship with her father. 'Do you know what the last thing was that he said to me before I went away?'

She gathered up their dishes and he followed her from the dining hall.

'I thought he was going to tell me something useful about estimating the range of artillery, or not looking over the parapet of the trench, but the last bit of advice from the old soldier was "Never marry a girl just because she says she's pregnant." I promised I wouldn't.'

Lucy wondered if that was why her father had married her mother. She'd always assumed he disliked her for being the cause of her mother's death. But perhaps he hadn't ever loved her mother. She knew she wouldn't ever be able to ask him.

The next days would have been the most joyful of Lucy's life if she hadn't been constantly living with the knowledge that they might be their last together. If only it was possible to live entirely in the present and not spoil the now with fears of what might soon be. But the thought of him leaving hung like a dark shadow over the sunny, fun-filled hours as Tom threw himself into sailing lessons, swimming lessons, cricket matches and PT. The children loved him for his enthusiasm, energy and laughter, and because he was a hero from the International Brigades, come from overseas to be the saviour of the blessed Republic, with an impressive red scar along his thigh. It was an equal joy and pain to Lucy to watch them with him and hear their squeals of laughter as he tossed them in the air or raced them up the beach with his new lolloping stride.

Alone with her he was more tender and gentle, laying his head in her lap and letting her stroke his hair, or watching her face intently as she rubbed a healing salve into the scar which ran almost the length of his thigh, and lemon juice into his insect bites. The smoke from his cigarette curled slowly into the still air, and sometimes he blew white rings and they watched as the circles lifted into the treetops and dispersed.

His nightmares reduced, and sometimes Lucy woke having slept all night in her own bed with Concha. She was glad that he was sleeping more soundly, but sad that he needed her less and desperately missed the feel of his muscular body against hers.

It began to seem that he was settling, becoming part of their community, and she had almost persuaded herself he would never leave, until one afternoon when they were under the pinos. He had kissed and caressed her to a fast-breathing fever pitch, and then she had drawn back as though from the edge of a precipice and now she was lying in the crook of his arm, batting away flies.

'The food supply lorry is coming tomorrow, isn't it?' he asked.

'Yes, we're almost out of rice.'

She heard the choke in his voice and knew what was coming before the words were even formed. 'Then . . . then I'm going to go back with it to Valencia, and from there to the Brigade.'

A little cry escaped her. 'Oh no. Must you?'

'You knew I would. My comrades need me.'

She twisted up on to one elbow and looked down at him, bleak with sorrow. 'I need you. The children need you. Please don't go.'

He wouldn't meet her eyes, but gazed up into the canopy of the pines. 'You'll cope. You are a coper, Luce. Always have been. But it feels like I'm betraying all those who died if I don't go back and try to finish what we started together.'

She sat up, wrapping her arms around her knees, her fingernails biting into the palms of her hands. 'You'll get killed.'

He sat up beside her.

'Very likely. The odds aren't in my favour.'

She was anguished. 'Don't you want to live? Don't you want to be with me?'

He jumped up. 'Don't make it any harder, Luce. Of course I want to live and be with you and make love to you every day.'

He reached a hand down and pulled her to her feet beside him and his eyes were black with despair. 'But this is my last night.' He laid one hand gently on her breast, and her knees were weak with desire. 'So, will you? Tonight? I want to know what it's like before I die.'

She wanted to scream with anguish, but she took a deep breath and said, 'That's blackmail.'

He tipped up her chin and kissed her till she was breathless. 'You know you want to as well. And then when the war is over you can marry Jamie and have four lovely Catholic children and forget about me.'

'I don't want to marry Jamie, and I could never, ever forget about you.'

'Is that a no, then?' He looked so sorrowful, so despairing, that she couldn't bear it. Was that the look she was destined to remember forever? Perhaps if they made love and it was marvellous he wouldn't be able to leave her. It was surely worth a try?

'It's a maybe.'

The evening seemed endless – dinner, and storytime for the little ones, and conversation and reading for the older children – until finally, one by one, everyone began to yawn and take themselves off to their beds. Tom went before Lucy, throwing her a pleading glance over his shoulder and carrying half a bottle of wine under his arm. Lucy undressed as usual, with a fizz of nervous anticipation running through her, touching her own body as though saying goodbye to her ownership of it, or to tell it what to expect.

Concha was asleep but restless as Lucy slipped in beside her and waited for all the creaks and footsteps of the house to settle. Finally it was quiet, and Concha was in a deep sleep. Lucy climbed out of bed and took the jam jar from the case in her wardrobe. Then she tiptoed to the door and closed it tight behind her.

She visited the toilet and pushed the vinegar sponge up inside her as far as her fingers could reach, where Tom soon would be, and that thought was thrilling and perplexing.

Then she crept to Tom's room, and he was awake, waiting for her. He opened his arms, but she shook her head. 'Not here. Down by the sea. The mosquitoes aren't so bad there. Bring a blanket, and be quiet.'

She led him by the hand through the pines, beyond the palms and left along the beach, where they could not be seen from the house. The moon was waning, and a thousand stars glittered above them. The sea was a dark navy, reflecting the flickering light from the sky, and softly lapping on the shore. A light breeze carried the fresh green scent of the ocean. It could not have been a more perfect night.

Finally she stopped. She could feel a trickle of vinegar running down her inner thigh and it reminded her what they were here for. Now or never, she told herself.

'Here. We can use these stones to hold down the corners of the blanket.'

They laid it down carefully, and he took a swig from the wine bottle and then handed it to her. She gulped it down gratefully, feeling its warmth spreading through her, and then he turned towards her, taking her two hands in his and spreading them wide.

'Will you let me look at you?' he asked. 'Please?'

It would feel strange to let her old childhood friend see her naked, but she pushed that thought aside and nodded imperceptibly.

He leaned forwards and raised the hem of her nightdress, lifting it clean over her head and scrunching it into a ball. She took it from him and wedged it under a rock so it wouldn't blow away. As she straightened she laid one arm across her breasts and covered her groin with the other hand. He gently took each wrist and moved them to her sides, then he turned her slightly to where the moonlight fell across her body, and let out a low sigh. His eyes were running up and down her as if he was memorising every curve and crevasse.

'Can you turn around?' he asked, throatily, and so she swivelled slowly, like someone showing off a new frock, looking out to the moonlight on the sea and then raising her arms and swaying a little in a mermaid dance in time with the swishing waves.

He stepped close behind her, cupping her breasts and sucking at the base of her neck, and she was filled with electrifying desire, running through her and through her. She turned in his arms and was kissing him urgently as he struggled out of his shorts and led her to the blanket.

Her fast, shallow breathing and the rapidly drunk wine were making her giddy as he lay her on her back, kissing her breasts and lips as he climbed on top and parted her knees. He pushed his fingers inside her and then kissed her more as he positioned himself, and she wanted him so badly and knew it would be now, opening to take the shock of him, and revelling in this complete joining.

He moved gently, and at first it was as though he was sending waves of sensation deeper and deeper into her. He was looking down at her and even in the darkness she could see his grin of sheer delight and it was her joy to be pleasing him so much. But then something changed, and he closed his eyes and began to thrust as if this was only about his brute gratification. Her body stilled and her mind seemed to be standing outside of them both, watching this thing which was being done to her, not with her, harder and harder. It was not making love, she thought. This was being fucked. She'd heard the word, but never used it – until now. He rammed into her with a strangulated cry, and then slumped down with all his suffocating weight on her.

Lucy trembled with rage. How dare he do this to her? He was always so selfish. It was only ever about him. She pushed him off her so she could breathe.

He inhaled, withdrew and flipped down on his back beside her.

'Well!' he said with satisfaction. 'Well, well.'

She turned her face away from him, too angry to speak.

He struggled up to one elbow to look at her, laying a hand proprietorially on one breast. She flicked it away in disgust.

'Good old Luce!' And then, catching the familiar scent of her disapproval, 'Did I hurt you?'

She struggled to control her fury and bite back the scathing words he deserved. This had not been the romantic, loving experience she'd hoped for, but it might still serve the purpose of keeping him from returning to the Front and being killed if she could only say the right things. Hesitantly she shook her head. 'Not much. I just didn't know what to expect.'

He was apologising now, but not for the act itself. 'I meant to, you know, pull out before, but you were too much for me.' He ran a hand down her flank. 'But I don't think it's possible to get pregnant the first time, is it?'

She forced herself to keep her voice steady and pretend everything was all right, explaining to him about Margarita and the sponge, and he laughed to think what Catholic Jamie would think of her precautions, repeating, 'Good old Luce.'

There was a throbbing discomfort between her legs. He had no idea of how she felt, and maybe he didn't really care. Maybe for him it had only ever been lust. She wondered if it would have been different with Jamie – more considerate and gentle, more loving? Or were all men the same in this regard? But she couldn't think about that. She had made her choice and now must play her final card.

'If you stay here we could do that every night.'

He flopped back on to the blanket, lighting up a cigarette and inhaling deeply. The tip glowed red and she counted three waves breaking on the shore before he replied, so quietly she could hardly hear. 'Don't ask me that. You know I can't.'

They lay for a long while looking up at the millions of stars, and an autumnal breeze off the sea shivered along Lucy's skin, warning of the magnitude of her misery to come. She sat up, reached for her nighty and pulled it over her head.

His mind was running on a different track, pleased with himself again. 'You've made a man of me, Luce. And I've made a woman of you.'

How little he knew, Lucy thought. That rutting wasn't what made me a woman. I became a woman the day I gathered up Jorge in the middle of an air raid and ran to the shelter with him.

'I can die happy now,' he said.

She snapped, 'I'd rather you thought about it every day and it helped to keep you alive.'

He took her face in his hands. 'I will think about it every day. And you. I'll think about you, Luce. And I'll do everything to come back if I can.'

They folded the blanket, and began to walk back to the villa.

Lucy felt cold spreading up along her spine, settling deep in the core of her. It was over, then. He was going off to get himself killed and there was nothing more she could do to save him.

20

By a steely effort of will, Lucy somehow held back her tears as Tom left, dressed again in his coarse, brown Popular Army overalls. She wanted his last memory to be of her waving and smiling. But after the lorry had passed through the gates, and there was no chance of him changing his mind, she ran to her room and sobbed. After a while Concha slipped in and sat stroking her hair, and when she had recovered enough, Lucy took Concha in her arms and they both cried for the lost things in their lives.

Although it was still only October, in Lucy's mind that was when winter began. Of course October in Benidorm was barely even autumnal by English standards, but cold had penetrated deep, wrapping around her heart. Every time she thought of Tom, she pulled down a shutter and forced herself to think of something else, something small, inconsequential and less personal: which child needed new shoes; whether there would be enough tomatoes in the market this week; how best to teach multiplication. Juan the fisherman was the only one who understood, and he would sit on the veranda with her and Concha in the evenings, each surrounded by their own ghosts. And once, when one of the boys was praising Tom's courage, she overheard Juan say, 'He is a stupid boy. To have thrown away so much.' As he stomped towards the villa he muttered, 'He does not deserve her.'

Juanita and Alfonso returned from Murcia with the proud news that they were married. A party was thrown to celebrate, and Lucy quietly presented Juanita with a sponge in vinegar. When it was found that the sound of their lovemaking could be heard all over the villa, she suggested they move into a room over the garage. Soon it was discovered that Pepe had moved in with them, claiming them as his family.

Lucy decided it was high time she helped Alfonso's artistic talent to develop further, so she went to see a respected artist living in Benidorm and took some of Alfonso's work. The artist spent a long time perusing Alfonso's drawings and paintings.

'He is good, but he needs training.'

Lucy turned her most beatific smile on him, the one few men could resist. 'But where would I find someone to help him here in Benidorm? He has no money.'

The artist's chest puffed up. 'It would be my honour to take the boy under my wing, Señorita. Send him to me.'

When she told Alfonso, he gripped her hand so tight she thought he had almost broken it. Tears stood in his eyes. 'It would be my dream come true,' he said.

So once a week he walked into town, and came back laden with art books and supplies. It seemed the artist had almost adopted him. Lucy released him from some of his duties in the camp to work on his paintings, and the room over the garage became his studio as well as their home.

Concha was also growing and developing greater independence. As soon as she had begun speaking, Lucy asked her what her real name was, but Concha had looked troubled. 'My baptised name was Ernestina but they always called me Conejito.'

Lucy's throat contracted at the thought of the loving family who had called Concha their 'little bunny'. She steadied her voice to ask, 'Would you like us to call you Ernestina now?'

Concha shook her head and frowned. 'I hate that name. I am Concha, who lives with Lucy.'

Now that Concha chattered all the time in her low, smoky voice, the other children had fully accepted her as one of their own. It was a joy to see her playing with them, singing with them and sometimes quarrelling with them. Lucy persuaded Concha out of her bed into a small one alongside, though she missed the comfort of the little, warm body. She knew now that she would take Concha with her wherever she went. The unconditional love of a child was a precious gift, and she must never let her down. She wondered if she had ever loved her father in the unquestioning way Concha loved her.

At the end of October Margarita wrote with surprising news.

My dear friend,
I have to tell you the most astonishing thing.
One evening the Danish Quaker Elise Thomsen came to our new headquarters, Luis Vives House, looking very troubled. When I asked her what was the matter she said

one of the mothers registered at her canteen was very ill and likely to die within days.

'She has a baby girl, Dorotea, only two months old,' said Elise. 'The sweetest thing you ever saw. Smiling already, as if fate wasn't about to deal her the harshest blow.'

I asked if the father was alive and Elise said he had been killed at Brunete.

'It will be sad to see the baby go to the orphanage,' she said. 'She's been bringing her to the canteen every day since she was born and everyone loves her.'

Her words clutched my heart. I can say this to you, dear Lucy, without you thinking I have gone mad – but it was as if my miscarried son was speaking to me and telling me I had to help that baby. I could hardly wait for evening when I could talk to Domingo. He was hesitant at first, but when he saw my eagerness he said if it would make me happier I could look after the baby for a bit while the mother was in hospital. I might not have told him how very sick the mother was.

So the next morning Elise took me to see the woman. She was slipping in and out of consciousness. The nurses were taking care of the baby which was crying and red in the face – hungry probably – but when I took her in my arms she quieted immediately and went to sleep. I felt an over-powering sense that she was where she was meant to be, and my son approved.

The mother woke up and saw that I was holding her baby and she reached out a finger to touch the little one's cheek. Then she looked straight into my eyes, and said, 'Take care of my baby.'

I nodded, and she insisted, 'Promise me.'

And I promised. Without asking Domingo, I promised.

The doctor arrived to check on the woman, and I walked away with baby Dorotea in my arms. On the way back home to Luis Vives House I stopped and bought a feeding bottle and a little dress for her as the one she was wearing was soiled. At home I took out the nappies and knitted hats and leggings I had already gathered together for our son. And I took the baby to show Domingo. He was very busy, of course, but dropped a kiss on the top of my head and said I could look after her if it wouldn't make me too sad when I had to give her back.

We didn't have a cot, so I cleared out a drawer and lined it with blankets and laid her in it beside the bed. And when I heard her cries in the night, I slipped out quietly so as not to wake Domingo and carried her down to the kitchen to warm milk for her. She began to cry quite desperately and when I put the bottle teat in her mouth she spat it out and seemed to be seeking something else. So I opened my nightdress and the little one gripped hard on my nipple with her lips, without any hesitation, but of course it was dry. I managed to slip the bottle teat into her mouth as well and she was drinking from the bottle, but sucking on me, and I began to feel a slight tingling in my breast. After a few minutes she pulled away, so I moved her to the other side, and she sucked again on the bottle and me simultaneously. And again I felt a tingling, like when my breasts leaked milk after we lost our son. Tears began pouring down my cheeks.

Each time she cried for milk, I gave her the bottle, but held her to my breast as well, and within a few days I was producing milk of my own for her — not much at first, but more and more each day. The more she sucked, the more I produced.

I kept this as a secret, wondering over it in my heart. But after she had been with us about a week, she was crying early one morning and I brought her into our bed and opened my nightdress without thinking.

After a moment or two I could feel Domingo had woken up. He raised himself on one elbow and looked at me.

'What are you doing?' he asked, as if it wasn't obvious.

'It's like a miracle,' I said. 'I have milk to feed this baby.'

He wiped a hand over his forehead and said uneasily, 'It isn't your baby.'

'I know that,' I said. 'I know this isn't our son. But it is a hungry baby and I have milk. Would you have me deny her?'

He looked doubtful and worried, but he pulled on his clothes and went to work, leaving me with the baby, learning the contours of her face, letting her hold my finger tight in her tiny hand as if she didn't want to let me go.

Later in the day Elise came to tell us that the baby's mother had died, and Domingo looked truly dismayed. Elise left us alone, and I pleaded with him, 'Perhaps this was meant to be? God has taken our son, but given us this little girl?'

'You knew the mother was dying,' he said, and I had to admit I had realised she was very ill.

I stood up and put the baby in his arms. He gazed down at the dark eyelashes on the whiteness of her skin, the eyelids blue with tiny veins. Then she opened her eyes and stared up at him, so serious, searching his face for an answer.

He looked up at me, awash with despair. 'I don't know what to say.'

'Say yes,' I said. 'Tell me I can care for this baby. She needs our love.'

His face clouded. 'There are so many children who need our love.'

'But this one is here.'

'Will it make you happy?' he asked, and I nodded.

'Then you keep the baby for now at least, until we find out if she has other family.'

I kissed him over the head of the baby, and he said, 'You have been so sad since . . .'

I told him, 'I will never forget our son.'

So, Lucy, I have a daughter. Dorotea, which means gift from God. She is the most beautiful creature on the earth, and so good. She only cries when she's hungry or dirty. Everybody loves her. I love her. It was true, what I said to Domingo: I will never forget our son, but love for this little scrap has filled up some of the terrible hollow in me.

I hope you will come for the conference in December and stay with us and meet her. Say you will.

Your friend,

Margarita

Lucy wrote back at once, telling Margarita she would come in December. It didn't seem so far away.

The leaves fell and the evenings turned chilly, and more letters came. Margarita wrote again about her adoration of the miraculous baby girl, and letters from Britain told Lucy about Captain Nicholson's new cooking skills and Mrs Murray's life in Lanarkshire. But the letter she most dreaded, telling her that Tom had been killed in battle, didn't come. His scrappy notes arrived sporadically from the Aragon Front, telling of the discomfort of trenches, of freezing nights and wet days, of boredom and terror. Through the same months, Jamie's weekly missives arrived from places all across Spain, as he followed in the wake of Franco's triumphs, but in early December he too said he was going up to the Aragon Front, to 'see for himself what was really happening'. He claimed to be in search of truth, but Lucy thought he was as blinkered as ever. In their letters both Jamie and Tom professed to think about her, but neither cared about her enough to leave Spain and ease the frozen band around her heart.

In mid-December Lucy travelled to Barcelona as Margarita had suggested, for the conference of relief workers from around Spain. She went with the American Friend Esther Farquar and on the long train journey Esther told Lucy she had taken over the running of the English Hospitals in Almería, Alicante and Murcia as well as the night shelters like Pablo Iglesias. She looked exhausted. In Murcia she was working with the local authorities to supply breakfast for four thousand schoolchildren each day.

'We start work mixing up the milk at half past six in the morning, and I have a team of eight women stirring and sweating over the vats.' She sounded awed herself when she added, 'We have to make a thousand litres a day. That's more than two hundred gallons. Every day. Imagine that.'

She said they had introduced free breakfast at many schools, and she laughed. 'I can't tell you how much school attendance has improved!'

Lucy was delighted to hear that 107 girls and women were now taking part in the sewing workshops she had started. The embroidered tablecloths and dolls they made were sent to England and the USA for sale. Esther told her the workshops had dedicated spaces which were used for evening and week-end clubs where women were taught to read and write or could gather to play board games. The idea had spread to ten other towns and the local authorities had promised to keep them going. It seemed extraordinary to Lucy that a simple idea of hers could have become as big as an oak tree growing from an acorn.

As soon as they arrived at Barcelona station, Lucy could see that everything had changed. She and Esther had to push their way through the crowds of refugees who thronged the streets, while in the restaurants people wearing elegant clothes were sipping coffee and eating cake, and on the roads highly polished cars mixed with the carts and wagons of the homeless. The flower stalls along La Rambla made it seem as if everything was normal, but the sirens and blackouts told the truth – this was a city under siege.

Thirty aid workers who had come originally from nine countries and were now spread throughout Republican Spain had converged on Barcelona for the conference. These included pacifist Mennonites from America and representatives of other Protestant groups. Somehow in this overcrowded city, Alfred, Domingo and Margarita had found accommodation and provided food for everyone. Lucy suspected Margarita had done most of the work, busying about the house with baby Dorotea strapped to her back like a peasant in the fields. She had ensured that Lucy was staying with them in the new Quaker headquarters, Luis Vives House, a white stone mansion behind high wrought-iron gates which had been owned by the Sagnier family before the war, in the aristocratic suburb of Sarrià overlooking the city. It was the kind of grand building which might have been an embassy or an art gallery in peacetime, and the Quakers had renamed it after a sixteenth-century humanist, Juan Luis Vives.

It was a joy to be reunited with Margarita, and they hugged for a long time before breaking into an excited babble of news and questions. When they were alone they talked about the horror of Margarita's miscarriage and the black despair which dogged her afterwards, and Lucy spent hours cooing over Dorotea, who had brought Margarita back to herself. Lucy felt the tension of the past months draining out of her as she sang softly to a baby who needed nothing from her. Snuggling this trusting, milk-smelling creature made her feel that love for men was just too complicated. She missed Concha with a small, sharp pain.

'You would be a lovely mother,' said Margarita.

'One day, perhaps,' smiled Lucy.

Margarita was gazing at her expectantly, teasingly. 'So?' she said. 'Did you use the sponge?'

Lucy played with the baby's fingers as she told her friend all about the visit to Jamie and then Tom nearly dying, and coming back to the White Villa to convalesce.

'And so, is he the one?' asked Margarita.

Tears began to slowly fall down Lucy's face, for the first time since Tom had left.

'He's determined to get himself killed. He loves the cause more than he loves me.'

Margarita reached over the baby and hugged Lucy as she wept. 'War is a vile, filthy thing.'

Baby Dorotea, half-squashed between them, sent up a sympathetic wail, and they broke free, laughed, and turned their attention to the affronted child.

At the conference, Lucy learned that large-scale US deliveries were filtering through, giving Alfred Jacob and his team the task of running a huge operation of budgets, colonies, canteens, supplies and a fleet of trucks for all the relief agencies. They heard about the work being done by city councils and government agencies, as well as religious groups from overseas. They talked about practicalities like where to obtain cooking pots which could hold more than fifty litres and how to find sufficient firewood. The wooden packaging which the food and soap arrived in was their principal source of fuel. Alfred summed up their task: 'Our job is to do the work of peace in the midst of war.' It felt like a tall order.

Cold was spreading through the whole country, and everyone shivered in the high-ceilinged, tile-floored conference room at Luis Vives House. It was heated only by two electric hotplates propped up on their side, and most of the delegates kept their coats on. Everyone agreed it looked set to be a dreadfully cold winter and the plight of the refugees was more urgent than ever. An American relief worker told about his trip to Oviedo.

'We had forty blankets to share out, but there were six hundred and fifty-two children who needed them.' He paused and took a breath, scanning their faces. 'Several of the little ones who did not get blankets walked up to them and felt them. One child petted the blankets then walked out into the night cold.'

Margarita's head drooped and tears dripped on to her lap. Lucy clutched her hand. The problem was so huge and what they could do seemed so very little.

The Barcelona canteens were now all being run by Elise Thomsen. She took the conference delegates to the Cantina de Sant Andreu, funded by Norwegian Quakers, where a young boy called Josep proudly demonstrated a huge stainless-steel boiler a metre high by a metre across, with a mechanism which mixed water with dried milk without making lumps. She told them they made butter out of any excess. Lucy admired her quiet good humour. She was obviously a born peace-maker who had smoothed over the condensed milk versus dried milk row by the simple expedient of letting the Quakers supply dried and Save the Children supply condensed. In Margarita's eyes she was the angel who had united her with baby Dorotea.

When the conference was over, Margarita begged Lucy to come back to Barcelona to live, but Lucy was not yet ready to leave the White Villa. She was eager to return to Benidorm and Concha.

As with the Great War, when the names of previously obscure villages and rivers like Somme, Ypres and Gallipoli were on everyone's lips, the whole of Spain now knew the name of Teruel, the centre of the fighting on the Aragon Front. Before Christmas Tom reported they were getting ready for the big push, and Lucy sent him a parcel of cigarettes, toothpaste, razor blades, chocolate and sweets. She even made him something resembling a small figgy pudding.

Christmas came and went, and was celebrated with joy by the children in the White Villa. Mateo organised a nativity play in which everyone had a part. Concha was an angel and tears stood in Lucy's eyes as she watched her little girl so seriously wishing them all peace on earth. Esther Farquar sent a consignment of toys and clothes from the American Friends, which were opened with squeals of delight and squabbling jealousies when the 'kings came' on the sixth of January. Francesca was in Spain for the Christmas holiday, and she came to celebrate with them, bringing Concha a pair of red shoes which she refused to take off, even at night.

Tom wrote that their quartermaster 'Hookey' Walker had rustled up a pig from somewhere and they had wine and nuts.

As the staff at the White Villa welcomed in 1938, Lucy prayed it would be the year in which she would persuade Tom and Jamie to return home. Eight days later the newspapers announced that the Republican forces had taken Teruel amid fierce fighting. Lucy held her breath, but no word came that either of the brothers had been killed.

Alfonso had somehow found out it was her birthday on the eleventh of January and he organised all the children to paint her special pictures, and Salvador brought rabbits for a delicious stew cooked by Juan. Mrs Murray and her father had remembered to write to her, though they weren't the letters she wished for most. The only gift she wanted was to know that Tom and Jamie were safe.

She looked about her at her new friends, her new family, gathered in the White Villa's dining room and thought how long it seemed since her twenty-first birthday in Welwyn.

Only a year had passed, but the girl she was then was long gone. Somebody new had emerged from the chrysalis of the 'foolish girl'. Somebody resilient, strong and decisive. But somebody much sadder.

She contemplated the children, helpers, Mateo, Valentina, Juan and Salvador who had gathered to sing 'Happy Birthday' to her and realised she wasn't the only one who had changed. Concha's face had relaxed and her eyes danced as she clapped her hands with delight; Alfonso had his arm wrapped around Juanita's waist and was looking Lucy clear in the face in a way he wouldn't have dared a few months ago. Emilia the cook had filled out and even dear Juan had lost his perpetually mournful expression. If only Tom was here with her. If only she knew that he was alive. She wondered what the next year would bring for all of them.

Eventually a note arrived from Tom, giving some details of the battle for Teruel and their losses. He didn't mention her birthday but wrote instead about fighting taking place in snow drifts two to three feet deep.

The Batallón Inglés is now half Spanish because so many English have died. We sleep jam-packed into Soviet trucks and try to dig trenches in frozen soil. We spent one night in a railway tunnel where the heat of our bodies melted icicles which dripped on us all night, soaking our poncho blankets. We cross trackless mountains. We fight in blinding snow-storms. Our tanks freeze to the ground. The Fascist bombers fly overhead in perfect formation, flashing silver against the deep blue of the sky. I have frost in my hair. Really. Frost. Can you believe that?

He was alive. That was all she needed to know. Relief made her briefly gay and she sang to the astonished Concha and whirled her round in a merry jig before slowly folding herself back into the quiet, frozen core Tom had left behind him.

The winter days came and went at the villa in a kind of noisy limbo. The storms of the children's joys and sorrows were like a tornado around her, while she held herself protected in a still centre. The daily anticipation of grief seemed to sap Lucy's usual energy, but of course she had a job to do and people who needed her. The girls and boys played on the beach, but only Lucy ventured into the sea. The Spaniards all thought it was a kind of English madness to swim during the coldest January for a hundred years, but the tingling of her limbs every day reminded her that she was still alive and would be for as long as those she loved remained in the world.

She took her lessons, and was pleased by the progress of the children, who seemed so changed from the wild cats she'd first brought up from Murcia. Concha could read now and she was very proud of the little girl.

Lucy used her spare time to gather up the pictures the children had painted for Alfonso, looking again at the images of terrible swarms of black planes raining death on their villages, the pools of blood and the lifeless, spreadeagled bodies, the running shapes, the fires licking into the sky. She sent the pictures to Francesca in England, who had a foreword written by a child psychologist and, with her usual magic, somehow managed to get it published as a book called *They Still Paint Pictures*, raising money for Friends Relief in Spain. Copies arrived at the villa and the children were astonished and full of pride to see their drawings in a published book.

On the twenty-second of February Salvador came with the grave news that Franco's forces had retaken Teruel and would now be pressing on towards the Mediterranean coast. It was said the Republic had lost six thousand men. The Republican government had already moved up to Barcelona, and Margarita's letters begged Lucy to return there to them before her route north was cut off. From Barcelona she would be able to escape into France if she had to.

With the fall of Teruel, Juan and Salvador added their voices to Margarita's, and as Franco's forces began their deadly sweep down towards the coast, Lucy reluctantly began to make her plans to leave the White Villa. It was agreed that some of the children would stay in Benidorm, cared for by Valentina and Juan. Others would return to their families in Murcia who might be wanting to start the long trek north together. The older boys would go up to Francesca's farm colony. Emilia took a job as a cook in Benidorm and Mateo found a teaching position. As for Concha, there was no question in Lucy's mind – she would come to Barcelona.

BARCELONA AND PUIGCERDÀ
March 1938

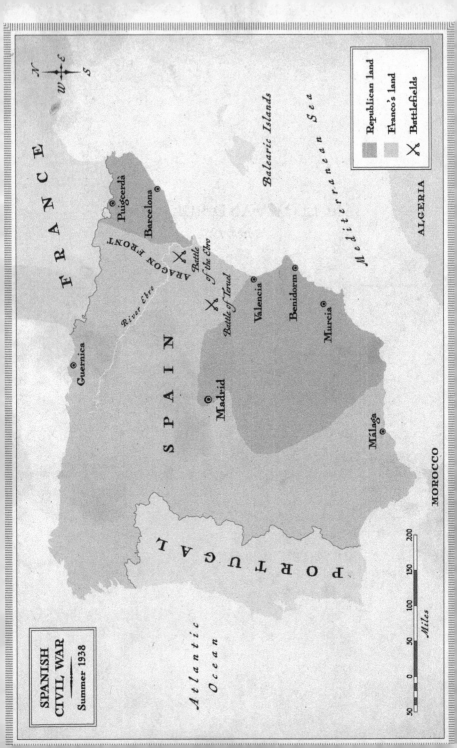

21

Lucy kept a firm grip on Concha's hand as they pushed through the milling crowds of refugees who thronged the streets of Barcelona. Very few people wore coats and many had bare legs although spring had not yet arrived. Children shivered in their thin clothes and it was clear from the smell of passing bodies that there was no soap. Concha stopped in front of a patisserie, gazing at the sweets piled high in the window. Lucy was ready to go inside until she saw the staggering prices. She was salivating herself as she pulled Concha away. 'I'm sorry, pet, but they are too expensive for us.'

Daily bombing raids had devastated much of the area around the docks. Houses were in ruins and Lucy and Concha had to pick their way through the rubble which had once been homes. And every day she knew more refugees poured in, surging north from Murcia, Valencia and Madrid.

As Lucy rang the bell of Luis Vives House, Concha pressed her face between the wrought-iron railings and looked up with awe at the place which would be her new home. Lucy knew that its arched windows, iron balconies and corner turrets must make it look like a fairy-tale castle to Concha. Margarita, with her baby strapped to her back, ran down the staircase from the front door to let them in. She kissed Lucy and then Concha, leading them back up to the entrance. Margarita was so delighted to welcome them that Lucy felt her heart begin to thaw at the prospect of living in the midst of such undemanding affection. Margarita untied baby Dorotea, who had grown a surprising amount in the three months since Lucy was last in Barcelona. She woke up and smiled at Concha, who was immediately smitten.

Margarita took Lucy and Concha up to their room in the attic, explaining that as house-mother she was in charge of who slept where and had chosen them a room close to her own, with spectacular views. Lucy dropped their suitcases and lifted up Concha to peep out of the window. The white city was spread before them with columns of smoke spiralling up from bombed buildings around the docks. In the blue of the Mediterranean beyond, the forms of low, grey warships sat ominously in the water.

'The Italian bombers come over from Mallorca all the time,' said Margarita. 'When they hit the petrol store a great plume of fire shot up into the night sky, and the whole town was under a fog of black smoke for a week. It wasn't so bad up here, but it was terrible down in the town. You couldn't breathe, and everyone was coughing.'

Margarita shook her head at the memory, and Lucy hugged her, wondering what dangers she had brought Concha into.

Then Margarita showed them around the gardens, holding her baby in one arm and Concha's hand in the other, pointing out the bitter oranges, tangerines, lemons, olives and figs which grew there.

'This is where you will play,' she told Concha. 'Nightingales sing here in the summer. It is a magical garden.'

Concha's eyes grew wide.

Margarita showed them the parking area for their six old Bedford food delivery trucks with AMIGOS CUÁQUEROS and the Quaker star painted on the side as well as six newer lorries donated by the Republican navy. Each one covered hundreds of kilometres each week, she said, distributing food to the colonies and canteens, with petrol provided by the Department of Transport.

She took a huge key from the bunch she carried around her waist and opened the door which led down to a cellar full of food.

'It's well known in Barcelona that we have supplies here,' said Margarita, with a sideways anxious glance at Lucy. 'All the staff have to work on a rota to stand at the gate and turn away hungry people. It hurts.'

Lucy bit her lip. 'I hope it'll be a long time before my turn comes up.'

'I'll see what I can do,' said Margarita, her dimples twinkling.

Lucy thought how good it would be to have someone caring for her for a change. Then Margarita turned to Concha. 'Would you like to come and help me with my baby while Señorita Lucy goes to do boring office work?'

Concha took her hand and went along with only one brief backward glance.

* * *

Lucy pushed open the heavy wooden door to an office which had once been a lavishly decorated ballroom or perhaps a formal dining room. The tiled floor and high ceiling made the space echo with the noise of people talking and the clatter and ping of typewriters. Alfred Jacob looked up as the door opened and a grin spread across his face as he hurried to meet her. His hair was beginning to recede and tiredness made him look so much older than when they had first met. She had to remind herself he was still only in his twenties. He shook her hand between both of his in an American way. She wondered if she too looked aged by all she'd seen. On some days she felt a hundred years old.

'We're so pleased to have you back. There's so much to do and it will be wonderful to have someone who can just get on with things. You can sit here.'

Alfred's refugee operation, which had begun with the one canteen at Barcelona station, had now grown to a staff of twelve overseas aid workers and sixty Catalan and Spanish people. Lucy counted thirty-two desks, nine telephones and twelve typewriters while she listened to Alfred warning her that they worked seven days a week for as many hours as they could keep awake and took three shifts for lunch. He also explained that back in England Edith Pye had set up an International Commission for the Assistance of Child Refugees in Spain. She had persuaded the British Foreign Office to pledge £10,000 if she could get other governments to do the same. Her efforts had succeeded so well that the commission was now based in Geneva and had money coming in from twenty-four governments. Lucy thought of the little ex-midwife with the Somerset accent who she'd first seen at Friends House with

Ruth, and was amazed that one middle-aged woman could achieve so much. Alfred said that although they now had large international donations coming in, the actual fieldwork was in the hands of volunteers – in Catalonia the English Friends led by Alfred, in southern Spain the Mennonites and the American Friends led by Esther Farquar, and in Madrid by the Swiss. In Barcelona alone there were now nineteen canteens feeding 3,500 people each day, distributing clothing and encouraging refugees to form sewing groups, choirs and dramatic societies. There were canteens in each city district: in restaurants, a hotel, the fire station, the town hall, an ex-seminary. He was proud to tell her that most of the canteen helpers were refugees, rewarded for their labour with a weekly food parcel. Lucy hid a smile. He'd won that argument, then. She knew they'd agreed a shaky compromise over the dried milk versus condensed milk battle in which the English Quakers still sent dried milk, though most of the refugees were fed on condensed.

'What should I do first?' she asked.

Alfred looked down at the piece of paper in his hand. 'The American Red Cross is sending six thousand tons of wheat flour. We'll need warehouses away from the docks, and you'll need to find bakers, and transport to get the wheat to the bakers every day and the bread to the canteens and colonies.'

Lucy knew who to approach in the city council and the regional aid committee from the introductions Margarita had made when she first arrived in Barcelona. She took the paper from Alfred's hand. 'I'd better get started then.'

At the lunch break on her second day Lucy sat next to Kanty Cooper, a dark-haired, vivacious Englishwoman in her thirties who spoke perfect Spanish and had only recently come out from England. Kanty wrinkled her nose over their meal of soup, with a plate of beans in sauce, lettuce, and an orange for dessert, and said, 'On Sunday we had dried cod and potato for a treat! The only thing there's no shortage of is oranges. But we are lucky. Most people are living on boiled turnips and rice.'

As they ate, Kanty explained she'd been a sculptor in England, who had studied under Henry Moore, but had to stop because of neuritis.

'It was like arrows of fire down my arms at night when I'd been working in stone or wood, or even just drawing,' she sighed. 'So I came here instead.'

Despite having to give up her art, Kanty was a cheerful, energetic person whose laugh echoed round the chilly mansion. She and her friend Audrey Russell were working on a scheme to focus extra canteen feeding on two-to-four-year-olds who weren't eligible either for baby rations or food in school. 'The trouble is we can only feed a third of the thirty-six thousand who need it.'

After a few days Lucy noticed that Kanty always wore trousers.

'It's much warmer, and more practical. You can wear thick socks too,' she said.

Lucy went out and bought some boys' trousers and found she didn't feel the cold so badly in the unheated office. Margarita put her head on one side to consider Lucy's new look and said, 'The anarchists don't like women to wear trousers.'

Kanty snorted. 'Funny sort of anarchism which makes more rules than before.'

'Hmmm,' said Margarita, and Lucy knew this meant she

didn't entirely approve of trousers either, or perhaps she feared Kanty was having too strong an influence on Lucy.

In Kanty's enthusiastic company and with the affection of Margarita, Lucy found her own drive returning, as the spring sunshine revived the trees in their garden. After all, she told herself sternly, neither Tom nor Jamie had been killed yet. It was a waste of energy to worry about things she couldn't influence or control, and somehow disloyal or bad luck to fear they were dead. She shook herself fully awake. There was so much work to be done.

A lorry arrived containing sweet oranges from the south, but they couldn't figure out how to unload it. Lucy noticed that the tail-gate was level with the first-floor windows of the office. So the lorry was backed up to the building, and they unloaded ten tons of oranges by hand on to the office floor. Everyone mucked in, and there was much laughter, especially when Kanty tried to demonstrate how to juggle with three oranges.

Lucy filled two string bags and took them up to the Los Cipreses colony in Pedralbes where Jorge was still living. This time she took Concha with her and introduced her to the serious little boy with the gold flecks in his eyes. He had lost another front tooth, and Concha showed him how wobbly her second incisor was.

'That'll come out soon,' he said authoritatively, and this seemed to seal their relationship.

He told them he was now in charge of the printing press because he was seven years old. He offered to show Concha how it worked. Lucy watched the two dark heads bent together and a surge of love went through her.

When they left she said, 'I will come back, Jorge.'

He smiled. 'I know you will, Lucy Yellowhair.'

On the way home to Luis Vives House Concha asked, 'Am I seven too?' and Lucy realised she didn't know when her birthday was. Concha screwed her face up in concentration, but couldn't remember the date.

'I think it might be in May,' she offered.

'May it is then,' said Lucy. 'What's your favourite number?'

Concha thought hard. 'Seventeen.'

Lucy laughed. 'I think you've just remembered your birthday!'

In their second week in Barcelona, once Lucy had organised arrangements for the American wheat delivery, Lucy and Kanty were each assigned three canteens to run. Lucy was pleased to have something practical to do which took her out of the constant pressure of the office. It seemed real to her to be back in the world of the needy.

One of Lucy's canteens was in a bombed-out slum district near the docks, and she had to step carefully through the rubble of the streets to reach it. There was a little cocoa left when all the children registered to Lucy's canteen had been fed, so she opened the doors to some of the old people who gathered outside for leftovers.

Earlier, as they served the queuing children, she had watched one skinny girl, dressed in black, being allowed to go to the front of the line and given several allowances of milk and biscuits.

The helper saw her watching. 'That's Marita. She's twelve years old, and she has five little brothers and sisters to look after. She leaves the youngest in the care of the older ones while she comes to collect milk for them all.'

A few days later Lucy saw Marita again waiting to be served. Marita raised her head at the sound of dull thuds in the distance, and they all stood quiet to listen. Then the sirens shrilled and Lucy jumped. Some people ran for the shelters, while others scrambled under the furniture. The crash of bursting shells came closer and closer. Lucy huddled beneath a table near Marita and gathered a trembling child below each arm. She tried to speak calmly to them. 'Don't worry, it'll be over soon. We are quite safe here.'

The ground shook and milk flew everywhere. Lucy caught Marita's eye, consternation and indecision written all over her face as she chewed her bottom lip. Then Marita moved – dashing out of the door crying, 'My children!' before Lucy could stop her.

Lucy let go of the two boys she was comforting and ran after her, but outside the dust in the air was thicker than a London fog and she couldn't see which way Marita had gone. She almost stumbled over a dead horse lying in the shafts of a cart which had been blown to smithereens. Whole trees lay across the square and a wall had been sliced off a house. Lucy covered her nose and mouth with her silk scarf, and went back inside the canteen to help clear up the mess, but for the rest of the day she worried about Marita and whether she had made it back to her brothers and sisters. She asked all the assistants, but nobody knew where she lived.

On her way back up to Luis Vives House, Lucy crunched through streets which were thick with shattered glass. Ambulances passed her with men clinging to their sides, blowing whistles. In other places, men and women were digging through the heaped remains of buildings to search for survivors. Marita might be under those walls, she thought.

Before she could reach home the distant thuds began again and the sirens sounded. Lucy raced for the nearby metro station. Her heart was beating hard as the *ack-ack* of the anti-aircraft guns started and when she glanced up she could see the silver specks of bombers in the blue sky. As she reached the metro, she shaded her eyes to watch the Republican fighter planes scramble to attack the bombers. They flew in low and at great speed, swooping like swallows. The noise was deafening. A middle-aged man was standing beside the station entrance, and as he looked up at the battle overhead tears poured down his leathered cheeks.

Lucy took his arm. 'You should come underground.'

He let himself be led down the steps by her, blowing his nose on a huge handkerchief.

As they sat on the platform together he explained, 'I have four sons. Two are in Franco's air force and the two others in the Republican air force. When I see the fighters and bombers go up together I know there is every chance one of my lovely boys will kill another.'

He raised his hands and wailed, 'My lovely boys!'

A woman on the other side of him shook her head sympathetically. 'This war is a bastard thing.'

Lucy dropped her head on to her knees, thinking of other brothers.

In the canteen a few days later, a woman was taken with labour pains while collecting her ration. Lucy took her home to a high block of tenement flats. They groped their way up a dark, smelly staircase, Lucy supporting the woman who had to stop every few minutes as pain gripped her. Lucy helped her into her flat, where her sister was waiting, and as she was leaving the apartment a door across the landing opened and there was Marita, her mouth wide in astonishment.

'Señorita, what are you doing here? You must come and meet my children.'

Lucy followed her into a small, light room with potted geraniums and ivy on a little balcony. A washing line dripping with clothes hung across the room, and in the centre, five children sat around a table, quietly eating milk and bread for breakfast. They were all neatly dressed; the girls' hair was plaited, and the boys' had been plastered down with water. The girls were clothed in black like Marita, even one who could not have been more than two.

As Marita introduced each of them, they stood up, shook hands and said, 'Good morning, Señorita.' Even the toddler solemnly held out her chubby fist. Lucy didn't know whether to laugh or cry.

'I try to keep everything as my mother left it,' said Marita, showing a darn in her brother's shirt which had been mended with stitches so small that Lucy could hardly see them.

'She would be very proud of you,' said Lucy, and Marita beamed.

A thought struck Lucy. 'What happens when an air raid comes?' She hated the idea of Marita shepherding the children down six flights of stairs in pitch-darkness to a dank cellar.

Marita shrugged. 'We sit under the table. We can only die once, and it's better if we all die together.'

313

Lucy shook hands with all the children again and dipped into her pocket where she kept a few coins. She laid these on the corner of the table without Marita seeing in case she was too proud to accept charity.

A new German word entered their vocabulary as they read in the papers that Herr Hitler had begun something called a 'blitzkrieg' on the Aragon Front. How could Tom survive bombing raids there in dugout trenches, without even a cellar or shelter to run to? Lucy shivered and crossed her arms in front of her. It seemed impossible that he could live through it. If he wasn't already dead.

In Barcelona, the air raids increased in frequency until they were coming at regular two-and-a-half-hour intervals. Everyone worked with their eyes constantly on the clock and their nerves on edge as they waited for the next attack. One week there were sixteen in thirty-six hours. If Lucy was at the mansion she gathered up Concha and they took cover in the cellar, but she was often out at one of her canteens, and ran to the nearest shelter or the basement of whatever building she was in.

At first her arms and legs trembled for hours after a raid, but soon she found she stopped worrying about herself. Her anxiety was all for her charges, the refugees and helpers, and for her friends and Concha back at Luis Vives House. If she took a direct hit herself – well, she shrugged, thinking of Marita, you can only die once.

When the bombing raids had frayed their nerves or tempers, or when they were just plain exhausted, Kanty entertained them over their meagre meals with stories of the scurrilous lives of famous artists and the details of flamboyant parties she'd attended in Chelsea. The stories might have been slightly shocking, but they certainly raised everyone's spirits. Lucy thought how much wider and more varied the world was than she had ever realised when she lived in Welwyn.

'You never seem to get downhearted,' she said to Kanty one evening.

Kanty looked at her shrewdly. 'The only thing I wanted in life was to be a sculptor, and when that was taken away from me I thought for a while that there was no point to living. Then I pulled myself up by my boot straps, and remembered something my mother used to say: "You can never be completely miserable when you are doing something for someone else." And by chance I met Audrey who was coming here. Well, chance or whatever you like to call it. So I decided to tag along. Not being able to sculpt was the worst thing I could imagine. And now the worst has happened and I've lived through it, and I've met you and Margarita and Concha, and found something I'm good at which gives me back my sense of purpose. So it doesn't seem so bad after all.'

It was the same for her, Lucy realised. Her world had revolved around Jamie and Tom and her mission to bring them back to England. But in Spain she had found other people who needed her and – here she thought of Concha – maybe who loved her even more than the boys.

There was still no word from Tom. In the evenings, if they were not too tired, Lucy, Kanty, Alfred and Norma listened to the Socialist and Communist Party of Catalonia radio station where Ralph Bates broadcast news stories in English about the International Brigades and read out letters from the Front. Another broadcaster was one of Tom's old comrades from the early days, Jimmy Shand, a student from Liverpool who'd been wounded. One night he announced that some International Brigade soldiers had been captured. Lucy hoped Tom was one of them and that was why he hadn't written. A prison cell sounded safer to her than a trench.

On 15 April the radio announced the news which everyone had been expecting and dreading – that Franco's Fascist army had reached the Mediterranean, cutting off Barcelona from the other cities of Spain. Lucy thought of her friends in Murcia, who were now at the mercy of the Fascists. She wished she had brought Alfonso, Juanita and little Pepe north with her.

Alfred raised his eyes to Norma and she reluctantly nodded. Lucy knew they had agreed that Norma would take their children out of Barcelona once Franco reached the coast.

A few days later they waved goodbye to Norma, four-year-old Piers and his three-year-old sister Teresa, who was nicknamed Terry. They were moving back up to Puigcerdà in the Pyrenees, close to the French border, which had been a prosperous ski and hiking resort before the war. John Langdon-Davies, the *News Chronicle*'s correspondent in Catalonia, had set up three children's colonies there through his own charity, the Foster Parents Scheme for Children in Spain.

Norma soon wrote that she'd found a house backing on to the River Reür, which formed the border with France at this point. Out of the rear windows she could see over the French town of Bourg-Madame. She said, rather wistfully, that there was plenty of room in the house for Lucy and Margarita if they wanted to join her there. Although there had been two

Italian bombing raids targeting the railway station, Puigcerdà was still much safer than Barcelona, and only a few steps away from France.

Do come, she wrote. *The mountain air is wonderful. So good for the children.*

Lucy bent over the sleeping form of Concha and moved a lock of hair off her face. Perhaps she should leave Barcelona for Concha's sake? But there were still so many people in need and so much work to be done.

She was finding it was becoming harder each day to make her way across the city. Refugees often blocked the streets with their carts piled high with bundles, mattresses, cooking pots and chickens. Horses and donkeys stood listlessly in the roads which stank of their shit, with their heads hanging down. But as Lucy waited for delivery trucks to bring the food to her canteens, underfed men would stop to help the driver unload, and nothing was ever stolen, not one bread roll, because the Quaker star on the lorry told everyone this food was for the children.

One Sunday evening Margarita took Lucy, Concha and Kanty to the Plaza de San Jaime, in the warren of slums which formed the old town.

'I want you to see something,' she said mysteriously. 'The Sardana.'

As they neared the plaza through the dark, canyon-like streets, they could hear the sound of a pipe or flute and a drum, and as the square opened out before them they saw circles of serious-looking people of all ages dancing hand in hand. The blue of the factory girls' overalls alternated with the brown of the Popular Army, the black dresses of the widows and the grey ragged suits of the older men. The music was jolly, but the dancers moved slowly, stepping to left and right, crossing and uncrossing their feet, raising their arms with dignity and grace. It had none of the skipping and bobbing Lucy was used to in an English country dance but the solemn circles seemed to be saying, 'We will go on. We will come through this.'

Margarita handed Dorotea to Lucy and took Kanty and Concha to join in. Kanty grasped the hand of an old man and a soldier and tried to copy the steps. Margarita's feet moved lightly and naturally in a dance she had obviously been doing all her life. This was where she belonged, and Lucy suddenly had a great longing to be in the place where she had grown up and everything was known.

When the music stopped Margarita returned to Lucy and put her arms out for Dorotea.

'You see,' she said. 'We die dancing.'

In May Norma Jacob wrote to say that scarlet fever had broken out among the refugee children in one of John Langdon-Davies's Puigcerdà colonies and the schoolmaster running it had been taken seriously ill. She was doing what she could, but was scared of catching the disease herself and infecting her own children.

'I had scarlet fever when I was thirteen,' said Lucy, turning over the idea in her mind.

Kanty grinned. 'Then it's obvious. You must go and manage the colony till the schoolmaster recovers. It'll be good for you.'

Lucy hesitated, thinking of her three canteens, until Kanty

cannily added, 'And good for Concha to be up in the mountains. She's looking very pale.'

Lucy chewed her lip. How much she would like to take Concha out of the constant danger of the bombing!

'But there's scarlet fever; she might catch it.'

Kanty raised her eyebrows. 'Much more chance of catching a falling bomb here. Just don't take her to the colony. Enrol her in a local school instead.'

Lucy pictured Concha running in the meadows below the mountains. It was an irresistible image.

She nodded. 'Just till the schoolmaster recovers.'

It took little persuasion to convince Margarita to bring Dorotea too, and soon they were packing, with all the anticipation of friends preparing for a peacetime holiday.

The relief of leaving the besieged city made them lightheaded, and though the train was dirty, slow and crowded, they giggled together like schoolgirls. Concha beamed from one to the other of them, filled with the novelty of seeing them so jolly.

As the train drew into the little railway station at Puigcerdà, Lucy's heart lifted. The mountains behind the town still had snow on their peaks. As they disembarked, scrambling over their luggage, the air smelled cold and clean. Norma met them on the platform, and en route to the house she showed them the centre of the town with its theatre, casino, tree-lined central square and an artificial lake surrounded by the turn-of-the-century villas of rich Barcelonians. In the water they could see reflected the china blue of the sky, a villa with an elegant square tower, and the trees just coming into leaf. It seemed to Lucy the most beautiful place on earth. Everything was calm and quiet, and far fewer of the people they passed looked ragged or starving. She hugged Concha and Margarita and realised she was completely happy for the first time since Tom had left the White Villa.

The children's colony was in another sumptuous home, the Villa San Antonio. John Langdon-Davies's charity had taken over the three-storey mansion which, like the house on the lake, had a tall square tower in one corner, topped with a pitched slate roof, and tiny windows looking out north, south, east and west. It looks like Rapunzel's tower, Lucy thought. When the scarlet fever was gone, she would bring Concha to climb it.

For now Lucy couldn't allow Concha to enter the infected villa, but instead she enrolled her in the school which occupied the ancient convent of Sant Domènec. Concha had never been to school before, and she clutched Lucy's hand very tightly as they stood outside the old building with its three tiers of arched loggias.

'You'll make some good friends here,' said Lucy, trying to sound confident.

'But I can't talk Catalan,' said Concha miserably, and Lucy's stomach twisted with guilt, as she wondered if she was really the best guardian for her after all.

'Give it a few days?' she pleaded, and Concha nodded slowly.

Running the Villa San Antonio colony felt like second nature as Lucy quickly learned the names of the boys and girls and their sad histories – those who had lost their parents on the desperate flight from Málaga, or who had been sent to a safer place by their families in Madrid. All of them hoped to see their mothers again – even those who knew them to be dead. She thought how she clung to the hope of seeing Tom and Jamie, even though she knew the odds were stacked against it.

The ten children who had caught scarlet fever had been moved into two back bedrooms and were kept in isolation. Two of the youngest had died before Lucy arrived, and the others were terrified. Now they were all covered in the livid red rash, but the worst of the danger appeared to have passed. Lucy divided her time between nursing the sick and teaching the healthy children alongside local women. One of the nurses was a middle-aged woman who had lost a child herself to scarlet fever and she slept in the dormitory, watching over them and praying fiercely. Every evening, Lucy would go to read to the convalescing children, rejoicing as they gradually regained strength and the skin began to peel from their faces and bodies, revealing shiny pinkness beneath. Within a week they all looked as if they had been sunburned.

Despite her concern for the children with scarlet fever, Lucy felt as if she could breathe more easily in the peaceful air of Puigcerdà. A tightness in her neck and shoulders which she hadn't even noticed unknotted as she slept soundly in the quiet nights, and she could see Concha's features visibly softening as she discovered the other girls at the school were vying to befriend her, and one little girl had taken her firmly under her wing. The teacher was asking her to assist with Spanish lessons. Lucy and Concha both began to gain weight on the food which was smuggled over the border from France.

'The border is permeable here,' Norma had explained as she unwrapped the first clandestine parcel of cheese. 'It follows the river in places but it mostly just meanders through fields, and there are many contraband routes – for food and people.'

How strange it seemed to Lucy that just there, over one of the bridges or across the fields, brother wasn't fighting brother, death didn't rain out of the sky, orphaned children weren't being cared for in colonies, ordinary people weren't seeking refuge in overcrowded, filthy shelters, and bereaved twelve-year-old girls weren't bringing up their siblings.

Lucy, Margarita and Norma settled into each other's company, taking turns to cook and wash for the household. Norma kept English bedtimes for Piers and Terry, so Concha too went to bed early and in the peaceful evenings the three young women would listen to music on the wireless while making clothes for the children and themselves, or read, or talk about the futures they planned. Norma agreed to help Lucy teach English to Concha, and Margarita helped her make a special birthday present for the little girl.

Piers and Terry were becoming like Concha's brother and sister, and as they only spoke English, she soon began to pick up words and phrases. She loved being the eldest and 'in charge'.

On the seventeenth of May they held a birthday party for Concha. Margarita made honey cake and Concha was given the rag doll which Lucy had sewn in the evenings and kept secret from her. The doll had straight black hair made of wool held in place with a slide, just like Concha's. And if the eyes weren't quite level and the mouth was a little wonky, Concha didn't notice, clutching it to her chest and swearing she would love it forever. Norma and Margarita gave her new clothes they'd made. They all sang 'Happy Birthday' in Spanish, Catalan and English and Lucy attempted to teach them to play 'dead lions', though Piers and Terry thought it was funny to tweak their noses and pull their hair to try to make them move.

'This is the best birthday party I've ever had,' said Concha. She thought very hard. 'I think it might be the only birthday party I've ever had.'

Whenever they could get away, Alfred or Domingo would come up to join their wives for a few days, and Lucy wished she had someone coming up to see her, to sit with his arm draped casually about her shoulders, to kiss her when he thought nobody was looking, and to make love in the depth of the night. Margarita was in the next room to Lucy and, though she tried not to listen, it was impossible not to hear the low moans and stifled cries of her pleasure as the iron bedstead creaked faster and faster.

On the day Domingo had left for Barcelona again, Margarita was washing up while Lucy dried, and Margarita blushingly said, 'I hope I didn't wake you in the night. I try so hard to be silent when . . .'

Lucy picked up a dripping plate. 'Can I ask you? About . . . that?'

Margarita glanced quickly sideways at her friend. 'Of course. Anything.'

'You like it, don't you?'

Margarita laughed. 'Better than honey cake.'

Lucy smiled. She knew Margarita could not resist honey cake.

Margarita glanced up again, frowning. 'It wasn't like that for you with Tom?'

Lucy shook her head.

'Sometimes it's not so good the first time,' said Margarita authoritatively. 'You have to get used to each other. Or maybe an eager English boy might be like a bull charging a matador?'

Lucy giggled. 'Something like that,' though she wondered if an eager Spanish boy would show any more restraint.

'Well, next time you must make him circle the bullring a few times until you are ready. You are the matador. You are in control. And men need to be told everything, like "yes, that's good", "stop that", "not there", "go slower".' She laughed her deep, throaty laugh and counted on her fingers as she listed the instructions.

Lucy had been telling Tom what to do all their lives. She didn't think she'd find that difficult.

'And try different positions,' continued Margarita, putting the last dish on the draining board.

Lucy's eyes widened. 'There are different positions?' This was something Mrs Murray hadn't told her.

'The one on top has more control,' said Margarita, and Lucy thought, yes, next time it would be on her terms. If there ever was a next time.

22

It was June and there was still no news from Tom, but a letter arrived from Jamie, forwarded from Barcelona to Puigcerdà. He wrote triumphantly that he had been vindicated in his support for the Fascist regime because Pope Pius had condemned the Republic's 'truly satanic hatred of God'. The Pope had formally recognised Franco, and the Holy Father could not be mistaken. Lucy shook her head and burned the letter.

But Jamie was following the advance of the Moroccan ground troops and was close to the fighting, and soon another letter arrived.

My darling Lucy,

Something most terrible. Oh, terrible, terrible!

I can hardly write it, but I will go mad if I don't tell someone, and who could I tell but you?

I might destroy this letter when I've written it. If I was going to post it I would have to smuggle it out somehow.

I am broken. Everything is broken.

Not in my body. I wouldn't mind that. But my heart is broken. Something has happened and the scales have fallen from my eyes.

I thought I was a crusader doing God's work against the powers of darkness. But now I see the powers of darkness are everywhere and my soul is black as night because I have been part of it.

I will try to write it.

The news crews and I were following the army as it pushed forward. At every step we were presented with grateful Catholics whose churches had been cleaned and reopened — ordinary people, Lucy, who just wanted to be able to pray in peace again. And I felt so good about what Franco was achieving.

And then, yesterday, we were closer to the line of fighting and I came into a camp of mercenaries. The men were resting after battle, eating and drinking. Then I saw their sergeant, coming down the road from the village they'd just liberated. He had two Spanish girls slightly in front of him, walking slowly.

When they came closer to me I could see they were pretty girls, about thirteen or fourteen, sisters perhaps. They were terrified, and one had a bright weal across her face. Their arms were behind their backs, and as they came level with me, I could see their hands had been tied, and the sergeant had a gun pointed at them.

'Help us, Señor. Please save us,' the girls begged me.

I held up my hand and stopped the sergeant. 'What have these girls done wrong?'

He looked slyly at me. 'They are Republican filth.'

I protested. 'But they are only children.'

'They are the children of Reds.'

The girls were arguing loudly. 'No we aren't. We are good Catholic girls.'

The sergeant swiped one of them across the mouth with the back of his hand, and when I jumped forward he levelled the gun at me.

The girls' eyes were wide with fear, as they looked all about them for somewhere to run and hide, for someone to rescue them. The one who'd been hit was crying.

I stepped back and raised my hands so he could see I had no weapon. I tried to keep my voice even and friendly.

'Come on now, sergeant,' I said, more calmly than I felt. 'Let me take them into custody, and I'll deliver them to where the other prisoners are being held for interrogation.'

The sergeant's eyes flicked to the encampment ahead. Some of his soldiers were standing now, watching us.

He shrugged. 'I have promised my men. They deserve some entertainment.'

My stomach lurched and I thought I was going to be sick. The girls were both weeping now. 'Please Señor, please Señor, save us,' they pleaded again.

I was begging too. 'No, no, you can't do this. They are someone's children.'

But the sergeant merely prodded his gun into the back of one of the girls to move her forward.

I took a deep breath and stepped in front of them, and he raised the gun to me again. 'If you interfere, my men will tear you limb from limb.'

I looked back over my shoulder and could see more of the soldiers were now on their feet, some with weapons in their hands. And, oh Lucy, I'm so sorry, but I was afraid for my life, and I stepped out of the way. The girls began to wail loudly.

'Don't worry,' said the sergeant as he pushed the girls past me. 'They will be dead in four hours.'

I turned away and vomited on the ground, trembling all over.

And once I had been sick, I ran back to the line, weaving between the tents, seeking out the most senior officer I could find.

I was out of breath as I told my story to the sergeant guarding his tent, and was then told to wait before I was ushered inside. The captain was urbane and immaculate. He invited me to sit down and offered me a glass of wine.

'No, no,' I spluttered. 'You have to go there now and save those girls.'

'You've had a shock,' he said soothingly, and pushed a glass into my hand.

I took a big swig. 'You have to stop what they are doing.'

'Tell me about it.'

I told him quickly, the words spurting out in disgust, hoping, expecting he would grab his gun and issue orders to stop the horror going on just down the road. But he raised his hands in a gesture of helplessness. 'What can I do? It's the same everywhere we go.'

I sucked back more of the wine. 'But they are innocent children. Madre Día. Please. I beg you.'

But he simply sat down and lifted his own glass to his lips. 'I would if I could. But we would have another civil war if I interfered.' He smiled at his own joke. 'One is enough. Please sit and talk to me. Where are you from?'

So I sat with him, Lucy. To my everlasting shame, I talked to him and tried to keep my mind from what those girls were enduring, and from my own cowardice in not being prepared to die for them.

We drank through one bottle and I told him about Oxford, and he told me about his university days in Valencia. In other circumstances I would have liked him.

He opened another bottle, and a man brought food to us, and finally I asked him about the German and Italian troops and why Moroccan soldiers were fighting for the Catholic Church.

'They are simply mercenaries,' he said with a dismissive wave. 'They fight for money, and the ridiculous hope that Franco will give independence to Morocco when he wins.'

He laughed, a humourless laugh. 'And the Moroccans think it a great joke, that we, their imperial masters, are paying them to kill Spanish people. Every chieftain who supplied 7,500 soldiers was given three anti-aircraft guns. They hate us and don't differentiate what kind of Spanish they are killing.'

It's in the Bible, isn't it: 'The scales fell from his eyes and he could see.' That's what it felt like to me. Suddenly I felt as if I'd been duped, taken for an idiot. My great holy cause, Lucy, was nothing but a sham.

I stumbled away from his tent, back to the journalists' camp, trying to reason with myself, to persuade myself that sometimes the ends justify the means, and the restoration of the Church to Spain was worth anything. But it wasn't worth the gang rape and murder of those two girls, was it, Lucy? And tomorrow they'll push on and it will be someone else's daughters from some other village.

My mind steamed with all the other things I've denied – the German bombing of Guernica, the reason all the German and Italian troops are here. Franco isn't fighting for God, but for power. For Fascism. This is not the holy war I believed it was.

I don't know how I went to sleep but I did eventually, and woke up with a thumping headache. All the other journalists and news crews went out interviewing the grateful Catholics who'd been lined up for them. I stayed in my tent and wrote this.

I thought I might burn it once I'd written it, but I want to get it to you somehow. I want you to know the truth.

I can't stay here. I'll file a piece for the Catholic Herald which tells what I know. Then I'll go up to the Ebro Front, and try to make my way to you. Perhaps I can help you with your refugees. Perhaps I can make amends. Perhaps I will try to go to Rome and tell the Vatican what's really happening.

Dear Lucy, can you ever forgive me for not saving those girls, even if it meant my own death? I know I will never forgive myself. I will see their faces to the end of my days.

I will pack my things now, and try to see if I can somehow make it across the lines to join you. I don't know how.

Oh Lucy!

Lucy crumpled the letter to her chest. How had it taken Jamie so long to see the truth? And what would he do now?

She was frightened by the thought of him trying to cross the battle lines. She wrote urging him to go straight home via Portugal, but knew there was little chance of her letter ever reaching him.

The schoolmaster at the Villa San Antonio colony had recovered enough to resume his duties by the middle of June, and Lucy knew she should return to Barcelona. Alfred had told them that Kanty was now supplying fifty-four canteens and feeding almost twelve thousand children a day as vast numbers of refugees continued to struggle in from the south. She had also set up feeding stations for the old and infirm. Barcelona was under siege and starvation gripped the city. Luis Vives House was beginning to seem too small to run the massive operation.

Lucy looked up at the mountains, and said goodbye to the peace which seemed to flow down from them into the town. With a heavy heart she made up her mind to leave Concha in the safety of the Villa San Antonio or with Margarita and Norma. Lucy explained to her that she must stay behind for her own protection, and assured her she would visit as often as she could, but a furious determination gripped Concha's features. Her catlike eyes narrowed to slits and her mouth set in a firm line. She planted her legs apart and folded her arms.

'I will not stay here without you. I will run away, and find a kind person to take me on the train to Barcelona. And if you bring me back I will run away again.'

'But the bombing – you remember what it was like. And next time you could be killed. You will be safer here.'

Concha's eyes flashed with fury. 'I would rather die than live without you.'

Lucy gathered up Concha's stiff, furious body and held her until she felt it soften in her arms.

Margarita waved them off at the station, saying she would be back in Barcelona soon herself. Concha sat close to Lucy, as if fearing she would be put off at the next stop. The train going south was almost empty, but on the roads coming north towards France there were uncountable numbers of refugees. Out of the window Lucy and Concha watched farm carts piled high with mattresses, saucepans, bicycles and sometimes live hens or rabbits.

'Look, look!' pointed Concha in amazement. 'A monkey!'

Lucy thought she must be mistaken, but sure enough, a tame baboon was sitting in the cart which passed them, its eyes full of infinite sadness.

'Can I have a monkey?' asked Concha, and Lucy laughed.

Later that evening, and not long after they had arrived back in Luis Vives House, the sirens sounded. As they hurried to the cellar, they heard the roar of planes above the rooftops, then a long whistle, and the thud of an explosion shook the house and blew out the windows of a neighbouring property. Lucy tried to cover Concha's body with her own as they ran down the steps to the basement, furious with herself for not leaving the little girl in Puigcerdà.

Underground, Kanty rushed over to them, swinging Concha off her feet and making her squeal with glee, forgetting the bombs overhead.

They settled down on boxes of oranges to wait for the all-clear.

Lucy noticed Kanty was still wearing slacks even though it was hot in Barcelona by now.

'Still annoying the anarchists?' she asked.

Kanty winked. 'Breaking as many rules as possible.'

She reached behind her for an orange which she gave to Concha. 'Shhh. It's stolen!' she said and the little girl's eyes glittered with fun.

Kanty's face was filled with its usual wound-up energy, but there were dark smudges under her eyes.

'You look so rested,' she said wistfully. 'That'll soon go, though we have Sundays off now. The London office sent a doctor to look at us all and he said we must have one day off each week. So the day after tomorrow we'll go to the beach. Would you like that, Concha?'

Concha clapped her hands together, and Lucy had a sudden lurching memory of her playing with Tom in the waves at the White Villa. She saw his lean, tanned body, and the livid scar down his thigh as he ran lopsidedly into the sea with Concha piggy-backing on him, her legs tightly gripping his waist, and her arms almost strangling round his neck. They were both laughing uproariously. Where was he now?

'Yes,' said Concha. 'I love the beach. I can swim, you know.' She turned to Lucy. 'See, I knew I should come back.'

'You were right,' said Kanty, tickling her.

'So how is it?' asked Lucy, when Concha's giggles subsided.

Kanty shrugged. 'Grim. We've got bread from American wheat going out every day to 93,000 schoolchildren, but there's terrible illness among them. In one of your old canteens we've got nearly five hundred on the books but a quarter of them are too ill to attend and collect their ration.'

Lucy wondered how Marita and 'her children' were faring. She promised herself she would visit as soon as possible.

'I'm glad you're back,' said Kanty, resting her hand briefly on Lucy's arm.

'I might get a pet monkey,' announced Concha. 'We could take it to the beach. I could teach it to swim.'

A few evenings later, they were listening to Jimmy Shand on the wireless when he announced, with crowing excitement in his voice, that the 14th corps of the International Brigades had carried out a daring amphibious guerrilla raid on Carchuna in the south, where 300 Republican prisoners had been held by Franco's troops. The rescue had happened on the twentieth of May, but it had taken over a month for the survivors to reach Catalonia, travelling at night and hiding from the Fascists. He began to list the names of those who had been rescued and made it to Barcelona. Lucy inhaled sharply and prayed that Tom would be among them. She told herself that if she could hold her breath until the list was complete, he would be on it.

Jimmy Shand continued to read the names, so slowly. Then, just as Lucy thought her lungs would burst, he said, 'Comrade Thomas Murray.'

Lucy leapt into the air, scattering the mending on her lap.

'Whatever is it?' asked Kanty.

'It's Tom,' Lucy stuttered, staring at the wireless. Kanty held up a hand for silence as they listened to the news that the rescued prisoners had been taken to Barcelona where

they would recuperate before being allowed to go back to the front line.

Lucy was already running towards the door.

'Where are we going?' Kanty asked, following her.

'To find him,' said Lucy. 'I'm going to find Tom.'

23

The man who sat in the hospital chair with his head resting in his hands was almost unrecognisable. The last time Lucy had seen him, Tom had been muscular and his skin glowed with a deep tan from the weeks on the beach.

Now she stood in front of a skeleton of a man whose bony, white arms poked out of the hospital pyjamas. Only his shock of dark, unkempt hair told her who this was.

She drew a breath and stepped closer. 'Tom?'

The man raised his head and Tom's familiar brown eyes stared out of a strange skull-like face. His tongue flickered over dry lips as he slowly focused on the figure in front of him. 'Lucy?'

She sat on the edge of the bed and ran her fingers through his hair.

'Who else would it be?'

He caught hold of her hand, turned her fingers over and brought her palm to his mouth, holding it there in a kind of kiss or blessing, or as if to prove to himself that she was real.

She laughed nervously. 'I heard it on the wireless. Jimmy Shand read out your name, and said you'd been rescued. I can't believe you are actually alive!'

He held tightly on to her hand and sat up straighter. 'Well, sort of alive. As you can see.' He indicated his wasted body.

She took in his translucent skin, and touched the stick-thinness of his upper arm where there used to be biceps. She wrinkled her nose critically. 'A bit scrawny and pale, but certainly alive. Are you wounded?'

He seemed to gather himself from a long way off and spoke like a bad actor playing the part of the boy he had been. 'No. I'm fit as a fiddle.'

'Hrmph. A bit out of tune, I'm guessing. What have they said?'

His eyes never left hers. 'They won't let me go back to the Front until I put on some weight.' He grinned in a way which was almost grotesque. 'I hope you've brought cream buns.'

'If you've got a small fortune to buy one!'

He lapsed into silence, as though speaking was a terrible effort, and Lucy studied him carefully. He seemed very young and very old at the same time. There was barely a vestige here of the boy she'd loved.

She spoke decisively. 'You'll have to come and live with us. I'll scrounge as much food as I can and I'll get Margarita to send cheese from Puigcerdà. We'll fatten you up. Will they let you come?'

Tom's eyes glimmered with a trace of his old amusement. 'They wouldn't dare refuse you.'

* * *

For the next few days Lucy visited him in the hospital, taking whatever tasty titbits she could lay her hands on. Though he was eating less than a small child, each time she came he looked more like himself, and less like a ghost who might vanish again at any minute. Or perhaps she was just getting used to his new appearance. He sat outside all day in the hospital gardens, and colour seeped back into his skin, like a watercolour wash over a pen and ink drawing. Each day he walked further. He didn't speak of his time in captivity, and Lucy knew better than to ask. He would talk about it when he was ready, she thought.

Meanwhile, she got everything prepared at Luis Vives House. She told Concha that Tom needed to sleep in her room while she nursed him back to health, and Concha was excited at the prospect of sharing a bunk bed with one of the other aid-workers' children.

Kanty stood in Lucy's attic room gazing at the two narrow, metal camp beds.

'I don't mean to ask a personal question, but my bed is a double. I could swap rooms with you while he's here?'

Lucy looked out of the window to hide her blushes. Nobody but Kanty would suggest such a thing to an unmarried girl. 'Yes please,' she whispered.

Kanty crossed the room in two strides and laid a hand on her friend's shoulder. 'Don't be ashamed of grasping whatever joy you can. In wartime every moment might be the last.'

On the day Tom was allowed out of the hospital Lucy brought him to the house by metro and tram, though he had to stop several times to catch his breath as they climbed the final hill.

He had no luggage. As Concha had done, he stood outside Luis Vives House in some wonderment, watching Lucy open the iron gates.

'Some place you've got here,' he said hoarsely.

'There's a garden you can sit in, but don't be surprised if you get given work to do. We are always short-handed. I'll show you our room and then I'm afraid I have to go to the office.'

She had tried to say 'our room' casually, but she saw that Tom had registered the words and she felt a hot flush creeping up her neck. Had she assumed too much? Nine months had passed since the night on the beach. They were both different people.

Kanty had found a bright cotton coverlet for the bed, and Lucy had arranged some flowers from the garden in a glass jar. The room looked welcoming. Tom acknowledged the double-sized bed, and walked to the window, looking down on the garden, at the wreckage of the city and the glittering sea.

With his back to her, silhouetted against the light, he said, 'Are you sure? About me being here with you? I look like a walking skeleton and you are more beautiful than ever. And . . . I'm not sure I can do anything . . . in that way.'

Lucy replied tartly to cover her embarrassment, 'You're in with me in case you still have nightmares. I don't want you waking the whole house.'

His head fell and his shoulders slumped. 'Yes, of course. Of course. And I'm afraid I do – have nightmares.'

He looked so alone. So vulnerable. Pity and love twisted free in her and she came up behind him, wrapping her arms around his skeletal frame, leaning her cheek on his back.

'I just want to be with you,' she said. 'I thought you were dead.'

He turned in her arms and bent his head to hers for the first time since his rescue, kissing her softly, with more sadness than passion. The familiar fire didn't leap up in her, but it was so good to feel his lips on hers and his arms around her. She rested her head on his chest and they stood for a long time, until she realised his legs were trembling with the exertion of the journey.

'Why don't you take a nap?' she said. 'I'll bring you some cocoa and call you when lunch is ready.'

For the first few days Tom rested in the shade of the garden. He spoke little, brooding and impatient to be back with his comrades at the Front.

'I'm like a fish out of water here,' he complained. 'I don't know how to be with ordinary people any more.'

Lucy made him cocoa three times a day with sweet, creamy condensed milk, and he joined them for meals, gradually recovering his appetite. He stood at the doorway to the office, hearing the hubbub of typewriters clacking, phones ringing and people making urgent arrangements which would save thousands of lives, watching Lucy's quick efficiency with awe. He began to understand the size and scale of the aid operation, and just how essential her work had become.

On the first few nights he was asleep long before she left her desk and slipped between the sheets beside him. He still shouted and writhed with nightmares and, though his terrible dreams didn't seem to wake him, he was still half-drowsy when she woke up and dressed to start work again in the morning. But on the fifth morning she was aware that he was watching her when she removed her nighty and stepped into her dress. As she sat on the edge of the bed to fasten her alpargatas, he ran his hand up her spine and she felt a tingling passing from his fingers into her skin. She swivelled to lay her lips on his forehead, but he lifted his face and began to kiss her like he had done on the day he left to join the International Brigade, pulling her down towards him, and her body responded with a rush of joy.

He cupped her breast, but she drew away laughing. 'You're feeling better!'

He sank back on the pillow. 'It seems I am!'

'Well, I have work to do. And if you are that much better, we'll find some work for you too.'

That night he was asleep before she joined him, but the next day was Sunday, and when she woke, she didn't have to drag herself out of bed to begin work, but turned to him and snuggled up close. He stirred and pulled her tighter to him and an answering eagerness leapt up in her.

He shifted and put a hand down to check himself. 'You've mended me,' he said with sleepy delight. 'For so long . . . I thought it would never . . .'

If only every element of a man was so easy to bring back from the grave, thought Lucy.

'I need to go to the bathroom,' she said, grabbing the vinegar jar from under the bed.

He sighed. 'Be quick.'

When she returned, he had rolled over, with his back to the door. She slid into bed behind him, with ripples of excitement and desire running through her, but he spoke to the wall in a harsh, strained voice.

'I can't promise you anything. You have to know that.'

She pressed her body into his back, spooning into him. 'I know that.'

She did, of course she did. But she wanted him so badly.

He continued, repeating a speech he'd obviously been practising, 'I have to go back to the front line. I expect I'll be killed. I ought to be dead already.'

She ran her fingers down the bony xylophone of his ribs, and whispered, 'But today you are alive and I am alive.'

He turned over and looked at her. 'Oh God, Luce, you are so beautiful.'

She stroked his stomach and he began to kiss her with a hunger which matched her own.

And this time she took charge, telling him to go slower or faster, sitting astride him and moving at her own pace until she knew why Margarita and Juanita had been unable to muffle their moans and cries, and at last she felt emptied out and at peace.

Afterwards he held her for a long, long time, and she thought he had gone back to sleep, but he hadn't. When she lifted her head she could see he lay with his eyes open, staring at the ceiling.

'I'm no good to you,' he said. 'Too much of me is dead already.'

She swung her legs out of bed.

'Cocoa,' she said. 'And today we'll show you Barcelona beach.'

*　　*　　*

There was a flurry of activity and excitement before Luis Vives House was locked up and the entire staff boarded a lorry and headed towards the sea. They laughed uproariously as their stress was released like steam from a pressure cooker. Kanty set up a game of beach cricket and the serious aid-workers became loud as children, running about the sand, yelling instructions and hilarious abuse at each other in a Babel-mix of languages. Lucy scored a six and danced a joyful jig. When they were all too hot, they ran into the warm waves, eager to forget all their pressing anxieties, living only in the moment.

At first Tom was reluctant to strip down to his borrowed bathing costume, self-conscious about his skinny body, but Concha insisted. He ran to hide in the waves and she followed him, shrieking like a demon. When Concha had tired of splashing him and ordering him about, Lucy wrapped her in a towel and then swam out beside Tom, doing a lazy breast-stroke parallel to the shore, keeping pace with him, until he tired. And then they lay in the shade and ate beans in sauce and drank red wine until their heads were muzzy and their skin glowed.

That night they made love again, tipsy and inhibition-free, exploring each other's bodies with their fingers and tongues and slipping into utter forgetfulness.

Tom began to put on weight and spent as much time in the garden exercising his body as resting. He identified the enemy planes which flew over Barcelona: Heinkel bombers, big with low wings, Heinkel and Fiat pursuit planes, and he knew before the sirens sounded when they should all run to the cellar.

343

Over the next two weeks, he gradually regained enough physical strength to offer to help the delivery drivers as they took food to the canteens and colonies. It was the first time he'd seen the devastation of the city as they steered around the rubble in the streets. Sometimes the roads were blocked by the wagons and carts of refugees. Other times they stopped to help people searching through the heaped brickwork of bombed houses for their children or parents.

It was also the first time he'd seen the relief work at the refugee canteens close-up: the desperation of the mothers, the stick-thin arms and legs of their toddlers, the listless babies with their too-big, knowing eyes, the enormous numbers of children Lucy was trying to save. Now he understood why the phones rang and the typewriters tapped and Lucy only came to bed when she could no longer keep her eyes open. All the International Brigade soldiers like him already gave a portion of their meagre salary for the support of hungry youngsters. Now he promised himself he would give more. Every penny he could spare.

But as his physical strength increased, Lucy felt Tom mentally retreating from her and, though she refused to let herself think about it, she knew he would not be with them in Barcelona for long. There was no yesterday, there was no tomorrow. She was determined to live only in each day, draining every drop of joy she could from her short time with Tom. She knew that he would return to the Front and she might never see him again, but she locked away this knowledge. And because she would never be able to say goodbye to him in so many words, she said it with her body, and he replied with equal tenderness. Their acts of love through the hot midsummer darkness were a long farewell, as they savoured each sensation in a slow leave-taking from each other and perhaps from life itself.

Through early July Franco's army was concentrating its efforts in the south, and the International Brigades had time to regroup and rest on the north side of the Ebro. Something began to harden in Tom's face as he listened to the news on the radio, as though he was steeling himself for his return. Lucy saw the echoes of battle flicker across his features, and sorrow solidified in her chest. Concha watched Lucy watching Tom, and reached out a hand as if to say, I will still be here when he has gone.

This time Tom didn't give her any warning of when he was leaving, knowing the pain of that would be too much for them both. But after breakfast one morning in mid-July as they sat in the dining room, he simply said, 'It's today, Luce. I'm going back.'

Her eyes searched his and she could see that he'd brought down a shutter to protect himself from emotion. There was no point in flinging herself on him and begging him not to go. It would make no difference. She nodded bleakly, and he continued, 'I've got to finish it.' She nodded again and studied his features, trying to photograph them in her mind: his mop of unruly hair; his slightly sticky-out ears and conker-brown eyes, knowing this might be the final time. He was looking at her the same way, committing her to memory, as if hoping her face might be the last thing he would see.

He refused to allow her to come to the army depot with

him. 'You've got work to do here,' he said. 'Important work. I'm so proud of you, Luce.'

She stood outside the gates of Luis Vives House and didn't cry as she kissed him goodbye, though it felt as if she had swallowed a lump of lead and it sat undigestible in her chest. This was too terrible for tears. Neither of them said anything. What was there to say?

His back retreated down the hill, step by rapid step, and she wrapped her arms around herself. As he reached the corner, he turned and waved, and then he was gone.

For a long moment she stood, taking in the empty space which had been Tom, and then, just as she was about to go back into the house, another familiar shape came around the corner, struggling up the hill towards her, pushing a pram. Lucy shaded her eyes from the July sun as the figure approached, and then ran down to meet her. Margarita! It was Margarita!

As they met, Margarita put the brake on the pram and held out her arms to Lucy, clasping her tight.

They spoke at the same time. Margarita said, 'I think I passed him. Was that him?' and Lucy asked, 'What brought you? How did you know to come today?'

Margarita loosened her grip around Lucy's waist and searched for a hanky. Tears were running down her cheeks as if she was doing all the crying for both of them.

'Kanty wrote to me,' she said, blowing her nose loudly.

'But how did she know? I didn't know myself till this morning.'

Margarita shrugged. 'She said she could see him withdrawing into himself, into a place where he could tear himself away.'

* * *

That evening Lucy and Concha moved back into their attic bedroom, but before she retired for the night, Lucy sat with Margarita and Kanty on Kanty's bed, and they shared a bottle of wine, and Lucy wept in the comforting arms of her friends.

When she couldn't cry any more, she told them, 'The truth is simply that he wants to die for the Republic more than he wants to live for me.'

'He's an idiot,' snorted Kanty.

Margarita shook her head. 'It's not about him or you. It's just war. This bastard thing.'

A week later Lucy received two short letters, from the opposite banks of the River Ebro. The one from Tom, on the north bank, said:

Forgive me for not saying goodbye. It was cowardice on my part. I thought if I had to say that word to you I would break down and not be able to do what I knew I must do. Please try to remember me as someone who loved you dearly, but owed too great a debt to his dead comrades. I hope you will find someone who can love you as you deserve. I was never worthy of you.

She noticed it was the first time he'd said he loved her but he was already speaking of himself in the past tense. A steel band tightened around her heart.

The note from Jamie, to the south of the river, said:

This is in haste, and I don't know if it will reach you. I am near the River Ebro now and I am determined to come to you, whatever it might take, to tell you what a fool I've been and beg forgiveness. I love you more than life itself.

She pictured the brothers on opposite sides of the river and was almost overcome with fear that they would die together, or perhaps even kill each other.

24

As thousands of refugees continued to arrive in Barcelona, the food supplies dwindled and the aid offered through Luis Vives House became the difference between life and death for so many people, Lucy threw herself into her work with absolute concentration. The refugees, her friends, and Concha. She allowed herself to think of nothing else, taking each day as it came.

On the twenty-sixth of July the radio announced that the Republicans had launched a great offensive, crossing the River Ebro on a moonless night to drive Franco's army south. Lucy was terrified that any day she would hear of Tom's death.

Sporadic notes got through from him. He wrote of intense heat, bare rock, the stench of blood, of harsh sun, dogfights overhead, pilots bailing out on parachutes, planes falling in flames. He didn't mention love.

Lucy was sick with anxiety about him, but she also had another thing to worry about. Her period hadn't come when she expected it. She didn't need to count the days, because all the women at Luis Vives House had slipped into rhythm with each other, and Margarita and Kanty both held their stomachs and complained of cramps on the same day each month. Lucy thought perhaps it was sorrow which had interrupted her cycle. She had heard of such things. Or, despite Margarita's sponge . . . might she be pregnant? There had been that time when the sponge was still in place from the night before but she hadn't refreshed the vinegar before they were overtaken by desire in the morning. Or perhaps the sponge was just an old wives' tale. Maybe her period would start tomorrow, or the next day. She shook herself. Worrying wouldn't help, and there was so much work to be done.

All through the baking heat of August, the battle of the River Ebro raged on. In July the Republicans had crossed the river and taken Franco's troops by surprise, but he quickly sent heavy artillery and planes to beat them back towards the water. The Republican air force was outnumbered by at least two to one and their pontoon bridges were constantly destroyed and rebuilt. Wounded troops had to be ferried north across the river at night in small boats.

Tom wrote of trench warfare, an inferno of continual fire and explosions, machine guns in the foothills, and bloody assaults as a few kilometres were won and then lost. 'They have tanks, while we have hand grenades and Molotov cocktails.' By September, everyone in Catalonia knew the Republican losses had been devastating, and Tom's letters stopped.

On 23 September at the League of Nations in Geneva, Prime Minister Negrín announced his intention to disband the International Brigades and send them home, in the hope that

Franco would also send home his German, Italian and Moroccan troops. The Republican government believed it could still defeat Franco if he didn't have the firepower from overseas. Lucy thought it would be a cruel fate if Tom had been killed in the last days before they were withdrawn from the Front. She remembered that the 25-year-old poet Wilfred Owen had died in the Great War just six days before the Armistice. But there was no indication of when the International Brigades would be removed from the fighting.

By that time, when the baking summer heat of Barcelona was beginning to be wafted by cooler breezes, Lucy had missed three periods, and her breasts were hard and painful, though she didn't suffer from any sickness. Certain now that she must be pregnant, and sure that one of her friends would notice soon, she took Margarita and Kanty to her room and closed the door.

Her friends sat side by side on one of the little beds and looked at Lucy anxiously as she paced up and down, wringing her hands.

'I've got something to tell you, but you must promise not to tell anyone else.'

They both swore to keep her secret.

'I'm think I'm pregnant,' she blurted out. 'That is, I know I am. I'm going to have a baby. In March, I think. Or April.'

On both their faces she could see the flicker of sympathy which told her they knew how hard it would be to bring up an illegitimate baby. A child who would be called a bastard. There was a pause.

'Didn't you use the sponge?' asked Margarita crossly.

'I did, but like you there was a time . . .'

Margarita flicked her expressive hands. 'You must write to Tom so he can come back and marry you.'

Lucy sat down with a thump on Concha's bed, facing them.

'I would have married him at the White Villa if he'd asked me,' she said, and it was hard to bring these words into the open, 'but he didn't love me enough.' And if he didn't love her enough at the White Villa or here, how would he love her enough to be a good husband and father when they returned to England? If he was forced into marriage he might always feel resentful and trapped. She remembered her father's parting advice to Tom: 'Never marry a girl just because she says she's pregnant.'

'You deserve better than that,' said Kanty, tapping her foot in barely controlled fury.

Margarita nodded slowly. 'If you have the baby here I could bring it up as my own. I would love it as I love you, Lucy. Domingo will agree. Nobody in England need ever know.'

Kanty clearly warmed to this idea. 'You could carry on with your work, and one day if Tom or someone is good enough for you, you could come back and claim the child.'

Lucy considered this for a fleeting second, but knew already that she would never be able to give up her baby.

'No,' she said firmly. 'It's my responsibility.'

'Or,' said Kanty, 'you could wear a ring and tell everyone at home you are a widow.'

Lucy met her gaze. 'I could do that,' she said, doubtfully. She had never been good at lying, and she knew that in the eyes of the world she had committed the sin of fornication, and would be made to pay the price.

Even so, she felt a lightening of the tension between her shoulder blades to have shared her secret with her friends.

When Margarita had left, Kanty stayed behind, hesitating in the doorway. She looked up and down the corridor to make sure she wasn't overhead and then searched Lucy's face. 'Do you need me to find a doctor who could end the pregnancy? It would be dangerous, but if it's what you want?'

Lucy shook her head. That was unthinkable. This baby was hers and it might be all she would ever have of Tom.

Pregnancy made her dreams extraordinarily vivid, and almost every night she had the same nightmare of Jamie and Tom coming face to face on the banks of the Ebro and killing each other in different horrific ways, with bayonets thrust into each other's guts, or gunshots which blew off the face of one or the other, or strangling each other with their bare hands.

During the day she thought little of them or her pregnancy. There simply wasn't time. More desks had been crammed into the office and they had reorganised who did what. Lucy worked with Kanty and her local helpers running the canteens for the Barcelona poor, while Domingo and his staff focussed on the refugee canteens. Other people arranged the purchasing and stores, supplying the colonies, managing the medical centres and keeping track of the finances, while Alfred took a general overview. The team struggled to keep supplies coming for seventy-four canteens feeding fifteen thousand children as Franco's army effectively blockaded Barcelona and starvation spread throughout Catalonia. Two of the Quaker lorries were converted into travelling dispensaries as disease spread through the overcrowded populations of the refugees and their weakened children.

From Murcia they received the terrible news of the

disappearance and possible shooting of the school inspector and chair of the Refugee Committee who had been such a help to them, and Lucy couldn't restrain her fury when she was told that the Fascists had closed the children's hospitals.

At the Ebro, the Republican forces had been backed to the river and suffered massive losses. Lucy hadn't heard from Tom for weeks and was in an agony of dread as she waited for news.

Finally, on the morning of the second of October, an official letter was delivered – the letter she'd so long feared. She took it out into the garden, away from prying eyes, and opened it with trembling fingers. The words swam out of focus and back in again. It said very little. Someone she'd never met regretted to inform her that Comrade Thomas Murray had gone missing in the valiant fight to keep Franco's troops from crossing the Ebro and he was presumed dead. That one word leapt out of the page as though someone had screamed it in her ear. Dead. Tom was dead!

It said he had been a fearless hero, always leading his men into battle. She crumpled the paper in disgust. She could see him at the head of a brigade, brandishing his bayonet, running into the face of death. She shook with rage, furious with him for loving his stupid cause more than he loved her or his mother. More than he loved the future they might have shared and the baby he would never know. More than he loved life itself.

She heard her voice crying, 'No! No! No!' and a wail like an animal in pain, and clapped a hand over her mouth.

Margarita ran across the lawn and folded Lucy in her arms. Lucy clung to her and sobbed. Grief was torrential as a tropical storm, wracking her whole body.

Kanty came out of the house and her two friends led Lucy back to her room, sitting with her until she had cried so much she felt there could be no more tears in the world and her face was red and swollen. But when the tears stopped, the physical pain of loss wrenched her stomach and chest, rose until it stuffed her throat and she swung her head in the effort of breathing.

How could there be a world with no Tom in it? He had been there for as long as she could remember. And now the world was shattered. She looked up at the careless sunshine and couldn't believe the birds were still singing. It was all wrong. How could she go on waking up every morning? She felt the weight of all the bereaved mothers and wives and sweethearts of Spain pressing down on her.

Somehow the day passed, in a blur of time that was no time. Margarita and Kanty took turns to stay with her. That night she realised Mrs Murray would have received the same letter, probably with a parcel of personal effects, the tattered remnants of a life. So she sat down to write, suddenly feeling how much she wanted to see the woman who had been like a mother to her. She held her pen over the page and considered whether it was time to admit that she was pregnant, whether it would be some comfort to Mrs Murray to know that something of Tom would continue. But she might be horrified, or insist that Lucy came home to be looked after, and there was still so much to do in Spain, and still a chance that she could bring Jamie back to his mother. Not yet, thought Lucy. I won't tell her just yet.

That night Concha crept into her bed as she hadn't done for months, and as she sobbed for the loss of her friend Tom,

Lucy wept too, for all the hopes she'd had that could never now come true, for the father of her child, for her lover who she would never see again.

And in the morning when she woke, the realisation of his death kicked her in the stomach, taking her breath away with its ferocity, but Lucy dragged herself out of bed, dressed and went back to work, because she had to, because the children needed her, because it was the only way to get through. She worked with fierce concentration, but her body knew Tom's loss. A weight sat in her chest and she felt too nauseous to eat anything. In the evening Margarita pressed a plate of food on her and Lucy pushed it away.

'You must eat,' Margarita insisted.

'Why?'

'For the baby. For Concha. For all the children.'

Reluctantly, Lucy lifted a spoonful of beans to her mouth. Chewed. Swallowed.

And so the rest of her life began. Her life without Tom. She had a sick emptiness inside, one which could only be filled by working until she was exhausted, and holding tight to Concha and her friends.

Two evenings after the letter about Tom, on the fourth of October, they heard on the radio that Republican Prime Minister Negrín had finally withdrawn the International Brigades from the front line. That night Lucy howled into her pillow. Too late! He'd taken them out of battle too late and her beloved Tom was dead.

In the days that followed, Lucy threw herself into work, from the moment she woke until she could no longer see straight.

She knew Concha was suffering too, but she could do nothing other than hold her and rock her to sleep. Her friends looked after Concha in the daytime and made sure Lucy took her meals, but didn't try to break through the wall of grief she'd built around herself. They were just there, as a steady presence, ready to catch her when she fell.

Late one afternoon, when her eyes were beginning to feel as though sand had been thrown in them, Lucy raised her head from the supply list she was ticking off, with that strange animal instinct which told her she was being watched. Across the jam-packed office Kanty was on her feet, talking into the phone. Then she twisted round and stared at Lucy with an unreadable expression. She scribbled on a piece of paper, hung up the phone and said something quickly to Alfred before she weaved her way between the desks.

Lucy stood up.

Kanty grabbed her hand, dragging her to the door. 'Come on, we have to go now.'

'Go where?'

But Kanty was already running round the house towards the undercroft. 'To a hospital. West of the city. We need to take a car. Alfred knows. I'll drive.'

Lucy kept pace with her. 'But who is it? What did they say?'

Kanty didn't slow her pace. 'Tell you in the car. Hope you can map-read.'

They sat in the car, poring over the map. Kanty jabbed a finger to a district Lucy didn't know, where an old nunnery had become a hospital.

As Kanty zoomed out of the drive, the wheels screamed and Lucy was thrown from side to side.

'Sorry,' said Kanty, slowing down a touch. 'It was a nurse on the phone. My Catalan is as bad as her Spanish but she said Señor Murray was asking for you.' She flicked an anxious glance at Lucy. 'I'm sorry, she said he's seriously wounded and there wasn't much time, and you should get there as soon as possible.'

Missing, presumed dead, the letter had said. So Tom wasn't dead after all? But probably dying. Maybe she would be able to save him again as she had done in Valencia. Her stomach tightened in terror, and sweat trickled down her neck. Although her four-month pregnancy wasn't showing yet, she laid one hand on her stomach where their baby was cradled.

'If he's asking for me, he isn't dead yet,' she said.

'Atta girl,' said Kanty, swerving to avoid a prostrate donkey.

Lucy concentrated on the map, though reading in such a violently driven car made her feel increasingly sick. She wound down the window. 'You'll have to go slower or I'll throw up,' she said.

Some roads were closed where bombed buildings had collapsed, and sometimes they encountered refugees who seemed to have made camp in the street. Kanty swung the car into reverse, driving as fast backwards as she did forwards, her face set in determination to get Lucy to the hospital in time to say goodbye.

Finally she pulled up outside the old convent, and Lucy flung open the door.

'Do you want me to come in?' asked Kanty.

Lucy was already moving away from the car, and called

back over her shoulder, 'No, no. Go home. Look after Concha. Thank you!'

The long ward was panelled with dark wood and badly lit. It had perhaps been the convent refectory. Lucy squinted up and down the beds for Tom's dark head on the pillow. A stocky nurse with cropped grey hair and a large mole pointed out the makeshift curtains around a bed in the far corner.

'Señor Murray is there,' she said in Spanish with a strong French accent. Her voice was hoarse with sympathy.

Lucy knew from the hospital in Murcia that curtains meant death. She almost flew down the ward, and for a moment couldn't find the opening between the curtains. Then she twitched them apart and she was standing at the end of the bed. But it wasn't Tom's brown hair on the starched linen. In the half-light she thought a mistake had been made and there was a moment of complete confusion, but then the head turned and to her utter shock she realised she was staring at Jamie's sandy hair and pale face.

His bright blue eyes filled with tears and he whispered, 'They found you! You came.'

Lucy hurried around the bed, and took his slender fingers in hers, bending to kiss his clammy forehead.

'Jamie,' she said, 'I'm here,' as her brain tried to re-compute. So Tom was dead after all. And now here was Jamie with that extreme pallor she had seen so many times on the dying. It was as if one of her nightmares had been a vision of the truth and the boys had somehow killed each other.

The curtains parted and an elderly doctor with white bushy

eyebrows whispered to her that Señor Murray had only a few hours to live, a day at the most.

'Please step outside for a moment while I tend to him.'

Lucy stumbled out into the ward, numb with grief for both her boys. She had failed to bring either of them home and hadn't been with Tom when he died. There was no question in her mind. She would stay with Jamie to the very end.

A Republican soldier in the next bed was talking to her and she forced herself to concentrate as he explained how Jamie had been fatally wounded. 'I saw it all,' he said. 'Señor Murray had successfully crossed the River Ebro himself, and he could have scrambled up the bank to safety with me, but he looked back and saw a family whose boat had overturned. The water was jumping with hails of bullets from Franco's troops and the father and mother were trying to shield their children. It was suicide, but he slithered back into the river to help them.' The soldier shook his head with a mix of admiration and contempt for Jamie's recklessness.

'Without a thought for himself, Señor Murray swam to the boat and hauled the whole family to safety but then was caught by sniper fire as he carried the last of the children to land. He's a hero. Needs a bloody medal.'

'Thank you,' muttered Lucy, thinking, a bloody medal for a bloody fool.

The doctor summoned her back to Jamie's bedside, and brought her a chair.

Lucy took Jamie's hand again. His fingers were cold, even though the October day was warm.

'I heard what you did,' she said, smiling into his dear freckled face. 'You idiot.'

His voice was weak. 'They had two daughters, you see,' he explained. 'Two girls saved for the two I allowed to die.'

He had succeeded in his ambition to become his father and sacrifice himself for others, Lucy thought bitterly.

'I know I'm dying, Lucy,' he whispered and his eyes were clear. 'I'm not afraid. But I would like a priest. Would it get you into terrible trouble to ask for one?'

She stood up. She knew Prime Minister Negrín was now allowing private Catholic worship in Catalonia and she would find a priest if it was humanly possible.

Two young nurses were rolling a patient to one side to remake his bed. Not them. She looked up and down the ward for the older nurse. There was something nun-like about her shorn hair and the length of her skirt.

The nurse was washing out a bedpan when Lucy came up behind her and coughed politely.

'Please can you help me?' she asked, and the woman turned.

'He wants the last rites,' she continued and the nurse wiped her hands on her apron, clearly sizing up this English girl and what risk she might present.

'Please, for the love of God,' urged Lucy. 'It would mean everything to him.'

The nurse's face softened. 'I can't promise, but I'll see what I can do.'

Lucy watched her hold a whispered conversation with the doctor who stared hard down the gloomy ward. She looked back pleadingly at him, and he gave a curt nod to the nurse who hurried away through a doorway hidden in the panelling.

When the nurse returned, she and the doctor carefully

lifted Jamie on to a stretcher. He bit his lips together but couldn't help a groan escaping and his face bleached of any remaining colour. Lucy's heart contracted with pity and love. The doctor and nurse carried him through the hidden door, beckoning Lucy to follow. On the other side was a small, dark room which might once have served as an office, but now it was empty apart from a bed and table. They laid Jamie on the bed and pulled a starched sheet over him.

The nurse took Jamie's pulse and his breath became increasingly shallow, but his hand reached out for Lucy's and she took it in her warm, firm grip.

'I'm here, Jamie. I'll never leave you.'

It was as Mrs Murray had said: the one who needed her most filled her whole mind.

His lips moved and she had to lean down to hear him.

'When the priest comes, after he gives me the last rites, if I'm still alive, would you marry me, Lucy? It would mean so much to me.'

Lucy looked into his lake-blue eyes and ran her finger down his face into the red stubble on his chin. He had been her dearest friend, who had known her better than anyone, who had guided and protected her all her life, whose love for her had never wavered. More than anything at this moment, she wanted to marry him. Not to please him, as she might have done in the past, and not because she couldn't have Tom, and not because he was dying, but simply because she had always loved the bright flame of him.

'I will,' she said, bending to kiss his mouth. 'Of course I will.'

The short, bald man who entered the office with the nurse

and doctor looked nothing like a priest. He was dressed in workers' blue overalls, and carried a large canvas tool-bag.

He took in the scene at one glance and smiled at Lucy. 'I am a carpenter now,' he said. 'Like Joseph.'

He unzipped the bag and lifted out a neat set of carpentry tools. From a hidden compartment below he pulled out a white stole rolled like a bandage, a black hat, a crucifix, a perfume bottle, a vial of water, a miniature wine bottle and something folded in a napkin. He laid these things on the table by the bed.

The nurse covered her head and drew her own crucifix out from the neck of her dress to lie on top of her uniform. The priest donned his stole, crucifix and hat over the incongruous blue boilersuit and stood over Jamie. While the priest heard his confession, Lucy whispered to the nun that if Jamie lived long enough they would like to be married. She patted Lucy's hand and hurried away again.

When she returned, the priest was giving extreme unction, anointing Jamie with oil from the perfume bottle, laying his hands on him. As he intoned the Latin words, all the tension seeped slowly out of Jamie's face. His eyes were closed and he looked so peaceful that for a moment Lucy thought he had died, but then his eyes flicked open and urgently sought her out. The priest unwrapped communion wafers from the napkin and unscrewed the wine bottle. Lucy smiled encouragingly at Jamie as the priest lifted his head, placed a wafer on his tongue and brought the bottle to his lips.

Jamie swallowed and smiled. 'Viaticum,' he whispered, and to Lucy, 'Provision for a journey.'

Tears sprang to her eyes and she dashed them away on her cuff.

The nurse leaned in and said something to the priest, who looked up at Lucy.

'Do we have a ring?' he asked the nurse and she held out a gold band on her palm. Lucy could see the indentation on her finger where the ring had encircled it for years. Bride of Christ, thought Lucy. How could she ever thank her? The priest could also see where it had come from and he pressed the nurse's hand as he summoned Lucy forward.

Jamie's breath was fast and shallow, and he was obviously in pain, but his eyes never left Lucy's face as the priest laid Lucy's hand over his on the sheet. He began to take them through the purpose of marriage, even though it was obvious that Jamie would never father any children. For the first time, Lucy remembered the baby inside her and wondered whether she ought to have told Jamie, and whether this marriage was a terrible disloyalty to Tom, but pushed the thoughts aside as the priest began to ask them to repeat their vows. Lucy's French and Spanish gave her an understanding of much of the Latin, but the nurse whispered a translation in her ear, so she was able to respond at the right times in Spanish. The ring was sprinkled with holy water and slipped on to her finger, and the priest laid a hand on each of their heads to bless them.

As the priest stepped away to repack his secret bag, Jamie reached up to her with both his arms and Lucy bent and kissed him.

'My wife!' he whispered. Joy radiated from his face, illuminating it from within. 'I wish Mum was here to see us. She would be so happy.'

Not if she could see you, thought Lucy, with anguish.

The priest left quietly before Lucy could even thank him,

because at the same moment a shudder of pain passed through Jamie and he cried out. Lucy looked helplessly to the doctor and nurse.

'Isn't there anything we can do?'

'Let's get him back to the ward,' said the doctor. 'We can make him more comfortable there.'

They fussed around him behind the curtains and Lucy could hardly bear the moans and groans which Jamie failed to suppress. It was a physical hurt in her chest to hear his pain. Her dear Jamie. Her dear husband. The strangeness of the ring on her finger compounded the unreality of the last half hour. When she'd left Luis Vives House she had no idea that this would be the outcome and yet she tested the flavour of it on her tongue and it felt right.

The nurse came out of the curtains, her crucifix tucked back in her dress.

'You can come to sit with him now. We've given him morphia. He will be drowsy, and please God he might slip away in his sleep with no more pain.'

Lucy sat down beside him and took his hand in both of hers, kissing the long, pale fingers. He was gazing rapturously at her and his eyes were bright in the dim light. He licked his lips to speak.

'You are all I ever wanted,' he said as his eyes slowly closed.

Lucy sat beside him all night, holding his hand. Sometimes she drifted into sleep and when she woke she found herself slumped over her forearm on the bed. Every hour or so the nurse came in to feel his pulse and one time she brought a pillow for Lucy to lay her head on.

Dawn came and Lucy stood and stretched. As he felt her

moving away, Jamie's hand fluttered towards her so she sat down again. The nursing shift changed and a younger woman brought her a plate of beans and a coffee. Lucy could hear the hubbub of the ward on the other side of the curtains. She didn't know how much he could understand, but she talked to Jamie quietly, about things they had done as children, about the damaged animals he'd brought home for her to mend, about her gratitude for the way he'd begged her father to let her train as a doctor and about her work with the refugees, but she didn't mention Tom. She led him on a mental walk through Welwyn, recalling every garden gate, every aubretia-spilled wall, where every cat and dog lived that they had petted in a childhood which seemed so long ago. Another life. From time to time someone looked in on them, and Lucy simply shook her head. The hours inched past, marked not by minutes and seconds but by the sound of Jamie's faint breath: in, out, in, out, as his body somehow clung on to life.

The longest day Lucy could remember gave way to night again and still his pulse flickered and his breath came and went. The effort of opening his eyes was too much, but she could feel the faint pressure of his fingers which told her he knew she was still beside him. And then her eyes closed as well and she rested her head beside his hand.

When she woke, she knew at once that something was different. He was still breathing, but the breath had a low, rattling quality.

'I love you, Jamie,' she whispered, and there was the only the faintest twitch of his hand in hers. After he exhaled there was a long, long pause before he drew breath. She leaned over and kissed his lips. The breath rattled out of him and she waited for him to inhale again. Seconds passed. And then a minute, and still he didn't breathe. She raised his hand to her lips and it was floppy. She kissed and kissed it, and let tears fall until Jamie's precious hand was wet with them.

When she lifted her head his mouth had fallen open and his eyes were less firmly closed, as though he had been trying to look at her for the last time. She dried her face on the sheet and went to call a nurse.

The older nurse was back on duty, and came at once, checking his neck for a pulse, closing his mouth and eyes and then allowing Lucy to kiss his rapidly cooling lips before pulling the sheet up over his face.

Lucy put her head in her hands and wept and the nurse helped her to the room where they had been married so little time ago.

When she had recovered herself, Lucy thanked the woman for all she'd done, and made to remove the ring to return it to her.

'No, no, it's yours now,' said the nurse, folding her hand around Lucy's. 'To remind you that it really happened and you are Señora Murray. You could stay in here till it's light. The morning shift comes on in an hour.'

Lucy sank thankfully on to the neatly made bed where Jamie had lain to receive the last rites and to marry her. At the door the nurse turned. 'I know the work you are doing at Luis Vives House, and I know it is holy work. God bless you.'

Lucy lay back on the bed and stared into the darkness. It seemed as though all the tears of her life had been cried when she'd heard the news about Tom and there were none left for

Jamie. Her eyes burned with the dryness of complete despair. She was physically exhausted, wrung out, utterly numb. Too tired to sleep, too tired to think, too tired to feel.

She watched the sky gradually lighten, and when it seemed another dawn had broken and the world would go on turning even without Tom and Jamie in it, she lifted herself from the bed and let herself out of the door where the priest had entered, out into the senselessness of a new day. Her mind had turned to stone, but somehow her legs carried her, one step in front of the other, towards the metro and home, though she would never know how she'd got there. The normality of walking back up the hill towards Luis Vives House felt completely surreal. How could such ordinary things happen in a world which was empty? She put out her hand to open the gate and caught sight of the wedding ring. The nurse had been right. If she hadn't had the band of gold on her finger Lucy would think it had all been a dream.

The way Margarita caught hold of her in the hallway told Lucy that the strain of the last two days and nights showed on her face and in every movement of her limbs.

'I just want to sleep,' she told her friend. 'I want to pull the blanket over my head and never get up again.' Margarita helped her to her room and knelt to untie her alpargatas. And then Lucy laid her head on the pillow and fell into a deep, dreamless sleep.

When she woke it was dark and for a moment she had no idea where she was or whether she had imagined the last days. A cup of cocoa and two biscuits had been placed by her bed. The cocoa was cold and had a skin on it. Pain lanced through her as she remembered Tom and Jamie were both dead.

She glanced over to the other bed and Concha wasn't there. She had a sudden need to see her and hold her in her arms. Lucy fingered the wedding ring. Was it wrong, what she had done? She tested her conscience and felt no trace of guilt.

The door opened a touch, and light slanted in from the landing. Kanty peeped in.

'Oh, you're awake.'

Lucy pulled herself up on to her elbows.

'Yes, come in, what time is it?'

'Midnight. I was just on my way to bed. You've been asleep for hours. Me and Margarita kept checking on you.'

'Where's Concha?'

'In with me.'

Lucy waved her over and patted the edge of the bed. Kanty sat and scrutinised her friend in the fall of light from the landing, her brow furrowed with anxiety.

'Are you OK?' She shook her head with irritation at herself. 'Stupid question. Would you like a hot cocoa?'

'I'd like a hug,' said Lucy, expecting the tears to come now. But she was hollow, sensationless and dog-tired. They held tight to each other in silence until Lucy raised her head as Margarita entered with tortilla, beans and cocoa, and sat on Concha's bed urging Lucy to eat. The food tasted like sawdust, but she thought of the baby and obediently chewed. She could tell they had both noticed the ring on her finger.

When she had finished eating Margarita said, 'You don't have to tell us now,' though her face was alive with curiosity. But Lucy found she wanted to share the whole story and see by their faces if she had betrayed Tom, or worse still been untrue to herself. They had to know that all was lost. She needed to hear herself say it before she could begin to believe it was true.

They were as astonished as she had been to hear that the Señor Murray in the hospital was not Tom, and that she had been married to Jamie.

'Was it wrong, do you think?' asked Lucy. 'It didn't feel wrong.'

'Then it wasn't,' said Kanty decisively.

Margarita nodded. 'Dear Lucy. Your heart was big enough for both of them. And both of us. And Concha.' She paused as a thought occurred to her, 'And the baby . . .'

She stopped herself, but Lucy knew she was thinking . . . now won't be born a bastard.

An immense wave of tiredness came over Lucy. She wanted to sleep and sleep and never wake up to the pain she knew would be waiting every morning of her life to come. Tomorrow she would have to write to Mrs Murray and confess that she'd failed in her promise. She hadn't brought either of her sons home, and both of them were dead. Everything was over.

25

7th October 1938
Barcelona

My dearest Mrs M,
   Writing this letter is the hardest thing I've ever had to do in my life. Perhaps I should have come and told you myself. Forgive my cowardice in writing instead.

   I know you've had the same appalling letter as me, telling us Tom is 'missing, presumed dead'. I know the terrible agony you will be feeling, and the cruelty of not even having his dear body to bury.

   And now I have to add to that unbearable pain, because I have to tell you that we have lost Jamie as well. There's no easy way to say it. I have written a dozen letters and screwed them up. I will post this one, however crass it seems.

   I don't know if it's any comfort at all for you to know I was with Jamie to the end. He had been fatally injured rescuing a family who were escaping across the River Ebro from Franco's troops. He got all the family to safety, but was badly hurt himself. I was called to his bedside in an old convent in Barcelona which is now a hospital. He was awake and knew who I was. He asked for the last rites and I was able to find a priest to secretly administer them.

And then he asked if I would allow the priest to marry us, and it was the only thing I could do for him, so we were married then and there. I don't know if it was legal without the banns and everything, but I truly believe we were married in the eyes of God. A nurse — or maybe a nun — who was with us gave me her wedding ring. I'm looking at it now.

I sat by his bedside night and day then until he left us. There was plenty of morphia and his passing was peaceful.

That was yesterday. I came home in a daze of pain, and my dear friends Margarita and Kanty are with me. Funerals happen quickly in hot countries, and it will be held tomorrow.

So I have failed you. Utterly. Utterly. I have failed to bring back either of your lovely boys. I am so, so sorry. I want to wrap my arms around you and weep with you for the boys we have loved so fiercely. I can't imagine how we will go on without them. I can't imagine how the world will go on. I feel we must go on living for them, but I truly don't know how.

I have something else to share with you. Something which may make you never want to see me again. I fear so much to tell you. My heart is pounding.

As you know, after Tom was wounded, he came to my beachside children's colony near Benidorm to recuperate. We became closer than ever, and — I am ashamed to say this, but I thought he might not return to the war if I allowed him to — you know. I have to write it . . . we became lovers in our bodies as well as our hearts. But even after that he still wanted to go back to the Front.

Then of course we thought we had lost him when he was captured, and finally he was returned to me in Barcelona and he stayed with us at Luis Vives House for two weeks. My joy in seeing him alive was so great that I wanted to spend every moment with him, day or night. I hope you will not think too badly of me when I tell you that we shared a bed. I hoped he might want to stay there with me and help with the work for the children. But he could hardly wait to return to his comrades at the Front. You know how obstinate he could be. Nothing I could say or do would change his mind. And now it is all as we most feared and he is lost to us forever.

But there are consequences of our time together, of our love for each other. I am carrying his baby.

Are you horrified? Are you shocked? Will you never want to see me again? Can you ever forgive me? I think my father will cut me off.

It sounds so awful when I write it down that I want to hide my head in shame — to be married to one brother while carrying the child of the other. But I had already been told Tom was dead when I married Jamie, and I knew Jamie only had a few hours to live, and he wanted it so much. And it feels so right to me to be Lucy Murray, not Lucy Nicholson.

Have I explained that properly? Do you understand? Do you despise me?

I tremble as I await your judgement because you are the mother I never had and your good opinion matters so much

to me. It will be a triple bereavement if you never want to
see me again. And yet I wouldn't blame you.

I hope you won't hate me forever for not bringing your
boys safely home to you. I tried so hard.

And I hope you will forgive me for loving both of them.
The world would not understand that. But I hope you will.

With so much love and begging for your forgiveness,
Lucy

It rained on the day of Jamie's funeral. Kanty and Margarita stood beside Lucy at the open grave. Margarita wore a black coat and dress and carried an umbrella. Kanty and Lucy were dressed in their sober Quaker greys and, though Margarita tried to share her umbrella, Lucy let the rain run down her face and through her hair as though the world was drenching her in grief. The only other mourner was the old nurse, who stood a little apart from them, and the priest who had married them, who wore his blue carpenter's overalls under a long dark coat.

They were invited forward to throw a handful of soil on the cheap coffin, and it seemed she was throwing the earth on both Jamie and Tom, who were wrapped together in a sleeping embrace as when they were very young.

*

Three weeks later, on Saturday 29 October, the 305 surviving International Brigaders who had been withdrawn from the front line were marched in a parade through Barcelona. Everyone wanted to be there to cheer them. Concha begged Lucy to take her and, though she felt she could hardly bear to see the Batallón Inglés without Tom, she knew he would expect her to be there to say farewell to his comrades.

Everything now seemed an enormous effort to her, as though she had aged fifty years, but she believed that this was the last thing she could do for Tom and it was her duty to go. Kanty saw how she was struggling and offered to come with them.

Since losing Jamie, Lucy had forced herself to focus only on her work for the refugees. Every time her mind veered back to the horror of the brothers' deaths, she slammed a door on the idea. Soon it felt as if she was in a long corridor of closed doors, with nothing to do but keep plodding relentlessly forwards, one grim step in front of the other, repeating through clenched teeth 'the children, the children, the children'. But now the day of the parade forced open a door, and the pain of the boys' loss flooded over her as if she was reliving the morning she'd heard that Tom was dead and the night she'd watched Jamie die. Her heart pulsed with grief as she set out with Kanty and Concha.

The parade was to take place at the Avinguda Diagonal, because it was the widest street in Barcelona, with broad tree-lined pavements to accommodate the spectators.

They could hear the noise of the crowds from a long way off, and they arrived to find the boulevard thronged with a crush of people and giant photographs of Stalin and Prime Minister Negrín hanging from the buildings. Bands were playing in riotous cacophony, and speeches being broadcast over loudspeakers. The uproar was compounded by the drone of Republican aircraft which patrolled the skies to protect them from bombers.

The crowd was many people deep, from the roadside to the buildings behind, as if everyone in Barcelona had come out to cheer the heroes of Jarama and Brunete and Ebro and so many other battles. Everyone knew what enormous losses they had suffered and how many foreign men like Tom would never return home to their mothers.

Kanty shouted, 'I've never seen so many people in my life. There must be a million. We need to move further down the avenue, or we'll never see anything.'

Concha shrank into Lucy's side, and Lucy clutched her hand tightly as they moved in the river of people behind the massed throngs and then tried to push forwards to where they might be able to get a view of the ranks of the surviving International Brigaders.

The crowd erupted and the bands stopped playing as Lucy recognised the voice of Dolores Ibárruri, La Pasionaria, as she began to make a fervent speech, which blared through loud-speakers on both sides of them. It seemed so long ago that she and Tom had gone to hear her lecture in London. Another life.

'You offered your blood with limitless generosity,' La Pasionaria declaimed to the remaining ranks of volunteers from all over the world, and her echoing words were like a knife in Lucy's gut. 'You can go with pride. You are history. You are legend.'

The crowd roared its appreciation but Lucy thought bitterly, better a live coward than a dead hero. Tom was gone forever and her baby would be born fatherless.

Only one phrase resonated. 'We will not forget you,' shouted La Pasionaria and the spectators erupted with whistles and stamping.

Never, thought Lucy, placing the hand with Jamie's wedding ring on to her slightly rounded stomach. As long as I have breath in my body, we will never forget you.

The International Brigades began to march through the crowded street and petals rained down on them till they were tramping on pink and red blooms and the bright flowers clung to their uniforms. The road ahead of the soldiers was strewn with flowers.

Women burst through the cordon of Spanish honour guards to kiss and hug the men who had protected them from Franco's Fascists for so long. Factory girls in their blue overalls planted lipstick kisses on the faces of the marching men and threaded blossom into their hair.

Lucy, Kanty and Concha were jostled from all sides and crushed tight to the packed rows of people in front of them who mostly blocked their view of the parade. Lucy lifted Concha into her arms so she wouldn't be trampled on.

'It's too dangerous for Concha. We should go,' she called to Kanty, but Kanty cupped one ear and raised her palms to express that she couldn't hear her over the racket around them. Kanty was a little taller than Lucy and much taller than most of the Catalonian crowd, so by standing on tiptoe and craning her neck, she was obviously getting glimpses of the soldiers between the heads of the women in front. Lucy could tell Kanty was thoroughly enjoying herself and wasn't going to leave for anyone. But Lucy herself could only see the occasional glimpse of a beret or a saluting fist beneath the much-repaired banners of the different brigades which one by one bobbed over the heads of the spectators. As each new banner appeared, the whoops and whistles of the crowd rose to a deafening pitch as they surged forwards. Lucy put her head down, and clutched hold of Concha. This would be over soon and she could go back to her desk, losing herself for a while in the urgent problem of feeding the refugees. She looked at the scruffy, worn coats of the people in front of her, and tried to concentrate on thinking about when she would have a new coat herself.

Then Kanty was nudging her and pointing over the heads of the people in front of them who were waving their arms with excitement, shouting themselves hoarse. Lucy looked up to see the tattered banner of the Batallón Inglés approaching. Red and pink petals rained down on the battalion from a window across the street. That banner would have been fluttering somewhere when her darling Tom was killed. A wave of sickness passed over Lucy and she hoped she wouldn't vomit or faint. She glanced back over her shoulder to see how far she would have to shove her way through people to escape. She wanted air. She wanted this misery to be over. But Kanty was cheering and yelling, and wresting Concha out of Lucy's grip to lift the child on to her shoulders to see over the heads. The clamour of the whistles and roars made Lucy's ears ring. Kanty was hollering and stamping and Concha was waving wildly and shrieking like a banshee.

Concha suddenly lifted herself up off Kanty's shoulders, straining to see better. As she lowered back down she drummed on Kanty's head with her palms and kicked Lucy's arm to draw her attention, shouting, 'Tom! It's Tom.'

Lucy and Kanty exchanged a quick glance of disbelief and astonishment, but Concha was pointing and screaming, 'Tom! Tom!' with such conviction that they were compelled to elbow a route between the people in front of them towards the parade, pushing the men and women aside.

Concha was bouncing with excitement on Kanty's shoulders and Kanty gripped her legs tightly.

Lucy scarcely dared to believe her, but Concha had been so fond of Tom, surely she couldn't be mistaken?

'He's there – there!' Concha pointed down the street as the men marched away.

'We'll never catch them,' said Kanty, and Lucy gripped her arm.

'We should go around, try to get ahead of them,' said Lucy, turning and shoving her way to the back of the crowd, who moved aside to let them pass.

Kanty lowered Concha to her feet, and Lucy took her hand, setting off at a run down side streets which had become as familiar to her as the lanes of Welwyn.

Concha was babbling with excitement. 'It was him! Truly! It was him! He isn't dead!'

Lucy knew they would be able to dash left, right, left, through the grid-patterned streets, zigzagging around the squares where roads intersected. Each time they neared the Diagonal they could hear the yells and cheers of the crowd, telling them the avenue was still thick with supporters of the International Brigades.

As they rounded yet another corner, Kanty developed a stitch and stopped still, clutching her side. Concha hopped impatiently from foot to foot as Kanty touched her toes, panting and blowing. But as soon as the stitch had gone they were off again, pelting through the streets with their hair blowing behind them.

When they had been running up and down the side streets for about fifteen minutes, the sound from the spectators seemed quieter, so Lucy led them back to the Diagonal, where the crowds had thinned to a few people deep. All three of them were breathless, sweating from their exertion. Lucy's heart was beating wildly when they emerged to a place where the marching parade had not yet arrived.

'*Por favor, si us plau*,' said Lucy, diving between the waiting people. '*Mi esposo!* My husband!' and in Catalan, '*El meu marit*.'

Men and women swivelled round, taking in the blonde-haired, light-eyed girl with such desperation in her voice, and they parted, telling each other to make way for the wife of the Inglés hero.

'Thank you, thank you,' said Kanty and Concha as they reached the very front of the crowds, behind the Spanish honour guards who were holding back the push of enthusiastic spectators.

The carnival atmosphere rose to a pitch of deafening excitement as the first International Brigaders marched into view in their ragged, mismatched uniforms, their banners flying ahead of each band of soldiers. Each man held his right fist to his temple, saluting the people who had come to thank them. Here was the Lincoln-Washington Brigade of American and Irish volunteers. Lucy had never seen so many black men. The cause of freedom must be close to their hearts, she thought. Now the Dimitrovs and the Paris Commune. And then, at last, the remains of the Batallón Inglés under their familiar banner, held aloft by the six-foot Jim Brewer.

Lucy's heart was hammering with hope and also with terror that Concha might have been mistaken. She thought now she might really be sick.

Lucy and Concha frantically scanned the faces of each line of men as they drew level. Many of them wore berets covering their hair, and some had their heads turned away, nodding to the crowds on the opposite pavement. Battle-scarred men, marching with their heads held high, grinning at the adulation of the women, their uniforms dotted with bright petals.

But none of them was Tom.

And then Concha shrieked and wriggled under the arms of the Spanish guards, into the parade. Her high voice carried over the din as she screamed, 'Tom, Tom!' and she hurled herself at a soldier who swept her up into his arms, looking all about him for Lucy. She felt light-headed, dizzy with disbelief. It was as if all the rest of the parade and the crowd melted away, all the noise and pushing and colour blurred to nothingness, and only Tom's face stood out in sharp focus. It was Tom. Concha was right. It was Tom.

Lucy dipped under the arms of the guards too and raced to him. If she pushed people out of the way in her desperation to reach him, she didn't notice. There was nothing in the world except Tom and the fact that he was alive.

And then she was beside him, gripping his arm, the solidity of it, and he was laughing down at her with his familiar conker-coloured eyes.

He slung Concha on to his right hip and embraced Lucy tightly around her waist with his left arm. The soldiers he'd been marching beside dropped back to make room for the new additions to the parade. Lucy skipped into step with the men, as, without breaking stride, Tom bent his head to kiss her on the lips. A wild cheer rose up around them from his comrades and the crowds. She clung to him and the softness of his mouth on hers was the only reality for a few long seconds until the awkwardness of kissing while walking forced them to break free. The soldiers who were close enough slapped them both on the back. She thought she might burst with the utter joy of feeling his arm like an iron band around her waist.

'They said you were dead,' she shouted.

Tom grinned his old impish grin. 'Not when I last looked.'

It was impossible to talk more above the cacophony of the crowd, but for these moments, nothing in the world mattered except the fact of his living, breathing body, welded against hers.

Lucy and Concha stayed with the parade until the spectators had dispersed and other hangers-on had dropped away, as they neared the outskirts of the city. Although she never wanted to leave him again, she finally forced herself to say, 'We should go back. We can't come all the way to France with you.'

Tom set Concha on her feet and kissed Lucy once more.

'I'll let you know where we are,' he called as he and his comrades marched away, out of Barcelona, up towards the mountains.

26

On her way back to Luis Vives House, her ears still ringing from the noise of the crowd, Lucy stopped at the post office, light-headed with joy, and sent a telegram to Mrs Murray.

TOM IS ALIVE! it said. And then, for good measure, I'VE SEEN HIM, because Mrs Murray might not dare to believe the wonderful news. She was leaving the post office when she realised she should also cable her father. Captain Nicholson had written to her most movingly when she'd sent the letter telling him Jamie was dead. His reply had said he was bereft at the loss of both his 'beloved sons'. He deserved to know that one of them was still alive. The telegram was quickly despatched. Concha danced and skipped beside her all the way home.

That night Lucy drank a toast to Tom with Kanty and Margarita, her emotions swooping between exultation at Tom's miraculous reincarnation, and bitter sorrow at the knowledge that Jamie would never reappear.

The following morning she received a formal letter from

the Batallón Inglés dated a week ago, telling her Tom was alive but had been concussed and laid up in a deserted farm-house, and a scrappy note from Tom saying the International Brigade troops were being taken somewhere near the town of Ripoll in the Pyrenees while arrangements were made to send them home through Puigcerdà. He hoped she would be able to see him before they left Spain.

'You must go to Puigcerdà,' said Margarita decisively. 'I will come too. Domingo keeps telling me it's time to leave Barcelona.'

Lucy's eyes flashed. 'We could take some orphans from the Barcelona colonies.' She turned to Kanty. 'What about you?'

Kanty considered. 'Not yet. We have so many good local staff, but there's still so much to do. Puigcerdà's got John Langdon-Davies's colonies and Save the Children and the Solidaridad Internacional Antifascista, so I don't think they need me.'

Lucy stumbled through the following days in a mix of exultation and despair. As she looked around her in the city, so many things mirrored her grief over Jamie: the closed shops; the ruin and desolation around the docks; the pinched, lined faces of the adults; the grey-white pallor and puffed eyelids of the children with clothes hanging off them. And yet she heard laughter and music too, and the familiar refrain of defiance, 'We Spanish die dancing.' And then she thought of Tom, and the fact that he was alive and she would see him again before too long.

October became November and the International Brigades were still camped at Ripoll in the Pyrenees, waiting to leave Spain. But Lucy barely had time to think about Tom. The telephones in the office were ringing constantly with new requests to evacuate this or that colony and take the children into the mountains or to France. The border with France was officially closed to refugees but there were many reports of the long lines of people queuing to leave Spain and people crossing secretly at night by the routes the International Brigaders had taken to enter the war. It seemed hardly anyone now believed a Republican victory was possible. Franco had not followed the lead of the Republicans and dismissed his international support from the Germans and Italians. It was only a matter of time before all Spain would be his.

Lucy and Margarita made plans to travel up to Puigcerdà, emptying their cupboards and getting their paperwork in order. Margarita would stay there with Norma Jacob until Franco took Catalonia, and then they would move to France to see how they could help the Spanish refugees there. Lucy would only stay in Spain until she had seen Tom leave. A great weight lifted from her as she made the decision to go home.

A letter came from Mrs Murray, which had been written before the telegram telling her Tom was alive, in reply to Lucy's letter of confession. Lucy opened it with great trepidation. Her heart beat hard as she slit the envelope. After all, she was carrying the bastard child of one of her sons and had married the other. She couldn't bear the thought that Mrs Murray might despise her. She scanned the single page of thin, blue paper quickly.

My darling girl,
  Thank you for your courage in writing to tell me about our sweet Jamie; it must have been so hard to do. And for

*telling me about the bairn. My grandchild. Tom's baby.
Something of him which will live on.*

*How could you think I might not want to wrap you and
the baby in my arms? Please come home soon and let me
take care of you. It's much too dangerous where you are. I
would have welcomed you anyway but the fact that this is
Tom's baby will make it infinitely precious.*

*I think you'll love it here in Lanarkshire; the air is clean
and we will have family nearby. The bairn will have cousins
to play with! But if you don't like it here or you miss your
friends too much, we can go back to Hertfordshire together.*

*I can't wait to meet Concha. She will be like another
grandchild for me. A ready-made family will be like a dream
come true when I've lived alone for so long.*

*Thank you for telling me about your marriage to Jamie.
It makes my deep sorrow slightly easier to bear when I
know you were with him to the last, and he died in the
happy knowledge that you were his wife. That's all he ever
wanted.*

*The loss of a child is the worst thing in the world, and
my heart goes out to all the mothers of Spain who are suffering with me. I know there will always be a rip in my soul
which will never mend. But there is still kindness and sympathy, in spite of everything.*

*It might seem strange to other people if you were ever to
tell them, but I understand completely that you loved both
of my boys. Of course I do. And I know they always loved
you, in their different ways.*

Please come home soon. Come today.

with much love, soon-to be-nana Murray

As she read and reread the letter, Lucy was overtaken by a great longing to sink her head on to Mrs Murray's shoulder and let herself be cared for, and at last to begin to think about her baby. If Tom had left Spain by then, she could go home in time for Christmas, and introduce Concha to Christmas trees and plum pudding and carols and Mrs Murray's shortbread. She would teach her to sing 'Away in a Manger'.

Once Lucy was in Britain, until the baby was born, she would work at raising money for refugees. She would speak at Friends Meeting Houses, WIs and trade union meetings. Francesca would help her. Maybe she would write a book. Perhaps after the baby came there would still be a way to train as a doctor. It seemed the future was rising towards her like an open road.

She decided she should tell her father about the baby when she next wrote to him. After all, it would be his grandchild too.

Lucy made certain that her two Catalan assistants would be able to take over all the work she would be leaving behind in Barcelona. They visited the colonies, where despite all their efforts the food shortages were becoming serious.

'We opened the beanbags they used to sit on, and cooked the beans,' one director told her. 'And then we used the material to patch their trousers. The children can't stay here much longer.'

Lucy told Concha that from now on they would speak only English, so that she would be ready when they both moved back to Britain. Concha hugged her tight, and Lucy realised that she had still been worried that she might have to remain in Spain when Lucy left. She raised Concha's head and looked deep into the brown eyes which welled with tears.

'I will never leave you,' she said. 'I love you like you are my own.'

The next day Lucy went to visit Jorge for the last time, half-thinking she might take him with her to Puigcerdà.

When she arrived, the colony matron was wreathed in smiles. She began to say something, then stopped herself. 'No, let him tell you himself! He's in the printing-press room.'

When Lucy pushed open the door she could see a change in Jorge which buzzed through every fibre of him.

'Lucy Yellowhair!' he yelled and threw himself into her arms, squeezing her so hard, she had to prise him away.

'What is it?'

'It came today. Just this very morning!' He fumbled in his pocket for a sheet of paper which was limp with being handled, unfolding it portentously, and presenting it to her.

But before she had time to read it, he burst out, 'It's from my sister. My big sister. She is alive, and is coming for me this very afternoon. She is taking me to live with her.'

Now it was Lucy's turn to hug Jorge. His whole body trembled with joy, and the gold flecks in his eyes glinted like treasure.

'I knew she was alive,' he said.

'Yes, you did. You were right.'

He had never given up hope. Perhaps she too ought to learn to believe in miracles, she told herself sternly. In all this destruction and devastation there could still be tiny pockets of joy, and when they came they should be celebrated and shouted to the rooftops.

Jorge's hand went to the printing press and a small cloud scudded over his beaming countenance.

'Do you think there might be a printing press near where she lives, which I'd be allowed to use?'

'I'm sure of it!' Lucy remembered what she'd been told when she arrived in Spain. 'Every school has one. Your new school will have one and be very glad to have a boy who knows how to use it so well.'

It was strange to say goodbye to Jorge knowing she would probably never see him again, and as she walked away she thought of all the others she'd left behind: Juan, Salvador, Alfonso, Juanita and all the children at the White Villa. She knew it was always like this in life, that you moved on and had to say goodbye, but the relationships she'd formed in Spain seemed so much more brightly coloured and vivid than any before, as though the nearness of death forced you into a new appreciation of life and a new level of love. She knew she would always carry these people with her, until the end of her days. They had made the woman she had become.

It took a few days before Tom's anticipated letter arrived from Ripoll where the International Brigades were encamped, awaiting the order to leave Spain.

November 1938

Dearest Luce,

Everyone's acting as though they are at a holiday camp, with games and football and knobbly-knee contests. I suppose we are finally free from the fear of dying at any moment,

*and you can't imagine how that lifts the spirits. It's as if
we are all slightly tipsy, just on the elation of being alive.*

*Most of the men are full of plans to return home, but
I'm sorry, Luce, I don't think that's where I'm meant to be.
Not just yet anyway. I've become very friendly with men in
the German, Austrian and Italian brigades who haven't got
a safe home like England to return to. For them the struggle
against Fascism is only just beginning. I'm sure you know
that Herr Hitler has annexed Austria and taken the
Sudetenland back from Czechoslovakia. I think England and
France may regret not stopping him and Mussolini breaking
the non-intervention pact here in Spain. They've become so
strong and learned so much about this terrifying new kind
of war from the air.*

*But I don't mean to be depressing. I am well, and full of
good spirits. I hope to see you in Puigcerdà before we finally
leave Spain.*

Tom

Lucy tested her feelings, as if she was poking a bruise. She
was not the slightest bit surprised that Tom didn't plan to go
home, but thought she could forgive him anything now she
knew he was alive. She hoped she would be able to see him
and at least tell him about the baby.

Eventually all the preparations were complete and Lucy,
Concha, Margarita and baby Dorotea left Barcelona for
Puigcerdà by lorry, taking with them a group of twenty
orphaned children from Barcelonian colonies. Their route
passed through the medieval town of Ripoll and it felt strange
to be so close to Tom, but not able to see him.

All the way up the slow ascent into the Pyrenees the lorry constantly sounded its horn to warn refugees to move out of the road ahead of them. Bundles of belongings had been abandoned on the verges as the incline increased and it became impossible to carry them any further. Their lorry overtook families who couldn't walk another step setting up makeshift camps for the night, with tarpaulins stretched over sticks to give them some protection if it rained or snowed. The luckiest people looked fat with the layers and layers of woollens they were wearing against the November chill. But many shivered in clothing which was completely inadequate for the altitude and time of year.

A boy of about ten was toiling up the road with his brother on his back. They seemed to have no other family. Two women with bare feet in alpargatas had sat down and pulled black shawls over their heads and shoulders. They held out their babies to Lucy as the lorry passed, calling, 'Please take them to France.' One of the babies lolled as though it was already dead.

Lucy clutched Margarita's hand as they drove past. There were too many of them. It wasn't possible to help so many people in terrible need. What could they do? Lucy frowned hard as thoughts leapfrogged over each other, and then turned to Margarita, her eyes aglow. 'We could set up a canteen. A mobile canteen which we can take to where they need it.'

Margarita nodded. 'That's a wonderful idea.'

All the rest of the way they talked about how it could be managed, until it was time to deliver the orphaned boys and girls to the colonies at Puigcerdà. Here they were safer from the bombing but the children were quiet and huddled close together as they were introduced to yet another new home.

At the Quaker house backing on to the river, Norma had cooked eggs and soup and the three women sat over their meal making lists of what they would need for a mobile canteen. Lucy sketched images of how they could convert a van. She was bubbling with enthusiasm and after dinner she telephoned Luis Vives House and spoke to Kanty, reading out their requirements in a way that brooked no resistance.

'You sound well,' said Kanty with a smile in her voice. 'I'll see what I can do.'

A few days later, a grey Bedford van with the red and black Quaker star painted on its side drew up outside their house, and honked its horn. Lucy, Margarita and Norma ran down the steps to meet it. Kanty leaned her head out of the driver's window and they crowded round, exclaiming in wonder.

'At least let me get out then!' laughed Kanty, shoving them aside.

She flung open the back doors with some triumph, and they saw the old van was loaded with sacks of porridge oats, dried milk, sugar and cocoa.

'That's just to tide us over,' she said. 'And underneath all that is a stove, a table and a sink. We got it out of a caravan. There's also a trestle table you can set up, and you can keep the porridge and cocoa warm on the rings. And there's two jam pans, two pails and three big saucepans. I didn't bring the big vats from the canteens because I didn't know if you'd be able to lift them if there are just three of you and . . .' she grinned at Lucy '. . . one is "embarrassed and creating".'

'It's perfect!' declared Lucy, hugging and kissing Kanty.

Norma looked decisively at her watch.

'If we unload some sacks here and take the rest to the storeroom, we could begin tonight.'

By nightfall they had heated up vats of porridge and cocoa and were ready to set out, in a state of high excitement. All four of the women wanted to go out on the first run, but someone had to stay home to put the children to bed.

'It's right you go,' Margarita said to Lucy. 'It was your idea.'

Kanty drove because she was used to the idiosyncrasies of the van, and they drew up on the roadside in a place they'd agreed with the Mayor of Puigcerdà. As soon as they opened the doors and the mouth-watering smells of cocoa and porridge wafted out into the cold night air, people hurried towards them.

Lucy, Kanty and Norma set up their trestle table and asked the first two men to carry the bubbling pans down from the van.

The refugees queued with tin mugs, handing them to Lucy to fill with a ladleful of cocoa, and held out bowls and plates to Kanty for a large spoonful of porridge. As they shuffled past, murmuring their thanks, Lucy looked into the eyes of young mothers struggling to carry huge bundles of all their possessions. Most had babies slung in shawls across them, or toddlers on their hips or small children grasping their skirts. She gazed into the wrinkled faces of old women and wounded men who had seen too much suffering, and wished each of them a safe journey.

When their supply of hot food and drink was exhausted for the night it was heartbreaking to fold the trestle table and close the doors of the van, telling the queuing people that there would be no more till tomorrow.

Lucy, Margarita, Kanty and Norma worked out a rota.

They needed two of them in the van at any one time, with the others at home stirring up the vats of milk and porridge, taking care of the children and trying to stop them 'helping'. Lucy preferred being out on the road.

She woke up each morning before dawn with purpose blazing in her head, alert and ready to go to work, knowing she had found her place in the world and was doing what she had always been meant to do. Jamie was dead, and the pain of that would never go away, but she was here and had to live for both of them. As she lay in the dark, cold mornings her heart thrummed out its beat, 'Begin! Begin! Begin!'

She pulled on thick woollen stockings under her serge trousers. Although she had become so thin during her time in Spain and her pregnancy was not yet visible to anyone who wasn't looking for it, her trousers wouldn't do up any longer. She used a piece of elastic and two nappy pins to hold the opening together. Her breasts were larger and hardly seemed to belong to her. She dragged a woollen vest and two jumpers she'd pulled from the charity bag over them. If she looked in the mirror she laughed at her shapeless body and rounding face. Despite the loss of Jamie and failing to persuade Tom to return home, she had never felt more alive, more necessary. Being needed was a form of happiness.

Day after day Lucy stood at the trestle table of their mobile feeding station with her back to the van where one of the others was stirring porridge. Her feet and lower legs were permanently frozen despite the socks she wore over her woollen stockings. She stamped to warm her toes, and turned her face up towards the mountains, grey with mist and snow, knowing she would leave Spain before long – as soon as Tom was safely in France. And when her baby was old enough perhaps she would resume fieldwork, finding Norma, Esther, Francesca, Kanty or Margarita or women like them wherever they were in the world, wherever there were people who needed the help of one foolish girl.

The snows began to fall thicker, and every day they heard that refugees were dying of cold and hunger beside the road. However hard they and the other relief agencies worked, they could never keep up with the avalanche of need. Lucy pressed another cup of cocoa into the hands of another hungry child.

On the morning of 6 December Lucy finally heard the news they'd all been waiting for – that the International Brigade troops had been moved up to Puigcerdà, ready to cross into France. She came flying through the town to the snowy field behind the railway station where the townspeople had laid on a feast, plying the soldiers with wine, ham, bread and butter smuggled over the border. As she approached the picnic laid out on long tables, she saw Tom stuffing a huge baguette into his mouth and laughing with his comrades. He hadn't seen her, intent on the food and the joke being made by one of his friends. She stood and looked for a few moments, pulling her coat and scarf a little tighter against the cold, then turned where she couldn't be seen and sucked the wedding ring from her finger, tucking it safely into her bra. Catching sight of the ring would be too thoughtless a way for Tom to find out she had married Jamie. She rubbed her finger to iron out the dent left by the ring.

Tom raised his head and spotted her, dropped the baguette

he'd been holding and ran towards her, lifting her off her feet in a great bear hug, and kissing her resoundingly on the lips.

The men cheered and she laughed. 'Let me down, you big oaf!'

He slung an arm round her shoulders in a proprietorial, brotherly way and as he led her to the feast Lucy noticed he still walked with a slight limp, but when he indicated a seat for her she thought he looked well, better than in Barcelona or even at the White Villa. He grinned at her with the old boyish glint in his eyes, as if here with his comrades he was completely himself. He swung himself on to a bench opposite her across the trestle table, and his friends crowded round, some looking Lucy up and down with frank admiration. She pulled her coat around her to hide her swelling breasts.

'Look!' he said. 'Ham! Cheese! Wine!'

He seemed much more interested in the food than he was in her.

She sat and watched him as he ate and laughed. All the light which had gone out of him when he was in Barcelona seemed to have returned, and she rejoiced to see it.

He suddenly reached out and twisted one of her curls around his finger in his old gesture, as if reaching into a half-remembered past, and she searched his eyes for anything which might have told her she meant more to him than the comrades who jostled around him. But he dropped his hand and picked up his wine.

'So what happened?' she demanded. 'They told us you were missing, presumed dead.'

He began to tell the story of the battle, and his friends couldn't seem to help chipping in, eager to add details about how calm, cheerful, courageous and selfless Tom was, to show him off in the best possible light. Lucy thought they could almost have been talking about Jamie. This all-for-one, one-for-all man they knew was not her old selfish Tom. Lucy was eager to hear more, to find out who Tom was when he wasn't with her, but he laughed it off as if she was someone who shouldn't be bothered with such nonsense.

'. . . Then I woke up in a bed in a farmhouse, with my head stitched up like Frankenstein's monster and no memory at all of the last two weeks.' He was playing to the crowd behind him as much as to Lucy and everyone listened with rapt attention. That at least was like the old Tom.

But Lucy hardly heard what he was saying because she was concentrating on sensations in her own body. For some weeks she'd been aware of fluttering movements like wind in the rounded lower part of her stomach. Now she had a rush of excitement as the flicking, fish-leaping feeling became more insistent. It was fanciful to think that the baby had somehow recognised its father's voice, but she caressed her belly with a cupped hand beneath the table, acknowledging the presence of new life.

'. . . And then we marched through Barcelona, and Concha saw me.'

She felt the flurry of kicks in her stomach grow stronger. You are going to be such a handful if you are a blend of us, she thought.

'Can we walk for a bit?' she asked, stamping her feet in the snow. 'My toes are numb.'

There were nudges and joshing from his comrades as he led her away to where they were out of sight, in the lee of the railway station. Tom pulled her into his arms, but it seemed mechanical, as though his mind was on something else.

'Will you go home?' she asked him.

He looked away, up into the mountains. 'I don't think so.' His eyes glanced off hers. 'There's still so much to do. Herr Hitler has to be stopped, or there will be so many Guernicas.'

She thought, what about your mum? What about me? But she didn't say it. Should she tell him about the baby? About marrying Jamie? She sighed. It didn't seem the time or the place. Perhaps it would be easier to write.

Lucy could see clearly that this was who Tom really was now – a soldier, most at home with his comrades-in-arms. Just as she was most herself when she was with her friends, focused and intent on helping others and relieving suffering. They were not so different, more like brother and sister than the twin souls of her romantic invention. She'd held on to an idea of him as the boy she'd grown up with, not the man he had become. Deep down she had known, even from the first time they made love, that Tom's true passion was the Antifascista cause and his brothers-in-arms, not her. As long as there was Fascism in the world, she would always play second fiddle. She might have expected to feel sadness at coming to this realisation, but strength and determination flooded through her and she knew she had the courage to go on without him, reliant on nobody but herself.

They returned to the feast, but one by one the soldiers around them fell silent, their faces turned a greenish pale, and they hurried away to the makeshift latrine as their bodies rejected the rich food. They had lived too long on rice and beans.

'Sorry, Luce,' said Tom, growing a ghostly white, and shouting over his shoulder as he hurried away. 'I've got to go.'

It wasn't quite the farewell she'd imagined.

The following day huge crowds turned out in Puigcerdà, lining the road which led to the bridge with the French border. School was closed for the morning, and all the children were given red-and-yellow-striped Catalonian flags. Lucy and Concha stood at the front of the press, waving, cheering and crying as one after another the brigades marched past them and out of Spain.

The Batallón Inglés banner came into view with Tom in the ranks behind it, scanning the clapping spectators for Lucy and Concha, and a great grin spread almost from ear to ear when he saw them. He passed close, within feet of them, and threw them a kiss. Then, with a military 'eyes front', he turned towards France and didn't look back. Tears rolled down Lucy's face as she watched his retreating back disappear into the lines of those who followed him. They were marching out of the country they'd fought so hard to save from Fascism, leaving behind the bodies of thousands of comrades who would never return home.

Twenty minutes later, when Lucy and Concha returned with their suitcases, the bridge to France had only a straggling queue of people waiting to cross the border. An old couple ahead of them paused for a moment as the man bent to scoop up a handful of Spanish soil and dribble it into his pocket.

Margarita, Kanty and Norma had come to wave them goodbye. Kanty squeezed Lucy so hard she could barely breathe and gruffly said, 'Don't worry, you haven't heard the last of me.' Then she swung Concha off the ground, making her squeal with pleasure.

Margarita wept and blew her nose loudly before she hugged Lucy and Concha for the last time. Bright tears stood in Lucy's eyes as she took leave of her dear friends. 'I'll write,' she said. 'I promise I'll write.'

Lucy showed her passport to the Spanish border guard and they were waved through. She took Concha's hand and smiled down at her as they walked across the bridge to France.

'Come on,' said Lucy. 'We're going home.'

Author's Note

In 1947 the Nobel Peace Prize was awarded jointly to the Friends Service Council and the American Friends Service Committee (the British and American Quakers) 'for their pioneering work in the international peace movement and compassionate effort to relieve human suffering, thereby promoting the fraternity between nations', which included recognition of their efforts in Spain during the civil war. It was given for their 'silent help from the nameless to the nameless'. But my research soon revealed that the aid workers were not 'nameless'. In this novel, I have tried to breathe life into some of them.

The Nicholson and Murray families and Concha are entirely imaginary, but most of the characters they encounter were extraordinary real people. Some of them are just names in the footnotes of history; others have been written about more fully, or left their own memoirs. In particular I have drawn heavily on the memoirs of Francesca Wilson and Kanty Cooper.

I have chosen to keep many people's actual names, even when I have had to invent and expand on what is known about them. Most of the acts attributed to Lucy in the novel were carried out by real people. For example: Francesca Wilson single-handedly undertook all of the work which Lucy helps her with in Murcia in this novel; Francesca also set up a colony on the beach near Benidorm, though that was in 1938 not 1937; Kanty ran all the canteens in Barcelona herself.

I would like to pay tribute to all the following real people and hope my imaginary expansion of what is known about them does none of them any disservice.

Friends (Quaker Relief): Francesca Wilson; Domingo and Margarita Ricart; Kanty Cooper; Alfred and Norma Jacob; Esther Farquar; Barbara Wood; Elise Thomsen; Edith Pye; Audrey Russell.

Minor characters: the Mayor of Murcia; the coastguard at Benidorm; Juan the fisherman; Harry Pollitt.

International Brigaders: John Cornford; Miles Tomalin; Ernest Mahoney; Charles Goodfellow; Frank Graham; Jimmy Shand.

Francesca Wilson had previously worked with displaced people in Holland, France, Corsica, North Africa, Serbia, Austria and Russia. Following the Spanish Civil War she went on to work with refugees in France and Hungary. She died in 1981.

Kanty Cooper went on to carry out relief work in Greece, Germany, Jordan and Amman.

Domingo and Margarita Ricart, as well as Alfred and Norma Jacob, spent time with the Quakers in England before moving to America. Norma continued to work for the American Friends Service Council.

*

Barcelona and Catalonia fell to the Fascists in January 1939. Franco finally took Madrid in March 1939 and then all Spain was his. There are tales of Republicans who remained in hiding until Franco's death in 1975.

During the three years of war, horrific atrocities were committed, 500,000 people were killed and millions were forced to flee their homes.

It is estimated that between 40,000 and 59,000 volunteers from overseas served in the International Brigades, including 15,000 who died in combat.

Accurate numbers are difficult to come by, but it is thought that by November 1938 there were more than a million refugees in Catalonia, of whom about half fled the country at the end of the war.

The Republican refugees who flooded into France were treated worse than animals by the French authorities. But that's another story.

Acknowledgements

First and foremost, huge thanks to Professor Farah Mendlesohn. In the middle of Brexit, I told her I was interested in writing about divided nations and she said, 'You should read my PhD thesis on Quaker relief in the Spanish Civil War,' and generously gave me permission to use what I found there. This novel is the result.

As the book was written during 2020 and 2021 when it was impossible to travel to Spain from England due to COVID-19, I am hugely indebted to the gorgeous travel writing of H.V. Morton as well as the memoirs of Francesca Wilson and Kanty Cooper, and the extraordinary help by email of

Josep Bracons Clapés, *cap del departament de colleccions i centres patrimonials Museu d'Història de Barcelona*

Mark Smith, the Man in Seat 61, for all my railway information

Miquel Serrano, *historiador i conservador, Museu Memorial de l'Exili*

Erola Simon Lleixà, *Arxiu Comarcal de la Cerdanya*, for all my information about Puigcerdà

Grégory Tuban, historian.

I am particularly grateful to my first readers, Farah Mendlesohn, Siân Lliwen Roberts, Rose Holmes and Erola Simon Lleixà, for correcting historical and geographical errors and offering advice.

My wonderful agent, Millie Hoskins, and the gifted editor Selina Walker have been at my side cheering me on as this novel took shape, and Selina and her assistant editor Sophie Whitehead, plus copy editor Sarah-Jane Forder and managing editor Rose Waddilove, have worked on the manuscript with meticulous care to help me get it as good as we could make it. I am indebted to them and everyone else at Penguin Random House who has been involved in this project. I can't thank them enough.

My darling family have been endlessly patient as I've abandoned them and taken myself 'off to Spain' in my head until the novel was ready for them to read and so usefully comment. To Tim, Katie and Amy – everlove.

Finally, I owe a huge debt of gratitude to the authors of all the Friends Service Council publications and the many other books I have consulted, notably of course Laurie Lee, George Orwell and Ernest Hemingway, but particularly

Bill Alexander, *British Volunteers for Liberty* (Lawrence & Wishart, 1982)

Kanty Cooper, *The Uprooted* (Quartet Books, 1979)

Ernest Hemingway, *For Whom The Bell Tolls* (Charles Scribner, 1940)

Rose Holmes, *A Moral Business: British Quaker Work with Refugees from Fascism, 1933–39* (DPhil thesis: University of Sussex, 2013)

Farah Mendlesohn, *Quaker Relief Work in the Spanish Civil War* (PhD thesis: Quaker Studies, Volume 1, The Edwin Mellen Press, Lewiston Queenston Lampeter, 2002)

George Orwell, *Homage to Catalonia* (Martin, Secker & Warburg, 1938)

H.V. Morton, *A Stranger in Spain* (Methuen, 1955)

Siân Lliwen Roberts, *Place, Life Histories and the Politics of Relief: Episodes in the Life of Francesca Wilson, Humanitarian Educator Activist* (PhD thesis: University of Birmingham, 2010)

Rosa Serra Sala, *Ajuda Humanitària dels Quàquers als Infants de Catalunya Durant la Guerra Civil 1936–1939:Humanitarian Aid from Quakers for the Children of Catalonia During the Civil War 1936–1939* (doctoral thesis: University of Girona, 2006)

Manuel de León de la Vega, *Los Cuáqueros y Otras Organizaciones en la Ayuda Humanitaria Durante la Guerra Civil de 1936* (M. de León, 2018)

Francesca M. Wilson, *In the Margins of Chaos* (John Murray, 1944)

J.A.W. (ed.), *They Still Draw Pictures* (The Spanish Child Welfare Association of America for the American Friends Service Committee (Friends), 1938); foreword by Aldous Huxley